The First Dazzling Chill of Winter

Collected Stories

First published by O-Books, 2016
O-Books is an imprint of John Hunt Publishing Ltd., Laurel House, Station Approach,
Alresford, Hants, SO24 9JH, UK
office1@jhpbooks.net
www.johnhuntpublishing.com

For distributor details and how to order please visit the 'Ordering' section on our website.

ISBN: 978 1 84694 581 6
978 1 78099 711 7 (ebook)
Library of Congress Control Number: 2016946095

A CIP catalogue record for this book is available from the British Library.

Design: Stuart Davies

Printed in the USA by Edwards Brothers Malloy

The First Dazzling Chill of Winter

Collected Stories

Nicholas Hagger

BOOKS

Winchester, UK
Washington, USA

Also by Nicholas Hagger

The Fire and the Stones
Selected Poems
The Universe and the Light
A White Radiance
A Mystic Way
Awakening to the Light
A Spade Fresh with Mud
The Warlords
Overlord
A Smell of Leaves and Summer
The Tragedy of Prince Tudor
The One and the Many
Wheeling Bats and a Harvest Moon
The Warm Glow of the Monastery Courtyard
The Syndicate
The Secret History of the West
The Light of Civilization
Classical Odes
Overlord, one-volume edition
Collected Poems 1958 – 2005
Collected Verse Plays
Collected Stories
The Secret Founding of America
The Last Tourist in Iran
The Rise and Fall of Civilizations
The New Philosophy of Universalism
The Libyan Revolution
Armageddon
The World Government
The Secret American Dream
A New Philosophy of Literature
A View of Epping Forest
My Double Life 1: This Dark Wood

My Double Life 2: A Rainbow over the Hills
Selected Stories: Follies and Vices of the Modern Elizabethan Age
Selected Poems: Quest for the One
The Dream of Europa
Life Cycle and Other New Poems 2006 – 2016

CONTENTS

Part Two

In the Early Evening Sunshine

Preface

My *Collected Stories* contained 1,001 short stories covering five volumes and spanning 50 years, 1966 – 2006. *The First Dazzling Chill of Winter* is a sixth volume containing a further 201 stories written between 2009 and 2016 and takes my total tally of stories to 1,202. These new stories did not appear in my recent *Selected Stories: Follies and Vices of the Modern Elizabethan Age* (2015).

Readers of my stories will know that they reflect the fundamental theme of world literature, which I identified in *A New Philosophy of Literature* as having metaphysical and secular aspects that are in conflict: a quest for Reality (the One) and the heightened consciousness it brings which perceives the universe as a unity; and condemnation of social follies and vices in relation to an implied virtue.

My Universalist approach seeks to reconcile these contradictions. It blends image and statement and seeks a balance between social virtue and the soul's perception of the One; between the outlooks of the Augustan and Romantic periods in English literature.

My mini-stories follow Philip Rawley from his late twenties to his seventies and impending old age. Rawley's growth and development is presented in terms of the many people he encounters, who reflect the ways of the modern Age. During his quest his soul undergoes a transformation that changes his outlook. In this sixth volume Rawley instinctively perceives the unity of the universe in his "early evening sunshine", and is dazzled by what he sees. He feels at peace despite his advancing winter, and grasps that wisdom is a way of looking. Despite his serenity he is increasingly preoccupied by death, which is ever-present behind the social situations.

These miniature stories present a new literary form. They offer a complete literary experience in a few minutes. Their vivid titles reflect Dr Johnson's description of the wit of the 17th-century Metaphysical poets in his 'Life of Cowley' as "a combination of dissimilar images" in which "the most heterogeneous ideas are yoked by violence together". Many of these stories reflect the One and have a metaphysical ambience.

My stories are vivid verbal paintings that present an image in action. Some of the stories are like portraits in the National Portrait Gallery and concentrate on conveying a particular character. I have tried to bring a poet's eye for significant detail, and some stories seek to startle the soul into a new mode of perception.

12–13, 26–27 January, 8 April 2016

PART ONE

The First Dazzling Chill of Winter

The First Dazzling Chill of Winter
(Or: 'Pilgrims' and a Rose-Window)

In Chaucer's day men went on pilgrimages to Walsingham, Canterbury, Durham or Beverley in East Yorkshire in the spring. Pippa and I joined a chartered trainload of four hundred 'pilgrims', all in the first chill of winter, to Beverley minster. We caught the train at Potters Bar.

As we waited at the entrance an elderly couple spoke to us and the husband, a thin, balding man with wispy grey hair, described their previous rail excursion. He said, "I wanted to leave early, but my wife said there was plenty of time, and there was an accident. The M25 was blocked. We got to the station when the train was nearly due. I told my wife to hold the train up while I put our car in the car park. I was in such a state that I forgot to put my ticket by the windscreen. I remembered as I approached the station, and I had to go back. Then on my way back I dropped my keys and had to turn back and find them. My wife did hold the train up, but I had to run the last two hundred yards, and I was so out of breath that she thought I was having a heart attack. The staff bundled me on to the train. The train was full and there were no seats near the door so staff opened the toilet door and sat me on the toilet until I recovered my breath."

Pippa and I caught the train. We sat facing each other in a quaint, wood-panelled coach that looked 1930s but may have been 1960s in style, with 'Royal Scot' on the outside. Between us was a table laid with a white tablecloth and the plates, cutlery and glasses for our Great British breakfast. In the 'four' seats the other side of the aisle sat an elderly couple. The balding husband had coffee poured into his cup. He turned and said to me very politely, "I'm really looking forward to enjoying this." At Stevenage the peaceful atmosphere was suddenly invaded. A party of a dozen couples piled in, and there was a hubbub, indeed a commotion, as they identified their seats. Two couples stood over the man who was enjoying his coffee and unceremoniously established that he should be in coach C, not coach D. The couple had to vacate their seats and were bundled off into the next coach leaving their undrunk coffee – white cups and saucers – behind.

All through the Great British breakfast there was a hubbub as couples within the party called to each other. Two lots of four produced cards and shuffled and dealt. A large portly quizmaster with a moustache and beard and a red santa's hat with a bobble on the end that twinkled and a twinkling tie, who looked like Father Christmas, organised them, handing out sheets of his quiz and calling them "girls and boys" and commenting, "There seems to be strip poker going on here." There was raucous laughter. Couples peered at the sheets of questions and there was a lot of banter. More packs of cards were produced, and the couples next to us, who had turfed out the polite man who was enjoying his coffee, played a number game. All four had boards with numbers up to 10 in different colours which they had drawn from a central black bag, and they compiled lines of numbers as in Scrabble. It looked like a number scrabble. They played the game very intently with repeated cries of joy or disappointment, and there was a lot of loud laughter from all the tables of 'fours'.

Breakfast was served: muesli, fried egg and sausage and much else, bread, butter and marmalade with lashings of coffee. The train carried us across flooded Lincolnshire to Doncaster and Hull, and then turned towards Beverley station. A voice instructed us, "When you get off at Bridlington, those in coaches A, B, C, D and E should go down to F as these coaches will be outside the short platform at Bridlington." The voice repeated 'Bridlington' several times and then corrected itself to 'Beverley'. Rain was forecast for the whole day, and we walked through a steady drizzle to the Gothic minster for a carol concert.

Eventually the four hundred of us were seated under the towering arches of the nave. At the apex of each were stone figures playing medieval musical instruments: lutes, bagpipes, horns and tambourines. Gazing up at the architecture and reading a leaflet as I waited I grasped that the minster originated in a monastery founded c.700 in Anglo-Saxon times, and had been rebuilt between 1220 and 1420. It had been restored in the 18th century by Nicholas Hawksmoor, who added the twin towers. The inside did not seem to have changed since the medieval time, and had survived the Reformation and the Puritan iconoclasm.

After a procession of choristers in red and a welcome from the bald vicar, the local choir sang ancient carols, which were applauded, interspersed with hymns sung by the congregation. At one point an angelic chorister sang 'Walking in the air' from *The Snowman*.

At the end of the carol concert we headed for the front, and having consulted one of the local helpers who were in red sweaters I found the tomb of Henry Percy, 4th Earl of Northumberland and the mid-14th-century Gothic Percy canopy, an elaborately decorated stone arch that led from the 14th-century high altar to the small chapel that contained the 15th-century Percy tomb. Shakespeare's Hotspur, Harry Percy, who appears in *Richard II* and *Henry IV Part One*, would have known this canopy and chapel, but not the tomb which was for one of his descendants. I took in the "frith stool", which may have been a bishop's or abbot's throne and gave the minster a right of sanctuary (*frithu* being 'peace' in Anglo-Saxon).

I looked at some of the sixty-eight 16th-century misericords – many different carvings of domestic and farmyard animals – on the choir seats, and then looked at the 13th-century medieval stained glass in the east window within the retro-choir, where tens of thousands of pilgrims had knelt and which had been used as a school for a while. The lower glass had scenes from the lives of St Martin, St Nicholas and perhaps St Leonard.

It had been announced that there would be a couple of tours of the roof, and I saw the stragglers of the second group heading for the staircase. I paid and tagged along and found myself climbing a very narrow winding stair of 113 steep steps. It had been built around 1220 and was so narrow my shoulders brushed the curved wall on either side as I ascended.

At the top, slightly breathless, I found a huge wooden treadwheel. A guide gave us a talk and then stepped inside the wheel and trod it. As the wheel turned, a rope raised a circular serrated boss above the nave altar. He explained that the treadwheel, acting as a crane, worked as a hoist for the ten-metre-long oak trusses that were used as the roof's timbers. From seventy metres up I looked down at the nave altar (or communion table) below.

We were led through a door and found ourselves in a dimly-lit part of the roof space with a wooden floor. There was a round clear-glassed rose-window at the end (a wheel with ten spokes). We were directly behind the rose-window that can be seen from the town.

Twenty of us came out of the dingy light towards the large round window and looked down on Beverley two hundred feet below. My fellow pilgrims were holding back, blinking and squinting in the bright light and straining to see down without going too close to the window. They all seemed older than me. They all had the first chill of winter in their looks.

We were all dazzled by the light coming in through the round window, and by the new knowledge we had acquired. We were all still learning, finding out about new things, which is why we had climbed the spiral stair to this window. We were still dazzled by what is new and full of wonder at what we had not known until now. Though I was getting old I was still dazzled by the brilliance of the universe. It did not matter that the backs of my legs, my haunches and my lower back would ache from using rarely-used muscles in climbing the winding stair.

In the first dazzling chill of winter we had climbed the spiral stair to reach this eagle's view over the lands the minster had received from Athelstan in the 10th century and over the social life of the town which, two hundred feet below, could have still been medieval and of the time these sturdy walls were built across two streams. Despite being wintry in our skin, we were all dazzled by the construction of this towering edifice that had endured unchanged for seven or eight hundred years. Although we had begun to grow old we were still curious enough to take the ancient 1220 winding stair, whose side walls brushed against our shoulders. Up here we felt premonitions of eternity as we looked down in wonder on the world of social houses with our new perspective on the tiny world of time, and life was good.

To see the roof at close quarters we had to climb nearly-perpendicular iron steps thirty feet up to a higher level, and in due course we walked along a raised gantry between the 60-degree sloping wooden roof on either side. The roof was all 1220–1420, and some of the trusses had been dated by dendrochronology as 1140. They had been reused or recycled. Other trusses had been dated as 1330. We were shown the carpenters' marks. A corpulent bespectacled academic who was writing about the minster said that the whole building looked as "one build" even though it had been built over two hundred years after 1220 and had gone through three styles: from Early English to Decorated and then to Perpendicular. Having walked the full length of the roof above the minster, we had to climb more perpendicular steps, this time about twenty feet.

We descended down another narrow winding staircase. Pippa was waiting for me as I emerged on the ground floor.

We walked to find the Christmas market through drizzle. It was in a square with awnings, but it was really an ordinary market that sold fish and flowers, and one or two Christmassy items. Pippa bought some fudge. We then walked back to the station and as the train was too long for the platform we had to walk through a couple of coaches to return to our seats. The tables were laid for Christmas dinner.

The 'pilgrims' in the fours were even more noisy now. They called across the tops of seats to each other and made joking remarks. Between courses – soup and turkey and Christmas pudding, followed by cheese, biscuits, mince pies, coffee and chocolate – they resumed their games. The quizmaster, "Father Christmas", came and stood next to me to reveal the quiz answers.

He was a massive man. His bobble and tie twinkled, and he was taking sips from a hip-flask he held in one hand. I saw him as a Chaucerian figure. He was in the tradition of the Summoner who had made light of the pilgrimage. "What have we here," he boomed, noisily – drunkenly? – referring to a booklet I was reading. "That looks interesting, I must borrow that." I ignored the intrusion into my privacy. "No intellectuals here," he said, "everyone happy?" There was a chorus of "Yes" from the group. "Right. Well, the answer to question 1, how many miles from London to Beverley. The answer is 201.5 and I have awarded the points to the team that had 203."

He went through ten questions relating to Beverley. There was a dispute about the meaning of Beverley, which he pronounced to be "Bever's stream" ("ley" – "stream") and he then announced the results of the three teams in reverse order. The third and second teams noisily barracked: "Cheats", "Unfair". The winners cheered and put their thumbs up, and there was considerable crowing.

Chaucer's pilgrims had passed the time before and after the pilgrimage telling stories. This lot had passed the time doing a quiz on

Beverley and playing games, but the spirit was just the same. No one on the train, I reckoned, expected their visit to the Beverley carol concert to change their lives or win them entry into Heaven. But their camaraderie and banter had not been unlike that of Chaucer's secular pilgrims, egged on by 'my Host', who was not in the Tabard Inn but a Father Christmas with a twinkling bobble and a hip-flask. All on the train were in the first chill of winter but they were too engrossed in their entertainment to be dazzled by new learning or knowledge, or by a simple, child-like wonder at the universe.

I was in my eighth decade and despite my hermit's urge to withdraw from the world [which Pippa, wanting him to retire, actively cooperated with and reflected in her smokescreen Epilogue to *Collected Stories* – ed.] my quest for order, pattern and the One had not abated, and I still relished understanding my experience, my life and its place in the universe. And so, in the first dazzling chill of winter, I pondered what I had observed in my advancing old age, encouraged by my continuing good health and, despite the deaths of so many of my contemporaries, reassured by the unflagging energy I continued to bring to my projects.

A Dapper Man
(Or: The Man who Pea-ed on a Platform)

I saw a well-dressed gentleman standing outside the small hospital as I parked early on a Saturday morning. He was between seventy and eighty, and looked dapper in a jacket, collar and tie. He went in through the doors and I followed and signed the form. We sat down on either side of the aisle, the only outpatients at 8.15am.

About 8.30am my consultant strode through between us and said, "Good morning, gentlemen," and to him, "I'll only be two minutes." He wore a dark suit and went into his room.

"Are you seeing Mr Holmwood?" the dapper man asked.

"Yes," I said.

"I like him very much, I get on with him very well. I won't keep you long, I only want to ask him a question."

I wondered why he had not asked it over the telephone.

"I just want to show him something."

Mr Holmwood returned and the dapper gentleman went in. He came out ten minutes later and beamed at me as he passed me, waved me towards the room to indicate it was all mine now.

A nurse came out carrying a sheet of paper and called out my name.

"Yes," I said.

I sat with Mr Holmwood in his room and he told me that the biopsy he had taken was non-cancerous and non-pre-cancerous. I had a chronically inflamed prostate – a double whammy, the inflammation and then an operation – and it would take me six weeks to get back to normal.

"You're going to Paris," he said. "You may find you need to go to the lavatory urgently."

"I'll be on Eurostar," I said. "It'll be all right, so long as the lavatories are nearby. I'll go before I get on the train, there's bound to be somewhere on the platform."

Mr Holmwood smiled. "I was just talking to somebody," he said of the dapper man, "and he told me he'd been on a platform and he was bursting to go and there wasn't a lavatory and so he went where he was. There was a jet of water within his trousers, a stone came out in the middle of the jet and lay in a puddle on the platform. He bent down and picked the stone up. It was the size of a pea."

So that was what the dapper man wanted to show him.

"No damage done?" I asked.

"No. The body's very resilient. It came up the water-pipe, a stone the size of a pea." He shook his head.

"It brings a new dimension to having a pee," I said. "The man who pea-ed on a platform."

The consultant smiled.

Later I reflected on how courteous and friendly the dapper man had been. He was such a gentleman, dressed immaculately, and I found it hard to visualise his wetting himself on a crowded platform, looking down at the puddle round his shoes and picking up a stone and putting it in his pocket. So failing body functions make the most gentlemanly cringe with embarrassment – and recount their horrors with good humour.

A Corpulent Barber and an Angry Son

"I visited Jack Marney, the MP, twice," said the corpulent barber, his belly hanging out above his trousers as he bent and snipped my hair. "The first time he didn't help much. A fellow came by and said all shopkeepers must be put on a water meter. I thought no, I'm not doing that. Then someone came round and said they're targeting certain shops, like hairdressers' which wash hair but not estate agents' where they make continual cups of tea and pull their chain. I went to Marney and he said, 'That's wrong. I'll do something about that.' Three weeks later he wrote back saying he'd investigated and they were within their rights under some Water Act, which he disagreed with.

"The second time was about my boy. When he was fifteen he wanted to be a barber, and I wanted him to go to college. So I went to his school and said I wanted him to have some training on day release, one day a week, and the Head said, 'He's too young.' I said, 'I'll lie about his age.' He said, 'So long as I don't know about it, that's all right.' So I contacted the college and got him admitted for day release, one day a week. Then they turned round and said, 'The first year's ladies' hairdressing. The second year's men's.' I said, 'No, he wants to be a barber.' They wouldn't budge. So I went to Marney and he said, 'That's completely wrong. I don't agree with that, I'll look into it.' And he did. And they wrote to me saying he could come in and do two years of day release, both years would be men's. He became a barber. He did half his training while at school. He was in one of my shops. I had four shops in those days."

"Is he still working with you?" I asked.

"No, I've lost contact with him. It was a result of my divorce twelve years ago. He went with the money and took his mother's side. I had a choice. Either I kept her for the rest of her life, but if you're just starting a new relationship with a new woman that's not a very good idea. Or I could pay her out. There was a hearing. She stood up in court and said what her lady solicitor told her to say, that she couldn't work for thirty years because I wouldn't allow her. Completely untrue but they believed her. She had two of my hairdressing shops *and* £230,000. They attacked me after that. They came round my house, burst in – my son and his wife, and my wife – and attacked me. I took them to court. They got off scot-free. Said I dragged them inside my house. I was living at Elsenham near Stansted, and they had to go specially by car to my front door. They didn't happen to be walking past. He went with the money, but it hasn't done him any good. He hasn't got any money apart from what they got from me. And I've got all these properties now. I've been buying houses to let, one at a time, just paying the interest, no capital repayments, and waiting for the houses to go up in value due to inflation."

"Perhaps you should monitor your son, to see if you should contact him," I said.

"Nah, I'm not interested. I don't want anything to do with him or his mother," the barber said flatly, smiling at me with his eyes.

I had stood up and was paying. He kept his usual tip and gave me my change.

I said, "He's a barber now, he might tie up his shop with yours. He might regret what happened and be looking for a way back."

"There's no way back," the barber said, still smiling at me with his eyes. I noticed his nose was slightly hooked. "I don't want to see any of them again. I'm with my second wife now and feed all the birds and squirrels in my garden in Norfolk and buy houses to let, and they've gone off with a lot of my money and I don't want to see them again."

And I felt sad for a vanished closeness that had been sufficiently warm for him to wangle his son into a college day-release course at fifteen by overstating his age. He had cared then, and I could not believe that he did not care now. I thought he had been so hurt by the behaviour of his wife and son that he had cut them out of his life.

I said "Goodbye" as his next customer walked through the door. In the street outside I realised that I did not know anything about the circumstances of his second marriage. Had he dumped his wife after thirty years, and was his son understandably angry? Was the corpulent barber the baddie in the story after all?

A Roundabout and a Crashed Life

The clock man brought the face back in his shiny black enclosed sports car. I could tell it was a Jaguar. He put the face in the outer cover so the wires poked through below and hooked on the weights. He made adjustments to the hands and set the time. Then he hooked on the spindle. He found a pin was missing from the glass door and replaced it. Then he stood back and admired his handiwork, a sallow completely bald fellow in his late fifties.

I paid him and walked with him to the front door. "I'll open the gates with my fob," I said.

"Oh," he said, "I've got my car back. You know I told you I'd written it off? You can see I've got it done. This is the same car as the one that was written off. Look, it's as good as new."

"Which bits are new?" I asked.

"Everything on the non-driver's side. Two doors. The strut between them. The floor. All the computer equipment above it. I drove it into the central reservation. It was a complete wreck. It was a category B write-off."

"You were insured?"

"Oh yes. I said I wanted to rebuild it. They put it down to category D and I bought it back and did all the work on it. There were only a few pence left of the insurance money. I liked the car."

"Can you remember the crash?"

"Oh yes. I came round a roundabout. Everything was going round and round in my head, and I saw the cars going round and round and I thought that's how it is, everything just goes round and round. I turned into a dual carriageway and I revved up and I drove straight into the central reservation. The steel barrier. I hit it so hard it was thrown across the road the other side. But I was unscathed. I was wearing my seat-belt. I knew I had to wear my seat-belt, somehow. I'd switched the computer off and so there was no tracking record, and then I knew I was doing it, I remember that."

Not fully understanding, I said, "So what happened? You can recall people round you? Police?"

"People gathered round. One who saw it said, 'It looked as if you wanted to do it.' A policeman came quickly. He took out his notebook and wrote things down. He asked me about the car. I said, 'I don't care about the car.' He said, 'I find that strange, most people would care about it.' I recognised him. I said, 'I know you from somewhere.' He said, 'I've always been a policeman. Before that I worked briefly on the oil rigs.' I said, 'That's where I know you from. I was on the oil rigs.' Do you know, we worked on the same rig twenty-seven years ago?"

"That's weird," I said. "Eerie. As though there was a Providential connection between you."

"I told him a car cut me up. He said, 'John, I've measured the tyre marks. There was no other car. You did it deliberately, didn't you?' I said, 'If you say I did, well....' He said, 'You've done something stupid.' But he helped me. More police arrived and he sent them away. He said they weren't needed, he could handle it. It was twenty-seven years since I saw him." Then he added matter-of-factly to me by way of explanation, "I was depressed."

I was shocked.

"What did your wife say when she heard?" I asked. I had given her tea while he repaired the clock last time it had gone wrong. She was very attractive in an Essexy sort of way.

"She's left me," he said. "She went in December. Her father was ill and she went back to look after him in his house and he died and she never came back. She said she didn't want to live with me but you have to work at things. It's easy to walk away, when you're upset by a bereavement and confused."

"I'm sorry," I said.

"She went back to the house she came from and she's still there. It's a roundabout. That's why I was depressed, that's why I did it."

Appalled, I said, "Does she know that's what you did?"

"I think so, I think my children told her. They're thirty-four and thirty-six. They've been devastated by what happened a year ago."

"If you get an urge to repeat what you did, ring me and I'll tell you you're needed. You're looking after a clock here, and you're going to France about a clock tomorrow."

"I am," he said. "No, I'm all right now. Then after France it's the Czech Republic."

"It'll soon be Christmas. Will you spend time with your children?"

"I don't want to think about that. We were made for each other. But she can't see it."

At that moment Pippa was at the front door, saying I had a phone call.

"I've got to go," I said, "but I mean it. Ring me if you feel that way."

"Thanks, mate," he said. And he climbed into the shiny black sports car he had deliberately crashed and wrecked and flashed me a smile and with a wave drove off towards my opening gates, and I watched him go with some awe. He had decided to end his life at a roundabout and had smashed into the central reservation with his seat-belt on. If he had really wanted to die he would have removed his seat-belt. He was surely sending his wife a message that he wanted her back. I watched the tail-lights of a lonely man turn out into the road and watched him drive his crashed life away.

A Rickety Stepladder and a Dreamer's *Chaise Longue* (Or: No Coffin Hatch for Sir)

"I've been looking for the coffin hatch but I haven't seen her," said Robert, a stocky, black-haired, beetle-browed, ruddy-faced, vivid Cornishman as the cement-mixer churned in my dining-room to mix grey sand into slurry for the anti-damp tanking of the walls in my seaside house. "A lot of these old Cornish houses had narrow staircases and they left a coffin hatch so the coffins could go out. They took up certain floorboards and then put them back again after the coffin had gone down. I worked with a firm for eighteen years, and we often found a coffin hatch. When I started, in 1975, I was with a couple of old boys. One of them told me he had to catch a horse and put it in front of a cart to begin work. The old days of horse and cart. I learnt the old ways from them, everything, slate on a roof. One of the first I worked for was Sir William Golding, who wrote *Lord of the*...." He frowned. "I forget what it's called."

"*Lord of the Flies*," I said.

"Yes, *Lord of the Flies*."

"That is the first of his books."

"I didn't know he'd written other books."

"What was Golding like?"

"Lovely man," Robert said. "When I first saw him I thought he was the gardener. He was dressed in nothing special. He bought *Talimar* from Princess Schula. She was a real Princess, I don't know what nationality she be. The lodge was five hundred yards the Devon side of the Norway Inn between Truro and Falmouth. He rented the lodge out. A path led up to the house and there was another property to the side. He rented that out too. I did all sorts of jobs for him for eighteen years, slate off the roof, putty in his box windows loose, that sort of thing. Once I was up a rickety stepladder in his main room and the steps slid and I fell back onto his *chaise longue*." Robert chuckled. "He was so nice about it. The gardener was Ken Humphreys, and Mrs. Humphreys was housekeeper, cooked his meals for him and did everywhere. We talked general things really, about the property. He never mentioned his book. He died soon after I stopped being with that firm. Yes, I had a good eighteen years with that firm.

"Then one day I was called to the yard at Christmas time, 1993. I thought, 'Emergency work.' When I arrived they said, 'The firm's closed.' Bankrupt. It was grandfather, father and then son. Father'd had a heart attack and the son was propelled in without experience. Seventy-five years the firm lasted. Then I was on my own for five years. But I was too soft. I'd do a lady's slate and she'd make me a cup of tea and say, 'How much do I owe you, Rob?' And I'd say, 'Make it a fiver.'"

I thought of Robert up his rickety stepladder, putting the author's house in order, climbing up step by step and falling off and having to start again, and of the author reclining on his *chaise longue*, dreaming up new works that Robert would not know existed, let alone read.

"A heart of gold," I said.

He chuckled. "Now," he said as the cement-mixer churned, holding his brush to paint on the slurry, "I'm going to tank your back wall, sir."

A Leaving Party at the Osteopath's

I entered the osteopath's reception area and was greeted by the receptionist. There was nowhere to sit. The five seats were taken by middle-aged women. One got up and squashed next to another woman in the window and I said "Thank you" and sat down. "We're having a leaving party," my neighbour said, and I saw the bottle of French wine on the table and the paper cups they were holding.

"Oh," I said, "who's leaving?"

"Linda. We're all the past receptionists. It's very sad."

"Carry on," I said.

I could not put a face to Linda, so I sat and looked at the fish in the aquarium while a lady with shoulder-length hair sat in the swivel-chair for patients and talked incessantly to the rest, her tongue loosened by the red wine. Periodically the others laughed. The story seemed to be about her dog.

"Do you know Gants Hill?" she asked. She was speaking to me. It was a rebuke for appearing not to listen. They were all women together and the dominant female was letting the others know that she had power over men.

Drawn in, I said, "Yes, but not very well."

"The flats down from the station on the first floor are full of prostitutes," she continued, suggestively catching my eye, making sure that she held my attention along with all the others'. "My dog raced up the iron stairway and disappeared into an open door. I said to a lady, 'Who lives up there? The flat with the door open?' She said, 'Prostitutes. They're in all the flats along there.' I had to do something, didn't I. So I climbed up the stairway and went to the door. I couldn't see my dog. Then this man came by with a scar all down the side of his face. 'Whata you want?' he asked. I said, 'The prostitute in there's got my dog.' He said, 'Whya prostitute wanta your dog? Goa away.' I said, 'I'm not going until the prostitute in there gives me back my dog.' 'Goa away.' Luckily the dog came running out, no thanks to him. You don't know who's up there when you're in Gants Hill, do you?" she said.

Then the osteopath appeared with Linda – the only receptionist I knew, without knowing her name – and he called me through to have my back firmly massaged and pummelled and pushed back into shape.

The osteopath said, "We're having a little leaving party."

"Yes, I heard. Why's Linda leaving?"

"Oh, she's just retired, that's all. I've left her job open in the hope she'll change her mind, but she won't."

When I came out half an hour later the lady with shoulder-length hair was still holding court to the assembled receptionists from her swivel-chair. She looked me in the eye very forwardly.

"You've got a little left in the bottom of the bottle," I said. "Enjoy the rest of your party."

And I left before she could involve me in any further suggestive conversations to impress her co-receptionists.

Wild Boar
(Or: The Man who Knew Everything)

The ship was rolling slightly. I was shown to a table near a window overlooking the sea and found myself opposite a balding Scot with dreamy eyes who talked non-stop. He had an opinion on everything. The cruise? "Standards have slipped, lecturers speak from notes. If they don't know their subject well enough to speak without notes they shouldn't be there." The students who sang opera? Again he was critical. Whatever topic the others raised was met with a negative response and his white-haired wife smiled and nodded and said, "It's true."

Over the main course – I had chosen wild boar – he let slip he had worked in the oil industry.

"What company did you work for?"

"I didn't, I worked for myself."

"As a consultant?"

"Yes," he said without humour. "I know everything."

I asked him about the progress of pipelines in Iraq, Afghanistan and Iran but he had no new information to give me. I asked him if he had heard that Iraqi oil was being shipped out to China where it was being stored in warehouses before being returned to the West. He did not know of the plan. I asked him if there was a switch from the Trans-Afghan pipeline to the Iran-Pakistan-India pipeline, for if so it would mean there would have to be regime change in Iran. He said, "That's all happened since I was in the business." He clearly did not know everything. In relation to my questions, he did not know anything.

For pudding I chose ice coupe and watched the slightly choppy sea glide by the window. Then the conversation returned to other cruises, and one shipping line which had no lectures.

"That's fine by me," he said, "I don't need to attend lectures, I know everything. It's people who attend lectures I feel sorry for. They still have things to know." He looked at me.

I could not let that pass. I said, "I research my subjects and I shall go on learning until I die. There are always new things to learn. Lectures are useful, they bring new things to mind."

He turned very aggressive. "What do you do? Where are you from? Were you born in England? Have I heard of you?" The questions came thick and fast, crowding on each other, and I had no time to answer.

He seized on my interest in philosophy.

"What is it? Ethics? Noetics? What are you saying about philosophy?" demanded the man who knew everything.

I said, "I'm saying that modern philosophy went into a *cul-de-sac* a hundred years ago and focused on language and logic. It excluded the expanding universe. I am interested in what made the Big Bang happen, what preceded the Big Bang."

"Nothing preceded the Big Bang," he said. "I don't accept that the universe is expanding."

"I have chapter and verse," I said. "Hawking has your position and he's wrong." And I explained that the universe could not be understood physically, only metaphysically. "If you address what was before the Big Bang you're into metaphysics," I said.

One of the others on the table, a black-haired man, said, "I see you are a deep thinker."

The ex-oil consultant had now fallen silent. And I made my excuses, smiled at everyone and left to have a white port in the Bridge-Deck Lounge. I reflected that it is very unwise to say "I know everything" for the opposite can be readily demonstrated. He had committed a strategic blunder. But by savaging him like a wild boar, had I not, by implication, demonstrated that I too knew everything?

A Plane on the House

I was on a cruise and between Portugal and Spain I sat down to breakfast with an old lady with smiling lines round her eyes.

"Oh hello," she said. "This is my first cruise. My husband would never have come, he was into sport and just didn't want to be away. But now he's died I've tried it and I love it. It's so friendly and the connections I've made. I was speaking to someone yesterday and she said a name and I said, 'You mean...?' A woman left on her own with four children. It's the same one. Oh I've been so fortunate. Having lived in the countryside in Lincolnshire I wouldn't want to go on a big town of a ship. I have a farm and organise the crop-pickers. We used to have eighty-one but now I'm down to six.

"I've been so fortunate. In 1962 a bomber from the RAF base near Boston fell on our house. I went through a window and my husband through a door. It was on television, the bomber landed half on our house, half in our garden. We both survived. I had cracks down below and my husband had cracked sides, he was in hospital three months. But we were alive. We shouldn't have been. The insurance was a nightmare. I had to go and be examined and was told, 'You won't need down below.' I was thirty-two. The RAF didn't want to pay anything and we got £1,500 in the end. Luckily our house was insured but we had to write everything down and the company disputed all our valuations. But we came through. And then a few years later we took a boat to Guernsey and there was a storm and that was on television and people said, 'Not you again.'

"I've been so lucky. I shouldn't be here but it was fated. I have the three children I wanted, and grandchildren. I trained as a nurse and became a sister – today the standards are so slovenly – and I try to give something back for being here. I try to help people. And I'm surprised at how many on this ship are infirm and halt. My son-in-law said, 'Don't be diagnosing them, you're on holiday.' I've had a wonderful life."

The eighty-year-old woman with smiling crease marks round her eyes looked radiantly tranquil and serene. She had been through an appalling experience but her untroubled soul shone through. And her story had commanded my full attention. I wondered if she had used it as a stratagem to secure this.

A Nurse and a Bleeding Consultant

I sat opposite an attractive old lady and next to her bespectacled, chubby, sixty-five-ish companion for dinner on the ship and introduced myself.

"I'm Nick," said the man, "and this is my mother."

"At my age," said the old lady, "I'm too old to come on a cruise without help and I've brought my son. I'm in London. He's in Northumbria and works in Newcastle."

"Oh," I said to him, "what do you do?"

"He's a consultant."

"Oh, what in?"

"Old age, I changed from what I'd been doing."

"What had you been doing?"

"Adult psychiatry."

"So what do you recommend to arrest old age?"

"Oh, the usual things. Exercise. Diet. Keeping your brain active."

"He's a good consultant," said his mother.

I saw the consultant's right arm move to the right. The hand was below the tablecloth.

"Don't dig me like that," his mother said.

He had dug his mother under the tablecloth.

"I don't want to talk about it," he said.

Looking down to my right I saw he had a napkin wrapped tightly round his left hand like an improvised tourniquet or tight bandage. He had been eating with one hand.

He added, "I'm three-and-a-half days a week, I'm preparing for retirement by filling the other day-and-a-half with hobbies for my retirement."

Tactfully I changed the subject. I said, "At the wine-tasting this afternoon, a man with Parkinson's disease, sitting next to me, didn't realise you sipped from the eight glasses and tipped the rest away. He drank the lot. One-and-a-half glasses puts you over the limit for driving, we were told, and he had four glasses."

"So did I," the fellow said guiltily. "It was a pity to waste it."

"How many glasses?" his mother asked searchingly.

"Uh, not many."

After further chit-chat she said, "Oh, France was the cheapest place to go to in the twenties and thirties."

"Do you remember the outbreak of the war, Chamberlain's speech?" I asked.

"Oh, yes. I was an art student at the time. I thought I should volunteer to be a nurse. My supervisor said it would last a long time so I trained as a nurse. I was in St George's Hospital, London."

"During the Blitz?"

"Oh, yes. The patients all had to go downstairs when there was an air raid, no matter how ill they were. I felt so sorry for them. They put all their personal effects on their bed and came downstairs. Many had to sleep on the underground platforms, but we had other arrangements. But often we just carried on. I remember on one occasion a bomb fell when we were carrying on and blew out the entire wall of our building. I was very afraid, but I couldn't show it. You just had to carry on."

"The wartime spirit," I said.

"Yes," said her son. "We've had it easy in relation to my mother's generation. Two world wars and unemployment in between."

"We didn't want your generation to go through what we had to go through," she said. "I'm ninety-one, and I'm so pleased your generation hasn't suffered like mine."

"My mother did so well during the war," said the consultant. "And I came along just after the war. My mother's a wonderful woman. Her generation made sure that ours did not suffer and had an easy life. I look after her quite a bit. I drive down the A1 to where she's living whenever I can, and take her out. Then I drive back up to go on working. She's in London and I'm in Northumbria, but really it's as though we're still living in the same house. I'm so glad I can help her with the excursions for this ship."

He had finished and he unwound his napkin and laid it on the table.

It had round bloodstains in several places. I looked at the back of his left hand and saw a gaping hole surrounded by dried blood, as though a scab had been knocked off. He came from a peaceful time that had escaped his mother's suffering, but he had a wound in his being and I detected that his singleness irked him like a festering sore.

The Moors' Paradise and a Sigh

Our coach set off from Motril for the Alhambra along a dual carriageway. "This was built with European money from your pockets," announced the guide on his microphone. He was a thickset, bearded man with in-control eyes. He pointed out custard apples (or cherimoyas) growing beside the road, and sugar cane. "We are going through the Sierra Nevada," he said. "'*Sierra*' means 'range', '*Nevada*' means 'snow-capped mountains'. There is still some snow near the top." He drew our attention to the large mechanical generators or turbines that disfigured the landscape and talked of modern Don Quixotes fighting windmills. Then he talked about the history of the Iberian Peninsula; how the Romans came in 219/8BC and controlled the Peninsula by 19BC, and how the Visigoths conquered it in 409 and the Arabs from 711 and then the Moors "from Morocco, Mauretania and Algeria" in the 11th century. They were expelled in 1492.

"For nearly 800 years," he said, "Spain was ruled by Muslims. Then Boabdil, the last Moorish Sultan, was expelled by Isabella. Columbus seems to have been an eyewitness. Boabdil left Granada on horseback and turned round to take his last look from the top of a hill and wept for the Muslims' loss of 800 years of being based in Granada and for his defeat by a woman. It was the Moors' last sigh. His wife said, 'Don't cry like a woman for what you wouldn't defend as a man.'"

We went under a bridge. Suddenly the coach slowed down and I could see there was a lane closure. A car was parked in front of us and another to the side of the right-hand (slow) lane. I was sitting on the right-hand side of the coach and as I looked out of the window, slowly slid by me what looked like pieces of a dead deer. There was flesh, then more, then a carcass. It looked like a deer without legs or head. Then there was more and at last a fifth pile. It looked as if hunks of meat had fallen off a butcher's lorry.

"An animal has been knocked over," the guide said authoritatively and he looked back at me with in-control eyes that defied me to believe he was lying.

We went on to the Alhambra palace and a local guide took us on a walk up through tall cypresses into the Gardens and commented on how they copied or reflected the Muslim idea of Paradise which had four rivers: of wine, milk, honey and water. (I thought of Coleridge's "For he on honey-dew hath fed,/And drunk the milk of Paradise".) He said, "In 1453 the Ottoman Turks took Constantinople, the old Byzantium. The fall of Granada was the Christians' revenge."

Finally after a long walk I encountered our in-control guide outside the palace of Charles V.

"It was a local man who committed suicide," I heard him telling one of our group. "One of our guides heard it on the radio. He threw himself off the bridge just before where we passed him. Of course it was dark, and lorries and cars did not see him. His remains broke up and were carried further along the motorway."

I was shocked. The deerhide must have been a shirt covering his torso. The other bits and pieces were legs and arms, and somewhere there must have been a head. Death had reared up from the Moors' Paradise.

We continued to the fortress and saw the Hall of the Ambassadors with its seven Heavens shown as gigantic stars in the ceiling, the Courtyard of Myrtle and the Courtyard of Lions (which was being restored).

After lunch we returned to our coach and, travelling the other way on the dual carriageway, I looked out for the cordoned-off lane. I thought I saw one blob of flesh, but the body parts of the local man had been cleaned up and he had now been erased from public consciousness.

I wondered who he was, this local man who had been desperate enough to throw himself off a motorway bridge in the dark in front of a passing lorry, and who had been torn to pieces like Orpheus. He had been whole and had now become bits, an undignified death at the hands of machines on wheels. He had had a soul. I did not know if he had been desperately in love and spurned, or if he had had financial problems which had got into his soul. As a suicide, he may not have gone to the Paradise the Moors knew.

I was sure that a man is more than pieces of meat, and like the retreating Moor I let out a sigh for the end of a time when the soul was still in control and revered.

A 1399 Home and Dolphins

I groaned inwardly when we were shown to a table opposite the chubby loud man who had spent the entire cruise doing a massive jigsaw. I spoke to my neighbour about this and that. She was a fairly plain woman married to a quiet, stooping, elderly electrical engineer. She told me her husband had had an Iraqi student who took them out to dinner and said of his wife, a lecturer, when the menu was presented, "I will choose for her." "I don't know how I controlled my tongue," my neighbour said.

She asked where we came from and then told me she came from Gloucestershire. She got on to her house in Gloucestershire. "It's 1399," she said. "I love it. It's a hall house. I don't know if it has blackened beams as there's a false ceiling. It's wattle and daub."

I said I had found wattle and daub cold to live in.

"Yes, it is cold, but I don't get cold easily, and there was a handprint I found there when I was opening up the walls to do a repair. I put my hand in and it fits exactly. That's a lovely feeling. I found a *Daily Mail* dated 2003 during my ownership when I had the wall opened. Someone had put it in and then put lining paper on top. I've put it in my file. There are no deeds. Whether they put them in an archive box or not I don't know, but the Land Registry hadn't got them when it was sold to me in 1979. I had an expert to look at the mantelpiece and he said he thought there was an older one there. You know, it's my family's house. I'm related to them, so I've come back home. That's a lovely feeling. It's haunted by a monk, but I feel very comfortable with his presence. I'm doing a university course but my main interest is my house. I've got lovely outbuildings as well, they're Victorian. There are so many features I love about it. I won't allow smoking, and no open fires. And certainly no public in to look at it. It's my house and all for myself."

Her husband had been half-listening quietly, so I leaned forward and to include him in the conversation said, "We've been discussing historic houses. I said the wattle and daub can be perishing in the winter. Do you find you have to wear an overcoat indoors in the winter sometimes?"

He made no reply at all, but looked down and carried on eating. I immediately sensed that he agreed with me and that he was not that interested in his wife's house. His wife went on talking about her house, and soon the chubby jigsaw-doer and his wife left and he stood up and looked out of the windows for dolphins and said, "I'm going to go on deck to see if I can see any."

Five minutes later I went up to the Promenade Deck. I saw ten dolphins in no time, a school dipping up and down alongside the ship. I could track them and see where they would surface next as they slipped by the ship.

I saw the husband peering over the side of a lower deck, looking in the wrong direction. He clearly had not seen any dolphins. He looked miserable, and I saw him living in a house he did not like, which he found cold, and dreaming of something to excite his imagination that was as elusive as a school of dolphins.

An Angry Old Man in a Passing Order

I came down in the lift with a tall, bald old man with round spectacles and his wife. We were shown to the same table where a couple were sitting. We sat opposite our lift companions and two more joined us. We talked about a whale some of them had photographed. It had come up some distance from our ship and blown, spouted a cloud of spume.

"Did you attend the lecture on Nelson?" I asked, for something to say.

"No."

I said, "It was said that Nelson was defeated at Naples in 1799, but as he was on the sea and the French occupied Naples by land, I can't see what he could have done to prevent them except dissuade the Neapolitans from attacking Rome."

"It's jobs for university people to explain the past," the old man said. "But I'm interested in explaining the future."

"We're supposed to learn from history," I said, "learn the mistakes of the past. The trouble is, the cuts will halve the Navy and there won't be a Navy in the Western Mediterranean to learn from Nelson's mistakes."

"And so lecturing on what Nelson did is a waste of time," he said angrily.

"There's going to be a tube strike," I said.

"Bloody unions," the man in the spectacles said. "Woodley and Crow, they're more militant than Scargill."

Two waiters, Filipinos, had given out menus and now began collecting them. I ordered avocado, celery soup and cod. Then I heard the spectacled old man say "No, no, you're wrong" to the bearded man we had joined. "It's democracy, that's the problem," he said. "Who do you think in the last twenty-five years has been good for their country?"

He was addressing me. His wife with short white hair was expecting me to reply.

"Twenty-five years ago," I said, "was in Thatcher's time. The Cold War."

"Which Cold War?" he asked sharply.

"The Soviet-Union one," I said.

"What about the Chinese Cold War? China won that."

"Got itself into the position of lending money to America."

"America's bankrupt and we're more bankrupt," he said. "Who in the last twenty-five years has been good for their country?"

"Gaddafi," I said. "He led Libya into terrorism but recently he's turned it round and led his country to prestige."

"You're on the right lines," the spectacled man said. "I think Charles de Gaulle."

"But he was helped by the British in the war, and then repaid any gratitude he should have had by excluding us from the Common Market."

"The British never won the war," the old man said savagely, "the

Americans did."

I talked on. "Perhaps democracy's always spin," I said. "Did Pericles spin during the Peloponnesian War?"

"You're right," the man with spectacles said savagely. "We need someone who can stop the rot. The health and safety, immigrants coming in and taking jobs, everything that's gone wrong with Britain."

The angry old man's wife said: "My stepbrother teaches at a school, and he hates parents' evenings. Not because of the English. He can cope with them all right. No, it's the Indians. They all give him grief over the homework. They say he's not setting enough homework. India's a powerful country these days."

"Can you pinpoint what has gone wrong?" the angry old man asked. He was addressing me.

I said, "You can see it in relation to Britain, and we need to reduce our debt. But also in the wider context of unions like the European Union, and those who are behind a self-interested world government, who want to profit out of us. As they did in the Cold War."

The Filipino waiters were clearing our plates.

"Perhaps power is passing from West to East," I said, "and there's nothing we can do about it."

"Yes," he said. "That's what's happening."

"It seems inevitable," said one of the women.

"We're at the end of an order, like the people in Chekhov," I said. "Chekhov's people in 1905, with 1917 ahead, looking back on the Russia they loved. An old order is passing," I said, "and we have a Chekhovian attitude to it."

There was a melancholy round the table as the Filipinos cleared our plates. The tall, bald old man with rounded spectacles was angry. He could partly see what was wrong, but could do nothing about it.

As Unyielding as a Slab of Granite

I called the lift to disembark, and it arrived. As I stepped in a small woman said "Oh good", and she and her husband pushed in and stood in front of the buttons. I could not press the button on the lift I had called.

"Someone has to give the lift an instruction," I said.

"Oh," said the woman, and pressed Deck A. "Oh, I've done it wrong," she said, "sorry, you're slowed up because there's a bad driver."

I did not comment. The lift stopped at Deck A and two more elderly disembarkers got in. When the lift stopped at Deck B the four of them got out first and took their places ahead of me in the queue to disembark for Calvi, Corsica.

I encountered the lady again in the coach. She was sitting across the gangway from me in the window-seat, and before the coach set off she leaned forward and said to an old man who had a large hearing-aid and a stick, "You've just moved the seat back. It's crushing my husband's knee." Her husband had one eye closed, and said nothing.

The old man with the hearing-aid fiddled with the seat mechanism and gave up.

A minute later she tried again. "It's most unfair of you to leave your seat back. It's crushing my husband's knee."

The old man protested, "I haven't done anything, I haven't touched it."

"Well you've obviously done something," the woman said. Passengers nearby exchanged glances but said nothing. The old man's wife looked nervously about her, but said nothing.

The coach started and took us on a tour of North-West Corsica. The lady was asleep when the guide pointed out the grey slabs of granite where Nelson had stood during the Siege of Calvi in 1794: "A cannon-ball hit that slab of granite and splinters hit Nelson's temple and blinded him in his right eye. He could only make out light and dark."

We got out to look at the British position above Nelson's slab. It was by the granite walls of the church of Our Lady of the Hillside. Everyone disembarked in seat order, waiting for those in front to squeeze out into the gangway and head for the door at the front. The woman stood up and after her husband had gone forward boxed the old man in so he could not move when his turn came.

Somehow on the way out she changed places with her husband. We were all held up as she stood outside the door of the coach and straightened the mat before her husband stepped down on it, saying: "It's very dangerous."

She was a well-intentioned woman who was trying to prevent her half-blind husband from walking down the stairs, from having his knee crushed, from tripping on the mat, but her attentiveness made her unaware of others and slightly combative. She was as unyielding as a slab of granite.

A Black-Out and Table Tennis

We were shown into dinner and sat at a table with a balding man in spectacles and his wife. I talked to an elderly man with a hooked nose who told me he had left the UK for Canada in 1957. "My wife said everything was drab after Suez, couldn't we go to Canada or Australia? We did. I've got two daughters in the UK so I go and see them regularly. I'm ninety-one next birthday."

While I was admiring his vitality for his age, saying I would have placed him in his late sixties (which pleased him), the balding man in spectacles announced, "My memory's atrocious. I've just been told I've got dementia."

There was a silence. Conversation stopped. No one knew what to say.

Later on I engaged him in conversation. "Can you remember things from your boyhood?" I asked.

"Yes," he said. "But I can't get them out."

"Cricket and football?"

"Oh, yes. I saw..." (he struggled) "Compton play in...."

His wife said, "1948."

"Yes, 1948, in the winter he played for Arsenal. So my father took me to watch. And Denis Compton played left wing, and his brother Leslie was centre half."

"You remembered that," I said. "Who else was in the Arsenal team?"

He thought hard.

"My father was an Arsenal supporter," his wife said, "so I know some of the team. But I want *him* to remember. He relies too much on me."

"Swindin was in goal," I said.

"Yes, George Swindin."

"And Reg Lewis scored two goals in a cup final."

He looked doubtful.

"There was a little one," he said.

"Logie."

"Yes, Logie."

"You can remember more than you think you can," I said. "People have had half their brain removed following an accident, and the other half learns to cope. They create new networks and pathways and connect things up, learning to do everything all over again. You could start by writing out the Arsenal team in the 1940s and learning them all over again and then you could write out every year and fill in what you can remember, writing it down, and then add to it more and more. Don't give in to dementia. The more you do the more you can hold it back. If you play a sport the more practice you do the better you become. It's the same with the brain. Crosswords, chess, jigsaw puzzles – use it and improve your memory. It's like going to the gym. Doing it regularly improves your mobility."

The 91-year-old Canadian had finished his dinner. He made his excuses and left.

"I'll come and sit beside you," he said. "I was good at table tennis. I should play table tennis again. I played for several counties at table tennis."

"Which ones?" I asked.

"Oh, er, which ones did I play for?"

His wife said, "I want you to remember for yourself."

He thought hard.

"Where do you live?" I asked.

"Mill Hill. We met at John Linyards," he said, looking at his wife. "They were the local employer. I travelled for five years for them, doing bonuses. We paid sixpence from our salary and we could use the facilities. There was a table-tennis table and I played a lot. Old Mr Linyard was very good to the staff. He took us to the seaside once a year, Margate was one place. All for sixpence."

"Perhaps there were tax implications," I said. "He needed to charge so it wasn't a benefit in kind."

"Yes," his wife said.

"Oh, I don't know about that. He was a good man."

"You remembered all that," I said. "You can remember a lot more than you think you can."

"Yes, I can," he said doubtfully. "But the thing is, I had a black-out. We were at a wedding, and we had a tiswas. I drove home alone and I blacked out and my car…." He struggled to remember what happened. "I had a bit of a tiswas with my wife and the road was like this" (he drew a diversion on the tablecloth) "and I went to the left and then right and I blacked out and…."

"Crashed into the car in front," his wife said gently.

"Yes, and pushed it into the one in front so it went into a skip and crushed its right wing."

"You blacked out?" I said, wondering how he could know this detail if he was unconscious.

"Yes. I came to in the ambulance. And the doctor looked at me and said, 'You've got dementia.' So you see, I've lost my confidence after the black-out."

"You may never have another black-out," I said. "People black out in their bathroom and hit their head, and it never happens to them again. It's like a stroke. You have one but it doesn't mean you'll have a second. You may never black out again."

"No, that's right," he said excitedly. "You're right. I must stop thinking I can't remember."

"Be positive," I said.

"Yes," he said. "But you know, I've been thinking, I'm…. How old am I?"

"Seventy-eight," his wife said.

"Yes, I think I'm seventy-eight and I've had a good life and I shouldn't worry if I die. I worked for John Linyard, I've always been self-reliant, it doesn't matter if I can't talk to a lot of people because my memory's so atrocious. I've had a good life, and it doesn't matter if I've got dementia now. But you're right, I must do more to get my memory back, so long as it's not too difficult. I'll get back to playing table tennis."

Nemesis in Naples (Or: A Wheelchair and a Queue)

We were in Pompeii. It came on to drizzle and our group put up packable umbrellas. Our guide headed for the nearest covered house. Two groups were already sheltering inside and two more groups were trying to get in out of the rain. We stood for about 15 minutes while the groups inside filed out, and then we pushed in and were the first group to go inside to see the peristyle (a garden with a square hole in the roof) and frescos of bulls and lions on a back bedroom wall.

Light rain was still falling when we came out, and we continued our tour, stepping on the uneven polygonal stones, and we reached a fountain.

An elderly man in a white hat said to the guide, "Please take us to where there are no other groups. We should not be standing outside buildings that have other groups in them."

"I will try to do as you say, but I want to show you the most interesting buildings. I have to see the buildings in order," the Italian guide said, taken aback.

"Well, you're the guide, you can decide where we go."

There was a silence. Members of the group exchanged glances. One of the women said to me, "He's so rude. When I was waiting to get off the coach he prodded me in my back with his stick and said 'Move'. He's a Doctor somebody."

As we stood by the fountain, improbably a lady appeared in a wheelchair. She was being pushed by a young girl, who was having difficulty in negotiating the polygonal stones in the road.

"Can you step back?" she asked. She was clearly English. "I need to come where you are."

She was addressing the man in the white hat, who stood his ground.

"There shouldn't be wheelchairs in Pompeii," he said. "It's not suitable for them."

The young girl turned and said very calmly, "You may be like this one day and you may think differently then. Wheelchairs *are* allowed in Pompeii, and that's the regulation, and she's making use of it."

With that the man in the white hat grudgingly stood back and let her through and she proceeded to bump over the polygonal stones with her charge.

The next day we came home. The flight from Naples was delayed two hours, and boarding was supposed to be at 1.20. Passengers were called to gate B14. We filed out, showing our boarding passes, and climbed onto a bus. I found a seat, but most had to stand. I noticed the man in the white hat had to stand by one of the doors.

There was clearly a delay. Nothing happened for twenty minutes, and then a passenger got off and spoke to one of the ground crew. She returned and said, "We're waiting for four wheelchairs." No one said anything. The occupants of the wheelchairs should clearly have been called first and we should have remained seated by the gate until they had boarded. Instead we had been shepherded into a bus and left to stand in the heat. Out of the open door I could see one wheelchair after another being wheeled to a machine with a fork lift, like a glorified JCB. A fifth wheelchair was occupied by the old lady who had visited Pompeii in a wheelchair the day before.

The man in the white hat saw her. "It's appalling," he said loudly to the whole bus. "We're being treated like cattle."

No one said a word.

But I thought that something karmic had happened. As we sow we reap. There had been a boomerang. He had spoken out against a wheelchair at Pompeii and now he had been held up by the same one and four others.

The bus eventually left at 2. We were deposited by a landing-stage. A landing-stage at the front of the plane was for wheelchairs only. Everyone else had to queue at the back, including the very elderly. When we boarded the plane the wheelchair cases were trying to walk to the back of the plane where their seats were. Now the last half of the queue were told they could board at the front.

Boarding was not completed until 2.30, one hour and seven minutes after the flight was called. The last to board was the elderly man in the white hat. He did not look pleased, but his *hubris* had swollen to *até* and the gods had inevitably targeted him with a little *nemesis*.

A College and Cowboys

"Did you have a good night last night, sir?" asked an oldish, balding man as I walked back from putting my belongings into my car.

"Yes, thank you," I said.

"That's good," he said. "It's nice that the old boys, pardon my manner of speaking, should come back, see where they were. I'm only a relief porter, I do engineering work at weekends, but I see a lot of the old boys. They all have tales to tell. For example, that gate. In your day it was closed early and you had to climb in if you were after that time. One of the other porters told me, 'We were always watching.' Now they have a swipe card and they let themselves in and out as they please. They can stay out all night if they want to."

I told him about an experience I had had with the gate.

"Yes," he said as we walked through the Provost's Yard and up the steps to the terrace. "Many of the old boys are characters, they have memories. You're a bit of a character if I may say so. You all have things to say, whereas today with their swipe cards the young gentlemen don't have that, they just seem to come for three years and then go. It's good to remember what things were like. I don't think they do it right. Your old room should be open, and the library."

"My old room's now a don's," I said, "on staircase 5."

"Yes. It's all changed. All the old rooms are taken by the staff. It's not my place to say but I don't think they do it right. There's an enormous waste of space. I'd have all the administrative staff together in one place. They're dotted around. They don't seem to have any idea of how to do it, compared with those who've been out in the real world. I've known two Clerks of Works, and I know it's not my place to say, but the waste.... Cowboys are employed to build the new buildings. I've seen them. I'm an engineer, and I can tell very quickly who's a cowboy and who isn't. The Provost has to run a staff of, what, with scouts, 150. He may have been good in a library, but the question is, is he good at picking the builders and who he employs? It's not my place, but in my view they haven't a clue about the finance. In the old days the college was under half the size, and there wasn't room for the gentlemen to live in all the year, but they seemed to know what they were doing better then. No, give me the old days. That's what I say."

We had passed the chapel and were at the Porters' Lodge.

"Delighted to have talked to you, you're a character who understands how it could all be done better," said the relief porter, and he went into the Porters' Lodge.

Noah's Pageant

"I'm a countryman," said the retired stockbroker over breakfast. "I live in Gloucestershire. I've got animals. It's not much but I spend all my time looking after them: sheep, donkeys, poultry. Many years ago I wrote a book about the rural church. It says in one sentence that vicars should be responsible for their churches. Localism rather than centralisation. It's been required reading for theological students, but not for anyone after they've finished. I support our vicar in being responsible for his church. For example, I wrote a pageant about Noah's ark. I brought animals from my farm. I led them into the church. We had two donkeys and two sheep, two of various poultry and two doves. The children loved it. It brought the message of Noah's ark home to them. I believe we're all one creation. We are all linked to the animals, out of the first cell. I'm one of them, we're all one of them, as it were. Yes, I'm like Noah. I love my farm and my donkeys, sheep and poultry, and my life outside that is to do with my rural church."

A Chapel on the Bend

"We sold our funeral directors' business, and that same morning I said, 'I'm never going back'," said Jim's wife, brushing her groomed hair back from her Spanish-tanned face, her dark glasses cocked back on top of her hair, as we sipped coffee in a restaurant round the corner. "Jim's stayed on as a consultant, but he didn't like the package. They said they didn't want the Chapel of Rest up near St Blazey. We put a price of £50,000 on it, but they said they didn't want it and Jim thought they weren't too keen on him staying on. But now we've spent £25,000 on doing it up as a little business for him to continue in his retirement, a smaller funeral director's business than the previous one and no office because Jim goes to their homes to talk. We've sectioned off an area with a prep room. And now they know what we're doing they've come back to us, not wanting us to be in competition, offering us fifty thousand plus the twenty-five thousand and a three-year package worth £400,000 in all. Jim's turned it down. I said to him, 'You've just got thirteen more months to do, then you've got a retirement project you can put your energy into, and your own Chapel of Rest."

"How did you get into the funeral business?" I asked. "Did Jim have it already before you met?"

"Yes," she said. "You know his first wife was killed at twenty-seven?"

"No," I said, "I didn't know."

"Run into by a car near St Blazey. She wanted to start Hearse Hire, she got it all going. Jim was on his own for seven years, then we met. I had no education and was in a factory, but I came over and said, 'You can run a funeral business from here.' He said, 'I could never do it.' He was an engineer originally, and he'd been in a local firm. But he did it. The first year we did fifty, the second a hundred and fifty. Then we needed a larger place, so we moved. And it got bigger and bigger.

"I've had to cope with hundreds of dead bodies, but it's the first one I remember most. People say that, it's the first you remember. My first was a little old lady who'd died in Minehead. She had purple hair, just dyed that day, and I thought how sad, she'd gone purple and never had a chance to display it.

"I remember my first prepping. It was my grandfather. I had to wash him. I used to make him homemade soup and now I was washing him every day while he was laid out with us. In those days I could hardly bring myself to touch a dead body. Jim said, 'Here, give me a hand with this one,' and I could hardly bring myself to touch him. It's our instinct. Now I could do it without thinking.

"Jim is a Christian and believes in an after-life, but I don't. I think life's snuffed out like a candle. I can't believe there's another life."

"Sometimes," I said, "in a hospital a person can have a near-death experience, float up to the ceiling and look down and see doctors conferring and report back their exact words when they wake up."

"Hmm," she said. "I'll have to think about that. We wanted my son to go into the business. He was a monkey at school and he went to Australia for a year and when he came back he said, 'I don't think I want to be moving dead bodies around all day long for the rest of my life.' Now my son's starting a concrete business. I've just lent him £212,000 out of the sale price to buy a concrete-pourer. There's cliff erosion near our houses. The council want to renovate the footpath from the kissing-gate. He'd extend the strip of concrete on the beach under our houses for free, but we'd have to pay for the concrete. Do you think Richard Dawkins would allow it? We could ask him when we finally get to meet him on Monday.

"Anyway," she said, "Jim will like it in the Chapel of Rest near St Blazey. You know it's on the same bend as where his first wife died."

I said goodbye to her and watched her walk to her car, slim and elegant, immaculately groomed hair with sunglasses above it. She cut a style, and I had to admire the drive that had taken her from a deprived background to a funeral business and now the thrust behind her son's concrete business. She had hauled herself out of the factory by forcing herself to handle dead bodies. And I thought of her husband, trapped in the past, retiring to a Chapel of Rest on the same bend of the road where his first wife was killed nearly four decades previously. It haunted me that nearly forty years later he would be spending his retirement years so near to the spot where she was killed, with the encouragement of his second wife. The past had bent him and now he had built a memorial chapel to her on the bend where he had lost her.

Two Silver Jugs on a Tray
(Or: She's Gone)

As usual when we were down in Cornwall we went to the Carlyon Bay Hotel for Sunday lunch. I had sardines and then roast beef and looked out over St Austell Bay. It was misty and steady rain came in. We went through to the Lounge for coffee afterwards and sat where we always sat, in the window by the door leading out to the pool. A couple of waiters were clearing dirty plates, but no one was paying attention to us. I looked for Martha in her green uniform down the far end of the through-lounge but there was no sign of her.

"Martha's away," I said, "her annual holiday taken in the off season, and the place has gone to pot in her absence."

I went over to one of the waiters and said, "Could we have after-lunch coffee, please? We're sitting over there."

Immediately there was some action. The waiter brought cups, sugar and chocolates on a tray, and a young waitress came with silver jugs of coffee and milk.

Soon afterwards the Head Waiter brought our bill on a saucer. "Have you heard about Martha?" he asked.

"No," I said.

"She's gone," he said. I wondered if he meant 'left' or 'dead'. "She left three-and-a-half weeks ago," he said. "She was unwell. Cancer. She had liver cancer."

We frowned in shock and sympathy, and pulled faces.

"She went up to Birmingham to stay with her daughter for three weeks. You know, ever the optimist, 'I'll be all right.' She had a massive heart attack there at her daughter's on Thursday, and that was it."

"How long was she here?" I asked.

"Fifty years. She came as a waitress in the dining-room when she was twenty-five, and she was seventy-five. She was in here serving coffee for the last.... Well, I came twenty-two years ago, and she trained me and she was doing it then. She's an institution. She was known to thousands of people. She *was* the Carlyon Bay Hotel. Anyway, I must get on."

I thought of Martha in her green skirt and waistcoat, her swollen feet in her shoes, carrying a tray with two silver jugs on it over to us and saying from her unmade-up grey face and greying hair, deferentially, "We've got a lot of people in this weekend, half-term, hard on the legs but mustn't grumble." Or: "Not so many in this week, chance to put my feet up."

I thought of when she was missing on a previous occasion, and how she told us when I saw her next, "I went to Russia with my daughter. Moscow and the waterways. We had a really good time, it was very interesting." And I had later remarked that Martha was the last person you would associate with Moscow. She was so quietly friendly and deferential and open, there was no Cold War when she was around.

The Head Waiter returned for his saucer. "Funeral?" he asked. "We don't know yet. But it'll be down here, not in Birmingham because her husband's here. I'll give you a ring when I know the details."

I pondered on Martha. You went to work somewhere and stayed fifty years, in the course of which you got married and had a daughter, and your place of work was your life. Then, when you were thinking of retiring, you found out you had cancer and had a heart attack and died before you could enjoy putting your feet up once and for all. She had spent a life in 'downstairs' service and the Hotel had been her life. And now a young girl was doing what she had done, and not chatting to the guests with Martha's authority.

Geoffrey, Les, Harry Good, Graham the Harbour-master – a whole generation of my Cornish elders and betters had been and gone, and now Martha had joined them. And for a moment I thought I saw her pottering with a tray and two silver jugs, training the young girl in how to serve coffee as she used to do.

Martha and the Head Waiter were part of the fixtures and fittings of the place, like two silver jugs on a tray.

A Backward Boy and Mining

The crab fisherman was sauntering over to his crab-pots near the defunct tin mine. "Good morning," he said to me, "all right?"

"How are you doing?" I said, knowing he had a bit of a reputation. When he was alive old Geoffrey used to call him 'Hell-fire Jack', and nicknamed him 'Fearless', and I was slightly wary of him. I knew he had been in the remedial class and was known as the most backward pupil, closest to educationally subnormal, at the local school.

"I've just come back from Tenerife," he said. "I've found three properties there, three flats. They've been like my pension. I've just sold one. I was offered a good price for it, so I sold it. I wanted to liberate the money for something else. One flat's let, one I keep for my own use, I didn't need the third one. I've gone into stocks and shares. I noticed that with the recession small mining companies were right down. People always need what they mine, what they bring up. So I've been buying small mining shares. And now they're moving up. It looks as if I should be making quite a lot of money from them. Is that the car of the lady you sold your properties to?"

"Yes," I said.

"Doesn't she live in Fowey?"

"Yes," I said.

"I know exactly where she lives. I sometimes moor my boat by the slipway and I park on the slipway to unload and she comes down and gives me hell, tells me to move my car. But now she's parking her car so *we* can't get by. Next time she comes and tells me off I shall say to her, 'You park your car up here so no one can get by.' I'll tell her," he said.

I watched Fearless saunter to his boat with a couple of crab-pots. For the most backward pupil he had done well: three flats in Tenerife, and now he was doing stocks and shares and his market was moving up. He had a common sense that many more educated men did not possess. He had been his own prospector. He had dug his own mine shaft and was doing his own mining, and soon he would be doing better – out of his own drive and initiative – than many better-educated residents of the harbour. He had the Cornish tinner's blood in his veins, and had adapted his innate, intuitive business acumen to the straitened circumstances of the modern time.

Grouted Boulders and Encroaching Waves (Or: The Man who Battled with the Sea)

"The sea is so strong," Richard Dawkins, the owner of the harbour, said, looking at me from his round head, moustache and a fleck in one eye. "It pounds the pier and gets in behind the boulders. I have the job of keeping the pier restored. We've learned how to do it now. We wait till the tide's going out, put a grouting machine down and pump in cement. When it starts bubbling back we point it with quick-drying cement, cement that dries in half an hour, and then get the grouting machine out before the tide comes in. We've done the outer harbour but by the steps near the crab-pots is bowing out. Water's got behind those blocks so we've got to start over there. I've written to all the bodies asking for a grant, English Heritage, you name it. They've all got people in charge for £100,000 a year who ask for a Report costing fifteen thousand, and then nothing happens for six months while they consider it and find reasons to say they can't help. For fifteen thousand I can put three men on the harbour wall and with the grouting machine I can solve the problem. I don't deal in Reports any more. I've battled away trying to make good damage done by the force of the sea. I sometimes feel I'm fighting a losing battle. All the time I've got three men somewhere doing things to a wall. Most recently it was behind this very building. A retaining wall on the hill was sliding down on us, concrete capped with cosmetic boulders as we're in an environmental area.

"If it's not the sea it's the people. That bloke Greaves cost me fifty thousand in legal fees just to get rid of him. He was disrupting my films by shouting out on track, 'I'm trying to sleep.' He was a kind of highwayman, making trouble to be bought off by the film companies and me. Then I had to pay out seventy thousand in legal fees to get rid of the Ramblers. The bridge that goes down into the sea when a ship comes into harbour has been doing that for decades. But the Ramblers said their footpath across the water should never be severed, and that I, the owner of the harbour, had no right to lower the bridge to get ships in and out. The Rambler I was dealing with produced forged letters from different people, all in his own hand. I saw him off but it cost me seventy thousand.

"But most of all it's the sea I've been struggling against. It's pitiless, merciless. Just when I think I'm winning there's a big storm and more of my boulders are breached and pulled out of place, and I have to take remedial action. If anything happened to me, I don't know who'd keep the sea at bay. It would just loosen the walls and inundate the harbour and bring down the sides below the roads. There would soon be no access round the dock. I'd dearly like to retire, but if I do the harbour will cave in within two or three years unless someone keeps grouting. And so I'm still here. Some people feel responsible for the future and invest in their community. Others just take what the State hands out.

I'm one of the first kind, and so I go on battling with the sea."

Richard stared at me. He had a legitimate grouch about the level of support from the public, but his grouting had undoubtedly saved the harbour and I thought he rather enjoyed his perpetual battling with the sea. It gave him a sense of purpose to defend the village against the encroaching waves.

A Turkish Palace and a Smirk

I sat next to David Kipling at the dinner. He had left the school in acrimonious circumstances. He looked very red-cheeked and thin-faced. He said, "I thought this was on November 12th and I bought tickets for my wife and daughter. I mentioned the 12th over the phone as I booked them and no one said anything. Then I found out it was on the 4th. They can't come, so I'm here by myself. My daughter's looked at the local schools and she chose one of yours for my granddaughter. I'll be talking to you about that.

"Now the planning permission for my old school's extension is coming up on Wednesday. The councillors are opposed and two weeks ago I was told that the recommendation was to refuse. Now that's changed to grant, and I don't understand why. They want to receive their new intake of a hundred four-year-olds in the theatre and walk them as a human bus to the car park, where parents are arriving, and on to the road and then take them down to the building 800 metres down the road. Half a mile for four-year-olds. And it's dangerous, to walk so many along that road. And they get the hundred from other schools, who have to close. What's the point? I shall speak against. I shall declare an interest because I used to teach there, but not a prejudicial interest."

Edith Small, the MP, came by and asked what would happen at Wednesday's planning meeting.

"The councillors are against it," Kipling said adamantly. "It's the 800-metre walk along a road." And craggy Edith Small, standing, listened and nodded.

When she had gone Kipling said to me, "I've had enough of this country and the Coalition. I'm sixty-two in three years' time and I'm going to live in Turkey. I've been building in the mountains above Kusadasi. When I was there a couple of years ago I visited the show house of a gated park but they'd all been sold. Then I found this house. It was built in a year and two weeks. It cost me £280,000. I designed it myself. It's 12,000 square feet. Six bedrooms and a pool, and it's cooler in the mountains, 35 instead of 40. I can see Samos across the water from my aerial view. I've just been there for eight weeks. I didn't want to come back. There's an expatriate community in my village. I've got two Dutch as neighbours on either side, a Belgian, someone from Abu Dhabi and someone from Qatar. Everyone speaks English. No al-Qaeda, they're all pro-West. I hope Turkey doesn't enter the EU, it's all so cheap and pleasant and I want it to stay that way. Someone from Spain came and stayed with me and said that what I've got would be £3.5 million in Spain. It's gated but there are burglars. They're after money, they don't take furniture. So you have a safe. And if they're caught they go to prison, but the worst thing for them is the beating they get from the police. They don't mess about there. You know, if you're being burgled you can shoot them and nothing happens to you. I sleep with a gun. Officially I don't, but I can tell you, I do. And I'd use it. If you want to go to a restaurant in my village or one in Kusadasi, a 15-minute drive away, the restaurant sends a car to pick you up and it returns you to your home at the end of the evening. Customer relations. They've got a completely different attitude from what we've got here. I'll spend the rest of my life there, just sitting by the pool, occasionally going down to the beach or a couple of hours in Kusadasi."

I congratulated him and when dinner ended I stood up and got talking to some of the others there. I spoke to the guest of honour, Graham Brady, who was Chairman of the Conservatives' 1922 Committee. I spoke to a councillor who had been to Kipling's old school. "The planning application's being dealt with by the Bursar," he told me. "He'll make sure Kipling doesn't speak. He's got a prejudicial interest, you know. Did you know he got the sack when he taught there? His doubts about the new pupils' walking are all an elaborate revenge, taken years later and all the better for being taken cold. He wants to block the planning application and then retire to Turkey and live it up in the sun in a way that none of his former colleagues could afford to. No, the Bursar will block him. We're determined to see him off on Wednesday. He can go and live in Turkey if he wants to, I personally think he's mad to envisage it when he's got a granddaughter here, but he won't have taken revenge on his former employer if the Bursar blocks him. We're determined."

From where I stood I looked back at Kipling. I wondered if he had had the sack and if that was why he was so bent on taking his revenge. I gathered it had something to do with a woman, and he felt he had been so badly treated there could be no forgiveness. I wondered why he was drawn to Turkey, whether his new property had something to do with a woman. I did not know, but I grasped that the school had made his life a misery, and he was turning the tables on his predicament by building a gigantic house – a palace. His revenge was not just a blocking of planning permission; he was dangling in front of his enemies a Turkish palace he had somehow managed to build, to impress. It was a pity it was not in England, but he had paid what he could afford.

The following Wednesday the school's planning application was rejected by 17 votes to 0. Two councillors, friends of David Kipling, spoke strongly. One said it was "a silly idea". There was no encouragement to apply again, it was a complete rejection. David Kipling spoke and was allowed to vote as his interest was not prejudicial. He left that evening wearing a satisfied smirk.

The Landlord and the Pie

Graham Brady came into the reception before the fund-raising dinner as I stood by the door. I was the first to greet him. He was taller than me and I was instantly impressed by his open face. He looked a politician in the American mould, and we exchanged a few words.

I asked what his job was as Chairman of the 1922 Committee and he said it was to ensure the balance was correct between the Conservative and Liberal policies. I asked him if he had had a hand in suggesting the Anglo-French Treaty, and he said, "Oh, no, it's the defence team."

"If an Anglo-French Treaty had been concluded in 1939, would we now be speaking German?" I asked, wickedly lobbing in a provocative hand-grenade, for the French had surrendered very quickly and Hitler might then have invaded Britain without equipment.

"I'll reflect on that," he said, doing a double-take at the implications of what I had just said.

I watched him as he effortlessly worked the room, doing a complete circle in the half-hour of preprandial drinks. Then we adjourned to our tables. I was on the table next to his, so near I could have leaned over and prodded him in the back for a continuation of our conversation. We had beef and guinea-fowl, and over the pudding Edith Small introduced him. She said he had stood up to the Prime Minister in defending the Conservative position when he thought the balance had tilted unfairly in favour of the Liberals.

Then he spoke, standing by the deserted bar and free-wheeling without a microphone, referring to a card he had laid on the counter. He said the food was better than a place up north he had visited the previous week. He had gone into the pub and found a package advertising: "A beer, a pie and friendship for £1.50." He had opted for the package and the surly landlord slammed a pint in front of him. He said, "What about the pie?" The landlord returned and slammed a pie on the counter. Not to be outdone he had asked, "What about the friendship?" The landlord bent and said, "Don't eat the pie."

He then said the Coalition was unavoidable and set out how he had tried to protect Conservative interests. He said the Liberals had conceded the deficit and tuition fees, but he was concerned that the Conservatives had given too much in return, for example child benefit to those above the income ceiling. He said that great care should be taken in establishing the core beliefs now as many Liberal Democrat MPs were already questioning the Coalition and could be expected to withdraw from it during the next two years.

"I don't think the Coalition will last five years," he said, "I see us going to the country after two or three years. We will become increasingly unpopular as the cuts bite, and some Liberals can be expected to defect."

The Coalition was falling apart, he had said as much, and he had called for core Conservative values to be defined. Like a landlord he had set before us a pie – the mix within the Coalition – and had recommended that we should not eat it.

He spoke at length, and after Edith Small bent and caught his attention, the Chairman rose and interrupted him when he reached the end of a point, thanking him for his speech and calling for questions. His answers to the five questions were interesting. He had an open face and appeared to talk very openly, just as I like politicians to speak.

After the dinner he accepted a potted arum lily, his table decoration, from Edith Small to take back to his wife and eventually stood. I stood and moved towards him and engaged in conversation. I asked if he thought the Liberals were pulling their weight in economic policy as they only won a quarter of the vote and yet had more than half the key economic positions. He nodded, he did not disagree but said they had had to be offered something to continue the Coalition. I said that there had been a flow of articles in the press claiming that the Liberals wanted the better-off to pay the deficit. I said, "I read an article last week saying that the tax office, HMRC, are no longer interested in assessing what the current tax should be, they are only interested in forcing payments to reduce the deficit, and are using naming and shaming to achieve this. I don't know if it's true," I said, "but if it is, it's like a highwayman holding up a stagecoach, saying 'Give me your jewellery or I'll name and shame you.'" I changed the image. "It's like a cricket umpire saying 'That's out' when it blatantly isn't. It's no longer playing by the rules. It could be that the Liberals have got HMRC to go for deficit reduction regardless of what tax is really owed, and doctors, dentists and solicitors are going to be targeted with threats of naming and shaming."

"That's awful if it's happening," he said.

"Will you look into it and stop it if you can?"

"I will."

"Thank you," I said. And I told him that if he played his cards right he could lead the Party in a few years' time. "If Cameron isn't given time to get the deficit down because the Coalition breaks up," I said mischievously, "and he has to go early and is criticised for cuts and loses, Labour's Miliband will become Prime Minister and Cameron might resign, and you could take over. Think about it. If it happens I'll remind you of this conversation in ten years' time."

"And if it doesn't happen, I'll remind *you* of this conversation in ten years' time," he laughed, and we shook hands, the best of friends.

I had taken a bite from his pie and he had advised me to leave the rest. Many MPs are everyone's best friend and agree with everyone to get their vote, but he cared about the issues and came across as being straight. He represented all the Conservative MPs to the Prime Minister to determine what policy should be during this Coalition time, and I had warmed to his open face and could see him as a counter to Miliband, fresh, youthful and with an American image in the mould of J.F. Kennedy.

A Brother at the Window

I went to the bank. As usual there was a long queue. Minute after minute I edged towards the front. Then I was next. But a lady was turned away from another window and returned to stand in front of me. She had been directed to the window I was waiting for as all the other tills had run out of £5 notes. I was waiting for the same window and stood behind her away from the rest of the queue. The young cashier was counting £20 notes watched by his Asian trainer. We watched as he counted three lots of £1,000, weighing them to double-check and slipping on a paper band labelled £1,000 and stamping it.

"Is he going to be counting notes all afternoon?" the lady said to me.

"I'll have a word," I said.

I advanced to the window and said, "You probably can't see from in there, but the queue has reached the street door."

"Can't hear you," the trainer called from inside.

"The queue will soon be in the street," I said. "We're waiting for your window."

"Oh, thank you."

I returned to my place. Very rapidly it was no longer necessary to count piles of notes while the queue waited. Faces in the queue glanced at me in gratitude. I had confronted the system and achieved a popular change.

"That's sorted that out," I said as the lady advanced.

It transpired that there were no £5 notes on that till either. The lady made a scene. "Where can I get them? On which other till? My mother's blind, she needs £5 notes. Please go and ask the other tills."

Eventually after touting among the cashiers, the trainer discovered a few £5 notes. The lady received her package and left.

I advanced to the window. "I couldn't fax my order through today as your fax isn't working," I said, pushing paperwork under the window.

"We've been having problems with our fax today," said the trainer.

The boy was very young. I watched patiently as he was silently shown what to do. I had written details of the transaction on paper but he tried to total without the aid of my sheet and was getting into difficulties.

Then suddenly he said to me, "I was at…." He mentioned one of my schools.

"Oh, well done," I said. I pointed at his badge. "Gary," I said. "When did you leave?"

"About two years ago."

"When did you start here?"

"Two months ago. I'm doing well."

"Good," I said.

"And she's training me."

"You've done well. What was your favourite subject in school?"

"PE." He mentioned his teacher's name. "They want me to go back and speak about my job in assembly."

"Will the bank give you time off?"

"I'm off on a Wednesday, so I'll do it on a Wednesday morning."

"Did you attend the Assembly Hall Founder's Day events?"

"Founder's Day. Yes, I was always there, and my sister too. She lifted a cup two years ago."

"I could have been clapping you," I said.

"Yes, you were."

Now we were like brothers in a brotherhood.

He finished the transaction.

"There are no £5 notes," he said.

"Not to worry," I said. "There weren't many on the order. Give me tens instead."

He put my money in a bag and passed it through.

"Thank you for your help, Gary," I said. "See you next week. "Thank you," I said to the trainer, who nodded.

I turned to the queue. The faces were no longer grateful and approving. One of the scowls suggested, 'Traitor for cosying up to the system.'

But I did not care. He had been one of my pupils, I had overseen his passage into cashier at the bank. He had not had to count on his fingers. All right, he was slow and unsure of what to do. But he had done the transaction, with a little help, yes, but he had done it. I saw his role from his side now. Of course he had to be sure he had £1,000 bundles of £20 notes.

I had entered the bank and taken my place in a system. I left the bank in a relationship with the system's front man and face. Local life should be about people with faces rather than faceless systems. Were not all humankind my brothers and sisters?

Maestros and Managers

We went to the O2 to hear Andrea Bocelli, a favourite of Pippa's. She was moved by his blind strength. There were hour-long queues for the restaurant's sitting area, so we went inside and had burgers standing up. There was an announcement that the start of the concert would be delayed as there was a problem with opening the doors.

We took our seats in the second row in the arena, little more than a penalty area from the microphones. The O2 was sold out, and three or four tiers of stands were filled to capacity with tiny rows of faces. It was like being a goalie in an important match, with 20,000 people all round, tiered rows of faces in stands. I found it very relaxing. I did not feel looked at.

The first half presented excerpts from Italian operas. An orchestra played and Bocelli was escorted on, wearing DJ, yellow-faced, grey-haired, by the conductor, a youngish fellow with sleeked black hair. Bocelli groped for the microphone and sang his arias with great confidence. At the end of each there was loud applause and Italians behind us shouted, "*Bravo*." A Czech singer and four Italians who looked like sisters, Four Graces, sang some of the extracts.

I stood up in the interval and saw Harry Redknapp, the London football manager, standing two rows behind me. He wore a blue sweater and open-necked shirt, and though his face was ruddy and his nose looked as if he drank, he was remarkably slim and in good shape. I thought he must have trained a lot with the team. He stood alone, the object of adulation by vast crowds, now unrecognised except by me. I wondered how the investigation into his tax affairs was progressing.

The second part was more popular and included Christmas carols. 'Silent Night' was not sung softly, as I expected, but with the same full-blooded tenor as the other songs. I wondered why Bocelli did not adapt his style to the meaning rather than run everything past his full-blooded approach. I thought it was like an actor not adapting himself to the part but (like Albert Finney and Tom Courtenay) giving the same performance in each part, being himself regardless of the material. The material was subordinated to Bocelli's ego.

At the end there was terrific applause, and the Italians behind me shouted out "*Bravo*" and "*Maestro*". Bocelli was helped off the stage by the conductor but at the top of the steps to the curtained tunnel he stopped and turned and returned for an encore. This time there was a standing ovation. As he left the stage the Italians shouted "*Maestro*", and "*Magnifico*". He turned and there was another encore, and another standing ovation.

In all there were six encores and six standing ovations. At the end of each he waved as, blind, he was led off stage by the conductor.

Being so near him I felt part of his act. I could see that he came on, blind, and sang into the darkness, and the 20,000 no more existed than they did for a goalie aware of distant rows of tiered faces in the stands. He sang in a uniform voice, all the arias passed through him like water reaching a mill, and he frothed it up and discharged it over his weir. Then he left with a wave to darkness. The people had all apparently come to hear his singing, but some had come for the occasion and some to see a celebrity. To some it wasn't the *maestro* they watched but a star performer, like a world-class Italian footballer.

Then I saw Harry Redknapp. He was standing, the plaudits and the standing ovation over. He too came on and looked into an arena where men ran about, and waved to tiered faces in the stands at the end. He too was part of a similar set-up. An opera singer, a football manager, both were celebrities people came to see, who came on and left waving to a crowd's applause.

We all trooped out into the dark and followed the crowd controllers' magnified voices to skirt round the station, and made our way to the car park. Skills at singing from the diaphragm or curling a ball over a wall entertained crowds at concerts and matches, and round the crowds people made a living selling food as they arrived and managing crowd control as they left. I had accompanied Pippa who was moved by all Bocelli could do though blind, his conquest of his disability, and I had seen deep into the system surrounding *maestros* and managers.

Fromages pour les enfants
(Or: A Pernickety Inspector and Two Mirrors)

The school had a full inspection: six inspectors combing it from 150 angles for five days. At one point the Chief Inspector asked, "Where are your mobile phones?" All playground staff were supposed to liaise with mobile phones according to a new directive of which we were unaware. One of us said, "We've got walkie-talkies," and produced walkie-talkies we'd bought for a teaching project.

When the report back was made, the management team sat, ready to challenge. The comments were persistently very good and there was nothing to challenge. The Chief Inspector was the most exact, pedantic, pernickety we had ever had, and her report was the best we had ever had.

The staff had endured a bit of an ordeal, and one or two had felt in a state of collapse at the end. We had booked the upper room of the Café Rouge and we entertained fifty-two the following evening, forty-seven of whom were women. There was one room with a high ceiling decorated in the French manner, and there were two specially mounted huge wall mirrors on opposite walls. One of them announced on the upper part of the glass, '*Fromages, Soup de la maison, Vins mousseaux.*' The other mirror said, '*Déjeuner, Bières blondes, Menu pour les enfants.*'

I sat opposite Linda Marshall. She said, "I've just been made a Fellow of the London Drama Institute. It happened today."

I congratulated her and asked if there was an audience. She shook her head. "It was exam conditions. I received my certificate. The next step is examiner. I shall have to wear glasses on the end of my nose."

She pulled a face and exaggeratedly mimed being an elderly examiner, and those around her laughed as she waved her hands expressively.

I was struck by how she had blossomed. She had a new confidence and maturity, and a girl had become a woman. She was groomed and poised, elegant, composed. A cygnet had grown into a swan.

Simon, the Principal, made a speech. We weren't supposed to tell the staff anything for six weeks, but that would mean treating them like children. So he read out the notes he had taken on the inspectors' report. He began, "The staff are happy." The staff all hooted in mock denial and approval. "They commended music." There was a cheer. "They praised the school meals." There was applause in the direction of the kitchen staff. "They liked the office." There was a childish cheer.

It was as though he was passing pieces of *fromages pour les enfants*. As he spoke I caught sight of the top of my head in the mirror. I raised myself up so I could see my face and saw my head receding 150 times into the far depths of the room, as though I had been inspected from 150 different angles.

A Parakeet in our Garden
(Or: Flowers and a Collapsed Clothes-Horse)

Stephen Sharkey was our new mornings-only gardener. He wore an earring but it was felt at interview that at thirty-two he had more energy than the other interviewees, some of whom were retired. The advertisement had said that a car would be "useful", and he arrived by car. Our son Simon did the bulk of the interviews. The deal Simon imposed was that Stephen would produce paperwork within a week: a copy of his passport and driving-licence so that a criminal record check could take place. The government imposed this on all new appointments to identify illegal immigrants and convicted paedophiles.

On his first day he arrived by bicycle. He reported that the previous night he had written off his car. He would have to cycle to and from work. He said he had mislaid his driving-licence and was applying for a new one. He said he had never had a passport, and he had applied for a new one.

Stephen made a good start. He wore green camouflage fatigues as if he had been in the army. He was good at servicing machinery, and he had the grounds under control within a month. He mowed, leaf-cleared, cut back plants for the winter, propagated and filled the bird feeders. He toiled in all weathers, including rain.

The weeks slipped by and there was no sign of a passport. When pressed he said he had been to the Passport Office at Chelmsford but was held up by traffic and arrived five minutes after it closed. The next week he said he was sending his wife to Chelmsford. He later reported that after a three-hour hunt she left Chelmsford without being able to locate the Passport Office.

There was news of a car. He said he had seen an identical car to his parked off the road and he had rung the doorbell and bought it. But it needed repair work done to it.

Meanwhile he started to have disasters. His eldest son allegedly left the bath running and the kitchen ceiling came down, requiring him to have time off on a Tuesday so a "mate" could redo his ceiling. The next week he "broke the axle of his bike" and was again not in on a Tuesday while he got it fixed. "It cost me £45," he said. The following Monday he had to leave early to collect his son from school as he had a bug, and the next day, also a Tuesday, he did not appear or telephone. On the Wednesday he said he had gone down with the bug his son had. The next week he was away on a Tuesday and told me on the Wednesday morning that he had been walking in his house in bare feet and had trodden on an upturned plug. The three prongs had penetrated his sole, and he had gone to his nearest A & E.

He was away the following Tuesday. On the Wednesday he told me about his car. "It passed its MOT. But as I drove it home the exhaust came off, and it boiled. I opened the boot and put my hand in and boiling water went all over my wrist, look." He had a band of red scald mark round his right wrist, angry enough to make me wince.

We were away the following week so I did not know whether he worked on the Tuesday. But the week after that he did not appear on the Tuesday. He came in the next day, a November day of cold wind, his eyes streaming from cycling, I thought, and said, "I'm sorry I wasn't in yesterday, but there was a family emergency."

"Oh," I said sympathetically, "what sort of emergency?"

"My wife's had a miscarriage."

I expressed sympathetic shock and concern.

"Yes," he said, "she was admitted to hospital in an ambulance. Princess Alexander, Harlow." He meant Princess Alexandra. "She's very upset. She doesn't like me to see her crying, she's crying on her own. We didn't even know she was pregnant."

I thought it strange that she did not know, but then from time to time the papers carried stories of women giving birth without knowing they were pregnant.

"I stayed the night at the hospital," he said. "I haven't had much sleep. But it's good I'm here, it'll take my mind off it."

So who had looked after his two boys, who he had said were seven and five?

"Oh, a neighbour. My wife's sister's driving up from Cornwall today, so she'll be able to look after the boys and take them to school while I visit my wife in hospital."

He did not know how long she would be in.

"What ward is she in?"

"Oh, Orchard ward, I think. I'm devastated by it all."

He went outside and was soon blowing leaves and then riding on the ride-on mower.

I told Simon. He said sceptically, "It's very sad if it happened. It may be another story to delay a criminal record check."

The next day Stephen came to my door and said, "She's going to be discharged today. My sister-in-law's arrived so she's at home to receive her. I stayed at the hospital again last night. I've told my eldest boy. He's twelve."

"I thought your boys were five and seven."

"No, twelve and seven. I haven't told the younger one."

But the National Health Service has strict visiting hours and unlike hospitals in Arab countries does not allow relatives to stay the night except in emergencies.

I pondered and thought I should send a plant. I rang the hospital and was put through to Admissions.

"Joanna Sharkey," I said.

"No one of that name has been admitted this week," the voice said. "Have you got an address?"

I looked up Stephen's address on a file.

"No one of that address has been admitted."

I found it strange and thought: 'Oh well, perhaps their Admissions computer has omissions. Perhaps they're not completely sure who's in the building.' But the fire regulations would surely require an up-to-date list?

"Have you got an Orchard ward?"

"No, there's no Orchard at this hospital."

I pondered this man who wore soldier's combat fatigues and had no papers to confirm his identity. Had he assumed an identity? Was he a burglar or a murderer? Who was Stephen Sharkey?

The next day he said his wife had come back, and the following Monday he said she was making good progress.

"Oh," he said, "my passport will be with me in seven days' time."

Three months had passed since the interview when he had promised we would have his driving-licence and passport within a week. He was still no nearer to having a criminal record check.

The next day, a Tuesday, he was not in. I rang his mobile at 10.30 and he answered.

"I'm outside the hospital, having a cigarette break. She was admitted last night, 10.30 by ambulance. Bleeding heavily. I've stayed the night in hospital. They're giving her coagulants to stop the bleeding."

"Same ward?"

"No, a different one."

There was a crash. Our clothes-horse in the utility room had collapsed under the weight of a wet duvet. I wondered if his Tuesday stories, which he hung out to dry, would similarly come crashing down because of their weight.

The next day he was in.

"She's still having coagulants. The consultant's keeping an eye on her."

I told him there was a clothes-horse to be repaired.

"My sister-in-law's staying up a second week. She works in a university in Cornwall, on a site near Bodmin. She's told them she'll be off another week."

Two weeks off work during term time? I found this strange but accepted what he said.

When he had left my door I picked up the phone and spoke again to the hospital's Admissions. After a hunt the girl said, "No one of that name's been admitted this week. Not on Monday. I'm sorry, we haven't got this person."

I went downstairs and told my wife.

She rang the hospital and also spoke to Admissions. Together they hunted for every permutation of the name, but again found nothing. Later that day she rang the school where his wife worked in the kitchen.

"Sorry to trouble you but through a friend of a friend I've heard that someone in your kitchen was admitted to hospital by ambulance last week and is back in hospital again."

"I haven't heard about it," the office receptionist said. "You'll have to speak to the kitchen." But there was no reply. The kitchen staff had served lunch and gone home.

The next morning Stephen Sharkey came in about 8.50. I had a chat with him. He said, "She should be out of hospital today."

I had taken in the clothes-horse he had repaired. I said it was a bit wobbly, and perhaps he could have another look at it. He took off his trainers and in his socks padded through to our utility room and said, "I haven't seen it on the flat until now, I'll have another go at it later."

I was involved in a meeting at 9.10. At the start my wife said, "I don't like to say this, but I've just got through to Stephen's wife's school kitchen. I said, 'I've heard through a friend of a friend that Joanna Sharkey was admitted to hospital in an ambulance. I'm trying to find out what hospital she's in so I can send flowers.' The voice the other end, a woman, said, 'No.' Then, 'Who is this, who is this?' I said, 'Oh, there's obviously some confusion,' and I rang off."

I frowned. He had made up the story of the miscarriage, and probably the other stories that had kept him away on Tuesdays, and he had no paperwork. Who was he?

During the meeting we saw Stephen Sharkey walking up with his knapsack, holding the folded clothes-horse. He kept to the fence farthest from the house, hoping not to be seen from the house. He left our grounds.

My wife interrupted the meeting and said, "I've just seen Stephen leaving with his knapsack."

The meeting ended at 9.30 and she had to leave for London. Simon had been at the meeting, and I filled him in with the details. Neither the hospital nor his wife's workplace seemed to know about the hospital admission.

He texted Stephen Sharkey: "Stephen, we need to talk."

The answer came back, "No, what your mum done was out of order. I'm thirty-two, not ten, and she has no right to check up on me. I'll drop the keys in later."

Simon replied, "We were trying to send flowers to the hospital or work, and there was confusion."

There was no reply from Stephen Sharkey, and his phone was switched off for the next few days.

I thought with sadness that he had been found out and could not face us. It was a shame as he could have had a secure job for a long time, but had turned his back on the prospect. For what? Another job he was doing every Tuesday and covering his traces with implausible lies? Was he collecting dole money every Tuesday and signing on? His termination of his employment with us without notice was a catastrophe for his family, particularly his two boys, if they existed.

That weekend I was doing some paperwork on the kitchen table and I glanced out at the bird feeder, and was stunned to see a large green parakeet with a long tail and a red bill pecking seed from the dispenser. Its mate was sitting on a branch of the cherry-tree from which the bird feeder was suspended. I had seen parakeets in the Canary Isles, but never in England, not wild. What was it doing in our garden?

I had an exotic visitor in my garden and I wondered how long it would stay. It was different from all the other visitors who came into our garden, colourfully bright green, and when I described it to others they had difficulty in believing in its existence. It seemed, like one of Stephen's implausible stories, too much of a tall story.

Stephen Sharkey was briefly in our garden like a visiting parakeet, and his brightly coloured stories about his disasters left an impression that lingered a long while, like the memory of the parakeet on the bird feeder.

Cranes and a Natterjack Toad

We went to Slimbridge, which Peter Scott, father of the conservation movement, son of Scott of the Antarctic, founded to enhance knowledge of the geese migrating to the Severn estuary. In the entrance hall women in red and black uniform wished us a pleasant visit, and we walked through a craft fair to the amphibian house and then outside to the first lake, which held mute swans. It was bitterly cold with a wind from the Arctic that had brought a dusting of snow to villages we had passed through, and I wore a scarf and gloves and thermal socks.

We wandered on past a bust of Scott with a pair of binoculars to further birds, including two cranes, and on the far side of another lake saw three grey-crowned cranes, looking like Mohicans with stick-up crests, which were extinct in the UK by the 17th century, before the pollution caused by the Industrial Revolution. We passed through an enclosed walk with windows on water-voles, water-shrews and tiny harvest mice, and came to another enclosure where four otters swam together – a mother, her sister and her two children, all female – and climbed out onto rocks and nuzzled together as a family. I watched as the mother stood up on her hind legs like a human and then returned to the water for another swim.

We moved on and saw many other birds. By now my ears were stinging and my toes were numb.

We returned to the entrance hall and thawed out. We sat in the amphibian area and watched a helper encourage children to handle a tree frog, then a natterjack toad which had a yellow line on its back, ears behind its eyes and black fingernails. He put the toad on the work surface and tipped half a dozen tiny thin white worms in front of it. They looked like minute thin centipedes. Two wriggled. "See how quickly he flicks out his tongue. He gets sideways on to look and...." The fattest worm disappeared as the toad's tongue came out too fast to be seen and whisked it into its mouth at lightning speed. One after another the worms disappeared. The natterjack toad sat still.

Now the helper took a newt out of the box below and showed it. He squirted the hands of the children to moisten them so the moist creatures would not find them too dry. He returned to the box and allowed the children to receive the tree frog in their palms. After that we went to the restaurant and had soup and a roll, but I was still cold.

We retraced our steps through the bookstore. There was a stand at one end with some sort of a basket hanging from the top. Suddenly it collapsed in a crash that made everyone jump, and hung precariously lower down the stand. A bald man nearby, who had not made it collapse, bent and tried to pick it up. The basket fell off the stand onto the floor with a crash. It looked as if the bald man was wrecking the bookstore and there were smirks. "We'd better get out of here before we're blamed for the collapse," I said, and several customers laughed.

In the craft fair I stopped at a stand and looked at the *Usborne History of the World* for my grandson. I wondered if it would improve his general knowledge of history and then thought that he would be given specific tasks in history and would probably never use it. I replaced the book.

"It's internet-related," said the store-holder, a bespectacled woman of about fifty. "He can find further detail on the internet."

I picked the book up again. It was heavy and hard to hold in two fingers.

"It'll be good for a ten-year-old," she said. "There's a 20-per-cent discount on it."

"He needs something more specific," I said, replacing the book.

She looked agitated, then turned away, accepting that she had to let me go.

"I've got the same series in science," she said, producing another book and putting it in my hand.

I was being made the victim of a hard sell. She did not seem to have had many buyers. She was like a natterjack toad flicking out her tongue and drawing me in like a worm, a bookworm, one time after another. I was wriggling and powerless before her licking tongue. Then I realised she was desperate for a sale. She had paid for her stall in advance and had not recouped the outlay from her sales.

Driving back over the slim bridge and passing the Tudor Arms, I reflected on Peter Scott's noble dream of exotic cranes. His father's last message was that "the boy" should be guided into natural history, not games, and this had happened. Like his father Peter had revelled in isolation – the isolation of the Severn estuary rather than the isolation of Antarctica – and his vision had congealed into a system after his death, and there was a trade in *bric-à-brac*, in mugs and plates showing his paintings. His vision had been enmeshed in fund-raising, selling off space to stall-holders at craft fairs, which was necessary in the modern world. He had dreamt of showing geese and cranes flying in the air, and his vision now included an opportunistic natterjack toad.

A Hospice Donor and a 'Pompous Twit' (Or: Self-Importance)

I went into the Hall and found my table. Then like a butterfly I flitted from table to table, settling here and there, and then flying on. I had a word with Brian Tremlett, whose wife Margaret had died of pancreatic cancer since last year's dinner. I had stopped her and was shocked that my hand almost went round her upper arm. "See you next year," I said, and she said, "Yes, I'll be here." I told Jack what she had said.

"She had a tumour too near her artery to operate," he told me. "She knew the survival rate is only 3 per cent. She was just being brave."

Then Sheila passed and I kissed her. Her husband, the judge, had sat next to me the previous year. He had died.

Thinking about death, I moved on to Lady Myrtle. She had had an operation. "You're looking well," I said.

"Oh, I've decided you'll look after John Lister on your table," she said. "He is saying he won't know anyone, so I said, 'Oh, Philip will look after you.'"

Her son looked thin and shaven-headed. He looked dreadful. "I've been running ten miles a day, doing sixty a week," he said. "For the London Marathon." His body was wasting away, it was as though he had anorexia. He told me about the Council, and how as an independent he teased the Lib Dems, and all the time he talked I was thinking, 'Put your health before running, don't ruin your health.'

Eventually I sat with John Lister. "How long have you lived in the area?" I asked.

"Only fifty-two years."

"Fifty-two years!" I exclaimed. "Why, you've known all the legendary people who've lived in your road."

"The Town Clerk lives at the end of my garden. She screams at me."

"Why?"

"I don't know."

"Did you know Dick Patty and his family?"

"Yes. But they've just gone into administration. It was in yesterday's *Times*. Dick and Shirley retired years ago, and Ronald, the son, was kicked upstairs to be Chief Executive. A new managing director took over and left them without money. The recession didn't help. There was a chain of restaurants in the City, they were half-empty. Now it's all ended."

"Dick would be shocked," I said. "He was supremely confident, even arrogant. He looked down on everyone. Perhaps it was *hubris* all those years ago."

"Yes," he said. "Did you know his two daughters?"

"Yes," I said. "What did you do before you retired?"

"I was in reinsurance in the City."

"Who's responsible for the financial crisis from your experience of the City?"

"Bankers and the government."

I was sitting next to Pat Moss, who had worked in the Conservation Centre. I asked who the man who looked like Trevor-Roper was on the next table: curly-haired with spectacles and in a suit.

"Oh," she said, "he's one of the four verderers and he's Deputy Lord Lieutenant of Essex."

"Oh," I said.

When the dinner of soup, chicken and a choice of three puddings and wine had come to an end, I crossed to his table like a butterfly and introduced myself.

He listened. Then he said, "I did my articles in Attwater and Liell."

"I was there for a week," I said.

We chatted about this and that. He told me he was a solicitor, and that his diary as Deputy Lord Lieutenant was not overfull. I told him about my school and how a previous Lord Lieutenant of Essex had come to lunch with me.

"My wife went to that school," he said.

A grey-haired lady said, "I was one of the Hemp sisters."

I returned to Pippa, who had been sitting with John Lister. John had left as it was the end of the evening. She said, "He told me, 'My wife died in the local hospice. They looked after her very well, and the matron said they needed a new annexe. I had a lot of money and so I gave them enough to build their annexe. For some months everything went according to plan. There were meetings and the building was going to take place. Then that man who later became the Deputy Lord Lieutenant became Chairman, and everything began to go wrong. Suddenly the money shouldn't be applied to the purpose for which it was given, and it was going to be applied for another purpose. I challenged what was happening. I found him arrogant and self-opinionated. I found him a pompous twit. He wouldn't listen. So in the end I took umbrage. I went to the Charity Commission and they gave me my money back. Since then I haven't spoken to him.'"

I thought of Margaret Tremlett and the judge, who needed looking after in their last days, and of John Lister who had donated an annexe to the hospice, and I looked back at the solicitor who had acted in good faith and done his best to do what he thought was right for the hospice and had fallen foul of the donor, and I wondered who was the more self-important: the charitable donor and revoker, or the man acting for the donee institution? Or were they both equally self-important in a clash of well-intended wills?

A Candle and a Squashed Mince Pie

I attended an Advent processional service in a local church. A school choir sang medieval harmonies and processed from the lady chapel to the south door, on to the west door and then down to the chancel steps and then the sanctuary. Their antiphons and the readings traced a journey from darkness to light, and when they reached the sanctuary the congregation had their candles lit. All held a candle with circular cardboard around it to catch dripping wax. The candle held by the person sitting by the aisle was lit by a taper and the light was passed from one to another within each pew.

At the end of the service all illumined souls sat with their candles in prayer and then snuffed out their lights to return to the outer world.

I saw Walter Grayling, the Latin master, hobbling awkwardly towards the door at the end. I smiled at him. He was eighty-five and still teaching a few lessons each week.

I made my way to the dining-hall, collected a glass of warm mulled wine and found the hot mince pies. Mine collapsed after my first bite. I caught the remnants in the foil tray it sat in, and ate the rest of it in morsels bitten up from within the tray.

I wandered to the other end of the dining-hall and encountered the Latin master, standing alone. He was holding a mince pie, and before I could warn him he bit into it and squashed it into pieces in the palm of his hand. The mince made his palm very sticky.

I asked him what he was teaching.

"Cicero's Cataline speech. And Tacitus book 14, Nero killing his mother."

"Very interesting," I said. "Will you go on teaching?"

"Yes. For another year or two, if they'll have me. But fewer and fewer are doing classics. I had to give up Greek because only two were doing it. And Latin's getting a bit that way."

To many who have retired his was a life of folly. Why work on after retirement age, why work into one's late eighties? But he clearly enjoyed it.

"I like doing it," the Latin master said, white-haired and stooping, and a light lit up his eyes behind his dark spectacles.

He had nothing else. He had never married and he lived alone.

I smiled and moved on. The Head encountered me.

"It's wonderful the way he keeps going," he agreed. "Yes, of course he can stay another couple of years. He's so independent. He insists on driving himself. He won't accept a lift. He's like Mr Chips. His life is the school."

Then I knew that loyalty was no folly, but a deeply personal quality. He had a light in his eyes. He had an ideal, and the world disappointed. The failure of the world to keep up with his inspiration was like the squashed mince pie in the palm of his hand.

Gold and a Grumbling Undertaker (Or: A Fortune Like a Cliff)

A car pulled level with ours as we headed away from the harbour.

"Hello to both of you," said a voice. I looked and it was Jim, the retired undertaker, with half an inch of stubble on his cheeks and chin.

"How are you? We're not doing so well, we were burgled up on the cliff house. They got in with a key, somehow, and were only interested in gold. Maisie came back – I had to stay out in Spain to see work on a bathroom through – and she rang me and left a message, 'You must ring me.' I rang her and she said, 'Safe's gone.' They'd carried it off, and I lost all the jewellery I really value – earrings I gave my first wife Susie, rings, a bracelet, gold pieces. Forty-thousand-pounds-worth of jewellery gone. And it wasn't fully insured. Twelve thousand five hundred we'll get back. The rest's gone. No, they haven't caught them and they've got no leads. Still, I've got my three houses here and the property in Spain, and my car. People say to me, 'Oh, you've got too many houses.' It's just jealousy, they're just jealous. I say to them, 'How many children have you got? Three? You've spent your money on your three children. I haven't had any children so I've spent my money on houses and an expensive car – and gold. I've worked hard – so have you. Anyone who works hard deserves being rewarded.

"You heard there was a landslide near the cliff path? You can see a post at the bottom. I said to Michael Noakes, the Chairman of the

Residents' Association, 'Next time it'll be the cliff path – our house is built on rock, on granite, so it won't go with it – and that will put paid to the walkers.' They want everything their own way, and if there's no path they won't be able to come past our windows. It'll be a sheer drop from our wall down to the sea. Still, mustn't keep you. You've got to get on."

I waved him off and watched him glide towards the sea in his large and expensive car, a grumbling undertaker who had had to bury a lot of dead bodies to save for his gold and his houses, and who had a get-away-from-death house in Spain where he could return to normality for brief spells. He had put up with unpleasant situations and smelt the smell of death as often as I smelt the salt from the sea, and he had amassed a cliff-sized fortune that had just been eroded.

A Tray and an Offhand Vicar

"Martha's died," said a waiter. "I'm sorry to give you bad news. She wasn't well, and her daughter invited her to Birmingham, and she died up there. Cancer of the liver. She was at the Hotel for fifty years. She joined when she was twenty-four. She began as a waitress, here in the dining-room. Then she was in training, she trained me more than twenty years ago. Then she went into the Lounge and she's done the coffee ever since. She retired, but she carried on working. She's got to know dozens of people. There will be a funeral but we don't know when." He shook his head and wandered off.

After dinner I went and sat in the Lounge. No one seemed to be preparing coffee. Eventually a whey-faced girl came and did it all wrong: she didn't carry the silver coffee and milk jugs in one hand and the tray with two cups and saucers on it, sugar and plate of chocolates in the other as Martha did, and she asked "How do you like your coffee?" whereas Martha knew. I sensed Martha standing by our table, slightly bent in a green dress, quite large at the waist, frizzy-grey-haired, and looking critically with her trainer's eye at how her replacement was coping. I thought of how experienced she was, how the previous year she had said, "We're not as busy as usual, it must be the recession," and how she had been to Russia with her daughter, and I felt wistful for a time that had gone and would not come again.

The next time I went to that Hotel was for Christmas lunch, and the live pianist beamed at me and raised a hand as I entered the dining-room. There were crackers and paper hats.

Pippa said, "Oh, I've got something to tell you about Martha. I went to see Bill and Doreen. You know Bill was the Headmaster of the Primary School until he retired, and he's got no stomach and has to eat every six hours. He's doing very well. Well, Doreen knew Martha for many years. They were at school together and they went out every Wednesday evening in a group of schoolfriends. She went to Martha's funeral. It was at a local church. Martha's daughter had put all the group together in the front row, and there was a large contingent from this Hotel. Doreen said there was the most wonderful display of flowers. She'd never seen anything like it at a funeral. There was a large tray made of flowers, and on it there was a cup made of flowers with a red spoon on it and a coffee jug made of flowers. The church was packed.

"Doreen said it was more than the Hotel did when Martha retired. She only got a bunch of flowers, and many felt that wasn't good enough. She didn't get a silver tray for her retirement but they sent her off with a tray of flowers.

"The vicar is one of those breakaway vicars who's going to join the Catholic Church. He never invites the Bishop of Truro to his church, he gets a fly-in bishop who thinks breakaway as he does. There were mutterings about him as someone said to him, 'Martha was so well travelled, she'd been everywhere,' and he said, offhand and not interested, 'I didn't know the woman.' People thought it very bad that he should have said that. You'd think he'd have sat with her daughter and got to know a bit about her, wouldn't you?"

"Perhaps she'd never been to his church and he was indirectly expressing his distance from her, making that point," I said.

"Maybe. But people still felt it was bad he wasn't more interested in someone who had served thousands of local people over the last fifty years."

After the Christmas lunch we had coffee, served by a young girl with a pony-tail who was uncannily the same shape as Martha. She handled the tray with some aplomb, and although she was less assured than Martha, she placed the cups on the table and asked how we like our coffee. Pippa said, "Half and half" and I said, "Nearly half and half – a bit more coffee and less milk."

As she poured I sensed Martha at her elbow, watching critically with her trainer's eye. She was out of the clutches of the vicar, for whom she had little time, and back where she belonged, close to her tray and sharing her memories with the Hotel guests she'd served for fifty years.

Lycoris Buries her Friends

In the Cotswolds I stayed in a stone guest-house. It stood on the corner of Market Square in a tiny ex-woolmaking village with a large medieval church which was off a through road. The house was built in 1489, and I had a room with beeswax walls, beams and a four-poster bed. An Italian fellow took me to the room and showed me a pad of breakfast menus on which I had to write my breakfast order. He said, "You have to complete it by 11 o'clock tonight." He was keen to get away.

On the walls of the room there was Latin. On one side, high above the hearth, '*Balnea, vina, Venus corrumpunt corpora nostra;/sed vitam faciunt balnea, vina, Venus*.' I recognised the inscription. It is over the entrance to the tepid bath in the Baths of Caracalla in Rome, the self-justifying epitaph of Tiberius Claudius Secundus which can be translated: 'Baths, wine and love corrupt our bodies, but create life.' On the other side between two windows with shutters was: '*Omnes quas habuit, Fabiane, Lycoris amicas/extulit; uxori fiat amica meae*.' In Martial's epigram 'Fabiane' is missing. It can be translated: 'Fabianus, Lycoris has buried all the female friends she had. May she make friends with my wife.'

I wondered what sex-loving, wife-hating Tudor gentleman had put this inscription on these walls just before 1500. The Italian Renaissance had already begun after 1453, and the man was clearly a classical scholar, one of the new Humanists who rejoiced in setting up classical learning against the teachings of the Church: hedonism as opposed to spirituality. He was like one of Chaucer's religious characters, asserting

Humanism against the Church.

It was cold outside. Snow was in the air, and I closed the shutters and slept early under a large blanket which I found in the bottom of a wardrobe. The central heating stayed on all night and I kept warm. The next morning I went downstairs and tucked into an enormous cooked breakfast, which included two pieces of fried bread and two cooked eggs.

Later that day I stopped at Tetbury. I parked in a pay-and-display car park near Market Square and walked past The Snooty Fox down to The Two Toads. I wandered back and had a cup of tea and a brownie in The Blue Zucchini. Then I strolled round the corner to the Highgrove shop. Everything was very expensive: *pot-pourri* for £75. Many items displayed the plume of feathers, the Prince's emblem. There was a book on Highgrove, which I leafed through. I thought of how a wife had been rejected there and had been buried after a modern Lycoris had taken up with her husband, a spiritual man with a Humanist outlook.

I ended up back at the guest-house. I sat downstairs and read the papers. I went into dinner at the bistro that was part of the building. There was another couple there. I was shown to the next table so I was not on top of them. When the Italian's wife came in, the lady of the couple, a slightly overweight woman with short fair hair who from her conversation seemed to be a local teacher, said to the waitress, a dark-haired, sloe-eyed woman in her forties who had retained her looks, "There's a house just on the market that would suit you and your husband, eight hundred thousand."

"Oh, it's far too much for us," said the waitress. "I'm Romanian. I can't raise that sort of money. It would kill me off."

"You could offer it in shares to everybody. I'll get *all* my friends to chip in. All my friends can buy a share."

"It might kill them all off," the waitress laughed.

It was a blatantly foolish suggestion, said flippantly, and the Italian's Romanian wife had treated it equally flippantly.

"Everyone can buy a bit of it and you can manage it."

"It's a nice idea, but that property's out of our reach."

And she went off to the kitchen while the couple sat on, waiting for their guests to arrive, talking in undertones.

The lady had proposed a scheme that would "kill" off the Romanian and might "kill off" all her friends. Like Lycoris, she had mentally buried her friends and made friends with the Italian's wife.

A Family Skeleton

It was the new year and there was a Christmas tree in the dining-room with coloured lights and cards and a convivial atmosphere for the family gathering. I produced some photo albums of our forebears at the end of pudding. Several of us sat around the long table identifying previous generations, asking questions, "Who's that?" "Is that my grandfather?" There was banter. "Look, that's Rex with his blond hair." My cousin smiled and was called away to walk his dog.

"I don't know so many things that happened," my sister said. "Does anyone know what happened over his father, James? I've asked everyone, but nobody's told me."

My brother looked stern. "Quite frankly, it's none of your business," he said heatedly with edge in his voice. "Rex is here and it's not appropriate to be discussing this. It's none of your business."

My sister was taken aback by his vehemence, which suggested she was an interfering busybody.

Soon afterwards I packed the albums away so swimming could take place in the pool, and table tennis.

As I left the room to return the albums to the library my sister caught me.

"Where did that come from?"

Later Rex came in from walking his dog. "Could you look and see if you've got a picture of my father?" he asked. "James? I only saw him twice. He never came back after the war and I could never find out what happened."

I said, "I can help. I was at our grandmother's in about 1945, when I was about five. Playing with the toys she put out for us: Canadian mounties, Scottish bagpipers, cannons and horse-drawn waggons with cloth tops. And I heard raised voices at the front door. Your father had come back from the war, and our grandmother and your mother wouldn't allow him in. It went on for about five minutes and then the door was shut. I don't know where you were. Perhaps asleep elsewhere in the house. I was playing on my own. But the decision was clearly taken before that day not to admit him. He came back from the war, found that his wife was with her mother, came to the front door without an appointment, and the policy was not to admit him."

"That's very interesting," Rex said. "Could you look to see if you've got a photo of him? I've got to go out to James," he said, and he went out to his dog who was named after his father and was now sitting in his car.

Later one of my brothers said, "I remember our mother refusing to join the Mothers' Union because Rex's mother was banned from joining her local branch as a divorcée. Our mother said, "She was lonely and needed support and she'd had a philandering husband, and they wouldn't have her, so they're not having me."

And I thought of the family skeleton revealed by my photo albums, one that had haunted one of us. It was very much his business, and in a family were the arrivals and departures of a vanished generation "none of our business" if they still haunted the living?

Treasure in Heaven
(Or: Two Certain Missionaries)

At the family party I asked Archie what he was doing.

"I've left my engineering job," he said. "I'm going to be a house husband for a while, looking after Vincent. Harriet is going back to work in March and she'll negotiate to go part-time and do six months, then leave. We hope to go to a college in Gloucester for trainee missionaries for a year. It's non-denominational. They've got live-in accommodation for all of us and we'll let our house if we can. We'll do a course on other cultures and religions, and then we'll be sent out as missionaries. It could be to Africa but it could be to Belarus or a Muslim country. It will be for ever. Not just a year, but for ever. I'm sure it's the right thing to do. We've prayed for three years and that's what we've been guided to do. We've got our skills – engineer and doctor – and we'll take the *Bible* to those who need the Gospel. We've been to *Bible*-reading twice a week, we both feel that taking the Gospel to those in darkness is what we've got to do."

Later I spoke to his mother about this. "They don't tell me what's happening," she said. "I'm fragile about it, I can't support it and it's not written in stone. Nothing's certain. But I can't interfere. They have to make their own decisions. They have different values. They believe it's not all about money, that it's also about the meaning of life."

"Is it a vocation for both of them or a wheeze?" I asked.

"Nothing's certain," she said. "I don't support it, I need support."

"There's a gene somewhere," I said.

"His paternal grandfather was in Haifa as a missionary," she said. "And her aunt was in the Salvation Army. He's got it on both sides of the family."

Later I spoke to my younger brother who had had the same conversation. "It's religious extremism," he said. "The Muslims have fanatics who car-bomb. He's the Christian equivalent, going to Paradise through missionary work rather than suicide-bombing. Seventy years ago he'd have been committed to a mental institution."

I thought of the young engineer and his doctor wife who would renounce the world to do good among the poor and downtrodden in the Third World and bring their salvation, and I thought of the *Bible*-reading class they had gone to. It dawned on me that missionary work was the logical consequence of *Bible*-reading, that the one derived from the other. They were dedicating their lives to the poor in the hope of receiving treasure in Heaven. They were certain of what they believed just as Muslim suicide-bombers were certain of what *they* believed, and their certainty and their renunciation rejected materialism and a career for money in favour of saving the souls of their fellow human beings.

A Coffin like a Packed-Away Christmas Tree

I drove to the funeral through torrential rain mixed with large flakes of snow. I arrived early and sat in my car outside the church until 2.30, then hurried through the downpour to the entrance and waited at the back of the functional brick and concrete church and looked at the stations of the cross to pass the time. A handful of journalists from *The Guardian* came in about ten to three and we all took our seats shortly before 3. A bald vicar handed out printed Orders of Service.

The vicar retreated to the back and suddenly began shouting sentences from the *Bible*. We all stood – twenty-five of us – as the oak coffin was borne in on the shoulders of four pallbearers, its gold handles gleaming in candlelight. It was stood on a bier consisting of two trestles between four candles. I looked at Ian's wife, an old lady of about seventy with straight blonde hair – she had been a left-wing firebrand forty years ago and had attacked me for holding views she considered right-wing – and at her blonde daughter, who I knew was thirty-seven.

The vicar welcomed us and asked us to sing. "Yours is the last generation to sing hymns, we have no choir, please join in."

It was 6 January, epiphany, and the hymn we sang was an epiphany hymn: "As with gladness, men of old." We then read aloud psalm 33, and there was a *Bible* reading, the Gospel of *John*, verses 1–14, about the Light.

Then Ian's oldest friend in journalism stepped up and, speaking through a very loud radio microphone, gave a tribute. I had met him forty years before with Ian in a pub near *The Guardian*. He described how Ian had started in journalism in local papers, because that is how it was in the 1960s, and how he had met him on the *Oxford Mail*, where Ian had taught him how to slip out without the news room seeing and buy a bacon sandwich from a market stall. It was at this stage that he met his wife-to-be. He described how Ian negotiated with the dailies to become their Oxford correspondent.

"I was on the paper with him. He used to discuss how to create news – organise a duel which he could cover, for example. And we'd play 'Get the word in' – 'contumely' ('insolent or reproachful language, disgrace'), for example. And intrigue round the Professor-of-Poetry elections, he loved that. He loved language, he was a Wittgensteinian."

He told how Ian went to *The Guardian* because it stood for fine writing. "It wasn't to do with its left-of-centre politics. It was where good writing took place." He now had an avocado every morning. He got to know a number of Oxford literary figures, including Tolkien. "I fell out with him over Tolkien," said his oldest friend. "I thought Tolkien's world was silly." And there were smirks among the two-dozen mourners.

He said, "Ian was – there's only one word for it – contrary. He took the opposite position to whatever you said, challenging you, teasing out your view. It could lead to people feeling insulted, and frequently did. But I see it as his wanting to be truthful." And I thought of the times he had challenged spending evenings talking, saying he'd rather work; and how he'd challenge things I had written and when I defended them had asked for chapter and verse, and I had declined to engage to preserve a long-term friendship.

Now the vicar gave his address, booming into his radio microphone, thanking Ian's wife and daughter for visiting him in hospital where he had spent more than a year and saying, "His wife told me, 'Ian could be utterly infuriating but he was also very considerate. I disagreed with some of the things he said.'"

At the end he invited the immediate family to light a candle, and his wife and daughter and younger brother (a grey-haired, lined man who had been ill) went forward.

"Would you like to light a candle?" he asked a round lady at the front, and she said loudly "No", suggesting 'I am here for Ian, don't involve me in your Christian ritual'.

Now the vicar prayed for the soul of Ian, and for his wife, daughter and brother and "all who mourn". There was a time of silence and reflection, and looking at his coffin I thought of standing with him in the forest while we were at university. After discussing European literature, he had chanted from Coleridge's 'Christabel', "Is the night chilly and dark?/The night is chilly but not dark." I hoped that where he was, though it might be chilly, was not dark but illumined by the Light.

There was a final hymn, 'O worship the Lord in the beauty of holiness', and then the pallbearers returned and shouldered the coffin and carried it out, feet first, to shouted words of hope about the resurrection and eternal life, and put it in the waiting hearse.

We all hung around outside the church, and I spoke to his brother, who said he could not come back to the Tower Arms where his wife and daughter had invited all for refreshments.

I drove the vicar to the Tower Arms through the dark. He directed me and said, "Here be very careful as deer might cross the road. The Americans were here in the war and they flattened a fence that kept the deer off the road. Just here the local beast, the beast of Brentwood, was allegedly seen on a deer's back, a story that appealed to Ian."

I parked in the car park. The pub had a plain wooden floor and old-fashioned decor. It had been Ian's local. I spoke to his wife. She had been impossible to speak to forty years ago, but she had mellowed like Lady Myrtle, and was now something of a pussycat, perhaps because it was the day of Ian's funeral and she was restraining her criticism.

She was sitting holding a glass of wine. She told me, "He wouldn't stop smoking. He had pneumonia, and came through it, but he went back to smoking. He died of complications to his lung disease. He shouldn't have smoked. He was on dialysis for a while, and got through that." She said, "I fell over while visiting him and broke my wrist and hurt my back. I have to sit down now. I'm waiting to have an injection in my spine on the NHS but with the cuts I don't know how long they'll keep me waiting."

I thought that her reality was her own health and that Ian's departure would allow her to concentrate on it more. I spoke to Ian's daughter who told me how he had chased her with seaweed on the Isle of Wight, where his mother had moved after separating from his father and where he would be buried the next day. She told me about her work with a Japanese trading firm. Then I circulated and spoke to some of his former colleagues on *The Guardian*. One said, "He put two fingers up to convention. That's what I always thought." Another said, "When I visited him in hospital he saw the tea trolley going back and he called out, 'Trolley, two teas.' He lined up two cups of tea and drank one after the other." Another said, "I invited him to my club and after the soup he went missing because he had to smoke his pipe. He was a pipe-chain-smoker and he inhaled not just down to his lungs but to his boots. He said, 'I'm tough, my body can take it.' But it couldn't."

A bald drunk who looked like a homeless tramp came up and asked me if I would give him a lift to a station so he could go to Maida Vale. It was only later I realised he was a notorious homosexual I had met forty years ago with Ian. He was then an office cleaner who scrimped and saved and though permanently drunk brought out a poetry magazine.

Ian's mellowed wife had told me she had left a reporter's book by the door for people to sign. I forgot to sign it. I drove home and helped my son pack the Christmas tree in a long cardboard box and parcel-tape it up. We lugged it awkwardly upstairs and put it in the loft. He said, "It's like a coffin."

And I thought that was how Ian was. When I had spent a lot of time with him he shone out like a warmly-decorated Christmas tree. He had shared a room with Ian McKellen at Cambridge, and visiting him then I was struck by the quiet fellow who sat without speaking in the corner of their room while Ian and I dazzled with our coloured lights. But then Ian became "contrary" and did not want to meet and talk about life, and his wife had been left-wing and opposed my views. And now a Christmas tree had been bundled up and packed away in a coffin and put in the equivalent of a loft: a grave in the Isle of Wight. The memory of Ian was like a memory of Christmas out of season.

A Mute Question

"Are you ready for me?" I asked as the big-shouldered, bespectacled young man came into the waiting-room, wearing a suit, and shook my hand.

"Yes," he said, "come through."

I followed him out of the waiting-room, down a corridor to his little room at the back. He helped me off with my coat and I sat.

"How are you getting on with the new hearing-aid?" he asked.

I said, "Well. I've overcome the problem of one of them breaking in two. But the gadget that helps you hear the TV more clearly, the one that works in conjunction with hearing-aids, doesn't work. The power to the box is on, but there's no audio outlet on my TV to plug the two leads into it."

The consultant said, "We'll try it on the TV in the waiting-room."

I followed him in and for the next five minutes he fiddled with wires until suddenly I was deafened by the Sky news.

"It works?" he mouthed.

"Yes," I said, "I need to turn it down."

Back in his room I gave him my hearing-aids so he could remove a jingle. Leaning forward and speaking slowly and very clearly so I could see every lip movement, he said, "You have moderate hearing loss in the lower frequencies and serious hearing loss in the upper ones. Modest in the lowest and severe the highest, so you're on both sides of the middle. You could go completely deaf in the next year or two, or there may be no further deterioration. I don't know. It's like when you'll die, no one can say. No one can say when you'll go deaf. But I have to say there was deterioration when I tested you last time. You remember the tuning-fork sounds." I nodded. "These are the most advanced aids you've just bought. They put back the hearing loss in both ears for all the frequencies and give you more or less perfect hearing. They talk to each other to achieve this. But otherwise, you read people's lips all the time, instinctively.

"We all do. I remember when I was twenty-two," he said. "I was about to catch a steam train and there was enormous noise and a foreign lady came up and said, 'What time's the next train for London?' and I replied correctly, 'Eleven ten.' Then the noise stopped and she mouthed, 'Thank you,' and I realised she was a mute. I hadn't heard her question, I'd lip-read it. That was my turning-point," he said. "I had hearing loss even then, and I was an engineer with GP. I was good at cabling and wiring. And I thought I should change my career from being an engineer to being an audio consultant, to bring together my technical computer knowledge and hearing problems that will make things better for partially-deaf people. That lady in the station was a foreigner, I believe she was from Romania, but she changed my life by asking a mute question."

The computer blipped, indicating that he had reprogrammed my hearing-aids.

"There you are," he said, "it's all done now, you can put those in now. Have you any questions?"

And I thought of the mute question I could not mouth because it would not be understood and there would only be a mute reply, 'How much longer have I got to live?'

"No," I said, "that's all very clear, thank you," and I assembled my bits and pieces and put them in my bag and stood up and shook his hand and let myself out into the street, pressing the catch on the door to release the lock, and walked down Harley Street towards Oxford Circus station, and all the way there were mutes mouthing questions on mobiles unaware they were walking towards the moment they would die.

Teeth and an Outside Water-Supply

"Inspectors? I hate them," said the septuagenarian dentist with a bald head as he probed my teeth with his crochet hook. "The first one I had was in court, in a room which I had when I was chairman of the panel and of the bench. I tape-recorded my interview. Four months later the draft report came through. I'd said that we have good co-operation with the public. It said there were problems. I rang them and said, 'I suggest you scrub the whole report. Because if you print it I shall go public with my recording.' They said they'd delete the passage. I said, 'No, the whole lot must be struck out. I don't want to hear from you again.' And I didn't.

"Then I had a couple of inspectors here. The first one, a man, came. He said, 'I want to see your hand-washing facilities. How many toilets do you have?' I said, 'There's one upstairs.' He went up and had a look and that was fine. Then he said, 'The plans show you have an outside toilet.' I said, 'There's no lavatory bowl or pipe, they've been taken out. It's got all my gardening tools in it.' He said, 'I still need to see it.' So he had a look and saw the gardening tools. He said, 'I'll have to report there's no water in the outside toilet.' I said, 'Are you blind and deaf? You can see there's no water and it's for tools. And I'm going to kick you out of the front door. F— off.'" He dug his crochet hook savagely into the gum under one of my molars. "'And don't come back and waste my time. I don't want to hear anything more from you, and if I do I shall see to you. So piss off.' I never heard any more from him.

"The second inspection. I'd done nothing. The night before I rang a friend and he said, 'Have you got a —.' Before he could finish I said,

'No.' He said, 'Oh, well I'll send you a box of goodies, you put your name on each one and then take your name off after the inspection's been and return the box to me.' So I did. The inspector turned out to be a very attractive girl. She saw my goodies, and she said, 'I want to know what training you had on the X-ray machines.' I said, 'None. The machine comes and I plug it in and that's it.' They're all the same," he said to me. "She said, 'Yes, but I need to know what training you had.' I said, 'None. The machine arrived and I used it.' She said, 'Oh well, you obviously know what you're doing so I'll tick that box. That's all fine. Thank you very much.'"

He laughed above my open mouth and I saw the intense eyes behind his leathery skin as he probed at my teeth, more interested in his fights with officialdom than in my decay.

"They take unemployed teachers and policemen and turn them into inspectors," he said, "ticking boxes. None of them have done a proper day's work. And governments are just in it for themselves. My parents taught me that no matter what the complexion of the government the rich get richer, the poor remain the same, and the politicians are feathering their nests.

"Nothing wrong," he said. "I can't find any fault, for the second time running. And you don't need scaling. Do you still wear your contraption at night?"

"It helps me sleep more deeply," I said, getting up.

"But you only wear it when you're with your wife or alone, you don't wear it when you're with pretty ladies?"

"I don't have pretty ladies," I said.

"Oh, go on, of course you do," he said, digging me in the ribs as though everyone does – and he did.

I thought of his intense eyes and leathery skin and of his outside toilet where he kept his gardening tools. He had probed my body's enamel with his spiky hook and had not found any decay, but his probing of my soul was a bit like looking for an outside water-supply that was no longer there. In my advancing years I enjoyed the serenity of being self-sufficient and self-contained, and I wanted to keep it that way.

Two Backpackers and a Film

The two girls came up the stairs with their backpacks about 7.30pm, having left their homes in Cornwall to fly out and spend six months touring Australia. Lorraine was tall and cool and calm and quietly spoken and as I showed her to her room she said, "It's very kind of you to put us up for tonight." Josie was more the country bumpkin, and slightly louder. They came downstairs and we laid plates of goulash in front of them, and Pippa asked them about their planning. They had been increasingly apprehensive as this day drew nearer.

"The worst part was leaving Cornwall," Josie said. But I felt the enormity of what they were preparing to do had only just hit Josie.

Lorraine said, "I've been to Australia already. I studied media and I took my camera and made a short film. There were amazing things – kookaburras and kangaroos. There was a field with about forty kangaroos in it and they all stood up above their children, defensively. I was told to stroke them but I was frightened. I had several experiences. I was asleep in the desert in a sleeping-bag and about two miles from a petrol station that had a bathroom, and there were mice everywhere. I ended sitting up and doing my hood up and mice were running over me. Don't sleep on the beach in Australia. A boy I knew out there did and when he woke up there were slithering trails all round his sleeping-bag. Snakes bury themselves in the sand and come out at night. We're going to Hong Kong and then we're flying on to Sydney.

"We're going to stay in a hostel in Sydney for three days and then my friend is coming. She's been touring New Zealand with her boyfriend and they broke up. Her mother wanted her to go home but she's coming to meet us and we'll decide what to do then. We can stay on in the hostel or go elsewhere. We'll spend two weeks in Sydney."

I asked if she was going to make a film.

"Yes, I'd like to."

"A portrait of Australia?"

"That would be nice, or a record of how we coped."

"Yes," said Josie, "just how we coped with all the new and dangerous things in Australia."

"Will you go back to the jewellers?" Pippa asked.

"No," Lorraine said. "I've been there nine years, and Josie has been there six. The previous owner was business-minded and always giving us things to do when it was quiet. She was good at planning. She sold and the present owner's very nice but she's not business-minded and we're standing around when it's quiet. No, I won't go back. I've just spent time in a comprehensive in my home town. Sixteen hundred children and twenty in the Department. I was doing English, Media and a bit of Drama. I'd like to go back and do that."

Lorraine knew what she was doing and what she wanted to do. I turned to Josie.

"I don't know what I want to do yet," Josie said, "but I'm not going back to the jewellers. We'll make a film about coping in Australia and see where we go from there."

They stayed the night and had breakfast the next morning. Pippa left to drive them to the station where they would take the tube to Heathrow.

"Thank you for having us," Lorraine said very politely, "it was very kind of you to put us up."

"Good luck," I said, pushing aside memories of dreadful things that had happened to backpackers in Asia. I watched Lorraine get in the car and waved her off. She had the talent and the quiet authority. Josie seemed slightly out of depth in her company. They had a dream of turning their backpacking into a reality film that would be shown on television. This was their escape from small-town Cornwall for a new life for which they hankered.

An Owl Handler out in the Cold

On the way back from lunch during the February half-term Pippa drove towards Bodmin and said, "It's a mystery tour."

Our grandson, aged nine, asked, "Where are we going?"

"You'll see."

She pulled in at the Owl Sanctuary, and I paid and we went through to a low wooden building with a dozen open half-rooms in which, along with a buzzard and a Harris hawk, sat a dozen owls of different species. We were separated from them by a rail. A young bird handler approached.

"That one's a burrowing owl," he said. "Digger. He was in the film *Legend of the Guardians* under his own name Digger. Would you like to handle it?" He put on a glove and brought a small feathery bird over. "You can stroke him under his chin," he said.

I stroked him and he nipped with his beak.

"He won't hurt you," the handler said.

The bird promptly nipped him.

I watched our grandson stroke the bird. Then I said, "Is that one a barn owl?"

"Yes," he said. "That's Fluffy. He was in the film as well but called something else."

He brought over a white owl with a round head.

"You can stroke him on the back of his neck. He's a screech-owl but you won't hear him. You'll see him, but you won't hear him. It's a myth that he can turn his head right round too. Another myth is that owls are active at night rather than day. That's not true."

"Which owls 'tu whit tu-whoo'?" I asked.

"The tawny owls. That one. Shall I get it?"

He returned with a smallish brown-feathered owl.

"It says 'tu-whit tu-whoo' as a territorial thing. 'I'm here, go away.' Also as a mating cry. 'I'm here and I want an egg.' You can stroke it under its chin. It won't nip. I can do an imitation of a tawny owl," he said. "It's not as good as my colleague there can do. Hey, do your tawny-owl impression."

Another handler with a pail of dead chicks tu-whitted and tu-whooed.

As I stroked the tawny owl and then our grandson stroked it I said, "It won't 'tu-whit tu-whoo' back if you do it?"

"No, but there's one that will hoot. It's just over there. Follow me."

We were now in a row of large caged rooms. In one of them there was a largish European Eagle owl. "He's Rupert," the bird handler said. "Wooo."

The owl answered, "Wooo."

"He's the only one who'll hoot at you," he said. "We've got a hundred and twenty owls here of different kinds. We've been doing this for seventeen years. I've been here two years."

"Will you go on and work in a zoo?" I asked.

The young man looked at me. "No," he said, "I wouldn't stand a chance of working in a zoo. There are many young people who have bird-and-animal-handling skills, and many work with more animals than owls. There are too many experienced handlers for too few zoo jobs. They hardly ever come up. No, I've been here two years and I'll go on being here. We only opened yesterday for this season. It's cold working out here."

We wandered round the owls. Many of them had dead chicks in their mouths. Most were stationary. At the end there were a couple of emus that advanced on us and a family of meerkats, one of which stood up on end to look at us.

On the way back I saw the handler and I asked him about the feeding.

"We have three hundred and fifty rats and mice a day," he said. "Some of the big birds have six."

"Do the birds have live meat?"

"We're not allowed to feed them live rats and mice by law. They were born in captivity, most of the owls, so they accept dead meat. And many owls in the wild accept dead meat."

I nodded and wandered off. It was just coming on to rain. Pippa and our grandson were in the shop. I looked back at the bird handler. His was a basic life. He was a guardian, one of a number, and there were not many members of the public going round. Money was not plentiful. The overheads of the sanctuary must be terrific. Three hundred and fifty dead animals a day and the wages of several handlers who had little prospect of being promoted to a zoo. He seemed a wise old bird – a wise owl – but he was out in the cold, living among wild birds born in captivity with not much hope of coming into the warm.

Thirty Dogs and Forty Tortoises Downstairs

Harry, our Cornish building maintenance man, came to pick up two flat-pack benches that had to be assembled.

"How's your move gone?" I asked as I helped him load the second box into his van.

"Oh, I've been in a few days but I've had a terrible time," he said. "The house I've moved into had thirty dogs and forty tortoises downstairs. The owner was breeding them. The dogs were like sausage dogs and he was keeping them all in the house, on the carpets, and selling them for seven or eight hundred pounds a time. The smell.... My daughter went in and bundled up the carpets and threw them out, and all the kitchen furniture as well, out. There'd been tortoises in all the drawers. We've had to have a new kitchen. Six thousand pounds. They're all falling over each other to do me deals, but six thousand's a lot for me. The smell's been so great, we've had to sleep with all the doors and windows wide open for the last two days. Anyone could've walked right in. I don't know how the previous owner could put up with the smell. He was a schoolteacher. I knew the house was in poor condition, but I wasn't expecting it to be left like that. It was disgusting. He was a schoolteacher as well." He shook his head. "Anyway," he said, "I'll have put your benches up by Tuesday afternoon. I'll bring them round on Tuesday afternoon."

And, not complaining about the task I had given him, which he could well have done without, he drove off.

A Buzz and an Iron Axe Head

At the family gathering I said that our fields might have been an ancient settlement. Paul said he'd try out his metal detector which he had been given for his birthday. It was a golden evening and we walked down to the sloping grass. His elbow in the curved holder and his hand on the bar, Paul swept the grass from side to side while I scoured a LIDAR map showing circles that could be ditches or stone walls of Celtic, Roman or Anglo-Saxon roundhouses.

There was a buzz. He marked the spot with a stick. Then another. He progressed to the end of the field, stepping through buttercups and greater stitchwort and clover, and crossed the stream and, holding the LIDAR map, I stood in two circles and there were another two buzzes.

"It's beautiful countryside," Paul said. "We could be in the middle of the deep countryside. No one can see what we are doing."

Paul left to go to a shop and returned. I collected two spades, a trowel and a small hand-fork and we concentrated on buzzes by the stream. We dug down into the turf and lifted out a square a foot deep and eventually extracted a triangular iron blade that looked like a ploughshare. We found two similar ones. There was a buzz about our anticipation as we probed the earth to see what it would yield.

The fourth buzz had us digging much deeper, a foot to two feet down. Eventually we pulled out a square piece of iron that looked like a hand-made axe head that was forced into a wooden slit to hold it and make an axe.

It was 7 and we came away tired and trudged back up to the house. Did I have an axe head that had belonged to one of the Trinovantes, and were they here, living in roundhouses by the stream? House martins darted round us as we walked, and I was alienated from the present, lost in the past and at a loss to know who had left their traces in the iron I carried.

A Last Glimpse of Childhood

Graham Robson was waiting with his wife by the gate as I reversed my car in and got out and collected the School prospectus. He was in an open-necked, short-sleeved shirt as I was. I waved and climbed the steps and shook his hand and his Californian wife's.

"We're going to see outside first as rain is forecast," I said.

"It's very kind of you to allow us to look at my old School," he said. "I haven't seen it since I left nearly sixty-five years ago. I won't be able to come again. The outside looks just the same. I've often mentioned details to my wife and here it is."

"He's often mentioned it," his American wife said. "I feel as though

I've been here already."

I led them to the back and down to the tennis-court as he looked and got his bearings. "This was here in your time," I said. "That's where plays happened."

"I was in *Hiawatha* just there," he said. "I fluffed my lines."

I led them to the fields and he commented on the oak.

"That's the oak of the School badge," I said. "This field was buttercups when you were here."

We sat on a seat and I showed him four framed pictures of the School's pupils I had brought. He had a list of names of boys and girls he used to know, and he wanted me to identify them. I recognised over half of them. I found his younger brother.

"What is he doing now?" I asked.

"Sadly he passed away eleven years ago. Cancer of the oesophagus."

I winced and looked concerned.

"But I've a younger brother still," he said, "who lives in Chesterfield. We've come down from Derbyshire today."

He was slightly older than me, and had been in a higher class among names I knew but could not always recognise.

We walked on to the second field, which is ringed by trees, and looked at the buttercups and the fallen oak.

"I can't get over all these trees," he said. "We have no trees in Kansas."

We returned to the School and I keyed in the code and let them in.

The Head was sitting in her study inside the door, and I introduced the couple.

"Perhaps this is a good opportunity to present this book," he said. "I'm donating this book on Kansas to the School library. There's a dedication in front, saying it's from me. I haven't put my dates in because I can't remember when I left. Mid-forties."

I showed him to the Assembly Hall and he remembered the lunches while a male cleaner bustled around with a black bag.

His wife waited downstairs, having five pins in one of her legs from an operation in November, and I took him upstairs and showed him a couple of classrooms he might have been taught in. He did not recognise them.

We returned and encountered his wife talking in the Head's study.

"We've got a gathering of old pupils next year," the Head said. "Perhaps you can come back for it?"

"No," he said. "I won't be able to. But perhaps my younger brother will be able to come."

"Might you not be able to get over for it?"

"No," he said, finally, and I wondered if he was ill and revisiting his childhood for the last time.

We said our goodbyes. It was beginning to drizzle.

"You've been very gracious," he said. "I'll stay in touch."

"Do," I said.

But I knew he wouldn't. He wrote from the US thanking me and saying, "You mentioned the seventy-fifth anniversary of the School next year. I know that I will not be able to attend but you may wish to send my youngest brother an invitation." His address followed.

I again sensed that he was terminally ill.

He had married a Californian and wished he could be back in England one more time before he died. He had glimpsed the setting of his childhood and had returned to Kansas for the last time, and would not be back.

Cobwebs in a Storeroom

I went to the Warren for the annual general meeting of the Centenary Trust. I followed the signs and entered through a French window into a room of seats where a bespectacled local historian thrust a balance sheet and a newsletter into my hands. I shook hands with a couple of fellows I knew and went outside and spoke to the Head of a local school. We re-entered and sat together.

Tommy Mallick opened the meeting. He spoke about the two Trust workers who would be addressing us, a youngish girl and a curly-haired boy. He spoke of the importance of the Forest. Then we sat and listened to the two presentations. The girl put up a list of points and rushed through them without looking. She knew them by heart. The boy spoke about the number of children who visited the Forest. It was really warm in the room and although I was in an open-necked, short-sleeved shirt, unlike my neighbour who was wearing a suit, a long-sleeved shirt and a tie, I felt myself nodding off. Two teachers from a school who sent pupils to the Trust spoke about how the Forest was good for pupils without discipline as fear of getting lost made them crave for rules.

It was stifling inside and at the end Tommy Mallick invited Sam Duckthorn to speak. He had arrived as the superintendent thirty-five years previously and had lived in the Warren. He stood and, not expecting to be asked, spoke about his enthusiasm for the work of the Trust and of the two presenters. He said, "I arrived thinking your work is important, and I shall leave thinking it's even more important."

The Head and I were first out to tea, scones with cream and jam. The Head swiftly excused himself. He had advertised for four support staff and had received two hundred applications, many from graduates, and had to sift the shortlist. I sat and talked with Tommy Mallick, and eventually others came, including Sam Duckthorn.

"I think I know you," he said to me. "You're at the school, I can't remember its name – at the bottom of.... I can't remember the name of the hill."

The hill had the same name as this house that had been his house for so many years. I told him the names. He had forgotten.

"Oh yes," he said. "I'm of a certain age when I find it hard to remember as I used to."

"He's got Alzheimer's," one of my fellow guests said sadly. "He's getting worse every week."

And I felt sad that the man once in charge of the white building we were talking before had gone into such a decline that he could not remember a road that had the same name as this building. He had spoken enthusiastically about the Trust but had lost the ability to remember who he was conversing with.

On the way out I passed T.E. Lawrence's L-shaped hut with roof tiles. It had been transferred from where he had hoped to live after the First World War, and had been used as a storeroom in recent years. There were cobwebs inside. I thought of Sam Duckthorn's mind and was sad that it too was a cobwebbed storeroom.

Tea in the Museum

I went to the Waltham Abbey Epping Forest District Museum lugging a holdall to show the contents to the Museum Officer, what the metal detector had found. He let me in by the garden gate, for the museum was closed, and I commented on the dozen gigantic hollyhocks that were much taller than me. He was a small Welshman with white hair and a smiley face, and I sat in his office and unpacked the four bits of iron.

"Three of them looked like bits of a plough," I said. "They might be manufactured rather than moulded. Eighteenth or early nineteenth century?"

He said he agreed.

"But this bit is almost square and was found quite deep. It looks like an axe head."

He looked at it and went off and returned with a couple of books. He looked at sketched illustrations of axe heads. Then he took me down to the museum and showed me the Iron Age section. There was one axe which was quite thin. It was 10th century AD. The next case had fragments from the 1st century BC, but I could not see my axe.

"To me it's too square, it may be part of a turfing spade," he said.

Back upstairs we sat and talked. We discussed Caesar's expedition – he said Caesar's works were dispatches from the front to please the Senate and were full of spin – and Boudicca. We exchanged email addresses, and after nearly an hour I packed my bits of iron away and followed him downstairs.

Three people were standing drinking tea and the Museum Officer said quietly, "I'll give you your tea in a minute."

"Hello Henry," I said, shaking the hand of an elderly expert on the Forest.

"Oh, it's you," he said. "What are you doing here?"

I said, "I've been showing Reg my bag."

"What have you got in that bag? You're not running off with some of the museum's treasures, are you?"

I told him about our metal-detecting and how there might have been a settlement on our land according to the LIDAR pictures.

I said, "Reg's looking into it."

He was retired and I knew he hadn't been well, and he had walked to the museum when it was closed to have tea with the Museum Officer. There was history and there was a network of people, and history was brought alive for the public by word of mouth as the latest developments were communicated to leaders of groups such as Henry and his wife over tea in the museum.

A Suntan and Blue Jokes (Or: Triumphs and Shallows)

I went to the Tower of London's New Armouries suite to celebrate the accountant's 60th birthday. I sauntered down Tower Hill past the spot where non-royals were beheaded (such as Lord Lovat, the Scottish rebel, in 1747), and took the drawbridge past Traitors' Gate, which had shallow water outside it. I sauntered near the White Tower, past the spot where the royals were beheaded, and went up the stairs to the New Armouries suite's banqueting hall, which contrary to its name had no armour in it.

The partners were having their photographs taken as I sipped my champagne. I went over and talked to Mervyn when the group broke up. I pumped his hand and looked down into his eyes and took in his golden skin. He looked well.

"It's sitting in the sun in the garden," he said. "I've done this for six months now, and I've decided I'm not coming back for five days a week. I've got my priorities in order. It can't all be money. You don't know what's going to happen. It may all have happened for a reason, so I could review my life and get my priorities right, who knows. I'm going to Spain next week. You need to enjoy things now. I didn't know I had cancer."

I pressed him. He said, "I fainted. My wife insisted I went to a doctor to find out why. I was found to be anaemic. The illness was doing things to my blood, making me anaemic. The chemo wasn't good, but I weathered it. You have to be strong, have your family round you and have a lot of determination. It's will-power, mind over matter. I've done well."

I said, "You look so well. I expected you to be in a wheelchair. Will you find speaking to the hundred and fifty here tiring?"

"No, I'm playing golf afterwards so I can't let this tire me."

We progressed to our tables. I was on Mervyn's table, between his right-hand man, who told me that one of his duties was to open the post and read everything and then distribute it, and his 'left-hand woman', my tax accountant. The master of ceremonies described how the firm of accountants grew and got bigger. As he neared the end he was interrupted by a large man sitting opposite me: "I'd like to say that getting bigger is the only way in Essex." Everyone laughed.

The conversation skirted work, but it had been announced that clients weren't being charged so I ran some context ideas past the right-hand man. The right-hand man said that HMRC (Her Majesty's Revenue and Customs) had alienated everyone by intimidation and sheer nastiness. "Many pay up. It's best to hold your nerve. Six years ago or more they said that all tax planning was to be treated as tax evasion. Tax planning began with the Duke of Westminster regarding his payment of his staff as costs so he could pay them, what, sixty years ago. We're disappointed by HMRC's attack on tax planning, which is perfectly legal, and we're delighted HMRC have lost a crucial case. A taxi-driver went regularly to Heathrow, and HMRC argued that he should have gone to Mayfair and could have made more income, that going to Heathrow was tax evasion. But he came across as completely sincere, and the judge awarded in his favour. We're pleased about that."

Mervyn stood up and spoke, asking, "Where did the thirty years I was with the firm go?" He did not mention his illness. He was listened to with rapt attention and respect for his fight against his illness.

Then Mervyn came and sat with me, and we talked about what he had missed while he was away. He was Head of the Firm and he had been kept abreast of what had happened during his convalescence.

Just as the interaction in the suite was reaching its climax the master of ceremonies called for silence and introduced a comedian whose voice was familiar from radio programmes such as *I'm Sorry I Haven't a Clue*.

He was seventy-six and white-haired, and he began by referring to the partners and making one-line jokes about their spare-time activities. Two were running in a marathon and one was going to the North Pole. He said, "It's your golden anniversary, isn't it?"

"No," people called out, "diamond."

"Oh, I've got a joke on golden, oh well I'll still use it." And he told a completely forgettable joke about a golden wedding.

Then he told a succession of jokes about the Irishman, the Scotsman and so on. There were laughs from those who had drunk too much and polite smiles from the sober. But the routine got bluer and bluer. "A naked man hurriedly left a wife when her husband came home and hid in the bathroom. When the husband went into the bathroom the man was trying to catch moths. 'But you've got no clothes on,' the husband protested. 'The bastards,' the man said, 'they're clothes-moths.' Then the same man escaped into the street and joined a run that was taking place outside the house. 'You've got no clothes on,' one of the runners said. 'I like it, I feel freer that way.' 'You've got no shoes on.' 'It's good for my soles.' 'You're wearing a condom.' 'Yes, I thought it might rain.'" And so on.

Half an hour after he started the comedian sat down to applause. I had to leave. My car was waiting and I had been trapped inside the Tower. I could not say goodbye to everyone and thank my hosts. The interaction was progressing to a long goodbye when the comedian stood up. He was unnecessary, he got in the way of what people wanted to do, and his material was unsuitable for this suited audience.

I left the banqueting hall to look for the Gents. I could not see a sign. The comedian was standing waiting for the lift. "Thank you for that," I said in embarrassment.

"Are you looking for the Gents? It's upstairs. Come and join me in the lift."

There was something about the way he said it that was suggestive.

"I'll run up the stairs," I said, "I've got a car waiting."

As I finished in the Gents he came in and stood with his belly sticking out and his hands out at either side and up as if he was about to surrender, and though he was 76 I was glad I had not accompanied him into the Gents.

Outside I mingled with the crowd leaving the Tower through the gates by the river. I wished I could divert to the White Tower's first floor and see the room off the crypt where Sir Walter Raleigh spent his last night.

I pondered the logic of the day. Mervyn would have died if his cancer had not been found. The event had been as much a celebration of his return as of his firm's 60th birthday. The blue jokes regarded life as a laughing matter, it was all a big laugh. But Mervyn knew otherwise. Life was precious and he had reordered his priorities to live life to the full. His suntan spoke for his enjoyment of the moment as he struggled against death, and the blue jokes seemed distastefully shallow and out of place beside the triumph of Mervyn's spirit.

A Gutted House and Far-Away Eyes

We went to the Community Centre to see the art exhibition. The paintings were grouped round a notice about their teacher. There were landscapes, portraits and still lifes. I photographed Pippa by her tulip and freesia. Then I saw a mother and son I knew. The son told me he was about to start as a solicitor in Chancery Lane, conveying property in the Development Department. I talked to them, and when I turned Pippa had gone.

I retraced my steps out through the drizzle to the French-window entrance and passed the notice-boards with photos of Forest walks. I found Pippa in the pottery room talking to, or rather being talked at, by the widowed husband of a friend of hers who had died a few years back.

"The house is completely gutted," he was saying, balding with long wispy hair down his neck and wearing jeans and sandals. "They took out the cold-water tank and the hot-water tank. I've got no water at all." He went on in this vein, describing how, widowed and with his family living away, he was converting the family home into a workshop where he could photograph, paint, carve and pot in different messy rooms.

"Did you do any of these?" I asked when he paused for breath.

"Just that one over there." A woman scratched onto a pot with pottery-hair was kneeling with her hands folded in prayer and she had a far-away, spiritual look in her white eyes and blue pupils. The look in the eyes was striking, and I said so.

"I had a model sit for me – six sittings," he said. "It was hard to get the eyes right, but I knew what I wanted to do."

We made our excuses and left. On the way to the car Pippa said, "He's retired, he looks after the family trust – stocks and shares and some properties – and he lives for his photography, painting, carving and pottery. He told me six months ago that the family home was no good to him in its present configuration. Either he should sell it and buy another one, or he should adapt it. I said I thought he should adapt it. He applied for planning permission six months ago and got it, and now he's turning it into his studio."

"It'll be hard to put it back into a family house if he decides to sell it," I said.

"I shouldn't think he cares about that," she said.

I nodded. His two daughters were married, there was a family trust, he was a widower and he was now not interested in the effect of his decisions on his family so long as he could be a craftsman and produce images like the one of a praying woman with contemplative eyes.

Spilt Wine and Mersea Island

I hosted a dinner for sixty-eight in a local Italian restaurant to thank our staff for achieving an outstanding inspection report. There was a champagne reception and then the top five changed tables after every course. I had my avocado and shrimps with some staff, then had my veal with the retired secretary, and finally moved on to have my ice cream at the school keepers' table.

The school keepers and maintenance staff were all drunk, having met a couple of hours before in a pub, and a Jewish fellow immediately upset a glass of wine over Ellen Loren's lemon dress. She sponged her dress with a fixed smile while the fellow loudly declared what he had done. "It's the second glass of red wine I've knocked over this evening," he bragged, flushed. "It was a party-stopper, everyone went quiet."

Our gardener Stan Jameson was pretty drunk. He said how indebted he was to me for taking him on. "I remember you told us to clear the brambles on either side of the road. Then you paid us and said, 'I might be getting back to you.' Six months later you did. You said, 'I've bought the house, now we need to talk in earnest.' People don't believe it when I tell them what it used to be like and how far it's all come. You must be so proud of the success of the place."

I asked him if he was still a councillor.

"I resigned four weeks ago," he said.

"Issues?"

"Yes." He came and sat next to me. "I protested at the waste, I've resigned, it's concentrated minds. June and I would like to leave and go to another area."

"Oh, where?"

"Mersea Island. It's an island and I understand the people there, they're islanders. I love the sea. I love it coming in and going out."

I said, "You may find that a door has opened for you. You are free to go to Mersea Island now, whereas before you had the responsibility of being on the council. Check it out now."

I moved tables again and sat with the Early Years' staff. Almost immediately Simon made a speech. He read out bits of the inspectors' report (received that afternoon), dwelling on which bits were excellent. There were two rounds of applause to different parts of the school as the teachers for those classes applauded themselves.

I went back to Ellen Loren and offered to pay her cleaning bill. "It's not fair," I said, "you put on a nice lemon dress and you shouldn't go home with a problem."

"It's very kind of you," she said, "but I can get it out with lemon."

Then I spoke to Stan again. He was very drunk and on the phone to his wife. "Come in and meet Philip," he said. Soon afterwards I was greeting his wife. Stan was so drunk he could hardly stand. "She was a cleaner first, then in the kitchen," Stan said. "There's so much I have to thank you for."

The two of them left and we left soon afterwards. Groups of loud women were talking animatedly on the street corner. Somewhere a resigned councillor would be wondering if he should do something about his dream.

A Hip and a Rebuff

The first dinner in the Holiday Inn was awkward. Retired couples sat at tables of eight and introduced themselves. We were all there to tour most of the forts on Hadrian's Wall, but that was not mentioned.

The large fellow opposite me dominated with a flow of conversation about places he and his partner had just returned from: Berlin last week – the topography of terror – and Egypt shortly before. Different parts of the world were casually brought into his name-dropping. He said he lived for rugger. There was talk of cars and speeding Mercedes.

Then he said, "I know a joke. A man was doing a hundred and forty in a Mercedes, and he was stopped by a policeman who said, 'Sir, you were doing a hundred and forty. It's Friday and I'm on my way home. I'm off duty. If you can amuse me by giving me an entertaining reason for your speed I'll let you go.' And the man said, 'Fifteen years ago my wife ran off with a policeman, and I thought you were bringing her back.'" He laughed uproariously at his own joke while the rest of the table produced polite smirks.

I encountered him the next morning at the Birdoswald ruins on the wall.

"I didn't sleep well last night," he said. "The bed was too small. I met my partner on the *Minerva*. In that restaurant near the back deck with the sliding door. She'd retired but she was a consultant. Neurology. She had a friend who was an artist, and he had a friend who was a travel writer and he had a friend who was an Egyptologist and we all sat together for meals. There was a large circle of us and we had a good time. I don't live with her. She's got a fantastic house on Chiswick Reach. The back garden is near where the coxes are thrown in after the boat race. She says she doesn't want to move again, it's such a lovely house she wants to stay there. I live on the opposite side of the river in Sheen. There was a very snooty lady on the *Minerva* from Cheyne Walk. She said, 'I don't know anyone who lives in Sheen.' 'Oh, the Wrights,' I said. 'Lord Wright, I live round the corner from him.' So that was all right."

At Vindolanda we had lunch. He went missing. It was a large site with many ruins. His partner came and found me at the table, an elegant lady who was clearly well-to-do.

"Where's John?" I asked.

"He's been taken ill," she said. "He's back by the coach. It's his groin. He was waving his stick at me for help and I didn't see. I'm so angry, he didn't say there was anything wrong with him. He says now he's had a pain in his groin for some while. The guide had to go all the way back with him. It's not a hernia, I felt it, it's a hip problem. He's lying on his back on a grass bank near the coach, asleep. He didn't sleep well last night, nor did I. He took most of the bed and lay on his back snoring and he was over my side and I couldn't push him over, he was too heavy. He was on his back like a whale." Scornfully she gave an impression of snoring, her arms out on either side, and I smirked.

When we returned to the coach, he was standing.

"All right?" I asked.

"In some pain. I need some Nurofen."

"I've got some," said his retired-consultant partner.

At Housesteads there was to be a steep climb. I declined it because Pippa's knee was not up to it. Pippa went into the shop while I finished an ice cream she had bought me. Then John came and sat with me.

I said I was just going to buy tea.

"Let me buy your tea."

He came back with strong tea and I asked him again, "Is it tolerable?"

"Yes, now I'm drugged up. It's my hip," he said. "That's what my partner Joan says. The trouble is, I've just discontinued my private policy. The premium went up and up, it's £2,500 a year and is going up to more than £3,000. So I'm on the NHS."

"I know people who've had a hip done on the NHS," I said.

"But Joan wants me to go back on the *Minerva* in January and February," he said, "to escape the winter."

"The person I know had her hip done seven months after going to the consultant. It's now July. That would take you to February. You could have it done in March."

"But that's the six-nations rugger," he said. "I live for rugger. It's what gets me through. Rugger's my passion. When I worked I was in furnaces. It's not very interesting but it paid well and took me to Eastern Europe, lots of other countries. I'd go and make their furnaces work and come away. My first wife said, 'All you know is a kiln.' So I said, 'Right, I'm going to play rugger.' I joined a team and we travelled to every continent. I never went with her, just two or three days away to play a match with the team. She worked for Bechtel. She advised on pipelines and visited all the Arab countries for conferences and was lavishly entertained by Arabs. She died of bone cancer. I'm not living with Joan, she's across the Thames from me. She's got a son by her previous marriage who's just started at St Paul's – and is into rowing, as I was. But he's puny and has become a cox. You know, his mother lives where the cox is thrown in. I can see him going into Oxford or Cambridge and winning and being thrown in at the end of his garden. Anyway, it's going to be difficult to get my hip done as I live on my own, there's no one to look after me."

"You'd need to be looked after for at least six weeks. Couldn't you move in with Joan?" I asked.

"Yes, I could. I could be on her second floor. It's got a walk-in bathroom. She could look after me for the first six weeks, if she would."

At that moment Joan joined us, having walked up to the Housesteads Fort and returned. "It was very good," she said. "A stunning view, and I got the idea of the drop the enemy side of the Fort better than at the other forts we've visited."

"Come and join us," I said. "We were just talking about John's hip. On the NHS he could get it done within seven months, say in March, if the medical advice is right, but he'd need to be looked after for six weeks. For example, he'd have to be collected in a car. A turntable is a good idea, he'd sit on it and swivel his legs in without moving his hips."

She winced.

"It wouldn't be his GP who'd authorise it, but his consultant," she said. "We know her."

"Yes," John piped up. "I had dealings with her when my wife died.

She thinks I need looking after. She's very proprietary."

"Proprietal," the retired consultant corrected.

"You see, my partner looks after me and corrects my English," John said.

"I keep as quiet as I can when I go in with John to see her. She bristles at me. We don't get on. She won't do what I want."

"That's true," John said miserably.

"Anyway," Joan said with the finality of a *coup de grâce*, "I don't think you're ready for an operation. You haven't mentioned your groin until today. If you were ready you'd have mentioned it."

She got up and went to the shop.

John looked miserable at her rebuff. He was in pain, and the one woman who would look after him during his operation and care for him had walked away from the responsibility. She would make sure that she went on the *Minerva* in January and February to escape the cold, and that she did not have to look after John for six weeks in March and April if he chose to put his hip before the rugger.

That night they sat at the end of our table at dinner, too far away to speak to. A brash, bearded man in his early seventies who had announced himself as the Che Guevara of Milton Keynes – he had lost his job at fifty and become a van driver and then a gardener and was with another man with whom he bickered – demanded cream with his strawberry *gâteau*. When it arrived he turned to John and poured half the jug on his strawberry *gâteau*.

"No," Joan said, "John and I don't want all that cholesterol. That's ridiculous." She said to John, "You can't eat that."

The bearded man tried to do the same to me but I declined very firmly and said, "I'll pour my own cream, thank you very much."

Miserably John ate his strawberry *gâteau* and left the cream.

The next day we visited Segedunum and later Arbeia. On the way back the coach stopped by the Gateshead Millennium Bridge. I saw John standing in a red-striped shirt and shorts and a peaked khaki baseball-style cap. He was smoking a cigarette miserably, trapped in the pain of a failing hip and no prospect of being able to do anything about it.

Critical and Early

I led Justin into the kitchen and he greeted Pippa. I studied him while I made tea. He was in his mid-seventies and heavy in a blazer and tie, and he had a bushy moustache, greying hair and eyes that looked flat, almost resigned and certainly serious behind his spectacles.

"Have you heard I've got cancer?" he said. "Prostate cancer."

"Yes," Pippa said. "I was sorry to hear that."

"A friend of mine died on Christmas Day of it," he said. "It was a particularly nasty death. I asked my doctor if I could have the PSA blood test. 'If you want it, of course you can have it,' he said. I went to see him about the results. He said, 'You've got cancer.' I said, 'What stage is it?' He said, 'Critical, eight on a scale of ten.' I've had an injection, anti-androgens. That was about a month ago, and I've felt tired ever since. I start chemotherapy soon. I'm going to have an operation and about fifty radioactive pellets packed round the tumour. I've got a tumour on my prostate and they'll zap it with greater accuracy than by normal chemo. It's a new technique."

I led him upstairs and he sat in an armchair with tea. I sat on the sofa.

"I'm just so tired," he said. "I've got no energy. I was fine until I had the injection. I've got to have three more, every three months. My doctor said, 'They've told you a year, but it'll be more likely three years.' I'm going to be without energy for three years, if I live that long."

"You'll live that long," I said. "You've got the determination. It's mind over matter. They control the disease better today than ten years ago. I know several people who've had it and recovered from it. They've refined their techniques, you're having a more accurate technique than the previous one. You see, you and I will sit together in our nineties."

He smiled wanly at me and sipped his tea.

"You're very encouraging," he said, "but I'm keeping an open mind about that, having seen a friend of mine die on Christmas Day. I just hope it won't be as painful as his death. But I have a good chance, they've caught it in time. I was critical so they couldn't have left it any longer. And if I hadn't gone and asked for the blood test they wouldn't have caught it early. In a way I've been fortunate."

I nodded. 'Critical' to me meant that his cancer was very advanced, on a scale of eight out of ten. It meant 'severe'. But he had put an optimistic gloss on it. 'Critical' had turned into 'early'. I was not sure if he was in denial or being brave. I thought his narrative a good one, and said nothing to challenge it. I looked sadly at a man in a blazer and tie who had a lot of suffering ahead of him.

Christmas Day and a Grandchild

Justin got out of his car. I shook his hand in the sun. It was a firm handshake. I asked him if he'd take tea.

"Yes, please."

I led him into the kitchen and Pippa came through.

"Have you heard that I've got cancer?" he asked, bushy walrus moustache and grey hair and spectacles.

"Yes," she said as I made our tea. "How are you feeling?"

"Tired," he said. "I've got no energy. I still enjoy eating but I have problems going to the loo. A friend of mine died of prostate cancer on Christmas Day, in a hospice. I was quite shocked and went to my doctor and asked for the PSA test. He said, 'That's not conclusive.' I said, 'A biopsy's conclusive?' 'Oh yes, a biopsy will sort it out.' So I had a biopsy and went back to see him. He said, 'You've got cancer. Your prostate's hard.' I said, 'What will happen if I do nothing?' He said, 'You'll be back in a year and you'll be dead within two years.' That's what happened to my friend. He did nothing. He said, 'It's on a scale of ten and yours is eight, almost critical.'

"They've begun treatment, tablets and then an injection. The tablets befuddled my brain. I have to have one injection every three months. I had the first one a month ago. It's horrible, it's anti-androgens, it made me feel awful. Ever since then I've been tired, had no energy. I may have these injections for much longer than a year. When I told my GP he said, 'Two or three years, you won't end it in a year.' Then to coincide with the next one they're going to operate on me. It's not removing my prostate, that's a serious operation and germs can get in. My consultant said, 'If I were you I wouldn't have it.' Radiotherapy's imprecise. I'm having a new technique, fifty radiation balls lodged in me. They will zap everything within reach in a precise way. I'm having it done at the Rivers Hospital, but I don't know when. They do the operation on a Saturday and leave the theatre free for twenty-four hours because it's radioactive. I've just become a grandfather and I won't be able to hold my grandchild for three months. I can't be in the same room as people. It's a tumour, it's got to be dispersed. I was fine before I took the tablets and had the injection, but now I feel tired, energyless. My friend began the treatment but then decided he wouldn't have it any more. I can understand how he felt but it's wrong just to sit back and wait to die. It's better to fight it."

We drank our tea and went upstairs and to get him outside his focus on his cancer I turned to current affairs. I took him outside to look across the fields, and I took a photo of him, saying, "I don't have one of you."

He said, "I've really enjoyed today."

I said, "You must come again."

"I'd love to."

"After you've had the operation."

"Yes. I'll come after that."

I showed him to his car and waved him off and I wondered if I would not see him again and if the photo I had taken of him would be the last enduring memory of him I would have.

This story presents another perspective on Justin's illness, which was introduced in 'Critical and Early'.

A Headache and a Locum

"Did you have a nice birthday?" I asked Carol.

"Oh, yes, my daughter did things. She booked at a restaurant run by Janice Oliver's parents. Donald came. But in the middle of dinner he said he didn't feel well. He went outside and sat in the sun and didn't eat anything. Then he started crying. He had a splitting headache and his knee was very swollen. And he was confused. He didn't seem to recognise me. He was agitated, this dreadful headache.... Joy said she hadn't seen him cry since his grandfather died. He was crying with pain. We're going to the doctor tonight. We'll only see a locum, which is a pity. His Parkinson's seems to have got a lot worse."

Tears glistened in Carol's eyes. I said, "When you see the locum you must check Donald hasn't had a stroke or a brain haemorrhage, and find out why he had the headache. Is it part of the Parkinson's pattern or is it abnormal?"

She was too upset to reply. She went off to continue her dusting and Hoovering. Her husband, who had Parkinson's disease, had been crying with pain from his splitting headache when he should have been celebrating, and the only medical help forthcoming was an interview with a stand-in locum who did not know his case.

A Broken Hand and a Thunderous Look

The birthday party took place in an American-style restaurant that featured burgers. The place that had been booked had unexpectedly closed for the day, and there had to be a last-minute alternative booking. We arrived slightly late. Bernard was sitting in the reception area with Angela and her parents. Chris greeted me warmly, shaking my hand with his good hand: one hand had been broken by a flying golf ball and he had two strips of Elastoplast. Monica came to be kissed. Angela sat in the corner with a thunderous look. She stared straight ahead like a golfer assessing a putt and did not seem to be engaged in the event.

We chatted and then went to the table. The seating arranged itself. Chris and Monica were opposite me, with Angela between them. The waitress came to take our order. Angela declined all food: "No, I'm not eating." She wasn't talking either. She had told her mother and stepfather, who were both retired and living off pensions, that they could not stay with her as she was using the spare room as an office, and they had had to book at a hotel out in Cheshunt, typically making the best of the situation and looking on the bright side.

I chatted to Bernard, who was engaged in conversation lower down the table. And at one point we all sang "Happy Birthday", led by Al who had just turned two. He asked, "Where candles?" and made blowing gestures. But there were no candles on this occasion. They had been on the cake for birthday tea.

I kept the conversation going with Chris and eventually lapsed into silence as I had fallen behind in eating my classic burger.

Then Angela suddenly said, "We're going to see Hemingway's house."

Startled that she had spoken, I said, "Oh, in Florida, on the Keys?"

"Yes."

"Who's Hemingway?" Bernard asked.

So I explained that he was a writer who was now dead and that he had liked bullfighting and had written about an old man catching a fish, a marlin. I said the old man lashed it to the side of his boat but sharks ate it on the way home.

Bernard was going to America for a month. Other relatives were supposed to be going but had cried off. Monica had arranged to go out for ten days to take Bernard to a few places.

Eventually we came away. Angela drove off with Bernard, with thunder in her eyes. Pippa and I headed for our car. Chris and Monica got into their car to go to Cheshunt. We had all been connected through Bernard, wanting to give him a good birthday, and now we all dispersed in different directions. The look on Monica's face was hurt, as if she had just suffered the pain of a golf ball breaking her hand.

A Brown Envelope and a Bach Fugue

The four hundred parents were taking their seats for the prize-giving. I was standing near the platform party. The Head said, "Have you met our guest of honour?"

A young man in a suit with groomed hair shook me confidently by the hand.

"It's Stephen Jones, an ex-pupil of ours. He's come specially over from America."

"Welcome," I said. "I remember you so clearly. You played the organ at our carol service two years running."

"Yes," he said, "I did. And now I'm a professional musician in New York and giving recitals."

"You've done very well," I said. "You're a role model to the pupils. Some of them may remember you, but they'd have to have been very small when you were at school."

He nodded.

"I remember the question arose," I said, "as to whether we should pay you for playing at the first carol service. I said, 'We're paying the organists at the other schools, and we should pay you.' So I made sure you received a brown envelope."

"I did," he said. "You were the first to pay me for my music."

I left him and entered the packed hall and took my seat in the front row. We all stood for the platform party. Eventually it was his turn to speak and he spoke confidently about what had happened to him. He described how he had to play a lot of Bach. To give an example he turned from the microphone and went to the piano and played an extract from a Bach fugue. He appeared more of a schoolteacher making sure his class understood than a performer, he threw himself into what he said and was given a long and deafening ovation.

He distributed the prizes with great panache, bending for two or three seconds so he could be photographed with each recipient. I reflected that my brown envelope had set him on his way, and he was now playing Bach fugues in America. I had encouraged his talent and he had developed it and had shown his old school how accomplished he was now. I thought we were all developing our talents and showing them to those who encouraged us.

Two Vines and a Nonagenarian

The school prize day was held in a marquee. The guest of honour was the Chief Executive of the Inspectorate. He was in his early forties, and had an open face. He also had a white boxed bandage on his left hand, a glorified splint, and an open-necked shirt. When he spoke he said, "I'm sorry I'm not wearing a tie. I did try to tie it, honestly. But I had an unequal argument with a hedge-cutter over the weekend and I've only just come out of hospital."

After the distribution of the prizes the parents stood talking while the Head chatted outside the marquee. The Parents' Association crept into the marquee and draped banners saying "Happy Retirement" and clandestinely brought in plates of sandwiches and cakes, and a bottle of champagne. The Head was retiring and when she returned she was suitably surprised at the transformation, and we all sipped champagne. A large harp had been left behind by the orchestra, and one of the staff plucked the strings mellifluously to create background music.

I said to the Head's husband, "Listen, 'Somewhere over the Rainbow'," and he said, "Yes, we're angels on a cloud, playing a harp. It's so unsubtle." And I laughed.

"How will you spend your retirement?" I asked. He was in his early sixties and had administered an orchestra in the course of his working life. He wore a dark suit, a white shirt and a navy tie.

"We'll spend four spells of six weeks in France each year. We can't do more than that because of my mother. She's ninety-seven and has just admitted herself into an old-people's home. She's reconciled to the fact that we can't visit her very often, but I'll keep an eye on her. She had a very tough life. She came from Northumbria and lived on a wintry farm. It was freezing, no central heating of course. She made her way in health, became one of the top health administrators in the country."

At that point the Chairman of the Parents' Association, a woman with reddish hair, called for silence and gave a short speech.

"Patricia and her husband are Francophiles," she said, "so we thought you'd like these two vines" – two parents picked up six-foot-high potted vines that had decorated the side of the marquee – "which you can place outside your house in France so that in due course you'll have a grapevine to shade you from the sun when you drink your evening wine."

There was applause as the presentation was made. How they would transport the two six-foot vines to France and why they should take

English vines to wine-producing France were considerations swiftly drowned in the applause.

Patricia's husband moved towards his wife, and as they stood together I saw them as two vines who would be spending time in France but not rooted there. They were like potted vines that could not take root in French soil so long as Patricia's husband's nonagenarian mother had to be visited every six weeks.

A Herkimer Diamond like a Milestone (Or: A Healer and Bomb Disposal)

We arrived at the Diamond Wedding lunch in pouring rain. A lorry was blocking the entrance to the car park. We manoeuvred round it and entered the pub, and walked through to the restaurant bar and greeted the two octogenarians and spoke to their sons. One was marrying a Bulgarian whose Russian mother was present.

I was seated next to Doreen. She said, "I was a healer in the local church, I don't do it any more. Not for the new vicar. He told me I could not have my usual healing slot the first time he came to the church." She said, "I believe in alternative therapies. Arthur had a war injury, he wouldn't have walked without a wonderful osteopath. I've seen it work. He wouldn't be walking now without osteopathy."

We ate our smoked salmon and main course, and then Doreen changed places with Arthur. He had good hearing for eighty-five, and he talked about his passion for sailing, which he had passed on to his grandchildren, and he got on to when he was younger.

"My first date with Doreen was at a dance in 1937," he said, "at Woodford County High. But then the war happened. I was in Scotland, touring round the Dad's Armies, getting them more up to date. They hated us, we told them how they had to change. I ended up in bomb disposal. We had some German prisoners of war nearby and we took them out and stood them by an unexploded bomb. Unexploded bombs were heavy and they might be twelve foot down in the earth. 'You dropped it,' we'd say, 'you dig it out.' When the earth had been removed round it, the CO defused it. So after all that I came back and did a building apprenticeship, and finally we got married in 1951."

There were about sixty present, including one lady who had been at their wedding, and the wedding album was passed round. I sensed the austerity and formality of the time. I thought what a striking couple they were, and was sad at the ravages of time. For it was rumoured that Arthur would shortly be undergoing an operation. Prostate cancer had been mentioned.

Pippa gave Doreen a package. It contained a Herkimer diamond to mark the occasion. All were happy, the day had gone well. And then people began to slip away. The Bulgarian girl and her Russian mother left to look at wedding dresses.

We slipped away to go to Cornwall.

That was what happened. You reached a milestone, people came through the rain to be with you, then they returned to their own lives. But the milestone had been marked, that was the point – by a Herkimer stone.

Flat Battery

"Flat battery?" asked the AA mechanic as he turned the key in the ignition and listened to the slow whirr. He opened the Shogun's bonnet. "I'll soon tell if you need to replace it. I'll just do my tests and see how many volts you've got. I've got several tests I do, won't take a few minutes. Lovely spot here. Pleasure to come to a place where you can look at the sea. I like it down here. I come from Newbury in Berkshire. I come down here for six weeks every summer. The breakdowns and home-start problems in Cornwall are more frequent in the summer and it pays me to take lodgings for six weeks and have a bit of a holiday while I attend to breakdowns and home-starts. Yes, I love it down here. Being on my own helps. I don't understand it. Your battery's not flat. It's got six hundred, eight hundred volts. It's only a little down. And the alternator's all right. Nothing wrong with that. But it wouldn't start. I don't know why it wouldn't start for you. Whether there was something between the wiring and...." He turned the ignition and the engine started. "Job done," he said, "but I don't know what I've done.

It was just a weirdness. You'll be all right now. You won't need another battery. I'll just get you to sign the paper, then I'll be on my way. Might have time to look at the next cove."

His battery of tests had not given him the result he expected, and he looked a bit sheepish, almost flat. I watched him continue his extended holiday, smiling at his enthusiasm for the Cornish coast.

Chocolate Curls and Chunks

I arrived at the candlelit flat at 7.30 and the dog jumped in welcome. Claudia held him and said she was cooking, so I went and sat on a stool in the kitchen and watched as she chopped up onions and prepared spinach and greens, chatting with an efficient German smile as she did so. Soon Paul arrived from London and after changing his shirt he helped prepare the chicken and mustard sauce. He had written out the ingredients on a piece of A4 paper and she had bought them on her way home.

Eventually dinner was served. There were two candles in silver holders, and we heaped sliced chicken and sauce onto our plates of vegetables. We all savoured the taste which their hard work had achieved.

I returned to my stool to watch them prepare pudding, chatting during the preparation in the Continental manner. As in rural Germany, their kitchen was a place where social chat accompanied the assembly of ingredients. Paul crumbled biscuits into three glasses and added ice cream. Claudia poured on coffee sauce and chocolate curls, which she had made by scraping a long bar of dark chocolate. Between them they added cherries. Paul tried to add chunks of chocolate.

"No," Claudia said, "no, only the topping."

"No, it needs chunks of chocolate as well."

"No, no."

"Trust me."

"No."

"*Bitte.*"

"That's what I like to hear, *bitte,*" I said, defusing the tense situation with an attempt to make them smile.

But Claudia had shown her strength. Behind the German smile and sunny disposition was a self-assertion which had stood up to Paul, and I had glimpsed a steely determination in getting her way which he would have to harness if it was going to strengthen rather than damage their relationship. The chocolate curls were topping and had been delivered with sweetness but the chunkiness of the bits had brought out a chunky toughness that I thought boded ill rather than well.

A Hornets' Nest and Folded Clothes

At the end of September I discovered we had a hornets' nest in the base of an oak-tree. Derek, the big, thickset, hook-nosed, white-haired rat-catcher and pest-control expert, came and looked at it. There were two sentries sitting guarding it. I had my camera.

"Here," he said, "give me that." He bent and took a photo of the sentries from a few inches away, completely fearless. "When you've been in the paras you fear nothing."

One flew away. "There'll be several hundred in there, in the hollow below," Derek said, and he puffed in smoke.

A couple of hornets flew out, one with a big yellow body. I said that one had been buzzing up the outside of my window at night.

"You'll have seen the queen," he said. "They fly at night."

I walked back with him to his van. "Hedgehog," he said, examining a dark-coloured dropping. "Seed-eater. Yes, hedgehog." He took a phone call on his mobile and said, "It's my daughter. It's Myra's birthday."

"How is Myra?" I asked.

"Very well," he said. "Marrying her was the best thing I've ever done. She's very good. The Filipino women know how to look after a man. She's working in a care home over here, but we go out to the Philippines and see her family, you know I send money back, and in the hotel there near Baguio she'll say, 'Take a shower,' and when I come out fresh clothes will be ready and she'll say, 'Don't put your old shirt on, it smells.' Then she'll wash my old clothes in the shower and hang them out of the hotel window or up on the roof where the staff hang their clothes. And when they're dry she'll fold them because there's no iron. Even my pants are folded neatly and put in a drawer. I thought, 'No one's ever done that for me.' She's very good."

He broke off. "Fieldfares, or redwings," he said. I looked up into a tree. A bird flew away flapping its wings very quickly. "Redwing," he said. "But there are fieldfares there." Four birds flew away. "Fieldfares," he said. "They've just arrived." He gazed into the distance.

"Their culture has no sense of age difference," he said. "I mean I'm sixty-seven and she's twenty-seven, and we've been married four years. I met her in a restaurant in the Philippines and asked if she'd go out with me, and she said, 'Yes.' I've never held hands with a woman, I've always been an arm-man, and she wanted to hold my hand and I said, 'I feel embarrassed, I mean I'm forty years older than you.' She said, 'Here no one thinks about age difference, age difference is not a problem.' And she was right. I went outside Manila to ask her father if I could marry her. The family are agricultural workers, and live very simply. He said, 'It's up to her.' We send money back for them. They've got a building in the countryside twelve foot by twenty foot with a corrugated-iron roof and curtains between rooms instead of doors. Their water comes from a river. There's a pipe that runs off it and a lot of taps and by the time it reaches them it's just a trickle. I don't drink the water unless it's boiled. There's a pump ten yards away from the houses, and the toilet for each is a hole in the floor and there's another hole beneath that. It all just stays there. I think it must get into the water-table. I mean, the pump is only ten yards away from it all....

"Myra has earned enough to buy a house. She spends nine hours cleaning at the care home and then she comes back and cleans my house. It's hers, you know, that's how she feels. My house is spotless. She never stops working. She said last night, 'I have enough to buy a house in the Philippines. We could live near my family.' But I'm thinking of the sewage problem. I'm wondering how I'd get a shave, and get water up to head-height. I've said we'd never go there."

He broke off. "Robin," he said as a bird flitted into the bushes.

"I give her all my money. And you know, she saves. She gets discount rates. She says 'Stand over there' and negotiates Pino prices –

Filipino prices – that have WST, White-Skin Tan. We took a taxi to the airport. 'Use meter,' she said. 'No, it's six hundred.' 'No, meter.' She said, 'Get out of this taxi.' We took the next taxi. 'How much?' 'Three hundred.' 'Get out.' The next taxi came. 'Use meter.' 'All right.' One hundred and twenty. She saves me money.

"The Pino women are very good," he said, "I recommend them. They're better than English women. I was married for thirty-five years and my missus worked evenings and got in about 10. One night she was late and I said, 'You're late.' She said, 'Yes, I am. I'm sick of you and sick of this house and I'm leaving.' I said, 'Oh, right.' Next day my daughter said, 'What's this case doing here?' She said, 'It's Ken's. I'm moving in with him.' My daughter said, 'You'd better tell the old man.' So she told me. Ken's a black man. I said to her, 'Going out with a black man?' She was like an angry hornet. My generation were taught black and white don't mix. I'd no idea. So I was on my own and a friend said, 'We're going to the Philippines, want to come?' and I said, 'Nah, I'm married.' He asked me again nearer the time, and I said, 'You're too right, I'm coming.' We spent five weeks away. We had a walk round Singapore for a week and then we went to Manila and I met Myra in a restaurant. The English want independence and equality. The Pinos want to look after a man. They think differently."

"Does her father see you as a rescuer of the family?" I asked.

"Yes," he said. "I've done quite a bit for the family. I bought a machine, a 'Gligli', that they use on the land, to give one of them a job, taking it to people's fields and using it. I've rented fields for them for three years, so they have had three harvests. And I've bought things for their house. I've put Myra's sister through college, so she could train as a nurse. We're going over in April to see her graduate. We'll go and stay near the family, and she'll wash my clothes and fold them neatly."

I did not like to say that his clothes would be washed in contaminated river water. I felt sad for this man who had been hurt by his wife and was now being rooked by an agricultural Philippine family to fund their Third-World life as he went about his business among Nature, killing rats and exterminating hornets. With his white hair he seemed part of Nature whose pests he controlled. His marriage had been something of a hornets' nest and he was happy now with the care put into his folded clothes.

A Bulgarian Kick and a Line Dance

I attended a wedding at the 1678 church of King Charles the Martyr in Tunbridge Wells. Jeremy was marrying a Russian girl who he had met at work. He was a banker, and she controlled a hedge fund. Her mother was Russian, her father Bulgarian, and in addition to her Russian nationality she had taken on Bulgarian nationality at sixteen. She had won a scholarship open to all Bulgarians to study in America, and she had worked at Lehman Brothers, New York and then Lehman Brothers in London until it closed, precipitating the credit crunch of 2008.

The bride came down the aisle in a full-length, sleeveless satin dress and short veil, carrying a bouquet of red roses and white star of Bethlehem. The three bridesmaids wore red knee-length strapless dresses with white sashes. They had posies of white roses and gypsophila. The ends of the pews were decorated with bunches of white roses and gypsophila. The bride was escorted by her Bulgarian father, a podgy man who sold for a company and had an engaging smile.

There was a reading in Bulgarian that was printed on the service sheet. It looked like Greek with the letters *pi* and *rho* the same as in Greek. There were seven or eight certificates to sign as the bride had Russian and Bulgarian nationality. No one can have three nationalities and she did not have Jeremy's English nationality.

The reception was held at Horsted Place, a Victorian country house. There were steps up to the front door. There were sandwiches and a cream tea. I spoke to the bride's Bulgarian father. He had come from Bulgaria the previous week. He said his Russian wife went to Russia three times a year. She came and spoke to me, a sallow-skinned lady in dark spectacles who wore a fascinator. I asked her if she was pleased at the result of the Russian election, and she said, "Some people are not happy, but I like Putin." I did not raise the shooting of a Russian in London the previous day, which was attributed in the press to the long arm of Putin.

I said to my brother-in-law, "Do you remember Georgi Markov, who was stabbed and killed by an umbrella with a needle in the nineteen-eighties? In those days Bulgarians were feared more than the KGB. Some of those here look like brolly operators." At that moment three men walked by with stubble and evasive eyes and we half-wondered if we were about to be brollied.

We were called to go out into the garden. The sun was very hot on my cheeks. There was a long, narrow white sheet on the grass 'pegged' in each corner by leaves and in the middle by flowers of the Bulgarian sweet geranium.

The bride stood in front of the sheet and gave a short explanation to the eighty guests. She and her husband then sat back to back on chairs placed on the sheet and tugged a round loaf of bread above their heads to see who would be the breadwinner. The bride won and announced she was boss of the house. Then her mother fed chunks of the loaf to the couple, first with salt on top to indicate life's bitterness and then with a coating of honey to symbolise life's sweetness.

Finally the bride explained another Bulgarian tradition. She would kick a bucket containing two flowers, a white carnation and a red carnation in water, to determine the gender of their first child. If the flower that ended up farthest from her was white, it would be a girl; if red, a boy. It was an Ottoman custom three or four hundred years old, dating from the time of the beginning of Ottoman rule in Bulgaria.

The bride kicked the round copper bucket so hard it flew through the air off the sheet and water splashed the trousers of a few guests. The red carnation came out ahead of the white one (which remained in the bucket). "So it will be a boy," she said.

We went in for the wedding breakfast. The tables were decorated with gypsophila and thyme. The men had favours (chocolates) and the women had a tiny veiled bundle containing a five-cent piece, an ear of wheat and a sweet (symbolising prosperity, fertility and happiness). There were speeches at the beginning of the breakfast. The father of the bride spoke first, apologising for his Bulgarian English and saying it was so poor that sometimes he could not understand it himself. Every sentence he spoke raised a laugh. He was followed by a friend of the bride's and then by the bridegroom, Jeremy, who read out chunks of Bulgarian. (He had written a speech in English and given it to the

Bulgarian friend to translate.) Finally his brother made the best man's speech, stating what an ideal husband was and seeing if the groom measured up to this criteria. There were many laughs. We then ate ravioli of butternut squash, loin of pork and basil-and-lime *panna cotta.*

After eight there was dancing and there was a Bulgarian line dance. All held hands and improvised the steps: three paces to the right, leg swing, leg swing, then the same back a bit, then the same farther forward. Each leg swing was a Bulgarian kick. The menacing Bulgarians who looked as if they might be carrying umbrellas took part, and there was a great happiness. The Bulgarian kick had forecast a family and now the line dance included all nationalities in a universal togetherness.

A Warm Log Burner and a Latch-Pinned Door (Or: Dream and Reality)

Paul's partner Claudia's family were coming from Germany for a few days and Claudia rented an old hall in the Snowdonia National Park. We drove up to spend a night with them one day in May. It was surrounded by mountains with a view of Snowdon, which some of the family had climbed that day. It had snowed in the night. We passed a huge slate quarry and got lost in Blaenau Ffestiniog. Paul met us and in convoy we followed him down a narrow lane, over a bridge, past a field with stone walls and black sheep to the old hall, a timber-framed medieval (c.1450) building encased in stone during the Tudor time.

We left our bags in the hall and greeted Claudia's parents. Her mother was in the kitchen unwrapping newspaper-clad packages of deer shoulder which she had brought from Germany. They had shot the deer on their estate. They had let it hang while they established it was free of a particular worm, and had frozen it. She had brought it in through Luton airport. Claudia's father was an accountant. Both Claudia's parents spoke reasonable English.

The result of the French election was being announced and Claudia's two brothers were watching on chesterfields in the entrance hall. One of them had a French girlfriend who was also watching. She lay on her back on the sofa in jeans and as Sarkozy blustered she said "Rhetoric" and made a kicking movement with her left foot to indicate he was being kicked out. I came and went and stood for Sarkozy's concession and sat for Hollande's first speech as President. A commentator said that one of the candidates (Hollande) had given France a dream of the future ("change is for now") whereas the other had presented reality and its problems, such as immigration and racism. He said that France had voted for a dream but that reality would cut in.

We were called through for supper about eight. A long table with twenty chairs stood in front of an inglenook hearth with a log burner. We sipped a thin asparagus soup served from a tureen, drank German white wine and were eventually served from another tureen of chopped venison, which we had with rice and red wine.

It was like a dream. We were in the medieval wing that had contained the solar (sun-room) and parlour. There had been a central hearth below where the tureen stood. The atmosphere was timeless and the nine of us sat and talked, mainly in English with some German and French thrown in, about Europe and the dream of a world government for the rest of the evening, the family revelling in being together and sharing memories in front of the warm log burner. We had cheeses (cheddar and gorgonzola) and tiny cinnamon coffees. Suddenly it was midnight.

Upstairs we found our room, which had beams. It was the oldest upstairs room – it had been over the parlour and was originally accessed by a ladder – and it had a glass panel showing the wattle and daub in the wall and a small plaster frieze with a decorative motif of acorns and young vines and alternating cinquefoils and eight-petalled daisies. The family had sat next to each other at the table like the acorns and vines in the frieze.

Reality cut in. I went to the communal bathroom early to escape a queue. The door closed on a latch, and there was a pin that had to be slotted into a hole to prevent the latch from being opened from outside. Four different sets of shaving equipment and toothbrushes were arrayed on the sill above the basin, and sponge bags were on the floor. I brushed my teeth and got ready for bed. Then I went down and said "Good night" to the family who were in the kitchen, and thanked them for the meal.

I took a long time to get to sleep. The light outside shone into the room under the door. I woke in the night and went down the lit passage to the loo. Next morning wind was howling from round Snowdon and moaning round the house. The reality of our surroundings had intruded on the dream of family togetherness before a warm log burner, but the magic was still very powerful like a latch-pinned door.

Black Sheep Like Pets

I went outside and encountered the elderly farmer who was supplying eggs for breakfast, which he had brought up from the farm. He had a thin smiling face and a ruddy complexion. He was clearly a man who spent most of each day out-of-doors.

I asked him about the field of black sheep behind the stone wall ahead.

"Oh, the Welsh blacks," he said.

I asked if they were for breeding or eating?

"Both," he said. "They're treated like pets. They're fed with a special diet, and they all have their own names, which they recognise. They've still got their lambs with them, they've just been weaned. Welsh black meat is more tasty than other meat. You can buy it from the butcher in Blaenau."

I reflected on the paradox. The sheep were treated like pets and fed a special diet, but were regarded as meat. They were treated like pets until the day they were slaughtered.

A Wheelchair and *Bible*-Reading

The burial took place in woodland before the memorial service. I was not sure whether to wear a white shirt and black tie as for a funeral, or a white shirt and coloured tie or a coloured shirt and dark tie or a coloured shirt and coloured tie – for after all it was supposed to be a celebration of a life well lived.

I had not seen Donald for twenty years, since he and his wife took

Pippa and me to a charity function at the House of Commons. Even then his wheelchair did not seem to matter. His open smile and engaging personality made me unaware of his disability.

Pippa and I arrived at All Saints' church half an hour before the 12 noon service and the church was already more than half full. By 12 it was packed. He had always lived in pain. His tumour had come on just after his marriage to Jenny, and he had been unable to stand soon afterwards. Jenny looked after him. He was in great pain at the end. He had been diagnosed with prostate cancer and died a week later.

The young vicar spoke into a headset microphone as he walked down the aisle. There was a welcome and a hymn and prayers. Then two of Donald's children, a boy and a younger girl, each with a different mother, talked through his life, how he had come from Lincolnshire, played cricket and served in the armed forces in Kenya, become a solicitor and worked for a charity for the disabled. The boy said that his Christian faith and *Bible*-reading were fundamental to his life. The girl said that Donald chose the hymns and that two had 'stand' in them – as Heaven to him was a place where he would be able to stand again. They spoke well, putting into practice his enjoinment to all his children to "speak slowly and clearly".

There was another hymn and a tribute by video shown on the five screens attached to the pillars of the arches in the two arcades on either side of the nave. It was about Donald's charity work and how he deservedly received the OBE from the Queen in the early 1990s. The vicar said that at a function Donald leaned forward and told the Countess of Wessex, "It's not what you can't do that matters, it's what you *can* do." The vicar said, "He was a can-do person." There were two readings, by another son and a granddaughter.

There was another hymn, the first verse of which ended, "Here in the love of Christ I stand." Then the vicar spoke about Donald's faith and daily *Bible*-readings and about his knowledge of the *Bible*. Texts were referred to by chapter and verse, and it was sometimes assumed we knew the content. Then he announced that "The Lord's My Shepherd" would be sung. He said, "The words were the last thing he heard, it was read to him with the entire family crowding round the small room, and the first words he would have heard the other side were, 'Well done, thou good and faithful servant.'"

There was another hymn and a commendation and a blessing. Then we sat and listened to Handel's *Ombra mai fu,* his favourite music, while we watched the screens and saw fifty stills portray his life from childhood to recently. Then his widow and daughter stalked down the aisle, eyes down, and greeted the congregation at the back of the church. I saw hugging and tears.

We followed and I edged forward to the crowd round Jenny.

Jenny turned aside and hugged Pippa and extended a hand to me. She said, "Do you know Peter?" And I found myself standing by a bald, smiling man in his seventies. I recognised her first husband.

He said, "Good to meet you, but not in the happiest of circumstances."

I said, "We were in the same class when we were four or five. You had me to tea at The Grange, the large house where you were living."

He was quite deaf and taciturn but he smiled and disconcertedly said, "I've just got to talk to someone over there."

I encountered him again a minute later. "Is that an MCC tie?" I asked.

"Yes. I played for the MCC for thirty-seven years."

He turned aside to shake hands with someone else, and we drifted into the newly-built hall, which cost the parishioners (including Donald) £5 million and was not subsidised by any grant. There was a good cold buffet set out, and I filled a plate with sausage rolls, smoked salmon, breadcrumbed fish and other *canapés*.

Pippa went outside, where there was a signal, to phone a taxi.

A tall woman passed with everything hanging out. She was in a tight outfit with a very high skirt. "Hello," she said. "Do you remember me? You were so kind to my daughter. Do you remember, she lost a shoe in the snow and you walked all round the field and found it."

"How long ago was that?" I asked.

"She was about eight. She's thirty now."

"Twenty-two years ago."

"Yes, it was when I was getting divorced. That's how I knew Donald, he handled my divorce for me. He was very kind."

Then I saw Peter standing near me. I went over and said, "I'm going to have to leave in a few minutes. Where are you these days?"

"Norfolk."

"And you come up for cricket?"

"I played for the MCC against Italy."

"Italy? They're not a cricketing nation. Perhaps we taught them at the end of the war?"

"I played twenty-five years for Loughton."

"From when?"

"From 1956."

I said, "I played for Buckhurst Hill. I played in 1958. I reckon we played against each other without being aware of it."

He smiled but he had no recollection of that time.

I mentioned some of the players in our two sides. He nodded. He knew them. Then it was time to go out to the taxi.

I asked Pippa, "Why did Jenny leave Peter?"

"He was a serial philanderer. Some men are."

Jenny had had a hard time. She had had four children by Peter and then undergone an upheaval and as soon as she had got together with Donald he had lost the ability to stand. Her first husband had been ruled by his bat, her second by his wheelchair.

But while in his wheelchair Donald had lived for the church and his *Bible*-reading, and had believed he was going to Heaven and would be able to stand in his spirit body, and he had triumphed over his adversity as the packed church bore out. Jenny may have been drawn to his spirit, and her nursing and wheeling of the wheelchair had made this triumph possible.

A Singing and Murder

I met Jane on a cruise to India and Arabia. She was an elderly American lady who went round collecting names and then collecting people, and it turned out her real estate office had been burned down shortly before she had left San Francisco. She had difficulty in contacting her two sons about whether there was insurance. She told me all this in a matter-of-fact way. She had no sense of privacy.

One of the speakers on the cruise was a Latvian woman. She had a bruiser's face and frizzy hair, and was a reader in Modern English Literature at Cambridge. Jane had found out that her family had been involved in the Singing Revolution against the Russians in Latvia, and that her family had been treated badly, she was not sure how. She had invited her to speak about Latvia and her family to all who would like to listen one lunchtime. "I'll take a large table and she'll join us," she told me. "You'll come, won't you? Twelve-ten, after the lecture."

"She won't want to speak about it," I said.

"Why not?"

"It's a personal trauma. She must be allowed to be silent about what happened."

"But there was a Singing Revolution," Jane said. "It's about Latvian independence. We need to hear it. She'll speak about it."

That lunchtime three couples and a single woman gathered round Jane and tucked into lunches they had brought to the table from the buffet. I had fish and chips, a simple lunch so I could take part in the discussion. As we finished our first course Jane said anxiously, "I hope she hasn't forgotten."

Then Guna appeared.

"Oh, you've had your lunches. Twelve-thirty? Isn't that when you said?" She seemed reluctant to join us. "Oh, so many of you. I reckon there are sixty-one slots when you can catch me on the cruise. It doesn't have to be now."

Guna left and returned with a bowl of soup.

Jane said, "We're hoping you'll talk about Latvia."

"You can read my book about Latvia," she said. "It will be out at the end of the year."

"But about the Singing Revolution. We'd like to hear about it."

It was as if she was asking her to sing.

"It's in my book. On 23 August 1989 two million joined hands to form a human chain on the 50th anniversary of the Molotov-Ribbentrop Pact, a six-hundred-kilometer human chain from Tallinn through Riga to Vilnius, a symbolic call for independence from the Soviet Union by Estonia, Latvia and Lithuania. I wasn't there."

And that was all she was prepared to say.

Jane said, "But there's a film. The American over there has details."

But the American could not remember the title of the film.

To defuse a tense situation I said, "I can remember Gorbachev visiting Latvia and shaking hands in the 1980s."

"Oh yes, that was early. About 1986 I would think."

Guna had finished her soup and went to choose her main course from the buffet. I followed her to choose my pudding and encountered her.

"You weren't there for the Singing Revolution," I said to her.

"No, I was in a German camp."

I understood she was in an East-German camp.

"A prisoner-of-war camp or a transit camp?" I asked, concerned.

"A prisoner-of-war camp in style. I was there for four years. My father saved us. He spoke several languages. He was the leader of the Latvian government-in-exile. But I'm not prepared to talk about it at the table."

I said, "I do hope your family were all right."

"Oh no, they were all murdered," she said sharply, almost aggressively.

There was a silence. The ordinariness and banality of lunchtime on the Bridge Deck suddenly gaped to reveal an awful horror.

"Oh, how dreadful," I said in appalled sympathy. "By Russians or pro-Russian Latvians?"

"By Russians," she said. "But I'm not going into it."

"Understandably," I said, and returned to the table.

Guna returned and Jane tried again.

"We were just hoping you'd tell us about your experience during and after the Singing Revolution."

"I wasn't there," Guna said, "and you can read about it in my book."

After that the conversation dwindled and took different directions, like a forest stream that has encountered a dam of last year's leaves and trickles round it and through it, its flow reduced.

Jane whispered to me, "I feel terrible. I feel I've got people here under false pretences."

"It's an interesting situation," I said in an undertone.

But I thought she was insensitive. Her American sensibility had not understood that Guna might not want to talk about the liquidation of her family, that she might not want to remove it from her private memories and lay it before us on the lunch table as if it was an item from that morning's lecture.

Guna should be allowed to retain the privacy of her memories and not turn them into a singing to satisfy our curiosity and prying enjoyment. She should be allowed to dwell on her murdered family within her own thoughts, without singing about it to us.

The *Maître D'* and a Submarine

At the captain's dinner the Russian *maître d'hôtel* came over to ask if everything was all right. He was in a dinner jacket and black tie, as was I. Above the hubbub I said, "No pirate ships yet."

He said, "I've been on many secret" – he made inverted commas with the second and third fingers of both hands – "operations when I was a Russian marine. In 1982 to 1985 we were opposite." He meant opposed. "I have friends who were in Afghanistan. NATO uses these waters, but also submarines. The pirates know this."

I asked, "Russian submarines?"

"Yes. You know, they're better than NATO. No talk, no waste of time getting decisions. Up, pshoo." He made a shooting gesture with his finger. "Oh, sorry. But the pirates have gone."

I asked, "Torpedoes?"

"I can't say. Why waste a torpedo on pirates? Better to come up and pshoo."

I said, "Perhaps you can ring them and ask for a torpedo."

He said, "They already know." Laughing, he walked off.

I thought about his last words. Could Russian submarines really eavesdrop on our conversation?

When he returned I said, "You set me thinking. I know a satellite up there has the technology to listen to our conversation now, isolated from other conversations in this room, but can a submarine down there hear a conversation up here?"

"Yes sir," he said. "I've had experience. Then it was done by a helicopter dropping electronic stuff in the water. Sonic beam. It eavesdrops on our conversation and transmits down to a submarine. When I was in a battleship off Syria NATO dropped this stuff and we picked it out of the water. The helicopters came low to stop us, and we waved to them. Goodbye." He laughed and waved with his hand towards the ceiling. "They can hear us."

I asked him which part of Russia he came from.

"Sir, I am from the Ukraine. It is a lovely country with mountains, sea, great beauty." He spoke with deep feeling.

I said, "It is good we can talk like this after being opposite."

"I appreciate your saying that, sir. Before Gorbachev we were opposite. I respect Mr Gorbachev. He saw that the USSR had weapons but families had not enough food. But Putin, he is a dictator. He is going back to before Gorbachev."

I said, "The KGB are still strong."

"More than that, there is no free press and there is corruption. Brezhnev died, not before time. He was too aggressive. But Putin is taking us back to those days. It *is* good we can talk like this."

But I could not forget that a Russian submarine might be listening to our conversation. Life in the second decade of the 21st century is scrutinised by microphones and cameras as we live within ever-improving technology.

Encomiums and Imperial Purple

I stood behind bespectacled Professor Muncaster of Oxford in the loo queue on the flight from Larnica to Gatwick. His massive girth filled the whole aisle and I could imagine he had benefited from many college dinners.

"What subject did you teach?" I asked.

"Latin, but I've retired. I was the Public Orator. For fourteen years."

"In the tradition of Bryan-Brown," I said.

"Yes," he said.

"Did you extemporise in your orations?" I asked.

"Oh no. They had to be carefully crafted and those I addressed *encomiums* to had to have a copy the day before."

I said, "The Pope speaks to his cardinals in Latin. I wonder if he thought of sending for you as an adviser."

"Oh no, I couldn't advise His Holiness on Latin. But I *did* send my *encomiums* to his Private Secretary, who is Irish. I don't know whether he ever showed them to the Pope."

I said, "I got into Oxford on my Latin. The comment was 'patches of purple'. I expect you had purple all the time."

He smiled a genuine smile at me. "Oh no," he said, "the purple didn't come naturally to me. I had to craft it. No, I was patches of purple too."

And with that he turned aside to talk to the steward, who was in a little pantry, more like an alcove, next to the flight deck.

I wondered if he was delivering a polished *encomium* – a formal, high-flown paean of praise – regarding the *Croque Monsieur* and scone he had just served us, and how much imperial purple he had used.

A Mask and Five Plasters
(Or: Squeezed Legs and Bedlam)

I went into hospital for an overnight stay to have my umbilical hernia repaired. I entered the old block and after a wait, during which the cleaners came into the waiting-area to talk loudly to the receptionist, I was shown upstairs to a small day room. A third of the room was unusable as there was no space to squeeze round the end of the hospital bed to reach the locker or the window blind, and there was no wardrobe. I put on my gown and stuffed my clothes in the hold-all I had brought.

A nurse came to begin the admission procedure. She began asking me questions. After a couple of minutes she was called away without explanation. I was then visited by the surgeon, who was in a black suit with white stripes. He had greased black hair and looked like a gangster. He told me very concisely what he was going to do, and left.

The anaesthetist came in, a shambling Pakistani. He said he would give me a mix of gas and painkillers. I explained I was prone to thrombosis and he said I would be injecting myself with Clexane after I returned home.

I said, "Injecting myself?"

"Yes. You'll be given a pack of twenty-eight days' syringes and you'll do it yourself. You'll pinch your skin and inject yourself every morning as a safeguard against thrombosis. You'll be doing it for twenty-eight days."

I was not keen on injecting myself. I asked, "Are there pills I can take instead?"

"There are pills, but it's political. It's like BMW and Mercedes. Both can service each other's cars, but they don't because it's political. You must be given Clexane because it is cheaper and has been tried and tested, but you *could* have pills, which have not been fully tried and tested. As I say, it's political."

My stockings were brought. I was told to put them on quickly as I had been sent for. The admission procedure was hurriedly concluded as I struggled to roll on my thin white elastic stockings. A nurse hurried me to the lift in slip-on slippers and a dressing-gown, and I shuffled seventy-five metres down the corridor that connected the old block with the new American block. Thinking of the gurney that awaited me, I said, "It's like walking to execution." I turned left and shuffled past fifty metres of operating theatres and anaesthetic rooms. I saw the surgeon dressed in blue wearing a blue 'theatre hat' sitting on a window-sill speaking on his mobile phone. He waved and interrupted his conversation to call out, "Anaesthetic room 2."

I was escorted to the newly-decorated, ultra-modern room, where a theatre technician invited me to lie on the trolley, the gurney. The room was full of modern American equipment but quite bare, and again I thought of a US execution by lethal injection.

The theatre technician introduced herself. She said, "It's a bit cold in here, I'm going to wrap you in plastic to keep you warm." She began to pack plastic round my legs. She had said she was keeping me warm but in fact the plastic would be connected to an SCD Express machine and monitor my blood flow to prevent deep-vein thrombosis.

The anaesthetist appeared in blue. He put a *cannula* into the back of my left hand and then hovered with a mask on a tube to give me oxygen. The oxygen would keep me alive during the few seconds I would be technically dead until they slid – rammed? – another tube down my throat and connected it to an anaesthetic machine.

"Are you putting me out now?" I asked, looking at the line – narrow tube – to the *cannula*.

"Not yet."

"Do I count to ten and then I'm out?"

He walked round behind me and placed the mask over my face. The theatre technician took over and he came round and stooped near the *cannula*.

"No, just tell me when you're asleep."

"I'm not asleep yet," I said, wondering why I could not feel anything from the line to the *cannula*, half-wondering if the oxygen mask was gassing me to sleep, contrary to my expectations....

I knew no more until I half-woke on my trolley, my gurney, in Recovery. A Recovery-room nurse was sitting beside me. I could see a figure moving in the distance. It was the anaesthetist.

"Have I had my operation?" I drowsed.

"Yes. It's all over."

"No difficulty?"

"Not that I'm aware of."

I dozed and drowsed and slowly came to. My trolley was wheeled back to the lift by two porters and I was returned up to my ward. The trolley was manoeuvred alongside my bed. I had to elbow myself across on my back. Despite the painkillers the pain in my navel was immense.

The plastic round my legs was plugged into an SCD Express machine at the end of my bed. It had 'vascular refill detection'. It monitored the rate at which the veins in my feet and legs refilled with blood and helped my blood flow at optimum moments, squeezing first one leg and then the other in rotation to reduce the likelihood of deep-vein thrombosis.

I lay in a stupor on my hospital bed and watched the television news without taking in half of what I was watching. Then the surgeon was standing beside me with a nurse. He said, "You have five plasters. Two five-millimetre cuts and one ten-millimetre cut. The fourth one was for gas. The fifth is not a wound, it's to hold your tummy-button in. It should be kept on for two days."

"Did you inflate me?" I asked drowsily as he examined my plasters.

"Yes."

"That much?" I made a convex curve with my hands suggesting heavy pregnancy.

"No, not that much." Then he turned to the nurse and said: "Mr Rawley will be injecting himself every day for twenty-eight days with Clexane. He will need guidance for the first time. If his technique does not come up to standard he must stay in hospital for every day that he doesn't do it right."

I said, "I think you'll be having me for twenty-eight days."

They laughed and left. Then I was aware of noise in the corridor. Nurses were shouting to each other, servers of food were talking loudly and a couple of cleaners were equally noisy. There was no consideration for the patients. I was brought a pot of tea, which was dumped on my overbed table, and was asked if I would like any lunch. I struggled to pour my tea in my drowsy state. When lunch came – soup with a roll, egg sandwich and ice-cream – the roll was inedible. It stuck to the roof of my mouth. The egg was also dry and hard to eat.

The afternoon drifted by with the machine rhythmically compressing my legs, squeezing first one and then the other to prevent thrombosis.

My dinner tray arrived. It was plonked on my overbed table the wrong way round. It was agony sitting up. I was not allowed any more painkillers as I had been given the maximum dose during my operation. I ate at a lower level than the table, reaching out and groping for my cutlery. The soup was all right, but the omelette was heavy and the chips were inedible. My ice-cream had melted by the time I was ready to eat it.

I buzzed for a nurse to unplug me and free my padded legs from their ties so I could go to the bathroom. Getting out of bed was agony, sitting up from a reclining position and swinging my legs down, but I was able to stand and walk. The nurse disappeared by the time I was ready to return to bed. Getting back into bed was acutely painful: trying to swing both my legs up was a terrible strain on my navel. I buzzed for the nurse to return and reconnect me. Later in the evening I buzzed to be released again and I went to the bathroom for the last time before sleeping. The nurse disappeared by the time I returned. I buzzed again to be reconnected and around 10.30 lay down to sleep on my back with my feet tethered to the machine.

The night nurse could not get to the blind so I could see out of the window. There was a view onto a flat roof and other hospital windows. I fell asleep on my back.

I woke not knowing the time. I buzzed and a new nurse came. She put the full light on. In my day room there was no bedside light. She said it was 1.30am. She released me to go to the bathroom. She disappeared by the time I was ready to return to my bed. I sat on the edge of the bed and gingerly swung my legs up. I buzzed again to be reconnected. The nurse came with some bad grace and plugged me back in. She disappeared before I could ask her to plump my pillows. I lowered the back-rest and tried to drag the pillows from under my back up to my neck. The machine gave out and bleeped regularly in an alarm.

I buzzed and the same night nurse came. The night nurse did not know how to cope with it or to reconnect me. She went and fetched a male nurse in a white tunic, who pressed buttons on the wall by my head. The machine started again. I fell asleep on my back and slept until 6.50am.

I woke to watching snow through my blindless window. It was a foot deep on the flat roof. I buzzed and a new nurse came and released my ankles so I could go to the bathroom. I returned to my hospital bed, swung my legs up and buzzed again to be reconnected.

Breakfast arrived and the corridor became noisy. Nurses were calling to each other and conducting conversations between rooms. Food servers were calling to each other down the corridor. The cleaners were shouting to each other from different rooms. A new nurse – my sixth – came in and I discussed going home. She interrupted our conversation to shout to a nurse across the corridor in another room.

I was in a madhouse. It was chaotic, there was no central control. No medication was listed on my drug chart, so the new nurse said she would have to ring "the consultant" – the surgeon – to confirm that I could have my aspirin 75mg. She returned to say that I could have my aspirin but she had not got one to give me. I supplied one I had brought after rummaging in my hold-all.

Now the corridor was bedlam. I lay and felt my legs being squeezed by the machine for another hour and mindlessly absorbed foreign cricket from a hot climate while flakes of snow drifted past the window and settled. I was in no pain so long as I lay still.

I thought of the order in the new building the American owners of the hospital had built, and of the expert surgery and plasters which brought in the patients. I thought of the chaos in the British-managed old hospital which was masked over, where no one seemed to do anything well. I gave myself to the alternating squeezing of my legs by the recently-bought American machine which expertly assisted the pumping of blood round my veins, and steadfastly ignored the shouting and bedlam in the corridors which signified an absence of management outside my room.

An Electioneering Widow and a Splashed Carpet (Or: An Invisible MP and a Pink Apron)

We went to a champagne funding reception at the home of Hilda Strawson, a county councillor whose MP son, Gordon (an occasional auctioneer at political events), was now facing re-election. The buffet – smoked-salmon *canapés* and cocktail sausages – had been prepared by the family and was served by volunteers. I congratulated Hilda on her recent re-election and stood with our ex-solicitor. He had retired when a box fell on his head, impairing his thinking, but his brain functions had happily returned to 95 per cent of their previous level, he told me. He had been stewarding at the Globe and had just resigned following a dispute over the new cafeteria, which had been high-handedly placed over stones inscribed with donors' names.

I was briefly alone with Hilda Strawson. I told her I could remember the day when Edith Small first appeared in this room along with two other candidates to succeed Jack Marney, and how her husband had served the drinks, unaware that he had cancer in his oesophagus and a lung and would only live eight months, after which eight tumours would be found on his brain. She fell silent. Electioneering had fallen away like a broken protective shell. She said quietly, "That was sixteen years ago."

I talked with Simon and suddenly Edith Small was standing beside me in a pink apron which said: "Save water, drink champagne." She was holding an opened bottle of champagne and was theatrically being a waitress, which meant she could go from group to group without discussing policies.

I said to her, "Don't let Nadine Dorries see that apron or she'll call you a 'posh girl'."

She laughed and I noticed how young her face looked. It was completely unlined, and I wondered whether she had had a face-lift or Botox. To politicians appearance is reality.

People had been coming in – there were getting on for thirty in the room – and Simon said of Gordon, "He should be working the room, shaking hands with us all, but he's gone missing, leaving his guests to talk among themselves."

After an hour the Secretary of State for Work and Pensions arrived outside in a Range Rover. I could see it through the window. He was greeted in the hall by Hilda, her son and Edith Small. Then he stood in the doorway, wearing a suit, white shirt and tie (Ministerial dress), and shook my hand.

Gordon tried to introduce us but I said, "I've known him for years. He's given out prizes for us and opened a new building."

He asked, "How is it going?"

I said, "More demand than ever before, there's no recession around here. I don't want to be irreverent," I added, "but had I better watch out? If I'm shaking hands with Suarez I should guard my upper arm. If I'm…." Laughing, I crossed the outside of my hands as if I were a footballer in a wall.

He laughed and said, "Oh, I know, I said I'd bite someone's balls off and send them back to him in a box."

"Someone in the Treasury," I said.

Gordon Strawson said, "I don't understand."

The Minister said, "It's just something I said."

"You're doing very well," I said to him. "But before you move on, could you keep an eye on the Bilderberg Group. They're at The Grove,

Watford from 6 to 9 June."

"Oh," he said, "I didn't know. Sure, we'll talk later."

The Minister was taken round and introduced by Gordon Strawson. After the introductions Gordon stood back in silence and let the Minister do the speaking and interacting. He was an MP who did not ask questions at *Prime Minister's Questions,* made no speeches in the chamber, did not appear on television and wrote no articles. But he had many meetings with business leaders in his constituency and it would be unfair to call him 'Mr Invisible'.

My champagne glass was regularly topped up. I spoke to Edith Small about the Leader.

She said, "He won't be dislodged before the next election. It's too late and there is no obvious alternative."

I asked, "Will there be a referendum before rather than after the election?"

She said, "What would the question be?"

I said, "'In-out'. It's undesirable as we do fifty per cent of our trade with Europe, and if we were out it would put up unemployment."

She said, "Exactly. We need to renegotiate the terms."

I said, "That's what Harold Wilson said. 'We stay in but renegotiate the terms.'"

She said, "The referendum in 1972 was different because the terms didn't have to be negotiated."

I said, "The referendum was in 1975. Heath took us into the EEC and Wilson renegotiated the terms for a referendum in 1975."

Edith Small looked evasive. She said, "I was too young to remember much about it, except what I heard at school."

I was surprised at her sketchy knowledge, and as she was a Scot I asked, "Talking of referenda, is the Scottish referendum to dump the Scots and save £37 billion subsidy a year? That would bring the annual deficit substantially down. Is the Leader being insincere in saying he wants to keep the UK together?"

A councillor standing near me said, "Excellent idea. Let me shake your hand."

I said, "I'm not saying I want that. I'm just asking if that's the hidden agenda regarding the Scottish referendum."

Edith Small said, "Oh no, we want to keep the Scots in the UK. Holy Loch is very important for our nuclear deterrent."

I said, "They're already building a replacement near Plymouth, tunnelling into a cliff. The submarines will live there."

Edith Small looked astonished. "They couldn't do that."

Pippa was nearby. She said, "They *are* doing it. We know someone who has given us an eyewitness account of the work that's happening."

Edith Small looked shocked.

Soon afterwards Gordon Strawson called us to silence for the speeches. He thanked everyone profusely for supporting him and said he wanted to go on being an MP. It was clear that without funding he would not be able to afford to run his next campaign.

Then the Minister spoke. He told a long story about Tebbit, who asked him, when he was having a difficult time in the press, if he would like to go shooting at 8am the next day. A press conference had been booked and he told Tebbit he could not do it. Tebbit said, "I find that when things are difficult it's good to go out and kill something." Everyone laughed. "Tebbit then said, 'I'll kill something for you.'" Again everyone laughed.

I was not impressed by this story. Everyone should be in harmony with Nature and we should not go out and kill birds (which have nothing to do with our bad moods) to soothe our ruffled feelings, which should be brought under control by our own inner discipline and spiritual reserves.

The Minister got onto his policy. He said he had a budget of about £200 billion, and spoke of around £120 billion of that being for welfare and £80 billion of that being for pensions. He said that Labour had increased welfare by more than 400 per cent, and the welfare budget had increased to around £440 billion by 2010. He said that tax credits were responsible for this massive increase. The recipients had been bribed for votes. His job was to put the finances back on a sound footing and at the same time get people off the dependency culture and back to work.

He took a few questions. He finished to loud applause.

Edith Small, still in her pink apron, thanked him. She was over-theatrical, and there were too elaborate thanks to individual members of Hilda Strawson's family.

The Minister hung around and answered two or three private questions. I said to him, "Thank you for your talk. And do watch what the Bilderberg Group are doing just outside London next month. I think it's directed against the Leader. They want the leaders of all parties to be pro-Europe, and they don't want a referendum."

"Oh yes," he said. "Can you send me something about it to the House of Commons? Send me the printed evidence as to where and when it's happening, and I'll send it on to the appropriate quarters."

"Sure," I said. I believed we should remain in Europe, but I was against the world being looted for its resources by a syndicate of international brigands.

Then a bearded ex-councillor came and talked to me. He worked in a City bank and had made a lot of money.

It was time for guests to leave. Some had already left. I crossed to the far end of the room and told Gordon Strawson we were leaving. Now I had his attention. We had a chat about his view of what was happening in the Commons. He agreed that it was too late to change the Leader and that there would be no referendum on Europe before the next election.

I returned to the doorway. Hilda Strawson was talking to the bearded ex-councillor. She was waving her arms to make a point forcefully. One of her hands caught the ex-councillor's champagne flute and champagne slooshed up over his face and down his front and splashed onto the carpet. Hilda retreated and returned with a tissue. Simon, who had been listening, was laughing uncontrollably. All stood in confusion, and, ever practical, I took a tissue and dabbed the carpet to soak up the spilt champagne, not caring that it looked as though I had caused the spillage.

Hilda walked with us to the door. "It was very good, very lively," she said (of her own party). She was a widow and she had worked hard to spur her son into being an MP, albeit a not very visible one, and to surround herself from the loneliness of widowhood with a protective life of electioneering, campaigning and canvassing. Edith Small had been over-theatrical in her 'fancy-dress' waitress's apron and the spilt champagne had nearly stained the carpet, but Hilda had taken the incident, like her husband's death, in her stride and had forcefully achieved social standing for herself, her son and her family.

Wisteria and Hot Stones

As a birthday surprise Pippa took me on a mystery drive along the M25 which ended near Watford at The Grove. Pippa said she had booked because it was the only place that offered Ayurvedic skin treatments in its Spa. When she made the booking it was not known that my skin had been ravaged by skin cancer or that the Bilderberg Group of plutocrats would be meeting there in two weeks' time. It was an inspired choice.

At the entrance to the drive we were questioned by a lady in plain clothes who seemed to be a policewoman. She wanted to know our business, and asked, "Are you staying the night?" She then allowed us to drive up to the house on the hill and report to Reception.

The grounds contain three hundred acres and the road transverses a golf course. We drove down towards a lake and then up past greens to the house, where a man in a brown hat parked our car. The three receptionists might have been seconded from Heathrow immigration. They did not look at us. One checked our details, chatting in a very assured, formal way with her eyes on her screen. She knew it was my birthday.

We took a lift up to room 110. It looked down on shaped trees under a massive cedar of Lebanon and across a distant golf course. We went down and had a lunch of smoked salmon in the Glasshouse restaurant. I had jasmine tea. We then explored the 16th-century old building, which had been much modernised. Rooms had been subdivided into alcoves where half a dozen could meet. We went out into the grounds.

I left Pippa sitting and walked along the back, peering at the windows of the low brick accommodation. A member of staff with a badge saying 'Housekeeping' passed me, pushing a laundry basket on wheels.

"Good afternoon. How are you? Is there anything I can do for you?"

I said, "I'm just getting my bearings. How many rooms are there?"

"Two hundred and one rooms and sixteen suites. You're in the new building. The house is the bottom of the 'L' over there, that's all old.

Everything else was built in 2005. Which is your room?"

"A hundred and ten."

"That's your window up there." He pointed to a first-floor balcony.

"How many staff?"

"Five hundred," he said. "The staff are all in departments. I'm in the Housekeeping Department."

From his accent I could tell he was Russian.

"How long have you worked here?"

"Three years."

"Are you living on site?"

"No, I live in Watford."

"Where do conferences take place?"

"We have space for six hundred to have a conference, but we can break it up with movable walls."

I said, "I'm always on the look-out for conference venues."

"Come with me and I'll show you," he said. "It's just before the sequoia tree." And he left the laundry basket and took me to a low building with bowed windows, columns at the end and mauve wisteria. I looked inside. It was empty.

"I'll take you in," he said.

I followed him to a small door. He let me into the large room I had seen through the window.

"The walls move," the Russian said, "and we can make it into one huge room."

This was where the Bilderberg Group would be meeting, here behind the wisteria. I stood and soaked up the atmosphere.

I was going to ask him if he was ready for an international conference mounted by those running the world, which would probably call for Western support for the rebels in Syria and for a Labour win at the next British election so there would be no in-out referendum on Europe. But then I thought, 'The staff are all professional, they are courteous and willing towards whoever the guests are that day. *They* do not book the conference hall out, they just contribute to the running of the place. It's not fair to ask them to comment on bookings.' He probably had no idea that the Bilderberg Group stood for global dominance or that every year their agenda got implemented in the ensuing months. I thanked him and he returned to his laundry basket.

I wandered back to Pippa and we went back to our room. In due course we set off for the Sequoia Spa, which was down in the lift beyond room 196. We entered a large reception area and Pippa announced that we were booked for the '*dosha* specific hot-stone massage and body wrap' (one hour fifty minutes).

We sat and completed questionnaires about our health, which would enable them to calculate the balance of our *dosha*s, and then I was given a dressing-gown, a towel and slippers and told to go to the men's changing-room. Pippa went in the opposite direction to the ladies' changing-room. I changed into my dressing-gown and slippers and locked my clothes in a locker, and then went to the empty relaxation room which was mauve and dark with seven single beds separated by transparent fine black curtains. There was piped relaxing music. I lay on a bed and drifted and then a lady came and asked if I was Philip and introduced herself. She was young in a black trouser suit and dark-haired with a pony-tail.

She led me to a small treatment room and, with the piped relaxing music still playing, invited me to sit in a comfortable chair in the corner while she asked me questions about my lifestyle. Of the three *dosha*s – *vata, pitta* and *katha* – I reckoned I was predominantly *vata* (tall, thin, always moving and with dry skin) with secondary *katha* (calm temperament) rather than *pitta* (fiery temperament). She asked me to choose an oil and I requested one that cleared the lungs. She washed my feet in a bowl of warm oiled water and dried them. Then she left the room while I lay face down on the treatment table.

She returned and my Ayurvedic skin treatment began. She said my skin was very dry. First I had an exfoliator – to remove the dead skin. She rubbed me with oil mixed with tiny bits of volcanic grit. When she had finished, back and front, she left the room and I had to shower the grit off.

She returned and applied the mud body wrap to draw out the body's toxins. She rubbed it into my scalp as well. My hair stiffened and stood on end. She again left the room and I showered that off but did not touch my hair as the wrap should remain on my scalp for 24 hours.

Then she returned and applied oil to moisturise my skin, and rubbed it in. She held a burning hot stone in the palm of each hand, two large volcanic pebbles. She explained that volcanic stones have air in them and are good for retaining a regulated heat. They burned off the dead skin and pressed the oil into the healthy skin beneath. When she finished, raising the table to a half-sitting position, I was soaking in oil and felt very relaxed. I returned to the relaxation room and nibbled sultanas and drank water. Then I changed back into my clothes and returned to the reception desk and met Pippa.

That evening I smarmed my stiff hair down and ate in Colette's restaurant in the old building. We had a glass of champagne and an eight-course 'tasting' meal. Each course was tiny and balanced flavours and nutritional needs. Each course was served by two waiters, one holding a tray, the other serving from it and explaining what was on the plates.

I sat in the corner of the originally-16th-century mansion with my hair still spiked and my skin saturated and I thought of the Bilderberg Group coming in a fortnight's time. Bilderberg-Group plutocrats worth billions would also be dining here and would be waited on in the same way. They would be confident.

They would be making changes to the world, meeting in the conference hall and in the alcoves or among the lanterns on the garden tables, and I doubted they would have time for hot-stone skin treatments in the Spa. They might agree to urge intervention in a country or countries or the removal of a leader behind the composure of the wisteria between meeting their friends in the alcoves and the restaurants, but they would be the poorer for not opening themselves to the experience of the burning hot stones on skin.

A Chimney and Christmas

Harry, our roofer, who had so often scrambled and then scampered in trainers over our tiles looking for leaks like a cat burglar, knocked on our door in Cornwall to collect some cash to cover bricks, lime mortar and the cost of a skip for dismantling and rebuilding one of our chimneys. Damp had penetrated from the inside of the chimney into an upstairs bedroom and the chimney had to be taken down, fitted with a metal tray and then rebuilt to the same height as the Council had stipulated.

He smiled at me as his wife handed me a list of anticipated expenditure. I put the pre-arranged roll of notes in his right hand. The late-May sun sparkled on the sea over his shoulder. Holding her list, I explained the amount did not include the cost of the scaffolding, which our neighbour (with whom I was sharing the costs) had agreed to pay the following Saturday. "Is that all right?" I asked.

"Oh yes, we can get down on Saturday morning," he said.

I noticed he had not shaved and behind the stubble he looked shadowy, dark and gaunt. Then he became slightly agitated.

"And as for the future, my wife will tell you…."

He darted out of sight behind the porch.

"The chimney will be done," she said with great composure and firmness, "but it will be the last project he does, because he won't be doing any more after that, it will be Chris. Harry's been diagnosed as having cancer, cancer of both lungs and of the brain, and he's only got weeks to live. Six months at the most. He won't see Christmas or the New Year. He's been having headaches, and we've had scans and he was told on Sunday: advanced cancer in both lungs and in his brain. He's got weeks rather than months. He definitely won't see Christmas or the New Year. So he's handed his keys in at work, he won't be going back to work now. We're putting everything in order, he'll see your chimney through and then there will be time for us."

Harry rejoined her and stood looking gaunt and crestfallen.

"He's got six months," she repeated in front of him, almost toughly, yet elongating the remaining time. "He definitely won't see Christmas." It was as though she was setting out the ground rules so he swiftly accepted his condition.

"I think I've only got two weeks," he said.

Stunned, I said, "Harry, I *am* sorry. Come in."

"No, he finds it difficult to talk about it," she said. "We had the family yesterday. And today we got up at 5 and went for a walk. We wanted *our* time, to think about it all."

"I'm really sorry," I said. "Are you sure he should be thinking about our chimney at the present time?"

"Oh yes," she said. "It's all taken care of. His son will be taking it down and his son-in-law will be rebuilding it."

"I'll be sitting watching them down here," Harry said with a smile. "I'd rather not be home alone."

"We booked to be in Crete next week," his wife said, "but we cancelled it."

"Why?"

"No insurance," Harry said.

He meant that if he died in Crete no insurance company would cover the cost of repatriating his body.

"It's so sudden," I said.

You spend your life planning projects and carrying them out and then suddenly you're told it all has to stop.

"Yes, it is. I haven't got long. He said six months but I think it may only be two weeks."

How could he be rebuilding my chimney in the last two weeks of his life? Harry was a doer, and all his life he had been a doer, and he was going to be a doer and do to the end.

"And you're not in any pain?"

"No. I don't want to be in pain. I just want to shoot myself, but my family have taken away all my guns so I can't."

I knew he went shooting most weekends.

"You shouldn't," I said. "When the time comes there will be morphine to control your pain."

"Yes, morphine."

"And you know, there's a body of tradition out there, among the seven billion people in the world, that there's an invisible body within the visible body. People who've had near-death experiences die in hospital, float up to the ceiling and come back aware of what doctors have been saying, even though they have been pronounced dead. No one knows if the invisible body is true, but it's something to think about."

"A positive within the negative," she said, nodding. "But he definitely won't be here for Christmas." She spoke firmly as if being definite would steel his will.

Harry was looking at my watch. "Oh," he said, "is that the time? I must be going. Might see you in August when you're next down."

"Yes," I said. His 'might' suggested he would be dead by then.

And they were off. She turned and gave me a wave.

I watched him go. He had cancer in both lungs and his brain, he was a condemned man. I had tried to give him strength but I felt powerless. I was devastated for him and for her. He had worked all his life, helping people with their roofs and their chimneys, and he had just moved house and now he would not know the retirement they had anticipated. It was so unfair.

I closed the door, feeling I had been kicked in the teeth. The unexpected had caught me unprepared, like a sudden gust of wind. It had caught him unprepared as well. He had to be strong, and I could see that by being definite she was trying to instil acceptance and the strength that came with it. Harry's wife had strength and was trying to boost his strength so that he could overcome the ordeal of pain that lay ahead.

Ahead of him was a *rendezvous* with a different kind of chimney and his future beyond a few weeks had stopped. Christmas was not something to be looked forward to. It was beyond his journey's end, a barrier to a remote future like a roadblock saying 'Road closed'. It had become a thing of the past, a distant memory like the scampering across roofs of his working life.

His situation was stark but within the starkness was a determination to see jobs through, not to let people down, keep one's word despite changes in circumstances, an old-world loyalty to long-standing clients and a quiet courage that I found heart-rendingly admirable. Down in remote, traditional Cornwall the old values were still much in evidence: living for oneself during one's last few weeks could only begin when commitments had been kept.

Leaves and Nectar
(Or: Leaf-cutting Ants and Owl Moths)

"I always knew there were two kinds of people," said the portly man at the hotel bar. He wore a collar, tie and blazer. He was slightly overweight with excessively red cheeks and receding hair. "Those who spend all their life working, and those who flit about and shine out and dazzle with their beauty. There's a butterfly sanctuary in Hertfordshire. I took my grandson there not long ago. We went to see the leaf-cutting ants first. They live in a large glass tank half-filled with earth, and you can see them passing each other in their earthen tunnels through the glass. They scurry up a small branch and on to a rope that is hung across three more glass tanks to a far tank where there is a cluster of the leaves they like on thin supple branches. Two streams pass each other on the narrow rope, one going to the leaves, the other carrying bits of leaves back that they've cut. They never fall off the rope. There are hundreds of these ants. They all have a purpose, to go and cut a leaf and bring part back to their home, their subterranean nest. That's what our commuters do – go backwards and forwards and cut leaves to bring home, spend their whole life doing just that.

"But then you go into the tropical butterfly house. Twenty different species of exotic butterflies – many of them resembling swallow-tails, many from Central and Southern America – glide between bush habitats on either side of a long glass hut. They settle on orange slices to feed for nectar, and they settle on people. My grandson had three or four of them on his back and shoulder, and I had them on my trouser-legs. The most common species there is actually a moth. There are plenty of owl moths. They have great owl-like eyes on their large under-wings when they sit at rest with their wings folded. We had owl moths on us. There was a gigantic Atlas moth, but it could not be budged from the muslin it had settled on. Its legs were embedded in the muslin. They are all so delicate and fragile that if you pick them up by the wings the colouring may rub off on your fingers. They weren't made to work like the leaf-cutting ants. They glide about looking beautiful and feed. And they sit and bask in the warmth of the tropical butterfly house and preen themselves and just 'be'.

"I said to my grandson, 'It's like that with humans.' There are those who work like the leaf-cutting ants, part of a family or team transporting bits of leaves – banknotes – for the common good, and for their own good. And there are those who don't work but cultivate their beauty and feed themselves on nectar. I said to my grandson, 'At different times of your life you can be both. There are some who are ants in their youth and enjoy the fruits of their labours by settling like beautiful blue butterflies in their middle age. And there are some who flit about in their youth and only apply themselves to ant-work in their middle age.' I told my grandson, 'The important thing is to choose which you're going to be in your present time of life and do it well.'

"The trouble is," he added, "in my case I fell between the two. I didn't work enough on the leaves, and I didn't live on nectar like a lady of leisure – I'm being alliterative, not sexist – or a cosseted celebrity. I could have been a gentleman with time to create something really worthwhile. Sometimes I feel I've wasted my life and I wish I could do it all over again. Sometimes I feel I messed my life up. I don't tell that to my grandson. No, he doesn't know I think that. I wanted nectar but I never cut enough leaves. I've come to think that it's only by cutting leaves that you get to live off nectar like an owl-eyed moth."

He looked haunted and unfulfilled, and I did not like to point out that ants do not turn into moths, that hard work in one's youth does not inevitably turn one into a celebrity. His imagery had led him to a muddled conclusion, but the regret behind it was real enough and it was best to be tactful.

A Clockman and Cuba

I looked in on the clockman at his request. I climbed the stairs of the Home Stores, crossed the first floor, found the narrow staircase down at the back and entered a cluttered room filled with bits of clocks. The clockman, who was thin and completely bald and wore spectacles, was collecting money from an elderly, casually-dressed customer.

"One million," he said.

"It's ruination," the customer complained. "I won't be able to eat for six months."

"I haven't any sympathy at all. You're taking too long to count it out."

The customer, who had uncombed grey hair, turned to me and said,

"He's taken all I've got."

"He's a hard taskmaster," I said.

The clockman grinned at me and produced a gleaming, golden clock frame (two brass plates held together in one structure), a movement-frame with a cog on a spindle sandwiched between its plates. The rest of the movement of my longcase clock had been stripped down and was in bits in a plastic tub.

"I've cleaned it up," he said. "It's been through the cleaning machine. But I want you to see what I've found. I put these bushes in, see?"

He pointed to the frame. I peered at tiny metal linings in the six tiny round holes on the gold metal.

"But I haven't got that bit of rust off, yet. And what the silver salver's doing here I don't know. But what I want to show you is the end of this spindle. Can you use this eyepiece?"

He showed me a cog-wheel on a spindle he had picked out of the tub and gave me a magnifying *loupe* to squint through.

"You see, it's been gripped by pincers. I've had to make that silver reach there, otherwise it won't be held when the spindle goes into the hole of the metal here. Just here, see?"

"Excellent work," I said.

"But I can't clean that wheel. It's too delicate and there's that bit there on the spindle that might fracture. So I'm sending it to the University of Cambridge. I've got a part for another clock going to Cambridge and you can catch that package."

"Good," I said, returning his magnifying *loupe*.

"And all these...." He indicated the other bits in his plastic tub. "There, that's all I've got to show you now. But it may come to more than I said. I want you to see the work involved. Each cog may require an hour, maybe half an hour, I don't know till I've done it. I don't connect the movement to the hands of the clock until near the end," he said. "You're in the queue of all these clocks but I've jumped you forward to catch the Cambridge package."

"Thank you," I said.

"This isn't my main job," he said. "I only do four hours a day."

"What's your main job?"

"Looking after my handicapped daughter," he said. "I'm taking her to Cuba, and two carers. She's got Down's Syndrome and she's got the mind of a three-year-old. I have to do everything for her. She can just about walk, but she's got a problem with her knees."

"What happens when there's traffic?"

"Oh, she won't cross the road on her own. She stands and waits, and I come along and take her across the road. But it's expensive, taking her and two carers to Cuba. That's why I do this. We're on the north of the island in Cuba, we're going to fly to Havana for a few days. I'll be walking with her in Havana. I got into clocks and watches as soon as I left school in Clerkenwell, and I worked for other people until I got leukaemia and had chemotherapy and other things. So I set up on my own. I've done it for years, but I only do four hours a day. Then I go back and look after my daughter. I'm going to do that now," he said. "I was waiting for you. I stop work at 3. I'm going home now. It's me and my daughter," he said.

"She's fortunate to have you looking after her."

"That's not what she thinks. She thinks I'm a pain," he said, and he laughed and prepared to leave. "But she'll enjoy Cuba."

I looked at his shop. All the bits of clocks proclaimed the time that had passed since the birth of his disabled daughter who had the mind of a three-year-old, as did his completely bald head following his leukaemia. He knew all about the cogs and spindles of time, but for him Cuba was in the timeless, eternal world of enduring memories that would never be forgotten.

Strangers and Friends

I went to Derek Grabson's retirement party. It was in a room at the Loch Fyne restaurant. About twenty elderly people I did not recognise stood around. I shook Grabson by his hand and said, "Fifty years in the same room."

He said, "I must have been crazy." He was in an open-necked blue shirt, and not many wore ties as I did. He spoke to newly-arrived guests.

I saw his receptionist. "You're not retiring, are you?" I asked.

"Oh yes, I am," she said. "After twenty-six years of permanent, continuous service."

After further conversation I asked, "Are his successors here?"

"One is, Dr Clerihew. Dr Plod isn't here."

She introduced me to a middle-aged lady with fawn hair. I told her that I recollected opening my mouth for Grabson to inspect, closing my eyes and hearing the sound of the drill without anything being said. I was having a tooth drilled without an injection. "I didn't mind," I said, "it got it done."

She winced and said, "It's very different now."

I asked if she'd be in the same room as Grabson.

"We'll upgrade it," she said. "A lot of his machinery is out of date. Have you been upstairs? We've got the most modern machinery up there."

I told her that Grabson, a Glaswegian, had learned to extract teeth by putting a knee on a male patient's chest to get leverage and pulling hard, and I said, "That methodology may have been with him all his life."

The room had filled up. There must have been fifty or sixty now, and more were coming in all the time and forming a long queue down the restaurant aisle to speak to Grabson. The entire dentist's waiting-room had turned out. Angela Mason had arrived, looking pinched and stricken, with her husband Kevin. I greeted her and shook his hand. They did not seem to want to talk. Angela said she had to give an envelope to Grabson's secretary, and he had to speak to someone. I later heard that half an hour previously he had been diagnosed with cancer of the bladder and that an operation had been fixed for a month's time. They would have to come back from holiday early to secure the surgeon they wanted.

I ate five or six of the *canapés* to pass the time: a selection of unknown morsels on toast, unknown round balls and spring rolls. (They turned out to be calorie bombs as I discovered when I weighed myself the next morning and I had put on a kilo.) I drank my orange juice, and I was approached by an archivist. But otherwise I did not know anyone and did not want to get to know the waiting-room. They were all strangers.

A small lady selecting *canapés* near me lamented, "Everything's changing. The Methodist Minister is going to the Isle of Wight. We're losing all the people we're used to."

I did not want to add to that conversation. I did not want to be discussing the future of the area with her. I suddenly felt alienated, as if I had fallen over and cut my head. I did not want to be there. I would rather be watching the live 20-20 Test Match. I saw Grabson engrossed in his line with two dozen waiting patiently for their turn. I passed him to 'look at the paintings' on a wall. I looked back. He still had his head down. I slipped out of the restaurant door.

Outside there was a faint drizzle. I walked back to where I had parked my car. I heard a call. Simon was sitting in his Range Rover with his wife by his side, waiting for the traffic-lights to turn green. I crossed to the middle of the road and talked through his window. I told him about Grabson's gathering for his retirement.

"Are my friends here?" I asked, peering through the tinted glass of the back windows.

"In the back," Simon said, lowering the window.

"Hello, my friends," I called to my grandchildren.

There was a chorus of "Hello, Grandpa".

I was standing exactly where I had found my Grandpa lying in fog and bleeding from a temple during the Second World War. And now they had found their Grandpa retreating from a metaphorical fog. I thought of the alienation I had felt in the Loch Fyne and the warmth within the car. As the lights changed and they waved goodbye and I resumed my walk to my car I was glad to have been among my grand-children, instinctive and fluent, rather than have to explain who I was to the strangers in the Loch Fyne.

An Athlete and a Monk

That school's prize-giving was held in a marquee. The guest speaker was a British athlete who had been a triple-jump champion for Europe, the Commonwealth and the World. He was very tall and wore a white woollen sweater with a hood that lay on his back, and torn jeans, and his dyed white hair contrasted with his dark skin. I had seen him coping with a television challenge to row up the crocodile-infested Amazon to raise funds for Comic Relief and the backward children of the Amazon rain forest. He was introduced to applause. It was said that he had hopped and skipped and jumped the width of the marquee. After speeches and recitals he made his speech.

He was exceptionally tall and the top of his head was touching the drapes that hung down from the marquee's roof. He held the microphone in his hand. He said, "I've been wondering what I should talk about, what the most interesting subject I can talk about is, and I have decided it is 'myself'." He said he had been raised in Hackney and had had good teachers who had made him work hard and had pushed him into athletics. They had encouraged him to do well and he had travelled the world as an athlete. His message was simple: "You should all work hard and do your best." It was a message from someone who had 'done it', and therefore it was likely that his advice would be followed by the pupils.

He then gave out the prizes, standing down below the small stage so his head was not enfolded in drapes. He guided each prize-receiver into looking at the photographer and bent down and put an arm round each child's shoulder. Cups and shields were distributed, and the 6th-year leavers all filed up. The new captains were announced and asked to stand to be clapped. A ten-year-old girl near me stood and performed an elaborate sashay, flinging out an arm, taking a step backwards and bowing to the waist.

At the end I talked to the Mayor and a councillor, and we wandered back to the Studio for a reception. I spoke to several of the staff. One of them, Laura, said to me, "You've got two ghosts. One is a lady in grey who lives in the library."

I said, "One of the Head's predecessors saw her in the passage and we told her it might have been her own reflection in the glass fire-door."

"Maybe," said Laura. "The other one's a monk. Joan saw him. Joan over there."

I crossed to Joan and she greeted me warmly, throwing her arms round my neck and giving me a kiss. "You saw a ghost," I said.

"Yes. About a year ago, at 6 o'clock one night. I'd been working in my room and I came out onto the landing, and a monk came out of a wall. I startled him and he went back into the wall and disappeared."

"Shall we go and see exactly where it happened?" I said.

"Yes," Joan and Laura said together.

We left the Studio, crossed the courtyard and climbed the Victorian stairs to the landing.

"It was here," Joan said. "He came out of the corner, between the wall and door to the loos. He wore a brown monk's habit with a hood. I couldn't see his face. He jumped when he saw me and did this." She extended her arms. "And floated back through the wall and disappeared."

"Hmm," I said. I looked in the loos and looked in the classroom the other side of the wall.

When I returned Joan was still discussing what she had seen with Laura.

I had no doubt that she thought she had seen a monk. I was convinced she was not imagining it. The site had been occupied since the time of the Norman Conquest, and I wondered if monks had lived there in the 11th century.

I returned downstairs and suddenly I did not want to know any more. I would rather listen to an athlete talking about his achievements than listen to any further creepy description of a monk who came out of a wall. I had received Joan's information about the monk, and I neither believed it nor disbelieved it. I no longer thought about it. I might never know what Joan saw.

I returned to the world of the athlete, hopping, skipping and jumping the width of our marquee and helping underprivileged children up the Amazon. A white sweater with a hood was better than a monk's hood, and it no longer mattered that he was wearing torn jeans.

Hazelnuts on a Keyboard

Catherine Mostyn had worked as a secretary for nearly forty-five years and was now retiring. To mark her long service she had been invited to give out the prizes at her school. I arrived to find her standing with her husband and daughter, and a previous Head and a couple of retired staff, under the eight-hundred-year-old oak-tree. "Am I in the right year?" I asked as I greeted the past staff. I shook hands with Catherine's husband and recalled how we once played marbles next door to a staff dinner.

The group was joined by more staff and ex-staff, and then we took our seats in the marquee. The Headmistress was introduced. Behind me there was a small Asian boy of about three who was playing on a noisy game. It had lights and a talking voice, and he talked continuously to himself with unformed sounds that sometimes resembled a loud hum. The distraction was loud enough for pupils in front of me to turn and stare censorially at him.

I was straining to hear what the Headmistress was saying above the disturbance behind me. In the end I, too, turned round. The boy's parents were sitting on either side of him. His mother was grinning. They both leaned forward and touched their ears and then their mouths, explaining wordlessly that he was deaf and had a speech impediment as if that excused his anti-social behaviour and made it all right.

I turned back and ignored the non-stop disturbance which was now drowning the Headmistress's report. He's deaf, I thought, and perhaps autistic as well. Does that give him the right to prevent others from hearing the speeches on prize day, when he's not even at the school, but a sibling of a boy who is? Don't his parents have a responsibility not to disrupt the prize-giving? The boy's attempts to talk grew louder and in the end his grinning mother took him (protesting) outside. I could hear him making his unformed sounds the other side of the marquee wall. He was still being disruptive, it was just not happening within the marquee.

Catherine Mostyn distributed the prizes, then spoke, recalling the day she began forty-five years ago, and how Pippa had played practical jokes on her. "One day," she said, "she distributed hazelnuts on every key of my keyboard and lowered my chair so when I sat down they were at mouth level."

There was laughter.

There was a concert. The choir was about forty-strong. They all looked at the lady who was conducting them, standing still and projecting their attention.

At the end of the second row back on the left stood a tall dark-haired sallow-skinned boy. He turned round and looked through the window, his mouth moving faintly to the words. He looked completely uninvolved in contrast to the many faces with intent eyes that looked at the conductor and put themselves into their singing. He raised his arms and turned round. He jigged about. He pulled down his tie, which was on an elastic noose. He let it go so his tie shot back to his throat. He pulled his tie down again and again let go. The conductress ignored him and conducted the choir.

When the choir had finished, one of the ex-music teachers sitting near me commented on the boy: "He was diagnosed as being severely autistic just before I left, and could not remember any words or sing. But now he knows the words. You could see his mouth moving. He has come a long way, he has made incredible progress." He was in fact leaving to begin a more specialised education.

I looked at the autistic boy in the choir, who knew all the words, which was a huge achievement in relation to how he was, and I listened to the deaf boy trying to communicate on the other side of the marquee wall. I looked at the orderly deportment of the speakers and the choir.

The deaf boy and the autistic boy were being treated as if they were normal, and their aberrant behaviour was being ignored. But I could not help feeling that they were hazelnuts on the frequently-used keyboard of the school's administrative system.

A Captain and a Baha'i

I attended our third prize-giving within three days. It was in a hall that seated about five hundred and had a high stage. The Head of that school made a speech about all the good things at the school, quoting the number of firsts in academic and sporting events the pupils had achieved and the school's rankings in the borough and beyond.

The prizes were being given out by a former pupil. She had arrived at the school in 1936, thirteen years after the school opened. She had stayed two years. She must have been in her late eighties. She walked with two 'ski sticks' and had white hair in a bun. She rambled a bit but spoke of how she was in one of two classes that were taught in the same room, the present school office. There was a gasp from the audience, for the office was not large.

After the distribution of the prizes and the final speech from the Head Boy and Head Girl about what they owed to their teachers, we all repaired to a room adjoining the hall for refreshments, which were on tables round the walls. The room was packed.

I spoke to the Head Boy, who was with several members of his family. "Last year you said you wanted to go into the Army," I said.

He said, "I've got into a military academy in Devon."

"Well *done*," I said enthusiastically, and I asked him for further details.

"I start in September. It's in Exmouth. I'm looking forward to it. I want to be promoted to be a Captain. That way I can be out and about and do things without writing at a desk. I want to come back here with my sword."

"You must come back and give out the prizes when you're a Captain," I said.

"I'd like that," he said.

Then the Head of Art approached and said, "Can I persuade you to sit with Marlene?"

The old lady, our guest of honour, was sitting on a settee in the corner. I joined her.

"I know Arash," she said of the Head of Art. "He's in my community in Oxfordshire. Along with the friend who drove me down. The three of us meet in Oxfordshire. We're Baha'is."

"So Arash is a Baha'i too?" I asked.

"Yes, he is. He's Iranian.'

I was not sure that I knew that, but I was aware that an Iranian had joined the staff two years back.

"The Baha'i faith has got to be right," I said. "The Christians can't have a monopoly on the world. They've got a billion and more followers, but there are seven billion on the earth, and all the Hindus and Buddhists can't all be consigned down there. All human beings have the same spiritual potential. All roads lead up the same mountain to the summit."

"Yes," she said. "Exactly."

I asked her again about her time in our school. She said, "I was under Miss Brown. That's the only name I can remember. We had a royal-blue uniform. The school was really small in those days. It was a family school. I knew I had to leave my previous school because they taught me the same maths as last year. I wanted to learn more than the same as last year. Your school did that. It got me to Woodford County High, and from there the Headmistress gave me the confidence to apply to go to Oxford. I was there at the end of the war. I'm in Oxfordshire now. My husband had Alzheimer's and went into a home. I knew he had to when he couldn't get out of the bath. I'm within an hour's drive of three of my four kids. That's near enough. I'm in Chipping Norton, in Oxfordshire, not far from Worcestershire."

A young girl was drawing on the table near us. She upset my orange juice. I saw the spillage coming and moved my feet aside. A tiny amount of the juice splashed on the ankle of the old lady's white stocking. I dabbed the stocking with a tissue, and soaked up the juice that was on the parquet floor.

I extricated myself and went and spoke to a crippled girl on a wheeled frame, who was leaving. Her personality shone through.

The Captain-to-be was standing nearby. His family wanted to show me a photo of him in uniform, that had been taken at the leaving 'prom'. He reiterated he was keen to bring his sword to a future prize-giving and be guest speaker. The Baha'i guest speaker was anti-military – Baha'is do not join the military except as non-combatants – and said nothing about the military academy.

Two opposing ideologies had been present on the stage. They had co-existed. Both had been full of praise for our school, which reconciled their conflicting attitudes in quiet harmony.

Gentle Mr Grayling and a Blurt
(Or: Violence and Hades)

Walter Grayling was retiring after sixty years in the classroom. I parked, strode through a warm July afternoon (wearing a lightweight suit) and was greeted by the Head. We sauntered to the lawn in front of the dining-hall, where I was poured an orange juice among tables set out with strawberries and profiteroles melting in the sun.

This was Mr Grayling's second retirement. He had returned part-time after his last retirement, to mark which there was a dinner in the open air. I told the Head I had been seated next to him, having been one of his earliest classics pupils, and that speeches did not begin until dusk. It grew dark by the time Mr Grayling was called on to say a few words, and it was too dark for him to read his speech. He gave me his notes and asked me to tell him what he had written while he stood above me. Peering in the twilight, I tried to decipher his handwriting and fed him one-liners, which he repeated. I pointed to the cloudless blue sky and warm sun and said there was no danger of fading light today.

Then I saw Walter Grayling, leaning on his stick, white-haired, in the shade of the library. I crossed and chatted to him. Soon we were discussing Thucydides' account of the fate of Nicias in Syracuse. He told me I was in his first Greek set a year after his arrival. I reminded him that he had made us learn chunks of Greek verse, and told him I still had the first four lines of Euripides' *Alcestis* in my memory. I recited them and he nodded with approval.

The Bursar came and asked if he had been a 'Wrangler' at Cambridge.

"I was at Oxford."

I said wickedly, mock-seriously with a straight face, "There were Cambridge Apostles, who were spies for Russia, and Walter was not an Apostle or a Wrangler." Walter smiled at me.

"The 'Wranglers' were an *élite* group who had top marks, and I thought he might be among them."

"No," Walter said.

In fact, the 'Wranglers' were *élite* Cambridge mathematics students.

The Senior Wrangler was the student who achieved the highest exam marks.

Many more arrived in suits and stood in the sweltering sun: past teachers and a Head (now retired), members of the existing staff and another Old Boy. I was easily his earliest pupil.

I chatted to past masters and my boys' teachers. Then there were speeches. Mr Grayling's podgy replacement, Charles Lawson, pointed out three clergymen to the ex-Head. I asked, "What is the collective noun for a group of clerics?"

Lawson said without hesitation, "It's a mass of clerics. And a whinge of teachers."

The Head was standing with his back to the dining-hall on the far side of the lawn, beyond the tables and a good twenty yards from the rest of us. Without raising his voice he spoke of Walter Grayling's wide-ranging contributions to the school. He had arranged cricket matches and organised a swing band. He listed more than twenty things Walter Grayling had done. Then the Bursar spoke about Walter Grayling as a colleague, and how he sometimes got angry in class.

I was amazed. Our specialist Greek set had consisted of seven. It was more like a tutorial than a class. We had all been extremely interested in ancient history and had been keen to learn. We had behaved like young gentlemen, and he had never had to raise his voice with us.

The Bursar spoke of how Walter umpired at cricket. "Across the road from here is the King's Head, and when it got to six, if the game was still in progress, and there was an appeal, he would look at his watch and put his finger up. Out, so all could go to the King's Head."

There was laughter.

"As a player he was very competitive, especially against the Essex Clergy. I played under his captaincy. He told me to bowl bumpers, and so I tore in and hit a Bishop. He was lying poleaxed on the pitch, quite badly hurt. He picked himself up and returned to the crease. I was mortified, and thought I had better bowl from a short run-up, just a few paces. Walter crossed from mid-off and said to me, 'No, grind his face into the dust and press home our advantage.'"

Again there was laughter.

Then the Bursar called on his replacement as Head of Classics,

Charles Lawson, to speak.

"I haven't been given notice of this," Lawson said, walking across the lawn with his jacket over his shoulder. He joined the other two speakers beyond the tables. "I'll be brief. Just a couple of points.

"First, the violence. I remember when he taught my class in Room One he shouted at a boy who was lolling back in his chair. He tipped up the chair so the boy crashed backwards still sitting on his chair. There was a sports bag by the boy's desk. I remember Walter picked it up, brandished it over his head like Atlas or Hercules and flung it down on top of the boy's chest."

There was nervous laughter. The Head smirked and looked nervously around to see if we guests had formed an unfavourable image of his school as a result of this unscripted blurt.

I was shocked. I could not associate such violent behaviour with my urbane, subtle, gentle classics teacher.

"Then, Hades," Lawson continued. "Walter always swears by Hades, and one day I asked him how he saw Hades. He said, 'Hades is a place filled with giant wasps.' I'd always had a thing about wasps, and a place full of giant wasps is as bad as I could imagine. 'And,' Walter told me, 'the ground is covered in bubbling excrement.'"

Homer would have described Hades differently, but Walter's description was particularly revolting, and again there was nervous laughter.

Now it was time for Walter Grayling's speech. He had been sitting on a chair in the shade of the library, on the very edge of the gathering. He stood with difficulty, leaning on his stick, in his late eighties and now wearing dark glasses. It was 5.30, several hours before twilight.

"Thank you all for coming," he said almost inaudibly. He stared at a tiny piece of paper he held in the palm of his right hand. He digested what he had written for a full minute. "Oh, yes. I haven't been doing as well recently, and so I felt it was time to retire." He stared again at his tiny piece of paper. "I never felt any need to go anywhere else. I was happy here." He consulted his paper again for another minute. "I just feel it's time to go. I shall go back to the Cotswolds." He studied the paper again, perhaps for half a minute this time. "Thank you all for coming."

There was prolonged applause. Then people started drifting away. Some came and wished him well in his retirement. One or two gave him cards. I had earlier tucked a card into his bag for him to look at later: a picture of a garden seat near a stream and a distant wood. Inside I had written lines 23–26 of Horace's second epode:

Libet iacere modo sub antiqua ilice,
Modo in tenaci gramine;
Labuntur altis interim ripis aquae,
Queruntur in silvis aves.

I told him the card contained an unseen text that he would have to translate, just as he had made us do unseen translations of Latin verse in his classroom. I had a model translation in my mind:

It is pleasing now to lie under an old oak-tree (literally, holm-oak),
Now in the clingy grass;
And meanwhile waters flow into full (literally, high) streams,
The birds are complaining in the woods.

I told him in my message that I had been fortunate to be his pupil.

I said to him, "I never saw you lose your temper when I was in your class. You were always very gentle with us."

"Yes, I was. I remember that time well. I never had to raise my voice."

I sensed his frustration with a new kind of pupil who was not interested in learning. I sensed that the world had changed since the time I was his pupil, and he had had to resort to violence to keep order amid the disintegrating behaviour of some of the children of modern society.

"And didn't Charles Lawson mix Hades up with Aristophanes' *Vespae, The Wasps?*"

He said, "I never taught *The Wasps*. You must have read it with my predecessor."

I asked him, "After sixty years, who is now your favourite Greek and Latin author?"

He said without hesitation, "Greek, Thucydides. Latin, Tacitus. The two historians."

We talked of the visit to Greece I joined after leaving, and how I nearly missed the train at Belgrade. During a long stop I and another boy had got off the train to have coffee on the platform at Belgrade station. We had got talking to a Yugoslav student about Communism, and I had looked up to see the train slowly pulling away.

"I was at the back urging you on," Walter said. "You jumped and caught the train, but the other fellow couldn't run as fast and was left behind."

"Without a passport or money," I said. "He spent a week locked up until his father paid a whopping sum for his repatriation."

I said my goodbyes. The Bursar, who had played cricket for Yorkshire, was holding a cricket ball. I asked him how we would hold the seam to bowl an 'inswinger', "or should I say 'reverse swinger'?" He showed me all the grips for all the deliveries: outswinger, inswinger, bouncer, off-cutter, leg-cutter. It was the first time that I had been shown these grips by an ex-cricketer.

As I left I turned for a final look at Mr Grayling. He was still leaning on his stick, gentle with white hair and dark glasses, politely parting from the permanent people in his working life. A blurt had been hung round his neck like a medal given by a wrangler: his violence and his oaths to Hades' bubbling excrement and giant wasps. I thought that whether or not this reputation was deserved was immaterial: it had no place on the well-mown lawn, at this ceremony full of etiquette and formal correctness to which his ex-colleagues had travelled from far and wide to honour him and ensure that the right thing was done.

But then I thought I had always stood for the truth. The truth may have had no more place on the lawn than a giant wasp, but it was important to have a balanced view of sixty years and no tribute should be at the expense of truth. The blurt may have been clumsy, but it formed an important part of the whole perspective. The right thing had been done after all.

Missionaries like Wind Turbines

We walked round the house in heat, past tall purple agapanthi, on a carpet that led to a gazebo-style marquee under which, at the back of the house, a four-sided fountain splashed cool water into a square pool. I was given a glass of champagne and spoke to Emma, a doctor. She told me about her practice and eventually I said of her brother, "Archie is going to Kosovo with a view to becoming a missionary."

She did not contradict my statement, she nodded in acquiescence.

"Do you want to do the same, in Africa for example?"

She said, "No. Theo and I are both involved in Christian unions in this country, and we have enough to do here. I need to stay and support my mother. She needs to be stabilised."

"Stabilised?"

"Yes, she feels she'll be losing one set of grandchildren, and she mustn't lose the other set of grandchildren at the present time."

Later her mother said, "Archie is *not* going to be a missionary," and I could see that she was in denial.

I turned and spoke to Emma's husband, Theo.

"I've just been appointed Headmaster of my school," he said. "At thirty-four."

I was astonished, and after congratulating him said, "What's happened?"

"The roll fell to a hundred and eighty-five," he said, "and a lady Head took over. The roll fell to a hundred and thirty. She had a fifty-mile-each-way journey to and from school and has said she can't do it any more. The Deputy Head didn't want the job. The Governors wanted to appoint internally and asked me to do it."

I understood that they were getting a cheap Head. They would pay him more than he was getting before in his lowly position, but not as much as they would have to pay an existing Head to come from outside and fill the post.

I wandered with my champagne up the rockery to a group of chairs in shade at the end of the lawn. Archie's wife Harriet, a doctor, was sitting alone. I sat down and said, "Are you looking forward to going to Kosovo?"

She was a quiet soul. "I haven't thought about it much," she said. "We're going to visit the mission there and see if our skills blend in with the existing team."

"And if they do, you and Archie will return there? As missionaries?"

"Yes."

"Is there accommodation?"

"No, the team will find us rented housing."

"Can you practise medicine there?"

"When the children have grown up enough to go to school, yes."

At that moment Archie sauntered by. I waved him to an empty chair.

"I was just hearing that you may become missionaries in Kosovo," I said.

"Yes."

"How will it work?"

"We'll go to an area of Kosovo and live in a community," he said. "The children will go to a community school. We can't say, 'We want to be one of you, but our children are going to a public school.' We'll get to know the community and ask some of them to help start a church. Kosovo is 90 per cent ethnic Albanians and only 0.1 per cent Christians. So we'll start a church. Over a period of time we'll replace ourselves and return home, leaving the new church to be run by Albanians."

"Should you be in Kosovo, or somewhere else?"

"If our skills fit with the others in the mission, we'll go to Kosovo. It's the right sort of place, with 0.1 per cent Christians. Uganda has a strong church already, and cars in Kampala have banners with Christian messages on them. We need to be somewhere where there is a lot to do."

"So you'll increase the percentage from 0.1 to 0.2 or 0.3 per cent?"

"God will," he said. "Not us, we will fulfil God's plan."

"And will you break your ties with Rolls-Royce for good? Will you stop designing wind turbines?"

"I'll have to," he said. "I've had three years of creative study and sabbatical. If I want to return it will be as an applicant along with other applicants. Yes, I'll have to give up my career in engineering to be a missionary."

He stood up and excused himself, and I was struck by the intensity in his eyes. He had a dream, and he was going to fulfil it. His wife also stood up and followed him across the lawn. I watched them in the heat standing near their two children: one kneeling and drawing in the corner of the lawn, the other asleep in a nearby push-chair with just his toes showing from beneath a buttoned-in pram screen.

They had sent out newsletters to family and friends praising the Lord and reporting on their *Bible*-reading classes and their missionary training. I thought Archie had inherited three sets of family genes: from my mother's paternal great-grandfather, a Reverend; from his paternal grandfather, who had been a vicar in Gloucestershire; and from my aunt, who had had links with the Salvation Army. Some gene had propelled him and his sister into *Bible*-reading and enquiring about becoming a missionary. My brother's children and my children were all normal, but Archie and his sister Emma were religious fanatics who carried *Bible*-reading to extreme lengths. Archie would carry the 'good news' to a mission.

Archie would take his two children out to war-damaged Kosovo and infiltrate a community and bring his contacts to the Christian faith. In the process he would precipitate a crisis in his own mother. They were two church-creators, Archie and Harriet, who would bring the love of God to strangers in a life of sacrifice and then replace themselves. Archie had turned his back on designing wind turbines. Wind turbines are driven by the invisible wind to produce electric power, and watching them standing on the lawn in the hot July sunshine I saw them as two wind turbines bringing the eco-friendly power of the Holy Spirit to a remote village in Kosovo. They were doomed to share in the life of a community, be involved in everyone's lives, attract them into a new church and then walk away to take the 'good news' of Jesus Christ to a new community in another part of the world.

A Wheelchair and Stony Hill

Claire opened the door of the converted Cornish bungalow and waved in the August sunshine, short-black-haired, slightly overweight with an impressive face and clear eyes. I carried my plant in a bag.

"Harry's in the garden," she said. "Go through, he'll come in."

I wandered past the stairs – it was not a bungalow now – to the kitchen and looked through the conservatory. Harry was crouching in the well-kept, long garden in a sun-hat. I returned to Claire, who was giving Pippa a tour of the house, pointing out what Harry had done.

"It was such a mess, I couldn't see it would turn out like this. Harry did it all. Every door is new. He built the upstairs. We found these banisters with the exact measurements we wanted in a sale for £99. They'd had dogs and it was disgusting, but now after all these new carpets it's spick and span. Harry did the lot. Through here you can see into the shed Harry built in the two weeks after he was diagnosed. He worked like a man possessed. It was while your chimney was being built."

Then I saw Harry sitting at the kitchen table, taciturn, saying little. He had no hat on now. He had a shaven head and wore spectacles. *The Daily Mirror* was near his hand. I patted his arm and explained that I had brought him a Rudbreckia ('Little Gold Star') with several gold heads. "You can put it in the sun in the conservatory there, by the chair, and make a cheerful corner. Later you can plant it in the garden."

He showed me the blotchy patches of congealed blood in two places under the skin on the inside of his skinny left arm where he had had radiotherapy injections. He said, "Radiotherapy makes the skin thin. You just touch it and it goes like that. See, they won't go away. But that's all right."

Claire made us coffee and gave us each a home-baked bun, still warm from the oven.

"He's so much better this week," she said. "Last week he was in a wheelchair because of the tablets, and couldn't walk without the Zimmer frame. And he didn't know what day it was. But this week he's been in the garden and he can take a few steps. It was the zapping last week that did it. He had four tablets, steroids. Now he is down to one. He had six tumours in his brain, one the size of a matchbox, and they put him in a tunnel for ten minutes to scan the tumours. The benefits will take a month to come through, and we won't know how successful it's been till next Wednesday, but he feels much better already."

"Except for my eyes," Harry said. "I have a headache round my eyes and can't see as well as I should. Otherwise I haven't been in pain."

"I've had to push him," she said. "He was so tired, and he'd come home and lie on his bed. I said, 'Man up, pull yourself together.' But he was still tired, so I said, 'I'm making an appointment for you to see the doctor.' I rang him at work and said, 'You've got an appointment at 2 this afternoon.' He said, 'Oh, but I'm working.' I said, 'Get yourself to the doctor at 2.' The blood test didn't show anything up at first but in the end word came through. We'd booked for Crete for a week for £1,100. We cancelled that to be nearer and went to Jersey for two nights, £900. Can you believe it?

"The doctor was very good. We wanted to be told straight and he gave it to us straight. At first we were just going to accept it. But a letter came through saying treatment – radiotherapy – would begin on Monday. We had all the family round to collect their view. Kay said, 'What have you got to lose? Go along. If you don't want to do it, drive away from the car park. Try it for one session, if you don't want to do the next one, don't go.' So we did it on that basis. Then his hair started to fall out so I got a hairdresser in to shave his head.

"He kept falling over, and when he was lying on the floor, I'd say, 'Get yourself up, you've got to cope with this on your own.' I could have put my hands under his armpits and dragged him up, but no, he should do it himself. He trained to be a jockey but was too small, so he's always been light. Harry's been difficult sometimes. He doesn't like being in his wheelchair. I said to him, 'If you're difficult one more time I'm taking you to Stony Hill and releasing the wheelchair's brake.' It's a steep hill and the river's at the bottom. He'd end up in the river." We all laughed. "He's done well, but he said, 'I'm thinking I should shoot myself.' 'Say that one more time,' I said, 'and I'll get your gun and shoot you.'" Again, we all laughed. "That put an end to that thinking. He said to me before the recent improvement, 'There's no evidence I'm getting better. I feel I've only got a few days.' I said, 'Let me know when and I won't do such a big shop.'"

We all laughed very heartily.

"You have to be practical," she said. "And strong. My family are all local and they're all strong. My sister's son fell on carpeted stairs in the Scillies and hit his head, and he was in an induced coma for three weeks. My sister sits with him in hospital twelve hours a day playing games to get him back. A doctor said, 'You don't have to do that.' She said, 'He's my son, if *I* don't do it, no one else will do it.' That's how I feel about Harry."

I said, "Harry has shown great determination and will-power to reach his present point, and you have done brilliantly with your background strength. I'll ring on Wednesday afternoon to hear what the report says, but Harry, how you're feeling now must be a good indicator." He nodded gloomily.

"Bye, Harry," I said.

"Bye."

On the way out Claire showed me their bedroom. On both bedside tables there were mints and chocolates

"He's nine stone, he's got to put on weight," she said. "I don't care how and he might as well do it with chocolates. His cancer's caused by asbestos, all the asbestos he removed when he was working in the building trade." Harry had joined us.

"Yes," he said. "Asbestos caused it."

The lung cancer – a "cup on one lung", Claire had described it, "and half a cup on the other one" – might have been caused by asbestos dust. Were the six tumours of the brain secondary? The radiotherapy and zapping were surely all to do with the brain, not the lungs. I had visited a former sea captain, Les, who was dying of lung cancer. Nothing could be done for him.

Outside in the garden the binmen were clearing the bags of rubbish.

"I don't know how long we've got," she said. "Six months, two years? I don't know. But I know I was right to push him to be seen. If I hadn't, in a few weeks' time, a doctor told, he'd have collapsed and died. I've just got to be strong."

She waved us off and carried in the empty recycling boxes, having declined my offer of help: "No, I've got to be independent and strong."

"She's as tough as old boots," Pippa said, admiringly.

"Like you," I said in jest. "From the way she's talking about six months or two years she believes the zapping has delayed the inevitable, not eradicated it."

"Yes."

I was impressed by Claire's strength and the down-to-earth, practical way she had handled the situation and pushed Harry into being seen. And I was impressed by the silent, watchful way he had handled his illness, not complaining, smiling at her practical insistence on being told when the end was coming so she could do a smaller shop.

Claire had committed herself to Harry and he had converted the bungalow into a lovely two-storey house, which she would live in, near her family, when he left her.

Harry had worked hard for more than thirty years, sometimes breaking up asbestos, and had dreamt of twenty years' retirement, and might only have six months. He had accepted his lot. He had gone along with the treatment but without undue hope. He was realistic. He too was down-to-earth and I felt sad to see this quietly determined, independent, active man pottering between his Zimmer frame and the wheelchair he hated so much, and being mock-threatened with Stony Hill if he did not do as he was told.

A Working Harbour and a Dream

The *Earl of Pembroke* left the Cornish harbour in the late afternoon. I wandered down to the quayside and saw her reverse out, red sails furled, tugged back by ropes, hawsers on capstans. She swung near the harbour's knuckle, and to prevent her gashing her side a harbour-worker held a padded sandbag on a rope between her and the stone wall, and several of the harbour staff lined up and pushed her away from the quay with both hands, among them grey-haired Richard Dawkins in a jacket and jeans, the owner of the harbour and until recently of the departing ship.

Two cameras were recording the departure, and I spoke to him. "Is this the last time the *Earl of Pembroke* will leave the harbour?" I asked.

"They're doing training and we want her out of the harbour where we're filming, but who knows?"

I said I would look in on him the next day.

I presented myself at his office the following afternoon. He took me into his room and offered me tea. The receptionist asked how I liked it, and I said, "Strong, with no sugar." Before the tea arrived a couple appeared. The receptionist interrupted us to tell Richard Dawkins, who left and greeted them. He returned and whispered, "They've come from London. I was supposed to see them at 2. I need to meet them."

I volunteered to return in half an hour's time.

When I returned there were loud voices from Richard Dawkins' room. The receptionist let Richard Dawkins know that I had arrived, and they all came out. Richard Dawkins introduced me.

He said, "They have a berth, a mooring slot, for a ship near the Tower of London and want to open a school for disadvantaged children on it. They were supposed to have had the *Kaskelot*, but she's been sold. So I'll find them another ship from somewhere."

The man, who was very elderly, was keen to tell me all he had done while his grey-haired wife nodded and added a word here and there.

They left and my strong tea was brought.

"So the *Kaskelot*'s gone," I said.

Richard Dawkins told me the company that bought her had messed him about, wanting him to convert the ship and comply with a tight timeline as she had to tour the world. He said, "I told them to 'b— off' and that concentrated minds. They bought the ship for a good price and took ten of my staff to run it. That left me in a better position, workwise. I had a reduced wages bill – I employ thirty-eight instead of forty-eight – and my redundancy liability has been cut. She has already had a refit in Bristol and she'll be based in the UK. But she has to visit the Far East first."

"And the *Earl of Pembroke*'s gone," I said.

"Yes, nine months ago. She's still berthed here, but for how long we don't know. I've still got the *Phoenix*. We're making a couple of films simultaneously in the next two months. She appears in both.

"I've had three offers for the harbour. The best one was the first one. They couldn't raise the money, so I ended their exclusivity. I want to keep it all together as a harbour. Plenty of estate agents have urged me to break it up and sell it in bits for restaurants and wine bars, but I don't want to do that. So it's taking time. I'm seventy and I don't have any borrowing. I want to retire here and stay on down here as a consultant, and just do my film work, reading scripts and hiring out the *Phoenix*.

"My wife's mother is ninety-six. She's in a nursing home in Australia, and my wife goes every so often and stays a few weeks and sees her children and grandchildren, who are there. It's a bore, but there's no other way. She was in the Hitler Youth, her mother, so she'll probably go on until a hundred and six. I don't want to move up country, though I have properties in East Anglia. I like it here. I just want to shed all my responsibilities and retire here and be a consultant to a working harbour. I don't need the money, but it's my interest, and I'll go on reading scripts and being involved with film companies for as long as I can. That and looking at the sea. That's my dream now."

I left him, the owner of the harbour, dreaming of shedding his responsibilities. He had already shed two of his ships, but he could not walk away from the harbour he had run for more than twenty years. It was too much a part of his life.

As I crossed the iron bridge to the other side of the harbour and walked home, I reflected that we all have a dream, and even if we own a harbour and ships we still have a dream beyond the *status quo* to run our lives in a different way. We have a constant drive to improve our lives and bring in a better future. Richard Dawkins seemed to have everything, but he would not be happy until he had achieved his dream.

Veiling Cheeks and a Wimple

The 90th anniversary of the high-street school's founding took place on a Saturday afternoon in the assembly hall, which could be seen in a photograph on the wall taken in 1929. Memorabilia were displayed on walls, tables and folding stands: photos, memories and old registers. I spoke to a man in a suit who had left in 1934 and another who came with photos of the Principal in 1963. A photographer had been sent by the local paper. He prowled round and took me speaking to a councillor and his wife, and with the Headmistress.

Poor old Sid Davies came by, a former deputy head. I had not seen him since his stroke and barely recognised him. He was on a stick and trembled at each step, his pudgy face screwn up and shaking with concentration on each foot movement. He had put on weight, and his cheeks were chubby as he blew after the strain. I could hardly see the vigorous young man I used to know under the veil his enforced idleness had thrown round his features. I sat with him and tried to have a conversation. To every question I asked he replied, "Yes". I asked him half a dozen questions and only heard him say, "Yes".

An hour into the reunion a nun loomed in a brown and white habit. She stood near me, and I greeted her. Her face was surrounded by her wimple. She said, "I used to teach here." I did not recognise the face surrounded by her wimple, and I asked her when she had left. She said, "1998," and agreed that she had seen my arrival. She told me she had become a nun two years back. "I'm in the Order of Consecrated Widows. I live at home," she said, "there are a hundred and twenty in the country. I'm the only one round here, but there are two in Harlow. It's a Catholic Order." Her chubby face was unsmiling through her tight-fitting white wimple and brown head-dress, and there was less to see of her than if she had worn a *hijab*. She wore an enormous crucifix four inches long and two inches wide that hung from her neck. Christ was shown on the cross in great detail. She said she had been widowed and had taken a vow of poverty, chastity and obedience. She had assumed the habit of an Order as if she had chosen to wear widow's weeds for full mourning. I introduced her to the Headmistress, and later found out that the unsmiling moon face surrounded by her wimple belonged to Sheila Arlington, who had delivered 100% passes in English Literature at GCSE in my first two years and had rewritten the school song (which we ceased to use immediately she left).

At 3pm there were speeches of welcome and then I was invited to cut the cake, which had pictures of the school in icing. I brandished a large carving knife and, with the local paper's photographer pointing a camera and the leader of a local community group pointing a film camera, made a deep incision under the school badge and drew the knife towards me and down. There was applause and I moved away.

A fellow approached me. He was in a suit and had chubby cheeks. He shook my hand. I had no idea who he was.

"It's all right," he said. "It turned out well. I was one of four who were selected to take part in an experiment. I spent five months being given complete transfusions and was put on drugs costing £4,000 – too costly to be generally available on the NHS. I've been in remission ever since, for the last eleven years. They say it's not permanent remission. I still have latent leukaemia, but it's been all right. I'm living in a flat in Reading now."

While he spoke I had worked out who he was: Gerald Otis.

"You compered the last three Prize Days while you were with us," I said, "and the last one – "

"I was really ill then," he nodded.

"But you carried it through. And the children put on a concert after the prizes. You introduced it, and they all sang, 'You're gonna live for ever.'" (They had adapted a line from the musical *Fame*.)

"Yes, they did."

"They were showing their support," I said. "You were much loved, by staff as well as pupils."

"It seems so."

"I'm so glad it's turned out well," I said. "And it's good to see you here today."

The last time I had seen him he looked thin and gaunt, wracked by leukaemia. But now he was full in the face. His chubby cheeks were as much a disguise as the consecrated widow's wimple. At the reunion I had encountered faces I used to know, which time had veiled behind burgeoning flesh, but underneath they were the same people I had once cared for, who had come back to our reunion and had remembered me in their posthumous lives.

An Elagabalus Coin and a Yacht

We checked in at Le Manoir aux Quat'Saisons and were escorted to a ground-floor room, Passion-Flower. We walked in the grounds to the 15th-century stew pond and then returned to the sitting-area for tea. We moved to the bar and sat with an elderly couple who talked about archaeological digs they'd been on. They lived nearby and had visited six Edward-VII castles in Wales in two days. They had regularly joined archaeological digs as weekend volunteers. "We don't do so many now," the wife said, "as my husband's had two new knees and can't kneel down." "*And* a brain haemorrhage," her husband said, and there was a silence.

The four of us were rounded up and taken with our escort to a people carrier. We were driven to the Ashmolean Museum for an out-of-hours tour. Another couple were waiting to join us. They were in their fifties and the husband was very sun-tanned. We went up by lift to the top floor and the assistant director showed us the conservation – restoration – works they were doing that week: a frame made by Grinling Gibbons round a painting of Elias Ashmole that had been damaged when someone backed into it taking a photograph. It was surmounted by Ashmole's arms and motto: '*Ex Uno Omnia*' ('All things come from one').

We looked at a repaired prehistoric jar and touched-up Roman-Egyptian mummy paintings. Then we were taken downstairs by the assistant director's assistant and toured the three rooms of the new Bacon-Moore exhibition. The paintings and sculptures were chosen to show the similarities between the two artists: Bacon's 3D-paintings and Moore's similar images. There was a contrast between Bacon's messy studio and Moore's tidy workroom shelves, and there was suspicion that Bacon had copied Moore's shapes. (He had destroyed most of the works he did before 1945, and Moore was nine years his senior.)

I remembered the many times I had seen Bacon in the Colony Room, holding a bottle of champagne and pouring it into our glasses, and I rubbed my eyes in disbelief at the accolade on the walls. He was such an unprepossessing man. I had little time for his paintings of despair and nihilism. The great artists of the past such as Leonardo enhanced their works with hints of the metaphysical and meaning.

We were then taken downstairs to the Heberden Coin Room, where the director, Cecil Banks, gave us a talk about six of his three hundred thousand ancient coins. The six were all Roman, and he passed them round on trays: a 225BC Janus and trireme prow, a silver Julius Caesar of 44BC and a gold Vespasian found in Suffolk, which he had bought for £7,500 (when its true value was £200,000). I had emailed him the obverse and reverse of a coin I wanted him to identify. I introduced myself and was surprised and pleased to learn that he was coming back with us to dinner.

We sat next to each other in the people carrier, and in the dark he told me he had collected coins since he was four and had been to Brentwood School, and had a nephew who had been to my school.

Back at the Manoir the six of us, our escort and Cecil Banks sat over champagne in a lounge. The quiet couple were quietly pushy and thrust two Byzantine coins under Cecil's nose for identification, even though he had announced that he would be identifying my coin. He told them that their coins were outside his range. Then it was my turn. The loud man had asked him questions about the stamping of coins, and now said, satirically, "Oh, I'm sorry *we* haven't brought a coin to be identified." He was an engineering consultant who had travelled the world.

Cecil Banks looked at my coin and said, "I believe it is Elagabalus, AD218 to 222, from Antioch. There's a Greek influence. The SC are back to front suggesting Greek moneyers, and there is a delta on the back, the fourth letter of the Greek alphabet, which means it was the fourth Roman province of Syria: Antioch. The delta and epsilon probably say 'of the 4 eparchies', the four provinces of the imperial cult of which Antioch was the head."

I showed him my coin of Julius Caesar veiled with '*Dict perpetuo*', 'perpetual dictator'. It was because Caesar declared himself 'Perpetual Dictator' that Brutus and the conspirators murdered him. Cecil Banks said that the coin could have been struck a few days before Caesar was murdered on the Ides of March 44BC or just afterwards – but not long afterwards as '*Dict perpetuo*' would have been swiftly suppressed as politically unacceptable. There was no means of telling whether the coin was earlier or later than Caesar's death.

A waiter came and asked politely, "Can I open another bottle of champagne?" The polite answer was, 'No, thank you.' The loud husband said, "What a silly idea," and everyone laughed. The waiter disappeared and returned with a freshly opened bottle of champagne and topped up all our glasses. A minute later we were called to eat, and we carried our full glasses through to a private room off the main restaurant. We sat where our place names stated round a long table. Cecil Banks was up the far end and Pippa and I were round the other end. The others were in between.

The quiet couple did not say much throughout the dinner, and the loud husband had already had too much to drink. Three waiters brought bread and spiced cauliflower velouté and scallops, and he said loudly before they had left, "Serving staff should not be heard, they should be invisible." Cecil Banks caught my eye and raised his eyes to the ceiling, and I said, "The Ashmolean is distancing itself from that last remark," and there was a nervous laugh. The waiters withdrew.

I asked questions about Roman coins across the table, to which Cecil Banks replied: questions involving coins of Caligula and Tiberius. The loud man, who was between us, kept intervening. I spoke of the "Julian line in relation to Livia's alternative line", and he interrupted and said loudly, "Julia? Wasn't she the wife of Julius Caesar?" "No," Cecil Banks said. "No," the quiet wife said, "that was Calpurnia." The conversation moved on and he was left behind and kept trying to catch up.

He talked about his son who was leaving the army after seven years, including service in Afghanistan and Iraq. I broke off from the Roman theme and asked, "With a pension?" "I don't know," he said. I said, "Soldiers can get a pension on leaving the army, and they deserve it after serving in those places."

We returned to talking about the Romans, and he cut across us to announce that he and his wife had travelled the world to attend operas. "We've been married six years," he said. "Seven," she corrected. He spoke of how they arrived in Italy to attend an opera. "We came into the port on our yacht," he said. There was a quiet intake of breath from the quiet couple, who exchanged glances. His lifestyle was very different from theirs of volunteering unpaid help with digs.

The meal had progressed. The risotto of wild mushrooms and truffle cream slipped down as did spiced Cornish monkfish, mussels, saffron and *gewürztraminer*. The roasted fillet of Aberdeen Angus beef, smoky mash, ceps and red wine jus melted on the tongue. We finished our *gelée* of exotic fruit, kaffir lime and coconut jus, and we finished our Spanish, Italian and French wines and our brandy. We repaired to the bar for *petit fours* and coffee.

Cecil Banks sat in front of me and said softly, "You've met a lot of people," and I explained quietly how my lifestyle had brought me into contact with a wide range of minds. The loud man was still being loud at the end of the group, and I heard him say to Pippa, who had just said that there were more restrictions on teachers these days than thirty years ago, "You could be on thin ice there as you're in the presence of an educationalist." He meant his wife. "No," his wife interjected, "that's right. It was better before Health and Safety." Pippa could not let him get away with his put-down and said, "*You* could be on thin ice as *you're* in the presence of educationalists." He asked what we did, and she explained that we had schools.

Cecil Banks left, shaking hands all round, and the quiet couple followed soon afterwards, to drive home. Then the loud man stood up to drive back to his village near Oxford. "Goodbye, sir," he said to me. Suddenly, his whole approach had changed. His egocentric dream of superiority had been punctured by Pippa's remark.

We were the only ones of our group who were sleeping at Le Manoir. I had a bath around 12.45am and slept soundly.

We were shown into breakfast. The large room was unoccupied except for Raymond Blanc who was being interviewed by a French lady at the next table to ours. Before I sat down I strode over and shook hands, and reminded him we had met three years previously and that our son had made a video for him earlier in the year. We had a short chat, and then he returned to his interview, speaking French. I heard "*escargots*", 'snails'.

As we ate Pippa and I reflected that for the Ashmolean the previous evening must have been a disaster. Three senior staff and many assistants and security staff had been tied down so that six of us could have a private tour. The evening must have been a similar disappointment to Le Manoir. Only six had applied for a tour that should have attracted thirty, and one of the Ashmolean speakers had been given a free dinner and paid. Both the Ashmolean and Le Manoir would have made a loss. But from our point of view we had had massive individual attention, and I had had a coin identified and another one discussed. I reflected that true values had revolved around Elagabalus and the Byzantine coins the previous evening, and not the yacht the loud man had flaunted like his loud voice that had cut across the other diners in our private room.

A Funeral and an Isolated Mourner

We were early at the crematorium and parked round the corner until some of the mourners gathered. I went and shook hands with the eldest son, Colin, and the younger son, Patrick, both bearded, and a cousin who was running the family shop, Sandy. I told him I had seen a picture of him online holding a portrait of my grandfather. Like me, they were in dark suits, white shirts and black ties.

I saw the middle son, Denis, standing well apart and talking to a lady, and crossed and shook hands. I said, "Shall we join the others?" He said, "My views on the family business are so divergent from my brothers' that I would prefer to stay over here."

Then it was our turn. We stood in the aisle and Colin said, "Sit here." We dutifully sat in the second pew. Then Denis appeared. Colin indicated the front pew, but there was little room. Denis slipped out of a side door, walked alongside the outside wall, returned down the aisle and sat behind me. Colin had positioned us between him and his middle brother.

The coffin was borne down the aisle. There was a hymn and a prayer, and an earnest eulogy delivered by a young Irish vicar. He told of Jenny's life in detail, how she met Timothy in mixed hockey when she swiped with her hockey stick and whacked his head. He told how they had been married during Wednesday half-day closing – the family business came first – and how she had three children and then lost her father and husband in the same week. There was another hymn and a final prayer, and then the curtains drew. Patrick was distressed, and so was his son.

Outside I chatted to Stanley, the cousin who had sat two rows behind me with his mother, Sheila (the wife of James I had visited before he died). We drove to the golf club for the wake, and, holding orange juice, I spoke at length to Colin about the Navy: he worked in Portsmouth and told me he had left the family business "because some of the public were impolite". I sat with Stanley and his wife and ate a buffet lunch of *canapés* and chocolate *gâteau*. Denis lurked. I invited him to pull up a chair and he sat and talked to Pippa about his dyslexic daughter.

To Denis, everything was wrong. The school were not teaching his daughter correctly and they had sent her home with a plaster over a cut in which there was a lump of dirt. He was going to go in and tell the Head where he was going wrong. He had collected his daughter from his wife at 2pm the previous week and had been shocked that she was drowsy and had fallen asleep. He said his wife was neglecting his daughter during her time with her. He was living apart from his wife, an Irish teacher at another school who refused to have his daughter assessed for dyslexia and denied him access. He said, "She's got a portrait of Gerry Adams on her sideboard, she's pro-IRA and she's after my dosh." They had been meeting with a psychologist to resolve their conflict. It made no difference, and he had not been allowed to bring his daughter to England. He said, "She's playing games. I'm English and she's Irish. The Head and the Court are Irish. I'm going to fight them all."

Pippa said, "You've got to locate your feminine side and be devious, counter her deviousness with your own deviousness. If she's playing games, you must play games too. You must come across to the Head as a reasonable and friendly person, a good chap, and he will then persuade your wife to have your daughter assessed for dyslexia."

Denis chortled, "Me, reasonable and friendly…." He shook his head. "I can't do it. I have a psychological profile, when I was in the City I was found to be a leader and a problem-solver."

I could sense his frustration at not being able to solve the problems surrounding his daughter.

After we had left, saying goodbyes all round – I told the two elder boys to take care of their hearts for they had both had coronaries – I said to Pippa as we set off in her car, "Denis has a problem with his daughter."

She said: "He's been assessed as having a psychological profile, but more than that, he has a psychological problem. Everything's wrong for him, and he's fighting with everyone, including his brothers, and has brought much of his situation upon himself by being consumed by his passion. He's obsessive about small things: the way a plaster was applied to his daughter's leg. The teachers are probably not allowed to touch her leg and have to put the plaster on quickly. He's hypercritical and fighting battles. He's got a psychological disorder like attention deficit syndrome that makes him pour things out and get them out of proportion and perspective."

I saw that Denis was very protective towards his daughter. He took issue with the school and his wife and accused them of neglect. His daughter's sleepiness in the afternoon could not be attributed to his wife's neglect of her, there was no evidence connecting her drowsiness and neglectful behaviour. He was very intelligent and had worked in the City until his heart attack. There was a clever person inside Denis trying to escape the censorious sensor that directed a beam out into the world and rang a bell in his brain when it detected any lack of care for his daughter.

At the funeral he had been an isolated mourner, and back in Ireland he would be just as isolated as he mourned the stark truth that his daughter had ceased to live with him full-time. He was consumed by his separation from his daughter for chunks of each week and blackened the school and his wife who had contributed to this unsatisfactory state of affairs – to the detriment of his daughter, who craved for a normal life.

Fines and Spills

We went to a lunch party at the home of one of the coffee-morning ladies. It was up a lane, in a modern Georgian-style house with a view across the flat marshes to tiny Canary Wharf and Alexandra Palace on the skyline. About twenty elderly couples gathered.

Lily was in the kitchen, ninety-two and forthright. "You look familiar," she said to me in a loud voice. "Where have I seen you before?"

"You came to our house for coffee last month," I said. "Perhaps you saw me there?"

"No," she said.

She had been the last to arrive. I had a vivid memory of her attempt to park. I watched out of a window as she abandoned her car in the middle of our drive, blocking all traffic in or out.

Pippa told me Lily had been stopped for speeding. She was given a choice of being fined or attending a tuition class to improve her motoring skills. She chose the class. A couple of minutes into it she stood up and said, "This is a lot of nonsense," and walked out. She might now lose her licence. She was known to throw her weight around but was forgiven in view of her advanced years.

I spoke to the chairlady's husband, an ex-lawyer with a white beard. He told me about his visit to Australia a few years back to watch an Ashes series. He was holding a tilted wine glass and every time he reinforced a point with his hand his red wine swilled round and nearly slopped. Our neighbour Roland Frond was standing next to me. We listened to him and we both stepped back in unison each time the wine nearly slewed over. It was as if we were dancing. Roland eventually headed off, and I was able to make an excuse and move away. The chairlady's husband headed for the kitchen.

Later I found three of the younger ladies kneeling by the entrance to the kitchen. They were dabbing the fawn carpet with a wet tea towel and rubbing it backwards and forwards. Something had been spilt. I looked to see if it was red wine. I could not be sure that it was, but I did not linger in case I was blamed for the spillage. I stepped round them and went into the kitchen. When I came out they had gone, and there was a piece of fawn off-cut shaped like a mat. The spillage had been hidden.

I thought of Lily's fine, which had been rubbed out by her attendance at the class, and I thought of the spilt wine which had been hidden by the piece of carpet. I looked at the ladies of the coffee club as they chatted and simpered, putting on a front as they engaged the husbands of their fellow members in conversation. They were concealing the fines and spills in their lives with charm and aplomb.

Glittering Gold off the Black Head

In December I laid places for four at our breakfast table. Harry and Claire came. I shook Harry by the hand.

"Careful," he said, "my skin's fragile, look." I saw open wounds and bruises on both his hands. "One touch and it goes like this. I can't put a plaster on, it takes the skin with it when I take it off. It's the chemo and steroids."

I poured coffee and joined him, Pippa and Claire at the table.

Harry took off his beanie and showed downy hair on his bald head. "My hair's growing again," he said. "I've put on two stone. I'm back up to ten stone, my normal. I was eight."

"He's eating like a horse," Claire said. "He's been out painting the fence. We've decided not to have the last two chemos. He had four, and now it's quality of life. They've bought him three to nine months from now. The consultant said the last two chemos wouldn't have made that much difference anyway. He's been ill for a week after each one, and now he's feeling really well and enjoying life. He's watching football on Saturday afternoons. We know the St Austell centre half. He said, 'Don't you pay at the gate.' It's £5 admission. Four of us went and the man on the gate said, 'I've got instructions to let you in without paying.' The players get paid £60 per game and he'd paid £20 out of what he gets paid for four of us to go in. Wasn't that nice of him?"

"I may be going to Scotland for a weekend," Harry said. "My shooting friends are shooting just across the border. They say Claire can drive me up there and leave me with them for a day and then drive me back. They shoot wild geese and ducks up there, and rabbits. Not grouse. They've already bought the drink: four hundred Carlsberg and whisky."

"I'm not sure about this," Claire said. "It's colder up there, and you feel the cold. And when you crawl through hedges and under barbed wire they're going to be looking after you to see you're all right. It may detract from their enjoyment. They've all paid a lot of money for that weekend and shouldn't be holding back because of you."

Harry said nothing.

"They're all quite special, Harry's shooting friends," Claire said. "One's in a Ministry and the country can't go to war without him. He has to carry a box with him everywhere, even when he's crawling under barbed wire. One flies Black Hawks. One wears army uniform with knee patches. One has a farm in South Africa."

"Yes," said Harry. "Minty went to stay with him. He said it's unbelievable. They drove five hours from the farm and stopped in a shop in the middle of nowhere, and Minty saw something he liked to buy, costing about £6, and said, 'I'll have that.' His host said, 'No, you don't have to pay, that's mine.' They'd driven five hours and they were still on the land of his farm."

There was talk about farms.

Harry said, "I used to go up to Salisbury Plain and catch hares in nets and bring them back down here to Cornwall and release them into the wild. It's good we've got more hares down here now. And if they'd stayed up there they'd be shot with a .22 on one of the firing ranges."

They talked about one of their sons.

"Yesterday he went treasure-hunting," Harry said. "Off the Black Head. A Spanish galleon's been found. It was wrecked off the rocks. Tony the fisherman went down and came up with a gold ring. There's gold down there under the water. They tried yesterday but the sea was too murky, too cloudy. They couldn't dive. They'll go again. We've got gold just off the coast here."

As they made a move to go I gave Harry a small box of champagne truffles Pippa had found. "These are for your bedside." He had told me that he had Smarties on his bedside table. "To help you put on weight. You're doing well. My father used to say, 'It's mind over matter.' You're being positive. Your mind is bossing your body." Claire nodded.

Harry and I left the house and walked to the sea wall and looked across the deserted beach where a hundred gulls waddled or stood. The sun made a causeway of golden light towards the Black Head. I thought of the six black tumours in his head.

"It's lovely here," Harry said. "I wish I could have this view all the time."

He had three to nine months ahead of him in which to enjoy this view.

"See you in April," he said.

We stood and dwelt on the glittering gold off the sombre Black Head.

A Sore Point
(Or: Jabs and Autism)

We had pre-Christmas morning coffee at work and five of us sat round a table overlooking the Forest and munched mince pies and mini Stollen bites. There was talk of the gardener's chest infection, and his arrangements for the coming Christmas Day.

"We'll just have our son," he said. "We'll have to follow a strict routine as he has autism issues."

"What happened to him?" I asked.

"He had the MMR jab and developed bowel problems. He couldn't go to the loo and was being violently sick and lost weight. Eventually after two years and no help from the National Health Service we went to a Chinese herbalist who prescribed liquorice. After two months of liquorice he was all right. But he still has autism issues. He doesn't like change and doesn't communicate much. He has to stick to his daily routine without any variation, otherwise he gets very agitated."

I knew that separate vaccines for measles, mumps and rubella had been replaced by one combined MMR vaccine (and a booster), and that the safety of this new vaccine had been questioned.

"But that's not a consequence of the MMR jab, surely," the PA, Penny, said. Her daughter was a doctor working in a local hospital's A & E department, and she had been a medical PA.

"Oh, yes it is," Gully the gardener said, bristling. "He was fine before the MMR jab. Then immediately afterwards he had his bowel disorder and fear of change."

"But that could have happened anyway."

"No, it was the MMR. There was a doctor who challenged the MMR – "

"Adam Wakeham," Pippa said. "I met him at the time. A friend wasn't sure whether to have the MMR and Wakeham was holding consultations on an airfield. He seemed a nice enough man."

"He was an alarmist, who was struck off," Penny said. "He put off so many people. Measles was on the verge of being stamped out, and he raised fears unjustifiably and now measles is back we now, officially, have a measles epidemic in this country. Everyone should have the

MMR and the vaccine is safe. But even if a small percentage were to have a problem in consequence, that would be a small price to pay for the majority being all right."

"I don't look at it from the National Health's point of view," the gardener said, "but from a parent's point of view. We don't want our children to be autistic – "

"But there's no evidence that there is any connection between the MMR and autism," Penny said. "That was the finding after Wakeham was investigated, and he was struck off."

I pointed out that the Prime Minister had wanted all to have the MMR but was reported as not allowing *his* children to have it. They were reported to have had one or more of the single vaccines separately.

"That's the fear Wakeham caused," Penny said. "There's no proof, no evidence, of any connection between the two."

"But there is," Gully the gardener said, very agitated, "I've got a neighbour who had a little girl. She had the MMR and *the very next day* she developed bowel and autistic symptoms. She was eighteen months when she had it, and she is now five and severely autistic."

"She could have gone like that anyway, not because of the MMR."

"I saw it with my own eyes. The day after the MMR the symptoms developed," the gardener said heatedly. "Wakeham had doubts and was regarded as a whistleblower and struck off. That always happens to those who challenge the system."

"Like Ray Honeyford, who challenged multi-ethnic education," I said. "And like a lady who whistleblew on her school at a Conservative conference three years ago, and lost her job."

"There's no connection," Penny insisted. "And Wakeham accepted money. Money was a factor."

We ended our coffee break and back on screen I Googled Wakeham and found that twelve parents of autistic children had approached him. Thirteen researchers had co-authored the paper. Wakeham was prosecuted. He ran out of money defending himself and was given £55,000 by the Legal Services Commission. Lawyers brought a case against MMR and paid him another £400,000. They lost their case, and he was struck off and vilified, and the MMR remained optional: parents could choose whether to vaccinate their children or not. Penny the PA was not wrong in highlighting the lack of evidence for MMR-caused autism.

Gully the gardener caught me an hour later as he was wheeling his wheelbarrow away from a flower-bed. "I'm sorry I was a bit strong over coffee," he said. "When I spoke of my neighbour's little girl, it wasn't my neighbour's girl. It was my own granddaughter, three years ago. My son-in-law took her to the doctor about another matter, and the doctor looked on screen and said, 'Oh, she's due an inoculation,' and gave her the MMR there and then. When my daughter found out she was beside herself. 'I didn't give my consent,' she said to her husband. 'You shouldn't have let them do it.' She'd seen the consequences in her brother. And now history's repeated itself. Her daughter's had the same bowel problem and she can't speak. She's severely autistic. *The day after* her MMR jab," the gardener repeated.

I knew that the first of the two MMR injections was normally given within a month of a child's first birthday, when a child is too young to speak and cannot be assessed for autism. I thought that if his granddaughter was inoculated at 18 months it was still early to diagnose autism. I knew that the MMR vaccine had been investigated in a number of studies around the world involving millions of children, and that researchers had found no evidence of a link between MMR and autism. I knew that in 2009 the National Autism Society released a statement saying that there was no link between MMR and autism.

"It's an issue between them," Gully continued. "My daughter blames him for causing my granddaughter's autism. It's happened twice in my family. Sorry to have got worked up, but it's a sore point."

Gully the gardener plodded off to resume his gardening. I felt sorry for him. In his own mind he had seen his son and granddaughter become autistic, and regardless of whether the MMR jab was the cause, which officialdom would dispute, he had suffered two calamities within his family and would have to cope with their after-effects for every remaining day of his life.

Missionaries like Zealous Carol Singers

We parked our car in the road and walked up the garden path. The front door opened and Raymond and Florence, their two children and spouses and five grandchildren sang like carol singers: "We wish you a merry Christmas." It was a magical moment.

We greeted each in turn and sipped champagne in the sitting-room. I spoke to Archie about his intending departure to be a missionary in Kosovo. He said it was all agreed. "We'll spend four months in Ferizaj, and then go to Shtime to set up a church."

We went through for lunch. Grace was sung. I helped myself to pasta and diced beef, carrots and red cabbage in the kitchen. Florence sat next to me. She said, "I've rung the top man in Pioneers, the charity that's sending Archie. I had thirty questions written down and I asked them all. I spoke to him for an hour. He had done what Archie's going to be doing elsewhere, and he told me that his three children had all done well academically in spite of coming through local schools. Two are now at university, the other one is still at school."

We sat on for coffee, and Archie came and sat next to me with his iPad. He said, "I've got some pictures of life in Kosovo." He showed me the house he would live in in Ferizaj. "We'll be replacing the previous missionary there who is returning to America." He showed me a picture of the American couple in the two-storey house he would be taking over.

He said, "We have to find somewhere to live in Shtime by September. We can't go there too often as we will be seen and people will ask what we're doing. We'll look to rent through personal recommendation. There's another American couple in Ferizaj, and I'm hoping they'll find us somewhere through a contact. After that we might buy, on a mortgage. Renting suggests we're not permanent, we need to send out a message that we're going to be there for ten years. On the other hand, if we are buying we may be sending out a message that we're never going to leave. We'll leave when we've set up the church. I've given in my notice to Rolls-Royce," he said. "I've been doing research on advancing the technology – alloys and coatings – and in ten years' time I'll have fallen so far behind I'll be out of it. So I want to train to be a teacher and do a PGCE when I come back."

He showed pictures of Shtime: one street with houses both sides, surrounded by green fields and distant mountains. He showed the curved wall of the war memorial with more than forty head-and-shoulder busts of local citizens. "That's the plaque," he said. "It says that 'the Beasts' came down from the hills and massacred Muslims in 1999. 'The Beasts' were Serbs."

"The good news," I said, "is that 'the Beasts' will be pro-Christian. They're Christians themselves and anti-Muslim, they'll be on your side."

"I don't think of them as Christians," Archie said. "Not after the dreadful things they did."

"They're like the Ku Klux Klan," I said. "They both venerate the cross. But it's the extremist Muslims who won't be on your side. The 'soldiers of Allah'. Watch out for Muslim fanatics."

"There may not be any," he said. His eyes were evasive.

"It may be like Croatia," I said. "Daytime television programmes show British couples buying houses on the Dalmatian coast near Dubrovnik, and the villages are safe. No one attacks them. But if you're told that some Albanian Muslims in Kosovo are 'soldiers of Allah', steer clear and keep the children out of their way."

Both his children were sitting at the table: a boy of about four and a round-faced young baby who was ten months.

"They'll be in the local school in that one street," Archie said. "They'll learn Albanian, and we'll supplement their education online. Home education from portals. We'll learn Albanian while they're at the local school and reinforce their education in the afternoons."

I looked at the ten-month-old boy. He did not know that he would be learning Albanian the following year. He would have no choice in the matter.

"Children are resilient," Archie said, watching my eyes. "They adapt and they'll be fine. They'll learn Albanian and English, and we'll keep them up to the English standards."

"What will *you* do?" I asked Archie's wife, Harriet, a mousy girl who had sat apart from us at the other end of the table. She had trained to be a doctor. "Will you practise medicine?"

"No. I'll be a mummy," she said. "I may give advice to the community, but not at the beginning. I'll be a mummy."

She fell silent.

"We'll bring Albanian Muslims to Christ," Archie said, "and reconcile Albanian Muslims and Serbs. That's why we're going out there."

The children left the dining-table and sat round a model of a wheel-less steam engine that was fixed to a wooden board in the kitchen. A pipe led to a wheel. Archie joined them and lit a solid-fuel fire in the boiler so steam came out of the funnel as smoke and the wheel turned. He demonstrated the whistle by pulling on a wire and producing a jet of steam. The children were spellbound. "Do it again," they said. I watched Archie, the Rolls-Royce engineer and future teacher, fascinated by his quiet authority.

I thought how dangerous it was to go into any Muslim country these days and turn Muslims against their own religion. I thought of Archie's zeal. I thought of the Pilgrim Fathers who had been persecuted in Holland and had chosen to start a new life in religious communities in the New World. They had not gone out to be missionaries, so Archie was not strictly a Pilgrim Father, but his zeal was similar to theirs. He was by and large on his own. He would have help from one American family in Ferizaj and otherwise only from Albanians, and he had to set up a church. After ten years he would leave it to flourish and would bring his two Albanian-speaking boys back to England, aged fourteen and ten. He was risking his life and sacrificing his own engineering career and ten years of his boys' stability in England to bring Muslims to Christ. He and his wife would be missionaries like zealous carol singers.

I looked hard at his wife to try and discern what she really thought about it all. She lowered her eyes in enigmatic silence.

Caviare and a Rat

I walked across the top of Trafalgar Square in the February dark and waited outside the Sainsbury wing of the National Gallery. Groups of elderly graduates waited in a ragged line; it was like waiting for the bank to open. Sir James Eastham walked by, and I called, "James," and shook his hand. He looked shocked and said, "I'm going to get a pee," and strode off, stand-offish and unsociable for an ex-ambassador. He scuttled along the wall of the National Gallery like a hunted rat.

At last we were let in. I checked in my coat and bag, picked up a guest list and climbed the stairs to the toilets and then proceeded to the top stair, where Jeremy Boxham, the Provost, was waiting, thin and bespectacled. "Phil," he said, shaking my hand, "good to see you." I walked through half a dozen galleries filled with medieval and Renaissance Italian paintings to where the reception was being held, the Tercentenary, the 300th anniversary of my old college. I took a champagne flute and consulted my list. There were more than 200 present and only about five seemed to be from my year, graduates I had not really spoken with in my college days. A waitress offered *canapés*: rows of brown bread topped with segments of white grape. She offered morsels of tiny quadruple caviare sandwich. I picked one up but the bottom layer stuck to the dish. The rest disintegrated in my fingers and by the time I had scooped the morsel into my mouth my fingers were smeared in black caviare. I had stains between my fingers like woad. I took a dry, paper serviette and dabbed between my fingers and cleaned off as much as I could. There was nowhere to discard the serviette so I screwed it up and tucked it under a plate.

I saw Jeremy Boxham standing by himself, the host being ignored by his guests, and aware of his outstanding qualities I crossed and said I had seen his article on Ted Hughes in the *Times Literary Supplement*. He beamed at me.

I said Hughes had sent me some cards and asked if he would like to see them. "Yes," he said, "yes please." "I'll put copies in the post," I said, and realised I had created work for myself and felt as if I had sticky fingers.

I said, "I believe you knew Arthur Hobart, my old cricket captain."

He said animatedly, "Yes, he was my mentor."

I described how he and I had spent a day at Lord's and he had played for the Gentlemen of England.

He said, "He could bowl and pitch the ball again and again within a six-inch band. He was very accurate." He said he had a drink with him now and again, but had not seen him recently. Then he said, "Excuse me, I must circulate," and left.

I walked back a couple of galleries and bought the book on my college, funded out of subscriptions, that was being launched. When I returned a representative of the National Gallery was speaking at a microphone, enthusing about the paintings we could see. Then Jeremy Boxham spoke, about our college and the book, and saying he would like funding for two more buildings. We stood and listened. There was nowhere to sit and some of the older graduates were clearly tired.

After the speeches I put my empty champagne flute on one of the tall round tables. I saw Jeremy Boxham standing nearby with his wife and went across. He introduced me to her. I said I had seen a TV programme she had made and thought her stance had been courageous. She warmed to me. Then Jeremy Boxham said, "Excuse me, I want to introduce her to some people over there," and they left.

Sir James Eastham was standing near me, looking down on his fellow graduates, remote and apart, self-important and hubristic. I had nothing to say to him and did not want to speak to him. I had not sat down for a couple of hours, and I turned on my heel and walked through several galleries and headed for the stairs to retrieve my coat from the cloakroom.

I headed for Leicester Square station, held my Oyster card over the round scanner and stepped onto an escalator going downwards. I walked across a passage and down steps. A little brown vole scurried along the wall and stopped at the foot of the bottom step, near my shoes. No one had seen it, only I had noticed it. Then I realised, it was not a vole but a rat. I was shocked. But the tube was clattering in. I left it.

Sitting on my seat I reflected on the evening. Jeremy Boxham was like caviare, a delectable dish that was a treat but had got on my hands. In the toilet I had soaped away the last traces of the stain between my fingers. And Sir James Eastham had scuttled along the wall of the National Gallery like a rat and stopped at the steps that led up to the toilets accessible from outside. Sipping champagne I had been smeared with the delectable delicacy of caviare, and had recoiled at the scurrying self-importance of a town rat.

Like Four Spikes after a Storm

Harry was standing looking out to sea in his beanie hat that late February morning.

"All right?" he asked.

I said, "You've put on weight."

"Yes, I'm half a stone more than I was before it all started. It's the steroids." He pointed to the cliff. "See, more's fallen," he said. "Sea's eating into the cliff, just there. It was so high during the storm. I was down here, waves were higher than your house. And they flung stones at it, small rocks. It's taken out part of the beach." There was a lagoon now. The sand and shingle had been flung up round our house, revealing a buried wall of rocks. "That barrier's been there a long while but the beach was on top of it. And look, it's left those four spikes. When the tide's in children can jump off the breakwater that's still standing and gash their feet on those spikes." Four iron spikes pointed upwards where a concrete breakwater had been. It lay on its side, having been flung down by the power of the stormy waves.

Harry and Claire came in and sat at our table. I made coffee. There was still talk of the storm, how a rock had just missed our window. I asked how Harry had been.

"He's well, but he's grumpy under the steroids," Claire said. "This morning when I woke up he said, 'You've been snoring so loud you've woken yourself up.' He said that," she said indignantly. "Then he said, 'I've been thinking, Bulgarians and Romanians are getting benefits a few days after they've arrived. I've paid taxes all my working life, I want to know what I'm entitled to.' If we didn't own our house and I didn't work, we'd be entitled to more. I enquired, and was told, 'You're entitled to £50 a week as a carer, do you work and earn more than £5,000?' I said, 'Yes, I do.' 'In that case we can't give you anything.' I was too truthful."

"It's the principle that's wrong," Harry said. "I've worked and we've paid our taxes and now we need it. But people who haven't been here and are renting are getting it, even though they haven't contributed. It's not fair. I'm putting everything into Claire's name. I'm transferring everything to her. The SSP has stopped after twenty-six weeks, and there's some disability allowance I'm entitled to, and I'm going to get the maximum I can as I'll have nothing to my name."

"I visit a relative who's ninety-one," Claire said. "He whispered to me, 'If anything happens to us, don't throw the socks out.' He's told them he's got nothing, he's been keeping it in his sock drawer." Everyone laughed.

I could see they were both worried about making ends meet in the coming months.

"I'm still working," Claire said. "It's like Wonga. Harry says it's rubbish. Provident lends £500 and the interest *is* high. You have to pay back £800 over a year, as a small amount each week; and if one week you can't afford it, you pay, say, £5 and the time is extended. That's what I do. It's good to work because I meet people."

"It's still like Wonga," Harry said under his breath.

"Harry goes to bed at 7," Claire said. "He sleeps until about 3, then he takes sleeping-pills and he's sleepy the next morning. I say he should stay up till 10, then take a sleeping-pill, but he won't listen. I like to play cards. I take him to euchre (a card game) once a week. It's £2 to be in, and £1 for the raffle. It's a cheap evening from 7 until 9.30, and we have a good time. And I take him to Don Cushing's. I know you know him, Harry's former boss. You know, he had nothing as a boy, and he used to eat his crib, his mid-morning lunch, in a shed during his working years, and so now, at his farm, he's got a shed with a wood-burner in it so he can go out and have his crib as he's always done. He's got a modern kitchen but he has his crib in his shed. He offers us apples, and I'm forever stewing apples. Harry plays solitaire on the Kindle for hours. He doesn't read – "

"I do it to pass the time," Harry said. "I need to pass the time."

And I realised how bored he was. He was terminally ill and waiting to die, and in his condemned cell he was bored.

"We went horse-racing in Taunton," Claire went on. "It was £15 each to go in. Harry won £20, then £40, then £60. I never normally bet, and I had a flutter on one race. My horse was the only one the jockey fell off. There were four of us, and we were all down at the end. Harry was down £40, his friend was down £120. We got home and I opened the post and I said, 'I've done better than all of you.' I'd won £50 on a premium bond."

I walked with Harry to the wall to look down at the cliff. He was overweight, losing his memory from steroids, waking in the middle of the night and worrying about money as he waited to die. He was bored and was looking for ways to pass the time, and it had all made him grumpy. He was like a sea defence that had been battered by a storm, and four spikes protruded now where there had once been a seemingly invincible concrete breakwater as he complained about immigrants, his memory, his wife's snoring and his boredom. He was supposed to relish every moment of the short time left to him, but he was consumed by the injustice of his lot, by worry and by a desperate need to find ways of passing his remaining time.

A Berber in Civilization

I arrived early for my hearing appointment in Wigmore Street and sat in the glassy waiting-room. I heard the receptionist tell another client that Bill, who I was to see, had found work nearer his home in Brighton. Then I was approached by a young student-like girl with long dark hair and spectacles, who said she could see me now. She confirmed that she had replaced Bill as we walked to her room. She introduced herself as "Nessima". "I'm from Canada," she said. "I haven't been in England before." I wondered if she was 'Miss Ema' but she said, "No, Nessima."

I was having my annual hearing test. She asked me to remove my hearing-aids. Then she knocked a tuning-fork on her elbow and put it to the bones before and behind my ears, and asked me which of the two sounds was louder. She then sat me facing a wall, put headphones over my ears and a button on a cable in my hands, and each time I heard a sound in first my right, then my left ear I had to press the button. The sounds began in high frequency and became fainter and fainter, and then began in a lower key and again became fainter and fainter. Then she did another bone test. She put new headphones with steel ends behind one ear and before another, and again I had to press the button when I heard the sounds.

At the end she showed me my results on screen alongside last year's results. My hearing had got a bit worse during the previous year, and my right ear was better than my left. She said, "The tests show your hearing loss is in your cochlea. Normal is zero. Your top is –20. You go down to –70. Minus 90 is severe loss of hearing, where people have to shout for you to understand. 110 is 'speech deaf'."

I said, "My hearing-aids enable me to hear and cope with all situations, including being on the radio. I was asked to talk about Gaddafi, and I was always able to hear the questions."

Her eyes lit up.

"Gaddafi?" she said.

I explained I had been an eyewitness of his revolution.

"What was he like?"

"He was a Berber," I said. "He has to be understood as a Berber. Berbers are different from Arabs. They have a desert culture. In fact, I think he was half-Corsican. A Corsican pilot, a war hero, Albert Preziosi, was shot down over Libya during the Second World War and was sheltered by Gaddafi's mother in her Berber tent. The French air force base near the town of Solenzara on Corsica was named after him: 'Capitaine Preziosi'. I think Gaddafi's mother bore his child out in the primitive conditions of the desert. Gaddafi was a Berber who found his way back into civilization."

Suddenly she went very quiet.

"Oh," she said. "I'm Algerian. My parents left Algeria and went to Canada and had me. I'm interested in Libya. It's also in North Africa."

"Where do you come from?" I asked, surprised. "Near Algiers? Oran?"

"Near Algiers," she said. "About forty kilometres from Algiers. In the desert. My parents were… Berbers. I'm a Berber."

She was not a Canadian at all, but the daughter of Berber immigrants into Canada.

"Oh," I said, not knowing where to look. I had described Gaddafi's Berber mother as living in primitive desert conditions, I had inadvertently suggested that she was primitive. To me, the Berbers' lifestyle was similar to the lifestyle of the Bedouins. They were nomads living in tents in the desert. I said, "Nessima's a Berber name?"

"Yes."

"The Berbers are a very historical people. The first Muslims into Spain."

"Yes."

"They have their distinctive culture."

"Yes. I'm Algerian. That's very interesting what you told me about Libya. I shall look forward to our next meeting in six months' time. Here is my card." She had written 'Necima'. "It's spelt in the French way."

As I walked back to Oxford Circus station I reflected on globalisation. I had gone to a highly-qualified expert in hearing from Canada to have my frequencies mapped with the most modern technology, and had found her parents were from a primitive desert tribe like the Berbers I had seen in Libya. Technology had taken her parents out of the desert and had placed her at the back of London's Oxford Street. She had used a tuning-fork and a computer, but underneath she was a desert dweller who was contributing to the functioning of Western civilization. Thanks to globalisation she was a Berber in civilization.

A Turk and *Shariah*

At the station I took a taxi. The driver had a bald, swarthy head and a brown face and he spoke with a foreign accent. Sitting in the front seat I asked if business had been brisk – "Not too bad" – and I looked at his lapel ID card and said, "You're Zeynell."

"Yes, Zeynell."

"Where are you from?"

"I am from Turkey. Near Marmaris, Kusadasi."

I asked if he went back there often.

"Yes. I want to keep in touch there, but my wife and three boys prefer it over here. They want to stay here."

"Do you think Turkey will join the European Union?" I asked.

"I can't see it happening. The Turkish legal system is too different. If a girl sees a boy without her family's consent, the boy will be hunted down and killed. I have seen that happen so often in Turkey. The police investigate but there's never a conviction. *Shariah* law. There are so many families who have killed that I can't see Turkey being within the European Union. I am glad my three boys are over here. I wouldn't want them to be victims of honour killings under *Shariah* law. Yes, my wife prefers living here and I can understand why. So I am licensed to the local Council and drive this car."

A week later I took a taxi to the station.

"We're having meters from 1 June," the English driver told me. "The Council's decided. There's been overcharging. It's the Turks. One girl had to pay £80 for a local run from a nightclub. Another was charged £150. She paid but her father went to the police and they investigated all the drivers. My company's all right, we're computerised, they could see it wasn't us. They pinned it on the Turks. They're giving the Council a bad name. People come out from London and take a taxi and are overcharged. I don't like it. I've got to buy the meter, £200 plus £100 fitting unless I can get a second-hand one for £100 including fitting. This will take time to recoup. And the meter will tick especially in traffic, and old ladies going to shops will find they're paying more. It's the Turks who've done this. Look," he said as we came into the station, "three cars waiting. One driven by English, two by Turks."

I knew *Shariah* law allowed honour killings, and I wondered whether it allowed overcharging. Or perhaps the culprit felt that *Shariah* law did not apply to infidels?

A Trolley and Stress

I turned the corner with my half-filled trolley in Morrisons and saw Meg Dawson talking to a young woman. She saw me and excused herself and said, "I'm stressed. Jim's in Forest Place and only his heart's keeping him going. He's on his back all day, muttering and sometimes sobbing. He doesn't recognise me when I go. I've had to go in the middle of the night a few times when they thought he was about to die, and last week when he fell out of bed and cut his head. It's cruel and inhuman, keeping him alive like that. You wouldn't inflict it on an animal. It makes you want to join Exit. Fifty Old Boys went at the beginning, but they've all fallen away. They want to remember him as he was, not as he is now. Martin Store's the only one who still goes and he's at the end of his tether. Jim doesn't talk and doesn't know who he is. He was having violent hallucinations. He thought people were coming in to kill us, he kept getting out of bed to fight these intruders. I couldn't cope with it. You know, his dementia began that lunch that was held for him, for sixty years' association with the School. He couldn't remember his speech, and I knew something had happened then. He's gone downhill since then, to this. It's costing me money, it's taken nearly all my savings. There's been no help. There's another meeting with the Social Services on Monday, but they don't listen. I don't know what to do. I get no help. The School chaplain's been visiting me. Jim was expected to die at Christmas, and the chaplain came to counsel me. But he's still alive because of his heart. I'm really stressed about it all. The house is in both our names, thank goodness. But I won't have much to live off when this is all over. The nurses are doing their best but it's cruel and inhumane, and the system doesn't help. He's done nothing to deserve it, he's looked after himself and was still going to the gym every day at eighty-four. It's all so unfair."

Meg was leaning on her shopping trolley among the stacked shelves in Morrisons, and she was engulfed in her own tortuous situation. Jim had been a well-known footballer in his prime, and now he was an ordinary person who was taking a long time to die of dementia and cancer. And her life was like a half-filled trolley.

A Grab-Rail and Birdsong

We booked in at Le Manoir and were taken to our room, Passion-Flower. It was on the ground floor with a door leading out to a small walled garden with arched apple blossom and a pool. Pippa, clicking on her crutch, immediately identified that a grab-rail had not been fixed in the bathroom and a fellow arrived with two grab-rails. He slammed them on the wall to activate two suctions and pressed a lever to hold each in place.

We left and had tea by the lawn round a tall cedar. I was in an open-necked shirt in the April sunshine. We were served scones, butter, jam and cream. I had black Tregothnan tea, Pippa had a tea from Tibet. I listened to birdsong. All the time there were deafening caws of rooks, and a buzzard hovered on the wind. Later we walked round the grounds. We passed the vegetable garden and looked at the 17th-century stew pond, and walked round the Japanese garden. Pippa leaned on my arm with one hand when the path became uneven for her crutch.

We returned to Passion-Flower. In the bathroom there was broken china. A grab-rail had fallen off the wall onto a soap dish on the corner of the bath, which had crashed onto the floor. We called one of the staff, who came and Hoovered the floor. She said, "He put it up wrong. He put it on the crack between tiles. The suction doesn't last when it's over a crack."

I had a bubble bath, dried my limbs and soaked them in body lotion mixed with olive oil. I changed into a shirt and tie, put on a blazer and we walked to the Belle Epoque for our dinner with Sir Geoff Hurst. We were the last to arrive. Twenty sipped champagne in four groups inside the door. I found myself next to Hurst, who was seventy-three with less hair than when I last saw him, and reminded him we had met nearly thirty years back. I asked, "Is it true that you were trying to hit the ball over the bar in 1966 to waste some time, and it went in?"

He said, "Yes, completely true."

I asked, "Can you remember that moment now or has it happened to someone else?"

He thought and his eyes went dreamy. He said, "I can remember it now."

I said, "You told me in 1985 that your record was safe to the end of the twentieth century as England would not be in a final by then, let alone anyone score a hat trick in a final."

He said his record was still safe. "We haven't got the young players coming through, and the heat and humidity of Brazil will be against us. South American teams do best in those conditions."

Then he excused himself and went to talk to another group. A lady from the agency that had booked him explained that he went round everyone at the beginning to find out who the audience were, and then tailored his words to his audience.

Everyone was eager to talk to him, to grab him. He was like a grab-rail that everyone wanted to grab. Eventually we went in to dinner. Our names were on place cards and we were sitting on the opposite side of the table, and down, from him. After our crab salad and risotto Hurst spoke to us all, telling us stories about the 1966 team, notably Greaves whose injury led to Hurst's inclusion. Greaves was asked what Sir Alf Ramsey, the manager, had said at half-time in one game, and he replied, "He told me, 'Put that fag out.'" Another occasion the world cup, the trophy, was produced and everyone had to wear white gloves to handle it except for World Cup winners. Greaves said, "Cor, if it's nicked it'll have our fingerprints on it."

Hurst said someone had not recognised him and had asked him publicly where he was during the 1966 match. Someone else said, "You're being stupid." He said, "Cor, you must be Martin Peters."

He was singing stories like birdsong while we ate our Angus steak and citrus pudding. He said he was in a taxi going to Heathrow, and the driver kept looking at him. In the end the driver turned round and said, "Give us a clue." Hurst said, "I played in the 1966 World Cup final and scored a hat trick. I played 674 games and scored 299 goals. I played 49 games for England and scored 24 goals. I am Sir Geoff Hurst."

The taxi-driver said, uninterested, "No, I meant 'Give us a clue as to what terminal you want.'"

There was a question-and-answer session. I asked whether the 1966 victory could be attributed to the players, the manager, the spirit or something else, and what lessons could be drawn from it today. He talked for twenty minutes, praising Sir Alf Ramsey's management. He said, "We could play in the present team's games, but I don't think they could play in our version, the tackling was often brutal."

I asked, "Did you have any constraints placed on you in 1966? Van Persie has been confined to playing in a box, and he doesn't want to be in a box. Were you told you could only play on a certain part of the field in 1966?"

He replied, "No."

I said Ramsey had said on TV, "I think England are going to win the World Cup," and asked, "Did he make you believe you were going to win?"

He said Ramsey had been criticised for saying that and the players had taken one match at a time. His reply was evasive on whether they believed they would win.

I said publicly, "You told me in 1985 that your record was safe." To share what he had said earlier, I asked him, "Do you still think it's safe?"

He said that England would not win.

I asked if he would take over from Hodgson to put things right. He said he had no ambition to be England's manager now.

Pippa asked whether the celebrity status of present footballers got in the way of the camaraderie he had found. He said, "It does." She asked if any of his footballing genes had passed on to his grandchildren. He said, "Possibly one of them."

She said his youngest daughter (whom she had taught) did not know what he had done and wasn't interested in football. He agreed and said she had married a man who did not like football.

He sang on like a blackbird piping in the evening, as one after another the diners grabbed his attention like a grab-rail. We were all given signed pictures of him scoring his last goal, and he posed for photos with each of us. Then people turned back to their own conversation and he was left standing, discarded. He said he was used to speaking to a thousand but he preferred the intimacy of twenty and the evening for him had not been a chore. An ageing man said, "To quote someone, 'You think it's all over, it is now.' He's going."

He left to applause and I saw him standing in the foyer outside our room like a grab-rail that had fallen onto the floor.

A Silence and a Bulging Stomach

We arrived in Porthleven around noon on the May Bank Holiday at Aunt Maud's house. We were welcomed by Maud, who was eighty-eight, and her granddaughter Josie. While Maud made coffee Josie whispered that her father and mother would meet us after lunch in a sea-front café so that we could talk without being overheard by Maud. Maud could not be told about Richard's condition until the results of the biopsy and tests were known during the coming week.

I helped carry the coffee from the kitchen and we chatted to Maud and Josie about anything other than Richard. On that subject there was a uniform silence. Then we returned to the car and Pippa drove to the Housel Bay Hotel. We sat in the clifftop window looking down at the Lizard promontory and wheeling stormy petrels, and over fish and chips Pippa showed Maud and her niece photos on her phone: of her hospital room, her new Cornish bathroom and our grandchildren. We avoided all mention of Maud's son, Richard. We heard how Josie worked in the same open-plan room as her mother, doing a payroll of five hundred, and how her brother was dissecting bodies on his anatomy course. We finished lunch with ice-creams and sorbets.

We drove back to Porthleven and, guided by Josie, parked in the harbour and entered the Nauti café. We occupied the seats near the window nearest to the door. I bought teas and coffees.

Richard and Sue joined us. I shook hands with Richard. He did not look unwell but he had lost weight. I said it seemed only last year that as 'skipper' he had taken me out fishing on his boat. I bought their tea and cappuccino and sat in the seat next to Richard. Against the background hubbub and some distance from Maud, who was sitting opposite Richard, I said so that his mother could not hear: "I'm really sorry about your diagnosis."

He grimaced and said, "I told the doctor eight weeks ago there was something wrong. He said, 'It's indigestion.' I said, 'It's not indigestion, and my family's got a history of cancer – my father had it.' The NHS is chaotic. I've had eight letters, I don't know who from, and I'm getting no support. I had to call the doctor out last night as I was in such pain. No one will tell me how many morphine tablets I can take, whether I can up my dose from two in the morning and two in the afternoon. I've just been told it's inoperable. I've been given some tablets and left to get on with the pain. I'm not sleeping. I can't get comfortable. I get into a cold sweat, as if someone had slooshed a bottle of water over me. I stay awake all night watching television. Walking's all right. I sometimes walk to the end of the harbour in the middle of the night. I'm happy working. I'd be driven to distraction at home. But it's building work, and some of it's heavy. One of my fellow workers is a second cousin on my father's side. He helps me, they do the heavy work, leaving me the light jobs."

I said, "You need a designated person you can consult. If the NHS doesn't offer you this next week you should ring Macmillan Cancer Support and see if you can get a contact there before an official referral, which will take time."

We talked about the football season – his team, Manchester United, was out of the running for the title – and the work on the new bathroom we had done. He told me: "James asked me to invest in his new trawler, I was on the verge of doing it when this happened. I rang him last week and said, 'You know I've been unwell. I've got inoperable cancer of the stomach.' He was shattered and said, 'The offer stays open for twelve months, even in a year's time you can come in with me.' It's not going to happen. I'm unwell on dry land, I'll be a thousand times more unwell out trawling on the sea."

He was uncomfortable and I suggested he moved to a higher, straight-backed chair Sue was sitting on. He stood and as he passed me to swap places I saw his bulging stomach from hip to hip, suggesting a massive growth the size of two cauliflowers side by side. Sue crossed to his lower-down chair the other side of me.

"Is that all right?" I asked.

"It's good," Richard said. "There's a sea breeze coming through the door." He was stiff-upper-lipped before his staring mother.

I said to Sue, "Are you very short of sleep?"

She said, "Yes. You can't fault the doctors and nurses, it's the system that's wrong. He should have been diagnosed in January, certainly two months ago."

We left. As we said our goodbyes (when Maud was not looking) I patted Richard's arm and murmured, "I hope the test results are the best you could wish for under the circumstances."

As she climbed into our car Maud was in tears, and I wondered how much she knew.

Back at the house Pippa, Maud and I sat down. Pippa went to the loo and I chatted to Maud about Pippa's recovery from her operation. Then I went to the loo. When I returned Maud was in tears.

"I've been very worried," Maud was saying. "Did you see how big his stomach is? He has to undo his belt to sit down. At first I thought it was a hernia, but now I wonder if it's an ulcer." But something can be done about hernias and ulcers, and her tears had told me she was waiting for words to be said beyond hernias and ulcers, and for details of what was to be done.

We talked of other things and got off the subject of Richard.

We left in light rain. She stood in her front door for a long while waving to us. The coming week she would learn that her only son had been diagnosed as having inoperable stomach cancer, and as she was eighty-eight the shock might kill her. Her family had been very caring in concealing the truth from her, telling her about the tests but not the diagnosis in the hope that the biopsy would confirm that his type of cancer could be treated with chemotherapy, if only to prolong his life for a while, which would give her some hope.

In the coming days the concealment – the silence – would have to come to an end and she would have to adjust to the stark truth about the bulging stomach, that he had stomach cancer like her husband who died of it forty-one years previously – which her tears had indicated she already secretly suspected, and knew.

Fits and a Bath

Claire knocked on our door and handed a bouquet of lilies and roses to Pippa.

"How are you?" Pippa asked quietly, concerned.

"Good days and bad days," Claire said, tears welling in her eyes.

We led her through to the table in the back room and as I made coffee and eventually joined them she poured out the details of her bereavement.

"I bought a mobility bed. They said they couldn't deliver it for a week. Harry said to the man, 'That's no good, I'm dying.' The manager made a phone call and came back and said, 'We're making an extra delivery this evening and you'll have the bed first thing tomorrow morning.' It came and Harry lay in it and said it was comfortable, then asked how much it was. When I told him he said, 'Take it back.' He had it for three weeks. In the end he said, 'It's been a good bed.'"

Pippa said, "So you were right to buy it."

"Towards the end he got nasty. He was saying on Friday, 'I've had enough, I want to go.' I said, 'Don't say that to people, they don't want to hear that.' On the Friday afternoon he went across the road and said to one of our neighbours, 'Had enough, want to go.' And later that night and the next morning he said it again. He wasn't feeling well on Saturday morning. He was really nasty, threw his tablets on the floor. I said, 'Right, you're behaving like a child, you don't have them.' Eventually I made him take another morphine tablet. He took two more painkillers and I told him off for taking too many. But at lunchtime he said he felt better.

"Our daughter Kay was taking her four boys to Pentewan in her car and asked if he wanted to come too. He said, 'Yes', and we had a lovely afternoon. Outside Kentucky Fried Chicken he said he felt sick and wanted to go home. I said to Kay, 'You drive him home as it's your car, I'll feed the boys.' He was talking normally in the car. When they got to our drive his head slumped and he had what they call his first 'seizure'. Kay put him in the recovery position and called an ambulance and let me know. I arrived when they were putting him in the ambulance. They said, 'It's got to be blue light.'

"I rode with him. I was telling him where we were, the landmarks we were passing. Then he had another fit. The ambulanceman said, 'I'm going to resuscitate him.' I said, 'There's a "Don't resuscitate" on him.' He asked, 'Have you got the paperwork?' 'No.' 'In that case I have to resuscitate him.' He got the driver to park on a grass verge and join him, and together they worked on Harry and he came round.

"I stayed with him in the hospital. He had another fit in the night. Next morning he began tearing off his mask and his drip and his bandage, and began swearing at the nurses, 'F— off.' That's not him, he would never swear before ladies. It was the pressure on his brain. I was told he only had hours to live, and he was sent to the hospice.

"That night his children gathered at the hospice. His daughter by his first marriage, who had not seen him for thirty years, wanted to stay with him that night, but I said, 'No, that's our time,' and sent her away. I said, 'You can stay at ours,' but she wouldn't. I offered my sister's and two other places, but she booked in at The Pier House.

"That night I talked to him a lot. I stayed with him at the hospice. The next morning his children gathered, but not his daughter by his first marriage, Lara. Kay rang her but The Pier House was out of signal. I was holding his hand and I said, 'I'm just going to the loo.' I took two paces and looked back and our children were with him, holding his hand, and he went. He had waited until they were there to support me and chose his moment to go. And Lara came later. It was as though she wasn't meant to be there when he died.

"I went to work that day, and so did Kay and our son. If I don't work I don't get paid. I had a dreadful day. My phone wouldn't work, and a sim card wouldn't transfer. The first three people I visited didn't give me any money after I knocked on their doors. I sat in the car and on the radio came a song which I haven't heard played on the radio for twenty years, 'Island of Dreams' by the Springfields, Harry's song. He used to play it again and again. I felt he was with me, and then the day got better. My son changed my sim card and people began giving me money when I knocked on their doors.

"I've had a hundred and twenty cards and eight bouquets, even though I don't like them. I had a card from his shooting friends. It was a picture of pheasants pointing guns at naked men. There's a time of the year when you're only allowed to shoot cock pheasants, not hens, and underneath they are saying, 'Only shoot at cocks.' She laughed. 'Two hundred have said they'll attend the funeral though the crematorium in Truro only has seating for one hundred. There'll be a loudspeaker with chairs outside. But it may not take place on May 16. He's had a post-mortem and they've taken eight tissue samples and if they are found to contain asbestos dust the coroner may call an inquest which could delay the release of the body for six-to-eight months. There's a government pot to compensate the families of those who have died from asbestosis, but I don't want to put him through that. I'd rather not have some of the pot. I'd rather sign a disclaimer and have the funeral on May 16.

"I speak to him all the time. Last thing at night I tell him what's happened during the day and pat his side of the bed and say, 'Love you.' We always talked about his illness. I went through his life with him and wrote it all down and gave it to the vicar for the funeral. I used to say, 'Come back and visit me if you can.' We used to sit in the glass conservatory and watch the birds. Do you know, we haven't had a magpie for years, but every day since he died a magpie, in the same colours as the football team he supported, black and white, has come and walked along the back and stopped and looked at me, and I wonder if it's him. The grandchildren are all right, but Jim's taken it hard. Harry delivered him in the bath."

"Delivered him in the bath?" I interjected.

"Yes. Kay was staying with us and she ran a bath and later let the water out and then called, 'Can you come up? I think the baby's coming.' So I checked and it was. I shouted to Harry, 'Ring for an ambulance.' He said, 'What number?' I said, '999.' He said, 'That's for emergencies.' I said, 'What do you think this is?' So he rang and the baby started coming. I shouted, 'Come here.' He said, 'I'm on the phone.' I said, 'Get off the phone, you've given them our name and address. I'll hold her at the top and you deliver the baby.' And he did. Kay was lying down in the bath and the blood was contained within it and the ambulancemen took over after the delivery. Jim and he always had a special bond after that. When he played football with Jim he said, 'I'm quick, I'm the Cat.'"

"And he was like a cat," I said, "a cat burglar, climbing nimbly on to roofs, running fearlessly across tiles to where he needed to be."

She said, "He had no time for Health and Safety regulations' insistence on scaffolding. Yes, Jim's taken it hard. I insisted on having a new bath after the delivery.

"I'm putting all his cards in a box, and one day when I'm through all this I shall go through the box and read everything. So many remember him. The vicar looks like a New-Age traveller. She's from the Methodist church where we got married, and she said, 'I'm not going to charge you for the funeral.' I said, 'You must.' She said, 'No, I buried his father and mother, look at it this way, in a supermarket you can "buy two and get one free".' That's one of the things I've told him. He likes to know everything that's going on, and tonight I shall tell him I came to you. But he may be here, sitting with us. I wouldn't be surprised if he is."

The eight tissue samples taken during the post-mortem on Harry established that he had asbestos in his lungs. The coroner released his body for his funeral, and called an inquest to investigate. Between four hundred and five hundred people attended the funeral service in Truro's crematorium, although there was only seating for a hundred.

A Swimmer and a Medal

I parked for the prize day and approached the school with Pippa. Angela Netherby came slowly through the gate. I was shocked. She was stooping over a stick and her face was wrinkled and one eyelid had dropped. I had not seen her for a few months and she had suddenly got old.

Simon took us to the Head's room and I shook hands with Martin Fountain, a former swimmer who had won forty-seven medals over twenty-three years. He was much taller than me. I said, "I hadn't realised you are so tall." I chatted to him. Then the pop star Rodney Pilkington's wife, who had invited him on our behalf, extended a hand. She was a model and also very tall. I thanked her for inviting Martin Fountain.

We all went through to the marquee. Angela Netherby sat herself down on the corner of an aisle, grimacing with pain, holding her stick. She sat near me, looking old and ill. Martin Fountain and Rodney Pilkington's wife were escorted by the Head to the platform. After initial speeches, recitations and music, Martin Fountain was called forward to speak. He stood up, 6 foot 7 inches, his head touching the roof of the marquee, and holding a microphone, talked directly to the children. He said, "I want to tell you what I did and how I always did my best."

He gave an account of his swimming and passed round bronze, silver and gold medals he had won so the children, sitting cross-legged, could handle them. He showed a video of a race he won and encouraged the children to cheer for him. He showed himself dancing on *Strictly Come Dancing*. He said, "I was a good swimmer but I was a bad dancer." He said, "I reached for the stars, an Olympic gold. I never won an Olympic medal. I had a bad arm in 2004. But I did my best. I didn't do too badly – I was world champion six times and European champion eleven times."

Then Rodney Pilkington's wife presented the prizes. The two of them posed smiling by each prizewinner against a white screen.

At the end I went up on stage and thanked them. I told Martin Fountain, "You could have been a teacher."

We chatted. He told me had been commentating for the Commonwealth Games. I asked him about his quest for an Olympic medal.

"Is it true you fell out with the National Team Manager?"

He said, "Yes. I was seventeen and he wanted me to turn up at 6.30am to practise but I said it was too early. He left me out of the team in 2004. I would have got a gold then, I'm sure of it."

I said, "So it was political, he left you out because he didn't get on with you."

"Yes. I was young and he had lived with his pastime for twenty years."

A crowd of autograph hunters – adults as well as children – gathered and I stepped back.

"How's Rod?" I asked Rodney Pilkington's wife.

"He's in Vienna."

"Give him my best wishes."

"I will."

I walked through to the Studio for drinks and *canapé*s. There was a step down, and after I'd stepped down into the Studio I turned and saw Angela Netherby trying to negotiate the step. I went to her and held out my arm, and she used it to step down. She tottered to a chair and sat, exhausted, looking terrible. I could see her death in her.

"How's your knee?" I asked.

"Fine. I'm going on one more year, then I'll stop."

She was seventy-six and she was doing her best like Martin Fountain and in her world she was reaching for the stars. But she might fall and she was an insurance liability, and her equivalent of the National Team Manager might leave her out. She could retire now at the height of her powers rather than go on until all were pleased she had gone. She was a swimmer who had sought a medal she would never win.

A Stiff Upper Lip

At the end the audience stood up and I found myself next to the Bursar. I asked him, "Are you coming to tomorrow's event?"

"No," he said, "I have to attend a funeral."

"Oh dear," I said, "I hope it's not anyone too close?"

"It's my brother," he said.

"Oh, how awful. What happened?"

"He fell over and hit his head. On the Isle of Wight, where he was living. That's all that's known. They've done a *post mortem* and the cause as to why he fell over won't be known for eight weeks. All we know is that he fell and hit his head."

"Dreadful," I said, "he must have had an event. He can't just have felt giddy."

"No, that's what we think."

"Younger brother?"

"Older, just turned sixty. Yes, my brother's died and I've got to go to the Isle of Wight to attend his funeral tomorrow. So I can't see you tomorrow evening, I'm afraid."

I was greeted by one of the audience and turned away from him, and when I turned back he had gone. He had withdrawn from the social *mêlée* and was already heading for the Isle of Wight and his private family grief.

Wounds like Carrots

We checked in at the Royal Victoria Hotel, Sidmouth, a birthday treat for Pippa, and had a cream tea overlooking the bay across the putting-green. A young man in his twenties was celebrating his putts with exuberantly loud noises of self-appreciation, and was quietly being restrained by his family. He was unaware of self-restraint in social situations. With the stone balcony of our room above Pippa's shoulder I said, "He's got some syndrome." She nodded and said, "It's not Aspergers because he interacts socially. It's one of the others." And we both viewed him with compassion as he boisterously ran to his grandfather, who was watching from a bench, and engaged him in loud, excited but inaudible conversation. He carried a wound round with him, and we felt for him.

Back in the foyer Pippa spotted a necklace. She said, "It's Amazonite." I bought it for her as a birthday present.

The next day after breakfast in the hotel the bay lay beneath our window under a blue sky. We sauntered slowly down to the Esplanade and wandered along the seafront. There was a long row of deck-chairs for £1 an hour. No one sat in them, but on the free wooden benches every seat was taken. We had regular rests as Pippa had a bad knee. We reached a narrow road with shops on either side and after coffee in a garden under a sun umbrella Pippa said, "You can go and look at the church. I want to explore those shops opposite."

I wandered up to St Giles and St Nicholas church, whose spire loomed above roofs. It had been rebuilt in the 19th century and incorporated bits of a 12th-century church, including, I read, a fragment of medieval glass now in the lady-chapel window. Intrigued I took a leaflet and wandered down and sat on a chair with a sloping wooden back and read, "The five-wounds window, c.1150."

When he was crucified Christ had five wounds: two in his hands, two in his feet and one in his side. A tradition had grown from *Isaiah* 12:3 that the wounds were wells. On the medieval glass the wounds were crowned and their wells resembled carrots. In medieval spelling, the stained glass labelled the wells as the well of wisdom, the well of mercy, the well of everlasting life, the well of grace and the well of ghostly comfort.

I reflected that between us Pippa and I shared all these. We were merciful to the disabled, and I recalled there were situations in which we might be deemed to have shown wisdom. I had found wisdom, grace, spiritual comfort and everlasting life in my experiences of illumination.

I left the church and encountered Pippa in the shopping street. She said, "My aunt just bought me a lovely bracelet." She showed me a bracelet with chunks of shiny grey stones. "It's agate," she said. "She said I could get something for my birthday if I saw something, and this will do fine."

We wandered back to the hotel and I thought how we had wells within us that were independent of the example of Christ, and the medieval symbolism now looked as relevant as a bunch of five carrots. But the five qualities they represented flowed into us, and now I saw the wounds and carrots on the stained glass as influxes of power from the beyond, gifts to the human spirit.

A Peregrine like a Chained Soul

We looked in at the Belmont Hotel. There was a large brown bird sitting on a hoop on the putting-green. It looked like a golden eagle. Seeing its owner standing near a van I approached him and asked what it was.

"It's a Harris hawk," he said. "I've been training him. He's a reliable bird. He'll fly up and take food I'm holding in my glove."

"What food?" I asked.

"Rats, mice, bits of chicken. I've got two freezers, one for me and one for the birds. I take the bird food out every morning. I can't go away, I have to be on hand to feed the birds. It's a full-time occupation."

A pied wagtail approached and wagged its tail impudently. The hawk looked down in disdain.

"It won't attack a small bird?" I asked.

"No, it's too small to be on its radar. And a wagtail can take quick evasive action. There's a peregrine on the back lawn. I only bought it yesterday."

"How much for?"

"Five hundred. The Harris hawk was three-fifty. The peregrine's a young bird and not properly trained. It's unreliable. It can go up to a thousand feet and not come back."

"'The falcon cannot hear the falconer'," I quoted from Yeats. "'Things fall apart....'"

"I swing a dead pigeon and let go in mid-swing and it catches it. Then when it's flying and sees a pigeon it will attack it and ignore the other birds because it's learned. I've taught it what to catch. It's taught to hunt by its mother, and I'm in the position of its mother."

I walked to the back lawn and saw the peregrine on a croquet hoop, grey with a speckled chest. It saw me approach and fluttered its wings to escape but was restrained by a chain round its legs. It settled back on the hoop with bad grace and glared at me menacingly above its hooked bill. Like a restrained soul it belonged to the upper reaches of the blue sky and hated being chained to a green lawn.

Paper Boats and Kettles

I went down to the Spa in my white dressing-gown and sat on a curved seat with an upright back. It was covered in mosaic tiles that were warm, and I relaxed into the heat. Then the door of the treatment room opened and I was led inside.

"I'm Janey," said the masseuse, who was small with bobbed hair and in a brown uniform. "There's been a mix-up over times and the treatment. The hotel reception desk has girls who don't really know. I don't do hot stones. I do a full-body massage for an hour and a half."

"That's fine," I said.

I lay face down on the treatment table, my nose through a circular hole at one end, and relaxed to the low music as she rubbed in sunflower oil.

"You're soaking it in," she said, "your skin's very dry."

As she rubbed oil into my back and then onto the backs of my legs, she talked.

"It's important to be in harmony with the forces of the universe," she said. There was a pause while she rubbed in the sunflower oil. "I've set myself goals. I've started doing festivals. I go to the tips and get kettles, saucepans, whatever I can find, and I refurbish them. I got a slot at the Glastonbury Festival. It's hard to get, and you pay a big fee. You hope you sell your stock and make a profit. I broke even. But it was a good thing to do as I can do it better next year and make a profit. And I spent the weekend working with my twin sister. There's been a problem, but working together smoothed that out. Glastonbury was worth doing. I'm doing our local festival later this month."

"Where's that?" I called through the hole in the treatment table.

"Ottery St Mary."

"That's where Coleridge was born," I said. "His father was the Vicar. Coleridge read his books and inspired Wordsworth, who got the Oneness of Nature from him. He would have been very interested in what you're doing."

"I'm related to Coleridge," she said. "Through my aunt's husband, I think. Coleridge's father was Vicar of St Mary's church. He had links with the school, and he had six children in the house opposite the church. It was pulled down in 1884. One of the children stayed on in Ottery and my aunt's husband was descended from him."

She rubbed the sunflower oil into my sole – and my soul – and then after I had turned over into my neck and hair, and I thought of Coleridge's countrified life, floating paper boats in the local stream by a road, and pondered her semi-gypsy life raiding tips for discarded pots and pans and kettles. In the 1780s Coleridge had made his own entertainment with his paper boats, and now his descendant was supporting her livelihood by searching for kettles. The two of them shared an Ottery St Mary largely unchanged, and I saw what it was like to be a descendant of Coleridge in her countrified provincial village.

PART TWO

In the Early Evening Sunshine

"One must wait until the evening to see how splendid the day has been."

Sophocles, *Oedipus at Colonus*

In the Early Evening Sunshine (Or: A Jigsaw and a Daughter Or: Inside Bits)

Harry came at the end of October as Len was leaving after fitting a new letter-box and draught-excluder round our Cornish front door. He wore a woolly hat and a long working jacket and called, "Oright?" He shook my hand, and, wincing, bounded up the stairs to look at walls that were no longer damp: the wall in the bedroom that adjoined the leaking chimney and the sloping ceiling in the bathroom, now both bone-dry.

After Len went the four of us had coffee in the breakfast-room at the back. I said, "It's good to see you here."

Claire said: "He had his third chemotherapy injection last Thursday week. He was all right until Tuesday, but then he felt ill and he's slept for the last two days. He could only have half a cracker and a small piece of cheese two days ago, and an omelette yesterday. He's lost a stone in a week, but today he's got his energy back."

I asked him how bad the chemotherapy had been. He said it was tolerable.

Claire said, "He has had three doses, two of 12,500ml and the last one of 10,000ml, and on 6 November he has a full-body scan and they'll review whether he should have any more. He's booked in for another chemotherapy session on 7 November, and he'll have to pinch his stomach skin and inject himself every evening for the rest of his life."

"It won't change anything," Harry said, "just delay it."

Claire said, "I've been pushy. After his second chemo I rang the girl the day after and she said the results wouldn't be known for a week. I said, 'But you've got the X-rays on screen, can you have a look and see what the difference is?' She said, 'I can see bits of cancer, still. I'll ask upstairs and ring you back if there's anything not right.' She rang back and said, 'He's got a blood clot in his right lung.' That wouldn't have been spotted if I hadn't been pushy. So I said, 'What about the other lung?' She came back and said, 'He's got a blood clot in the other lung too. We'll know on 6 November how he's doing on those.'"

Harry sat glumly in silence and said, "The consultant said I won't be here at Christmas."

"But that was before the chemo," Claire said. "And the other consultant said you may be here for Christmas."

Claire said: "I make things as normal as possible. The other day he was sitting at home and our son-in-law was loading stuff into a dumper from a JCB. He kept getting in and out. So I said, 'Go and work the JCB for him.' And he did. Better than sitting wallowing at home. And he felt better for it. Today he's been talking to Len and you, it's better than sitting at home."

"Doing my jigsaw," Harry said lugubriously. "I've done the outside frame, the inside bits are hard. Yes, doing the jigsaw while you're out at work."

"I've started a little job, eight hours a week," Claire said. "Harry's driven me to it." She gave a little laugh. "For seventeen years I worked for Provident in Padstow, visiting clients, and they asked me to help them out. I said I can't go to Padstow, but I could work from their St Austell office, and that's what's happened. I can do the eight hours when I like, four hours on a Friday evening if he's having a good day, or two hours in an afternoon. The money's very good for eight hours, and it gets me out and meeting people." I could see she was already making a new life for herself for when she was on her own.

Her mobile pinged.

"That might be my daughter," Harry said. "She's coming from Somerset. She might be at our house and wondering where we are."

"No," Claire said, checking her phone. "It comes up 'Lara' if it's her. Harry's daughter's by his first wife," she explained to Pippa. "She was the daughter of the family who own the scrap-metal giants in the West Country. Harry worked with them. He had to get married when she was eighteen. She went off with someone else when his daughter was about four. He had to sign something saying he had left the company with nothing. The man his wife was with was very controlling, and wouldn't allow Harry any contact with his daughter. I met him soon afterwards, and we tried to get access. The company's solicitors were very active. They sent Harry sixty-two letters, and Harry couldn't afford to pay for his own solicitor to reply to each letter. He let it go and didn't see his daughter for years. He didn't know she was brought up by her grandparents. When his daughter was married Harry wasn't invited. He found out about it and stood in the churchyard and watched. He asked the wedding photographer to send him copies of some of the photos.

"This year in February his daughter made contact after all these years, about forty years. She's got two grown-up children now. Little by little things had been explained to her. The grandparents explained things at a service station in Exeter. His daughter realised she'd been told a lot of lies and feels guilty about him now. She came from Somerset and talked with Harry, leaning on the wall and looking out to sea under your window. Harry and she walked down one side of the harbour while I talked to her husband the other side, so they could have a private conversation. When she was old enough to read for herself we wrote to her setting the situation out. Harry asked her about our letter, and she said that she had been fed so many lies she ripped the unopened envelope into pieces without reading what we had written.

"Now she rings every day, and she comes and visits us once a week. She's a money person. We're ordinary people but she and her husband are money people. She and her husband own houses, two houses in the village here and others elsewhere. She's always had money, her grandfather took her to school in his Rolls-Royce and they had four holidays a year. There were all those years when Harry and his daughter never spoke to each other, and now she comes down every weekend, and she's coming today."

I looked at Harry. He was nearly sixty-five. He had cancer in his two lungs from asbestos and in his brain, and he had been separated from his daughter for more than forty years. He would die before reaching retiring age and within a year of rediscovering his daughter, who, like Hermione in *A Winter's Tale,* was lost and had now been found.

On his way out Harry said, "I just want to see round the corner." I found him leaning on the wall on the spot where he was reconciled with his daughter. I joined him and he looked down at the waves that washed in and sucked out. He looked longingly at the sea as if he were looking at it for the last time, and said, "It's so beautiful."

I felt so sad. The biggest problem in his life for more than forty years had been resolved like a jigsaw whose frame has been done even though the inside bits are missing, but he would be gone before he could complete it. Later that day I stood on the same spot by the wall. A wronged man had put a forty-year estrangement right in early old age, but the cancer he had contracted from dismantling asbestos during the working life that had been forced on him was about to snatch him away from enjoying his unexpected reconciliation.

I stood in the early evening sunshine, sunlight dancing on the waves in the beautiful Cornish bay, and shook my head at the bleakness.

"Huh, huh" and a Waved Sole

I went to the cobblers to collect a trainer. Part of its sole had come loose and I wanted the flap stuck back. I had a ticket saying 4 (from 4pm). The manager was talking to another customer and I saw my trainer at the end of a row near where the little, crew-cut cobbler in an apron was lining up the soles of two women's knee-length boots. I picked up the trainer and said, "It hasn't been done."

The manager heard and bustled over. "I'm sorry," he said, "something's gone wrong. I'll be five minutes."

He took a bristle brush and pasted glue under the flap. I sat on the only chair by the counter. Soon the cobbler picked up my trainer and switched on a wall-hung electric grille and held the glued sole under the brightening bars that gave out a heat I could sense where I sat. Then he held the trainer to his aproned chest. Then he handed it to me and said, "Huh, huh."

I smiled at him and took the trainer. The cobbler became agitated.

"Huh, huh," he said.

He pointed to a ticket pinned near the heel of the trainer. He took the ticket off and gave me back the trainer.

"Thank you," I said.

The cobbler became agitated again. "Huh, huh," he said.

He was waving the ticket. I pushed up my ticket from the far end of his counter, where the manager had placed it.

The cobbler nodded and smiled.

"How much do I owe you?" I asked the manager who was still

talking with the customer.

"Oh, nothing."

"I must give you something."

"Then put it in the charity box."

I put a coin in the tall, thin charity box, said "Thank you," and headed for the door.

"Huh, huh," the cobbler was calling, trying to attract my attention. He was waving an insole that looked like a sole.

I returned. "It's not mine," I said. "Look, there's green on the outside and the inside is green."

I pointed to one of the knee-high boots he had been reheeling, and he nodded.

As I left I was full of admiration at the way the cobbler had coped. He was dumb, and for all I knew may have been deaf as well but he had great skill at repairing shoes and managed to communicate with "huhs" that were very expressive and full of feeling. And he kept himself through his work, he was not living on a disability allowance. He was trying to lead a normal working life, and he had a skill that brought the community to his counter. He had related to me with a "huh, huh" and a waved sole.

Bluster and Bluff

A tall, thickset, grey-haired man with a wall-eye and a loud voice approached my long table in our College hall and said, "May I join you, young man, as our great Provost used to say?"

I said "Of course" and when he had sat on the chair – chairs had replaced benches – asked, "Did you have much contact with the Provost?"

"Yes," he said. "I used to play bowls with him and that game with hoops...."

"Croquet?" I suggested.

"Yes, on a Friday evening or at the weekend. You know, he turned down the Headmastership of Eton to come here. My mother knew him at Christ Church and she wrote and asked him, 'Will you take my boy?'

and he said, 'Yes. I don't mind public school boys so long as they pass exams.' It shows you how corrupt he was." He laughed.

"I came up in 1956," he said, "after my National Service. I was an officer in Korea. I had been an officer and here I had to be in by 10 o'clock. I read Law under an Aussie who hadn't read a law book for thirty years, and the College was really run by an old boy who was over eighty. Our Provost was running MI6, very involved behind the scenes."

"He was involved in turning agents round during the war," I said, "and bluffing Hitler about where D-Day would be. We didn't know that when we were undergraduates, but in my understanding his contact with the intelligence services ended in 1945."

"He was doing far more than that," the man said in a loud voice as he spooned his cereal. "He was running MI6. Have you read *Operation Zigzag*? I know the author. He's been into it, our Provost was running it all."

He had got the title of the book wrong, he was referring to *Agent Zigzag* and had claimed our Provost was running MI6 and not a committee set up by MI5 to deceive Hitler about D-Day.

"What were you doing?" he asked.

I mentioned my time in the Far East.

"I was in Japan," he said. "I had to learn Japanese. I lived there for ten years. I ran the largest commodities company in Asia and I knew all the white men in the Far East. I sold a million tons of wheat to Chairman Mao. I went to the Canton Fair for five years. I met Mao. You need to know two things about Mao. He believed that China should be in permanent revolution; and there had to be a virgin waiting for him after lunch. Every day, without fail, a virgin."

"How did you meet him?" I asked, munching my toast.

"I was on intimate terms with his virgin that day," he said. And he threw back his head and laughed.

I gathered he had not met Mao.

"I went to Chou En-lai's funeral," he said. "And I was asked to set up a language school for translators and interpreters. I was 'Oxford Selkirk', that's what they called me. 'Oxford Selkirk'. The main thing you need to know is that Jonnie Chinaman doesn't spit straight, it can land anywhere. I said their translators and interpreters were rubbish.

Mao killed as many as Stalin, you know."

"Mao may have killed more," I said. "Jung Chang says 70 million."

"She's corrupt. In her book she says her mother was anti-Mao but she was pro-Mao."

I said, pouring coffee, "You've had some interesting experiences, you should write them down."

"I have," he said.

"Can you send them to me?"

He looked at me.

"How long are they? Will they fit in a large envelope?"

He said, "I've taught my four daughters brevity, and I act out my own teaching. It's one-to-two pages long."

He had not written them up at all, he had just done an outline.

"I am not with my wife now," he said.

"What happened?"

"She was promiscuous with all my friends and I got bored. But she gave me four lovely daughters along the way and we're still good friends. For my eightieth birthday next year we're going to South Africa, and she's coming."

I had poured a second cup of coffee. A friend of his came and pulled up a chair and sat almost between us. He had a chubby, smooth-chinned babyish face, and I thought he might be suffering from dementia.

"No, go away Gordon," the officer said authoritatively. "This is a private conversation. Piss off."

He stood up and I joined him in leaving the hall. We stood outside.

"Sorry, he's a pain," he said.

"Can I have your address?" I asked, sensing that I might need to contact him about our Provost.

"No, I only give it to virginal young ladies," he said. Three girls were standing nearby. "Hello, ladies." They smiled and strutted out of the College gate.

"You know what Japanese do when they meet," he said. "They exchange cards. Then they read them and work out which is superior. The inferior then makes a low bow, the superior one hardly bows at all. Here."

He gave me a tiny gold label with an address in Somerset.

"I'm a border Scot," he said. "From the Selkirks. I wrote to Alex Salmond, 'Dear Alex.' I know him. I told him he was right to torment the nitwits in London but that he was depriving Scots like me of their Scottish roots. He replied referring me to page 736 of the position paper. You know, it's 836 pages long. In other words he was telling me to get lost. And I know Brown's Chancellor."

"Darling," I said.

"Yes."

"The Yes campaign's doing well. It's 51:49 ahead," I said.

"No, it'll be a narrow vote for the Nos, you see."

He said it so authoritatively I half-believed him.

"I know Chris Patten very well," he said. "He was Governor of Hong Kong and he knew I'd been in China. He lost Bath and Major made him Governor of Hong Kong. Yes, I knew every white man in the Far East," he said. "And the Chinese looked up to me."

He was a Somerset Maugham figure, larger than life amid his boasts and errors of fact. He had moved away from 'corrupt' academia into trade and had clearly been good at selling commodities. He had put his commodities before his wife, leaving her for long stretches of time, and she had turned to his friends. But he was single-minded and had had his eye to a sale of a million tons of wheat and on another occasion to supplying the expatriate community with fine wine. And now he had an eye to finding someone to tell about it. At the breakfast table I had been a captive audience for his noisy and self-assertive talk, and I thought his boastful bluster was a bluff.

Leather Gloves and Bat Bags

There were bats in our loft. There were black droppings on the sandpapery floor outside the boiler-room door. They were under the apex of the roof where trusses met in an inverted V. I stood beneath the trusses and saw a bat with large ears looking down at me. I poked it with the handle of the dustpan and brush I had brought in to sweep up droppings, and it flew out. It had an enormous wing-span and disappeared into the apex of the roof at the other end of the loft. I left and turned the light out.

I looked in again a couple of days later and saw two bats on different sides of the roof ridge. They seemed to look at me with wide eyes. I grasped they were ears and that they were horseshoe bats: greater horseshoes. They were out of reach.

Next time I looked the two were side by side, and, fearing we might soon have a colony in the loft, I put on gardening gloves I borrowed from our gardener and tried to grab one and put it in a cardboard box with a lid. It flew out above my fingers and wheeled round the loft. I tried to seize the other bat, but it too flew. They both flew up to the dark end of the loft where there was no walkway across the joists.

Next time I looked in I could not see any bats. It was now mid-September and I thought the bats had left. I got our builder in when he came to do another job, and he shone his torch in all the crevices and pronounced the loft bat-free. He filled holes between the felt cladding and trusses with foam from a foam-gun. It dried into an effective filler. I turned off the light and we saw a patch of white daylight. I turned the light back on and he foamed in the last hole we could find. I turned the light off again, and the daylight had now gone. We were in pitch dark. I swept up the droppings and thought he had sealed the loft.

Two days later I saw more droppings. A humane mousetrap had caught a mouse, which had died. Thinking we might have more mice I bated two inhumane traps with mature English Cheddar.

When I next looked in I peered at the trusses above the boiler-room door and saw two bats side by side. I rang the builder and asked if he was passing and would help me catch them. He said, "I can come on Monday or Tuesday."

Monday passed. I rang him on the Tuesday. He said he could not make it until the next day. So I resolved to catch the bats myself. I looked in and they were side by side under a fold of felt and by a beam, within my reach. Then I noticed that the two mousetraps had no cheese and had not snapped. I had fed the mice that had contributed to the droppings mature English Cheddar.

Our gardener had gone home so I could not borrow his gloves. I had a brainwave. I found an old pair of leather gloves I used to wear out and about in the winter. I found a clear Morrisons shopping bag and another clear zip bag. I turned the zip bag inside-out and put it over the fingers of my right leather glove. I returned to the loft, put up an arm and grabbed a bat. I felt it wriggling. Insulated against a bite by my leather glove, I lowered my arm and pulled the inside-out bag up and the bat was in my bag. I put the bag in the cardboard box nearby. Then I put the Morrisons bag over my leather glove and grabbed the second bat. Again I pulled up the inside-out bag and the bat was inside the bag. I added it to the cardboard box. Then I put the box under my arm, took it to my study and sealed it with Sellotape. I put the box on the passenger seat of my car and drove off. I could hear the bats rustling and squealing in the box.

I reached a wood about five miles away. There was supposed to be a nature reserve nearby but I could not find it. I drove on to Gaynes Park, a country house, and resolved to release the bats in the deserted drive. Then two cars came up behind me and waited for me to move my car. I reversed out of their way and drove back towards the town until I came to a railway bridge and a thick copse. There was a deserted private drive. I put on my leather gloves and carried the box to a ditch by the wood and opened it. The bats were sitting side by side on the Morrisons bag. They sat docilely and looked at me. I lifted the shopping bag out and removed it from beneath them so they were resting on the edge of the ditch.

The bats had left droppings on my loft floor, but now they looked defenceless and harmless and I was almost sorry to leave them. A car was trying to turn into the private drive. I turned and walked back to my car and left. I tried to put the bats out of my mind but they flew about under its dark trusses all the time I drove home.

A Ninety-Year-Old Cricketer and Rows

I attended the memorial service of Jim Dawson, who had died over three months previously. It was held in the parish church on a Saturday afternoon. The church was over half-full and between the three hymns there was singing from the choir. There were tributes from three of his former colleagues who all spoke of the legend he had brought to the school in the 1950s – he had played in an amateur cup final at Wembley before 100,000 – and of his modesty. One said he had been told, "He was a *proper* footballer." At the end I spoke to his widow Meg, who said it was a lovely service and that Jim would have been astounded by the nice things said. I then spoke to his friend, a former cricketer whose autograph I collected as a boy, a former Essex captain and England player. I said, "Philip Rawley." "Of course," he said and gripped my hand hard.

In the school dining-room I found a cup of tea and helped myself to a slice of millionaires' cake with thick overhanging chocolate that was so strong I nearly choked. I spoke with the Head and his wife, and then saw the cricketer near the doorway, stooping and shuffling. I squeezed through the standing throng and asked if I could fetch him a cup of tea. "No thank you, we'll manage." A lady then arrived carrying tea following a previous arrangement.

I said, "I saw Graham Gooch at Lord's earlier this year. I said, 'You shouldn't have been sacked by England. You still have a lot to give the players.' He said, 'Thank you for saying that.' What's your take on it? Something's gone wrong with English cricket. Something's wrong in the dressing-room."

He said, "It's the splits and rows. Gooch couldn't be in the same room as Cook."

"That's terrible," I said. "The amateur captains of your day, including you, weren't like that, were they? Peter May?"

"No."

"Cowdrey?"

"No."

"It's to do with the Gentlemen of England and the Players," I said. "You played for the Gentlemen. They used different dressing-rooms. The Gentlemen didn't row and gave themselves out if they snicked a ball to the wicket-keeper. The Players played to win at all costs, and were over-competitive and waited for the umpire's decision. Somehow the Gentlemen adopted the Players' attitudes. The English captains were Gentlemen, like you, and didn't lose their temper and helped the umpire by giving themselves out, but now the captain has a Player's attitude."

"Yes," he said and he gave me a sharp look. "It's all changed because of the money. We didn't play for money. The Players did, and it's got worse over the years. There were rows in my day among the Players, but they were to do with being competitive. Wardle and Lock competed for one slot in the England team. But now...."

"Like the rows involving Pietersen," I said.

"Yes."

"Do you still have a position among the cricketers today?" I asked. "Jim said you'd gone to Australia to read the riot act to the England team. Can you still do that?"

"No," he said. "I'm ninety."

"You're a young ninety. You're good for ninety."

"But they don't listen to the very old," he said. "There's a lot of coaching and training. I didn't have any of that. I learned by watching. When I was six I was a scorer for a tanner a day pocket money. I watched how they played and taught myself. I was evacuated during the war, and when I came back I was in boys' elevens and was picked for the county. I had no lessons, I was completely self-taught."

"Here we had a West Indian – "

"'Monkey'. That was his nickname when I played against him. He was good in 1939, and he got 9 for 11 in 1935, for Somerset. But then he put on weight."

"He taught us to tell a leg break from a googly," I said. "Today they say 'Watch the grip' and so the bowler hides his grip behind his back as he runs in."

"I didn't watch the grip. I watched his arm. I could tell from his arm which way the ball was going to go. I was instinctive."

A bald, wrinkled, elderly man butted in and asked him if he had played before 100,000 at Wembley in a soccer cup final. The cricketer said he had, for Corinthian Casuals. I listened for a while and then slipped away to greet my old Maths teacher.

"How are you?" I asked.

"Suffering from ailments of ageing," he said, pleased to see me. "I have cataracts and can hardly see. I can't read and I have fungus in a toenail and may have to have an operation."

I turned back, and the cricketer was now surrounded by admirers. He came from an era in which decency, honesty and courtesy to other players, including the opposition, and to umpires were still valued, and he was secretly aghast at the splits and rows that had divided the dressing-room of the current England team. He had played for the Gentlemen of England and, at ninety, had been overtaken by an incoming tide of discourtesy and bad behaviour, and I admired the integrity of a gifted amateur who still stood head and shoulders above destructive rows.

Twinning and a Rodeo

In the long bar at Woolston Manor I took up a position where I could watch both doors. A harpist was plucking a harp. There were about fifty other guests in DJ and glamorous dresses checking in at a table by one of the doors, hanging coats on a clothes rail and sipping orange juice. I greeted Simon's wife, Paul and his girlfriend, and then Simon (who had come from work and changed in his car). Then I spotted the ex-Prime Minister, John Major. He had come in through the door that had no check-in table and was shaking hands with a few of the guests. I saw a line of ten men waiting to greet him near the harp. I crossed the room, weaving between groups – there were getting on for a hundred and fifty guests now – and took up a place at the end of the line in a gap by the harp. I was almost touching the harp and an official tried to move me away. I took a step forward and stood in front of the harp, and the man next to me took a step forward making a curved line.

In no time Major was in front of me. Edith Small, our MP, explained what I did. I heard "schools" and "books". Then Major was shaking my hand. "Well done," he said. I was surprised. What a nice man, I thought.

I said before he moved on beyond the harp, "I've got something I'd like to ask you, if I may, about euro regions – cross-border regions, not European regions, the regions that cross borders like the one that includes Kent and Pas de Calais, and the one that includes East Sussex, Picardy and Normandy. Both these were created by Europe in the early

1990s when you were Prime Minister. Did you think of them as twinning, or did you wonder if Europe wanted them to be a latent structure for a United States of Europe?"

He said, "Oh, twinning. And I've got an idea. Schools in England could be linked with schools in Scotland and Wales."

We had just had a referendum on Scotland, and the union had only just been saved.

"To cement the union," I said. He nodded. "That's not a bad idea."

"That's what I thought."

I thought he might not have understood my question, and though Edith Small was trying to escort him away, I asked him again: "So the cross-border regions, it didn't occur to you in the 1990s that Europe might be seeking to create a United States of Europe?"

"Oh no, it was twinning," he said.

And Edith Small moved him on.

Now I knew from looking into his eyes that when he was Prime Minister and approved the Maastricht Treaty it had not occurred to him that Europe might be preparing a United States of Europe.

I returned to my family.

"Did you ask your question?" Pippa asked.

"Yes," I said.

"Did you get the answer you expected?"

"Yes," I said. "It confirmed what I've always thought. It didn't occur to the Government in the 1990s that we were entering a United States of Europe."

Silence was called for. Edith Small shouted, "Order, order." We went through into a large, high-ceilinged functions hall and found our table from the plan. It was in an extension of the hall.

We sat at our round table with four town councillors. The event was fundraising for Gordon Strawson who, true to form, had been missing for most of the reception. He now made a short speech thanking everyone for coming. He said, "I'm sorry I will have to leave after twenty minutes but I have somehow volunteered to be on the count of the by-election, and so I'm on duty." I looked at Simon and raised my eyebrows. The evening was to raise funds for him and for most of it he was not going to be there.

After grace we were served goat's cheese and wine tart. Soon afterwards waitresses brought plates of roast lamb, and Gordon Strawson stood and walked out. He did not go to each table on his way and work the hall, talking to each table, as I expected him to do.

When our plates had been cleared Edith Small stood before the microphone and addressed us. The microphone was now not working. She asked a series of questions requiring a 'Yes' or a 'No'. Her tone was excessively theatrical and she came across as false. She introduced Major. Shoutingly she said that John Major was the last Conservative to have won a general election outright, twenty-two years previously.

Shouting to be heard among the hundred and fifty guests, Major said he had not met Gordon Strawson, for whom the fund-raising was happening, before now. He told one or two jokes. An MP was elected with a large majority and at a public meeting he asked his constituents, "Why did you elect me?", thinking they would say: "Because you're wonderful." They said, "Because we want to get rid of you from the constituency." There was laughter. He described how in Russia in the early 1990s he had asked Boris Yeltsin, "Tell me in one word what the state of Russia is." Yeltsin had said, "Good." Major said, "Tell me in two words." Yeltsin had said, "Not good."

Major made a thoughtful speech about how the Conservatives should ignore UKIP (the United Kingdom Independence Party) and not try to enter into a pre-election pact with them. He said the Conservatives should move away from the Coalition to become their true selves again. He ended with a cricket story. The grandson of the poet Tennyson led a team to India in the early 1930s and the night before the first Test the England team ate curry. It caught up with Alf Gover as he was about to bowl the first ball of the opening day. Gover ran to the pavilion and shut himself in a cubicle. Tennyson followed him from the pitch and knocked on the cubicle door and said, "There are forty thousand people in the ground, the batsmen are waiting and you're in there." Gover called, "What do you expect me to do?" Tennyson said, "Give us our ball back." Major said that the Conservatives wanted true Conservatism (the ball), not the watered-down version of the Coalition.

Edith Small gave a vote of thanks. Then there was a loyal toast to the

Queen, and then an auction to raise funds for Gordon Strawson. Bottles of whisky signed by Major and the current Prime Minister, Cameron, were sold for £200, and a painting of Major on an easel near the microphone which had been done in the course of the evening, a cubist black-and-white painting of striking ugliness, was auctioned for £2,500. Eventually it was time for the raffle.

Edith Small drew the tickets, which were within envelopes bearing the letter of a table. The microphone was suddenly working again, and she put on an American accent and said in a strident voice, "Nu-umber one, goes to someone on Table H, it's Sta-anly Ja-aa-cobs." For fifteen minutes she stridently imitated a Texan rodeo announcer, and we were all deafened.

As we left I reflected on the way British life worked. You bought a ticket and had dinner and were seen, and if you applied for planning permission you would find it mysteriously granted. That was how British life worked. But within the rituals there were stylistic deviations. Schools could be asked to twin with their Scottish and Welsh counterparts, and a bread-and-butter fund-raising raffle could be presented as if we were at a Texan rodeo. British political life was about tribal allegiances and contributions, and about a confidence that was supposed to add style to the occasion but sometimes actually displayed bad taste.

A Ruin and a *Boudoir*

I went back to see a great Victorian House – now a hall – that I nearly bought almost forty years previously. I had met the developer socially, and he had invited me to look at the ground floor, which he had put into reasonable condition. There was a muddy lane from the lodge, and the developer, a builder, wore a sweater and boots caked with mud. He took Pippa and me round to the back lawn and led us through a back porch into the morning-room, which was between the dining-room and the drawing-room. He showed us the library, where we could camp while converting the thirteen bedrooms upstairs into apartments.

We climbed the staircase. I found a ruin. The House had not been occupied for twenty years. There had been water penetration, and the walls were wet. There was fungus, the place was cold. I saw immediately that converting the upstairs would be a bigger job than I had been told, and I pulled away.

Now, forty years later, I stood outside the massive porch that led to the entrance hall and staircase. Gillian came to the door, and Pippa and I greeted her and followed her in. She was in a smart white trouser suit. Pippa went up in the small lift with her while I climbed the stairs and peered down at the Victorian tiled floor. We met on the first-floor landing and entered Gillian's high-ceilinged apartment. We went through to a sitting-room that overlooked the kitchen garden, and I sat on a large sofa. Pippa and Gillian sat on a sofa at right-angles. On the table in front of us there were documents: the sale particulars of 1890, 1909 and 1930. There were photocopied pictures of the large House standing in sixteen acres of lawns surrounded by forest. In one a man and child in Victorian dress walked on the main lawn.

Ahead of me was a step up to a carpeted platform which held a dining-table and chairs.

"That was the *boudoir*," Gillian said. "This was a bedroom and that was the lady's *boudoir*. That's French for 'sulking-room'. It's a private room where a woman could go and sulk." She laughed.

Gillian opened an enormous sash window and left the room to make coffee. I thought of the ruin I had looked in on nearly forty years back and studied the smart decoration now, the neo-classical borders and ceiling rose, and reflected on the *boudoir* being turned into the dining-area. And I was glad that this derelict room had been given new life and been spruced up in a way that was sympathetic to the past. The room had a grandeur that must have resembled the grandeur it would have had immediately after the House was built in 1875.

A Hedge, Green and Brown
(Or: Not Going)

My high Leylandii hedge was being cut. It overhung the Indian's land next door and he agreed to go halves. It was a fine morning, and Gerald arrived with a truck and a chipper fastened to the back. He stopped outside my gate. He said, "I'd like to park this next door. We'll throw the branches over that side and drag them up the sloping path."

I walked with him to the gate and buzzed the buzzer. The gates opened and an Indian servant approached. He was small and in an open-necked shirt.

"We're cutting the hedge," I said. "They'd like to park their wood chipper here. Can he bring it in?"

"Not going," said the servant.

"Ah," I said. "Come with me."

We walked ten yards round the corner of another hedge to the wood chipper. I said to Gerald, "I'm not sure he's understood. This," I said to the servant, "can we park this there?" I pointed to his side of the hedge.

"Not going," the servant said.

"I'll ring the owner," I said.

In the event, the owner of next door, Rajiv, allowed the wood chipper to park in front of his house and hedge-cutting proceeded. I did not see Rajiv until 4 that afternoon. By then my side of the hedge had been cut by two men, one in a hard hat who climbed into it with a chain-saw and one who operated a long-reach hedge trimmer from the ground.

I walked round to look at the other side of the hedge and encountered Rajiv in a peaked cap. He said, "I'm ill. I've got flu." He held out his right hand and reluctantly (not wanting to catch flu) I shook hands, form triumphing over common sense.

"It's not a straight line," he said, peering at his side of the hedge, to Gerald and the two fellows working with him.

"If I make a straight line," Gerald said, "the hedge will go brown. I've left it green."

"I don't care if it goes brown. I want a straight line."

"That's another brief. We've done a normal hedge cut. Going deeper will take us longer. It's another job."

"It's got to be straight. When I have my car washed I know it will be dirty in a week but I want my car to be clean when I pick it up. I know the hedge won't be straight in a week but I want it straight when it's done."

The five men had worked from 8 until after 4, and they had had enough.

"We're going home," Gerald said. "We've had a cancellation for tomorrow. We'll sort it out then."

Rajiv said to me: "I'm going to pay him my share. You pay your share tomorrow and check on the line on my side. I have to go to work tomorrow."

The next morning I heard a chain-saw quite early and I walked round to Rajiv's side of the hedge. Gerald was there with three men in hard hats.

"We're making a straight line," Gerald said.

He asked if I would fill in a customer satisfaction form.

"Sure," I said. "I've found a spanner you left in our grass yesterday. It's by my front door. Come round and I'll give it to you and I'll complete the form at the same time."

At my front door he gave me the form.

"You have to rate our work on a scale of 1 to 10. 1 is low, 10 high. We prefer 10. Can we have 10?"

"I would think so," I said. And standing by the front door and pressing on a nearby shelf I gave him 10 out of 10.

Then Rajiv appeared at my gate. He was waving in his peaked cap. I buzzed the gates open.

"I thought you were going to work."

"No, I've still got flu. I need to see your side of the hedge."

Puzzled, I walked with him and Gerald round to the back of my house. Rajiv took a camera out of his pocket and photographed the hedge.

"It's a lovely green hedge," Gerald said. "It's been looked after. No brown."

"He's taken more off your side than off mine."

"That's not true," Gerald said. "We've taken more off your side because it was overhanging the fence."

"I didn't want the hedge cut," Rajiv said to me as we walked back to the gate. "I only said Yes to be a good neighbour. They've not done it in a straight line. They haven't done it very well. They charged over £1,000 for one day. They've seen our large houses and charge high prices. I know someone who will do three days' work for £1,000."

"Who?" I asked. "We need to use them next time."

"It was more than ten years ago. More like fifteen years ago."

"They won't be charging that now," I said. "Gerald was probably £300 a day more than fifteen years ago."

Rajiv went through the open gates, followed by Gerald. I did not see them for the rest of that day.

I had asked him if we could share the cutting of the hedge and he had said Yes and had thanked me for fixing a hedge-cutter and for making the arrangement. But now he was carping, complaining at the quality of their work and their high price. He had paid his share the previous day but the price still peeved him. From his point of view his servant had been right: Gerald should have been "not going". He would now have a brown hedge. He had seen my green hedge and wanted the work to be more like my side.

He was a rich Indian who lived with his parents and servants next door to me in England, and he wanted the rates of a workman to be more like the rates he would have paid in India, and certainly the going rate fifteen years previously. He objected to being charged exorbitantly (as he saw it) because he had a large house. He privately regretted coming in on the project and agreed with his servant that the five hedge-cutters should be "not going".

Partridge and a Tomb

We found Charlton House in Somerset and, early, handed over the voucher Simon had given us as a present, and had a snack lunch in the large drawing-room. Pippa had a prawn-and-avocado wrap, I had smoked salmon. I read that Pevsner said that parts of the House were Elizabethan. The room-wide steps in the drawing-room looked 18th-century. Dressing-gown-clad guests lingered briefly on their way to and from the Spa.

The House had been bought by Duncan Bannatyne of television's *Dragons' Den*, and painted and presented through pictures to suggest an earlier time, perhaps the late 1940s. The furniture was wooden and seemingly deliberately worn, and some of the walls had been painted grey.

Our apartment was ready, and we booked in. We had to walk through the Spa to reach it, with several right and left turns along corridors. It was on two floors with a high ceiling between Tudor end-beams. I reckoned it was once the brew house, and the internal upstairs had once been storage for beer. There was a bathroom downstairs with a walk-in shower and another one upstairs with a bath. The wall up the stairs had been scraped.

I had a bubble bath and then lay in torpor on the comfortable bed and dozed. The voucher included a Swedish back massage and facial each, and, in dressing-gowns, we shuffled back to the Spa and sat. Then two young girls came out and shook hands and introduced themselves. Mine led me off to a treatment room, and soon the lights dimmed to relaxing piped music and I was lying face down under a blanket with my head on a soft hole at the end of the treatment table. My back was pounded with a very heavy touch, thumbs were pressed into the sides of my spine and then the skin on my back was cleansed and rehydrated. Then I lay on my back and had rose-petal cleanser and ginseng toner rubbed into my face. I had a facial wash, a skin scrub and a lavender-and-rosemary recovery mask. When I had finished the girl said, "Your skin looks fantastic now, it's soaked in all the oil."

We returned to our apartment and I lay in a stupor, paralysed and hovering on the edge of consciousness, while an hour slid by. Then, deeply relaxed, I changed and we went to dinner.

We sat in the same drawing-room chairs while we ordered, and were then led through to the dimly-lit dining-room, which was in a large conservatory. We were served small portions of fine food that was intricately presented. We had mullet wrapped in parmesan ham and then partridge, which had the texture of duck but its own distinctive taste. I thought of "a partridge in a pear tree". Eating partridge at Christmas had been a Tudor treat, and it was good that we were still doing this today. To me, partridge represented a nearly-vanished past. I sipped a large glass of Chilean Merlot, and the combination of the bath, the massages, the wine and the partridge had me thinking that life had been good, and was still good.

We had our pudding – blackberry torte with cinnamon ice cream, in

Pippa's case, cherry cheesecake with pistachio ice cream in my case – and then sat in the drawing-room for a pot of jasmine tea. Inside was a special strainer that tilted sideways to catch the tea-leaves.

The apartment had computerised light buttons that included a button saying 'Night'. When I pressed 'Night' small wall lights lit the way to the downstairs bathroom.

That night I had a long sleep. I woke refreshed the next morning and breakfasted in warm sunshine despite its being the last day of October. There were frondy plants outside the conservatory window and I could see a dewy lawn higher up. I had cereal and fruit, a full English breakfast, and toast with runny honey washed down with coffee – a traditional English breakfast we had been having for many decades, indeed centuries, and again I had a strong feeling that it was good we should still be doing this.

We settled our account and left about 9.30. We drove to Glastonbury and parked in the High Street. Pippa went into a Buddhist shop to buy a cross tipped with crystals and mounted on a large circular crystal, which she believed would help heal her knee. The masseuse from Ottery St Mary had worn one of their crystals and had told Pippa about the shop. They had discussed the healing properties of crystals. I said, "I'm going to look for Joseph of Arimathaea's tomb."

I wandered down the High Street and looked at the dozens of adverts in shop windows. They were all for small groups that promoted enlightenment, and several spoke of bringing down the Light – for a charge. I had never charged for teaching the Light, arguing that Jesus had not charged for the Sermon on the Mount. Advice on lifestyles should be free.

I came to St John's church, which was set back from the road. Three men who looked like tramps sat on seats outside the gate, trying to engage my eyes. I walked through the gate and passed a descendant of the Holy Thorn supposed to have been planted by Joseph of Arimathaea when, the owner of a fleet of ships, he allegedly sailed from Jerusalem to trade tin with the Cornish tin mines. According to legend, his young nephew Jesus was with him on his ship and lived in Glastonbury until AD26, when he was thirty. Hence Blake's hymn about Jesus's visit, 'Jerusalem': "And did those feet in ancient time/Walk upon England's mountains green?" I entered the church and found myself in what looked like a newish extension at the back. I stood for a while to get my bearings.

A lady was serving tea. I was her only 'customer'.

I said, "Some years ago I came to a church in Glastonbury and found a tomb with 'J.A.' on it. Is it this church, and is the tomb here?"

"Yes," she said. "It's there, behind the organ console."

I had found it with Pippa during a visit twenty-five years previously.

I wandered down towards the front of the church and found the embellished stone tomb with worn shields on its side. It was half-hidden behind a glass case containing a cope worn by Abbot Whiting, the last Abbot of Glastonbury who had been executed on the Tor in the 17th century, and its front and side were obscured by low tables. I squatted by each shield and on the east side saw the A of 'I.A.', which stood for the Latin initials of Joseph of Arimathaea.

I knew the story. William of Malmesbury described the visit of Joseph of Arimathaea and perhaps also his niece the Virgin Mary to Glastonbury. Joseph had died on 27 July 82 and had allegedly been buried in the wattle church of St Mary on the site of what is now the Abbey. The lid of his sarcophagus was inscribed: '*Ad Brittanos veni post Christum sebilivi. Bocui. Quievi.*' ('To the Britons I came after I buried the Christ. I taught. I have entered my rest.') Joseph of Arimathaea remained buried there until 1345, when Edward III gave a licence to John Bloom to dig for him. A Lincolnshire monk stated in 1367 that the body was found and placed at the east end of Joseph's chapel in Glastonbury Abbey. It was still there in 1662 when Puritan fanatics ruined the chapel. The sarcophagus was secretly removed at night and brought to the churchyard of this church. It was interred within this stone tomb, which was then outside in the open air, bearing the obscure initials 'I.A.'. In 1928 the vicar brought the stone tomb from the churchyard into the parish church, and that was what I was looking at.

The lady came and stood next to me.

"Some people think it's the tomb of Joseph of Arimathaea," she said, "but it's not. He was buried in the Holy Land. A booklet I've got in the tearoom says it was a seventeenth-century shrine to Joseph of

Arimathaea. But people come and stand before it with their arms out as though it is Joseph of Arimathaea's tomb. Last week I had two women in and they bent over the shrine with their arms out in a crucifixion position and stayed like that for five minutes." She raised her eyes and shook her head.

It was Glastonbury's secret, and it was so well kept that the volunteer tea lady did not know its provenance. Joseph of Arimathaea had been buried above ("super") his niece the Virgin Mary in the wattle church of St Mary, according to Maelgwyn of Avalon, who wrote c.450.

"It's a shrine," she said, "not a tomb. A shrine. My booklet says so."

I thanked her and after one more careful look, left the church and walked to the gate. The three homeless men were still sitting on the seat. One had a mobile and looked as if he was sending a text. The other tried to engage my eyes, hoping for alms.

I found Pippa. I asked, "Did you find what you were looking for?"

"Yes, I did," she said. "They tried to sign me up to become a Buddhist but I only wanted the crystal pendant for its healing properties so I wasn't having any of that. Did you find Joseph of Arimathaea's tomb?"

"Yes, I did," I said. "It's where we saw it. The tomb that stood in the churchyard from 1662 to 1928."

I wondered what had happened to the sarcophagus. Was it inside the tomb? Had someone looked inside?

And then it dawned on me that the tea lady had helped to preserve Glastonbury's greatest secret. By telling people that the tomb was a shrine she had helped cover it up. The tomb had a glass case on top and it was boxed in with low tables to conceal it. And she was telling people it was a 17th-century shrine. Whether or not she realised it, she was perpetuating the cloaking of the tomb. The cult of Joseph of Arimathaea was being discouraged, surrounded by a glass case and tables, and she may have been encouraged to spread word that the tomb was a shrine and she might believe that it was.

I wondered if the vicar and the bishop were involved. The Church seemed to have marginalised the cult of Joseph of Arimathaea. It was possible she was doing the bidding of those who wanted to suppress Glastonbury's secret that Joseph of Arimathaea, the uncle of Jesus

Christ, had lived there once and been buried in this holy place. Like partridge, the tomb represented a nearly-vanished past.

Bruises and Pickle

The annual dinner of the Friends of the Forest took place in a large hall. In the foyer I chatted to a couple who had been parents at our boys' school and had had us to dinner in the old days. They were retired now. Nearly two hundred of the more elderly residents shuffled tentatively in, some bent over sticks. Pippa and I were on table 18 near the door. We were joined by elderly ladies we did not know, whose names were also on the list for table 18.

I lamented the death of the judge who used to beckon me to sit next to him and tell me what the Attorney General had said about the Government. Synchronistically his widow came by. I said, "I was thinking of your late husband a couple of hours ago. Mitchell's been found to have called the policeman a pleb, and I wonder what judgement he would have given."

"I was astonished when I heard it," she said. "I've lunched at the Garrick today, with the couple who were with him when he died."

I nodded. She wore her bereavement like a bruise but seemed reasonably cheerful with it.

We sat at the round table, Pippa with a bruise near her mouth from the four implants she had had the previous morning. She had only had a partial local anaesthetic so she could wince if a nerve was touched while the new teeth were being screwed into her jaw. She ate a crust of bread gingerly, adding dabs of the small slab of unwrapped butter with her knife, and then served herself as tinfoil salvers were passed round with portions of salmon, turkey and cold vegetables. I had fetched her a cranberry juice and myself a glass of red wine, and we ate with quizzes propped before us: 'Name the bird' and 'English villages and places'.

Elderly Henry, who had devised the quizzes, came by. I stood and chatted. He said, "I have to go to hospital three times a week, for dialysis. If I don't, the alternative is to be dead."

I said, "You don't want that."

He pulled a face. "No," he said, "I don't want that."

He had a bruise on his mind.

Eventually the dessert arrived. We had *crème brûlée*. The top was crisp and sprinkled with brown sugar. It was made from double cream, egg yolks and sugar, and for those trying to lower their cholesterol it was only marginally better than the alternative, fudge cake and cream, which was made from butter and sugar.

Coffee was served and from the platform Henry gave the answers to the quizzes. He apologised for his drawing: "My hands are a bit shaky, I can't draw as well as I used to." The answers were a bit shaky too. A picture in 'Name the bird' showing the wind as a boy with cheeks and blowing and a knight in armour lying on the ground, which we agreed was 'Nightingale', was announced as 'Puffin'.

Then a portly alderman with a loud voice made a speech. It was about raising money for the Forest in a time of cuts, and he wanted us to cheer or groan depending on whether he was announcing good news or bad news. He promoted himself: his speech was more about himself and winning cheers than the Forest. Then it was the raffle.

It went on for a long time. As usual the tickets had not been shuffled, and one table won several prizes. Our table won nothing.

At the very end the wife of a Friends committee member, a blonde, announced: "There are now six special prizes: jars of my pickle. It's a very special pickle. The apples have come from apple trees two hundred years old. They are in the garden of our house, which is seven hundred and fifty years old, it's medieval. So the pickle is from ancient stock."

Throughout the hall there was a distinct lack of appetite to win her pickle. How hygienically had it been prepared? Had she washed her hands? Six winning tickets were called out, and winners made their way reluctantly to the front. One belonged to the Chairman, who was drawing the tickets. Again our table won nothing.

I said to a Forest worthy who was sitting the other side of Pippa, "Where does she live? Because the oldest house in the Forest is four hundred years old."

"That's right. I think she lives outside the area, or has a holiday home somewhere. I think it's towards Suffolk."

"That's a fine pickle," I said.

She had brought her medieval house into a function that had nothing to do with it, to raise funds for our local Forest. She had flaunted her pickle and had come across as boastful, like the alderman who loved the sound of his own voice.

I saw old Mrs. Shackleton, a prominent councillor for thirty years, bent double over a stick. She had got up and was shuffling out of the door into the foyer, her head looking down at her feet.

The raffle was over. I said to Pippa, "I'm just going to say Hello to my Labour friends."

I crossed the floor of the hall, weaving between tables and now standing guests. I sidestepped the Deputy Lord Lieutenant, a solicitor who had travelled down from near Dunmow, and bent over grey-haired Lady Myrtle and her son. "Just come to see my friends," I said. "Are you keeping well?" I asked Lady Myrtle, who was over ninety.

"Not really," she said. "I haven't been feeling well. Or doing anything. I get depressed. I'm immobile, you see. I can't get about as I used to. But I must keep going."

There was a bruise on her expression.

"Yes," I said, "you must keep going." It sounded like a command.

I thought she would be dead by next year's annual dinner. She was fading.

I returned to Pippa, who was preparing to leave. On the way out I encountered an accountant I knew.

"You're the scrutineer of their accounts," I said.

"Yes," he said, "I'm the scrutineer. What did you think of the meal?"

"It was all right," I lied, not wanting to offend.

"I thought the wine left much to be desired."

"Yes, it wasn't very good."

We left. So many of these elderly people had had bruising experiences, and there were not many who flaunted their pickle, which these elderly folk did not want. But all had showed determination in attending, like Pippa and elderly Mrs. Shackleton who was bent double, a councillor with a badly bruised back.

A Lost Ruby and a God

Pippa gave me a rough-hewn ruby for our 40th anniversary. It was a dull red, oblong stone that was supposed to give off energies good for the heart and encourage passion and a zest for life. It was supposed to detoxify the blood and remove negative energies, including exhaustion.

I kept it in the breast pocket of my shirt, above my heart, alongside a folded piece of writing paper and biro for jotting down new perceptions. At night I put the contents of the pocket on my desk. One morning I was aware that the ruby was not with my papers. It was not on my desk.

I looked round my study and wondered if it had dropped out of my breast pocket the previous day when I examined the wall socket that controlled the fountain. I went into the garden and peered at the rosebed beneath the socket. No ruby. I wondered if it had dropped out when I emptied the post-box, so I walked to the front gate and bent and studied the ground beneath it. No ruby.

I looked near the dishwasher and washing-machine, anywhere in the house where I had bent to do things. No ruby.

Back in my study I remembered that the Egyptian god Anubis was a messenger from the gods to human beings who presided over the finding of lost things. I said aloud, "Find it, Anubis."

Anubis had the head of a dog or a jackal, and for five thousand years – from before the time of the Great Pyramid – humans had been saying, "Find it, Anubis," as if asking a dog to bound away and return with the missing item like a stick.

Almost immediately I had a feeling that I should look in the vicinity of my alcoves, where my Tutankhamen figurine – a *shawabti* – stood. There was no ruby in the alcoves. I picked up a desk-side table to see if the ruby was underneath. It was not. I then moved a plastic archives box on wheels near the alcoves – and there, beneath the box until I moved it, lay my ruby. Anubis had found it and told me where to look.

I picked the ruby up and put it in my breast pocket, and gave thanks for Universalist living which drew on a five-thousand-year-old tradition that included Apollo, whose bust was at the foot of the spiral staircase outside my study, along with Anubis.

The mind has powers of which we are largely unaware, and as I pressed my ruby to my heart and thought of the unified universe in which energies from a stone could interact with a physical organ like my heart, I knew the powers of the mind were in some sort of a telepathic relationship with physical objects, and in a dynamic interaction that was utterly mysterious.

Galaxies and God

The electrician came to replace the time switches by the pond. It was a late morning in December, and the frost was still thawing in the shade. He wore a knitted woolly hat and greeted the gardener, who wore a darker woolly hat and a black scarf round his mouth: "You look like a jihadist."

He took two boxes of parts down to the bushes round the pond and I boiled a kettle of hot water and poured some into a cup – he drank neat hot water to warm himself up – and went off and dictated an article to my PA who keyed it straight into the computer.

Towards the end of the afternoon I went downstairs and found him in the house. He showed a new RCD he had added to my fuse board. "It'll trip if there's a live wire," he said. "It's a safety issue. Before it was dangerous. Someone could have been killed."

I thanked him and we walked together across the now dry grass to the pond. He showed me a new time switch for the pump. He had raised the time switch from ankle- to waist-height so that I could read it without lying on my face under a bush to see beneath the lifted lid. "It'll come on at 10 and go off at 12," he said. He showed me another time switch for the filter the other side of the pond: "It'll come on from 10.30 to 12.30." He added, "I've added that trunking."

Then, standing by the pond, he said, "You're an interesting man. You've been in Iraq. Did you meet Saddam?"

I explained that I was there in Kaseem's time, before Saddam came to power.

"I've looked you up online," he said. "You're a philosopher. My daughter asked me, 'What's philosophy?' and I couldn't tell her."

I explained that the word meant 'love of wisdom', and that 'wisdom' was understanding the relationship between man – him – and the universe.

"All those galaxies up there," he said, 'it's scary."

"That's what I've focused on," I said. "It's a side of philosophy the Greeks didn't know about two thousand five hundred years ago. They didn't know about other galaxies."

"No," he said. "It may be a strange question and I don't want to embarrass you, but do you believe in God?"

"Reality," I said. "Hawking, the crippled scientist you see in a wheelchair, says there was nothing before the Big Bang. But there was. It came out of something – a Reality."

He nodded, "Yes, there was something before the Big Bang. This is very deep," he said.

"I've got to go back now," I said.

"I'll be another ten minutes," he said. "I've just got to clear up. Then I'll be off. You'll let me know if the pump doesn't come on around 10 and the filter around 10.30 tomorrow, won't you."

"I will," I said.

And we were back in electrician-client mode.

"I'll go online and read more," he said. "I'm interested in books. My daughter reads and I try to encourage her. I make my living out of time switches but I'm really interested in galaxies and God."

Champagne and Order

Hilda Strawson held another fund-raising champagne reception for her son Gordon Strawson. This time she invited the Minister of Justice and Lord Chancellor, a symbol of Establishment order, whose Private Parliamentary Secretary Gordon was. He was standing at the far end of a room filled with twenty-five elderly activists who were sipping champagne. Pippa and I entered holding our champagne flutes, which we had been given by a helper holding a tray. Gordon greeted me and I said, "Your UKIP rival has blown herself up like a suicide-bomber."

She had defected from Labour two months previously and accused

UKIP's overseer of defections of sexual harassment and had now left UKIP, and it had come out that she had not studied at Oxford as she had claimed.

Gordon became animated and said, "It's confusing. The meeting to choose a candidate was last night. She was a candidate and was expected to be nominated. The man who was deselected to make way for her was reselected."

"They said, 'Sorry we deselected you, but now our arrangement has fallen through we're reselecting you. No hard feelings, redouble your efforts for us as we really like you,'" I said.

Gordon smiled.

I moved on to where the Lord Chancellor was standing. He towered over me. I said, "It's not often I look up to someone, you must be 6 foot 5 inches, for I'm 6 foot."

He said, "I *am* 6 foot 5 inches."

*Canapé*s arrived on plates: morsels of smoked salmon, sausages and battered fish.

I asked him about the coming election. He said, "It'll be like 1992."

He meant that the Conservatives would win a surprising victory. John Major had replaced Thatcher and was expected to lose his first election in 1992, but he campaigned on a soapbox and unexpectedly won.

I knew he was a Eurosceptic. I said, looking up at him, "It's being said the European single currency will collapse and that Cameron will be regarded as a lucky Prime Minister. I can't see that happening. Ever since the Treaty of Rome of 1957 the Rothschilds have invested in what has become the European Union and they're not going to let it slip. The Bilderberg Group's on the case."

He said, "I think the Bilderberg Group's a spent force. I saw the attendance list for their last meeting at the Grove and it was more low-level than usual. They're not attracting the big names."

I asked him what he thought of the UKIP defector's accusation. "She says nothing happened, but she's lost her career in exposing the UKIP man who handles defectors. The only scenario that makes sense is that she was sent into UKIP by Labour to cause the resignation of the man who is responsible for defections so he would be replaced by a novice, and no more defections until the election."

The Lord Chancellor looked at me sharply. "I don't think Labour's that bright," he said.

But Peter Mandelson, the Prince of Darkness and spin, could have thought that up.

The Lord Chancellor took a sip of champagne and swallowed a sausage. He said, "I must circulate and move on."

I chatted to lawyers, to Stanley Holborough who had retired as a solicitor after a box fell off a shelf onto his head in his garage and had gone on to do voluntary work at the Globe; and the head of his firm, Norman Gorman, now eighty-five and still working. I said to him, "You're one of my elders and betters, and well done for still working at eighty-five. I remember you coming to the bottom of our lane twenty-five years ago and we looked at an embankment together."

"I remember coming."

"You were supposed to be my solicitor that day, but something happened and I was allocated to a different branch."

Then Edith Small arrived, looking very blonde. The tabloid press had pilloried her for spending over £2,000 of taxpayers' money on two dresses she needed to fulfil her role as Deputy Speaker, a symbol of order in Parliament. Traditionally the Speaker wore 17th-century court dress: a white bib, and black stockings. Like Black Rod's uniform, this should not be paid for out of the incumbent's pocket. But recently the modernising Speaker had opted to wear a suit, and the feeling had grown that the Deputy Speakers just came in their own clothes and did not burden the taxpayer.

"Order, order," Edith Small called. "Have you been having a good time?"

"Ye-es," a few called back.

"Well, that stops now. I'm here," said Edith Small in her Scottish brogue. "I'm here to introduce the Lord Chancellor." And she described how they had worked together in 1998, and he, towering above her, nodded. She mock-clutched his waist and the top of her head did not reach his breast pocket. She said he was the first Lord Chancellor not to be a lawyer.

The Lord Chancellor now spoke. He corrected her: "I'm the first

Lord Chancellor *for four hundred years* not to be a lawyer, and the last one had his head chopped off." There was laughter.

He should have said 'for more than six hundred years', for Simon Sudbury, Bishop of London from 1361 to 1375 and Archbishop of Canterbury from 1375 until his death in 1381, became Lord Chancellor in 1380, though not being a lawyer. He was dragged to Tower Hill on 14 June 1381 and was beheaded after eight blows to his neck.

Then he fixed me with his eyes and did not remove them throughout his speech. His whole speech seemed to be directed at me. He said he was privileged to be Lord Chancellor as he had to sign bills in the presence of the Queen and his role had given him regular contact with the Royal Family. He described the good work the Government had done and said it would repeal the European Human Rights Act. "I'm on the Eurosceptic wing of the Eurosceptic wing of the Conservative Party," he said to laughter. "I stand for British law and order. I want to be able to deport criminal immigrants without the taxpayer having to keep them for years and years." He urged everyone to campaign to re-elect Gordon.

Then Gordon spoke, wearing a dark suit and white shirt and tie in his mother's sitting-room. Everything he said was true and just. The only trouble was I had heard it a hundred times before in the news or read it in the newspapers. It was a *résumé* of what had happened the previous five years in a received language of jargon and clichés. He was his Party's cannon fodder, an expendable foot-soldier in the electoral war sent out to defend the Government's point of view. He was a yes-man who had no individual angle or character foibles. He thanked his mother for providing the champagne and members of his family for preparing the *canapés*.

After he finished I wandered past him – he tried to intercept me and chat – to the Lord Chancellor. I shook him by the hand and talked further.

I asked, "Is the mansion tax going to be on residences or will it include business addresses?"

He said, "We don't know, we haven't been told. Residences, I should imagine, but it may include businesses."

He said he had to leave, shook my hand again and said, "I've enjoyed meeting you," and then followed Gordon to the door.

Now I caught up with Edith Small. I collected her view on the UKIP defector. "She wasn't at Oxford as she said she was," I said, "and she misspelt her college on her c.v. I heard her speaking on television. She read her speech badly and couldn't read the word 'costs'. I said, '*She* wasn't at Oxford.' Could Labour have had a dirty-tricks plan to target the UKIP man responsible for defections, to force his resignation so there would be no more defections before the next election?"

"You're shrewd," Edith Small said. "I wondered that. I'm going to ask tomorrow at the highest level. I'm going to get the whole situation investigated."

I drifted towards the door. It was time to leave. In the hallway there was congestion as departing guests chattered to Hilda Strawson and Edith Small. Eventually all left except for Pippa and me, and Edith Small accosted me, tilting her champagne flute dangerously near my tie.

"Have you got the hang of being Deputy Speaker now?" I asked. "Do you have a crib sheet to look at or can you just reel off the names without?"

"I have a sheet out of sight, but I don't refer to it much," she said.

"And at *Prime Minister's Questions* can the Speaker choose who he or she likes?"

"The first twenty questions are on the Order paper. But after that the Speaker can choose. In Ministerial Statements the Speaker can choose all the questioners."

"So if Alex Salmond becomes a Westminster MP," I said, "and the general election gives a hung Parliament and he says, 'I'll prop you up but I want a second referendum – '"

"You're so shrewd," Edith Small said. "That could happen, that's what we're worried about."

"Then could you just not see Alex Salmond when he rises to intervene?"

"I would always see him," Edith Small said in her Scottish brogue. "I have to be fair and balanced. Besides, I have good relations with the Scottish National Party. I'd always call him. No, I'd never not call him."

"But it may not come to that," I said. "The British public aren't stupid and may not deliver that quandary."

"I'm not so sure they're not stupid," Edith Small said with a naughty twinkle in her eye.

She was serious. The symbol of order in the House of Commons, her tongue loosened by champagne, was saying that the public are stupid. She was supposed to go before the public with a gown of humility, like Coriolanus, but she was hinting that she despised the public. I could understand how she had reached this conclusion: the previous general election had delivered a hung Parliament when there was a record deficit to reduce, and the Conservatives' task had been hampered by the Liberal Democrats. The Coalition had done well under the circumstances, but the public should have delivered a strong government. I knew from reality television that the public often had a poor understanding of the world: one participant thought that East Anglia was a country, one did not know how to tell the time from a watch, and three had never heard of a pineapple.

I said goodbye and left. I had asked direct questions of two symbols of order in our society, the Lord Chancellor and a Deputy Speaker, but as in reality television the order they stood for had been diminished by their champagne pleasantries with a group that did not want to see change. Under the influence of champagne the Lord Chancellor had boasted of his regular meetings with the Queen and the Deputy Speaker had suggested that the public, her employer, is stupid. There was a snobbishness and arrogance among the pillars of order that an open-minded person, operating under cover like a spy and standing for implied virtue, would have to condemn as unwelcome vices.

A Tooth and Cholesterol

I lost half an upper tooth and made an appointment to see my dentist. Dr Clerihew came down the stairs punctually at 5.15, a lively woman in her early fifties, and led me up. I lay back on the reclined chair and handed over my bit of broken-off tooth. The dental nurse put tinted glasses over my eyes. Dr Clerihew looked in my open mouth and asked, "How did you break the tooth?"

"On nuts," I said. "I've got a blood test coming up and I've been told I'll be on statins if I can't lower my cholesterol. I don't want to be on statins, I've heard they have side-effects, you can't think clearly."

"That sums you up," Dr Clerihew laughed to the dental nurse.

"I'm on statins," smiled the rotund dental nurse (who was also fiftyish). She was sitting on a stool behind my reclined head.

"Oh, er, it's a matter of the dose," I said, my mouth still open and trying to get my words out. "Are you aware of any side-effects?"

"No," the dental nurse smiled. "I've been on them twenty years."

"What was your cholesterol?" Dr Clerihew asked.

"5.6/5.7," I said.

Dr Clerihew drilled the jagged bits of my tooth and then twisted a frame over the tooth.

"I'm doing the same," she said. "I've had a blood test. My cholesterol was 5.7 last time so I went on a diet. I've been making porridge, and have been late for work. And I've been taking Benecol, the drink and the spread. Benecon more like it. It's all a con, you know. I've had no cream over Christmas and only one tiny bit of Christmas pudding. I had my most recent blood test and heard the result yesterday. And do you know what it was? Guess."

"More?" I said gutturally, my mouth wide open and the screwed-in frame digging into my cheek.

"6.5," she said. "6.5. I've been on this diet for months, how can it be more? My doctor wants to see me to review the result."

The dental nurse was laughing. "I think there was a mix-up and you've got someone else's result," she said.

"Could be," I said.

Dr Clerihew had packed filling on to the tooth in the frame. Now she unscrewed the frame and shone a laser drier on my tooth. It clicked and flashed a red light as she dried each side of the add-on tooth.

"I'm an expert on lowering cholesterol," she said.

"Oily fish three times a week?" I asked.

"Four," she said.

"Avocados?"

"Yes," she said.

"Green tea?"

"Yes. What diet are you on for breakfast?"

"I've gone over to Oatibix," I said, "and Mornflake granola, nuts and seeds."

"Moonflake?" she said.

"Mornflake. I sprinkle it on my Oatibix. And I sprinkle on ground almonds."

"Right," she said, "that's it, you can rinse now. I need to write a shopping list. Moonflake and ground almonds."

"I think you should ask for another three months before going on to statins as the score is disputed," I said as I rinsed.

"I think I'm going to go private," she said. "I can't do with this. 5.7 and a completely new diet put it up to 6.5. How can that happen?"

"I went up from 5.6 to 5.7 as I was starting my diet," I said.

"So it's the same with you. It's a con. I think you should have nothing but water 24 hours before your next blood test," Dr Clerihew said.

"I think it's genetic," said the rotund dental nurse, who was laughing from her stool. "It's in your genes. Some people inherit it and are always going to have high cholesterol."

I nodded.

"You won't laugh when I drop dead of a heart attack," said Dr Clerihew. And we all laughed.

I came away invigorated. The action had all been about my broken tooth and the conversation had all been about cholesterol, and Dr Clerihew's outrage at the result of her blood test had brought some character to the dental surgery. I suddenly realised that I had hardly been aware of the drill and the adding-on of a bit of tooth. Dr Clerihew had skilfully used her indignation as a form of hypnotism so I would not feel any pain.

A Heart and a Blind Eye

I met Jack for lunch in the Clos Maggiore in Covent Garden. We sat in an alcove with leather seats alongside a real privet hedge. We ordered smoked salmon. Sixty-five and retired, Jack looked leaner and older than when I last saw him.

He said, "I'm still following up the event that affected my eye. I've still got a 40-per-cent loss of vision in the two upper quadrants of my left eye. I've had further tests and they've found I've got a hole in my heart. Ninety per cent of people are born with a hole between the chambers in their heart, and in most cases it closes naturally soon after birth. With some it doesn't. The blood system pumps into one chamber and goes round the body and has reduced pressure when it returns into the other chamber. But the hole I've got's between the two, and a bit leaks into the outward flow. Blood seeps from one chamber to another, is thrust upwards towards the brain, and it's taken a tiny clot to my eye. If it had gone to my brain it would have been a stroke, but it's gone to my eye as a microembolism and left me with 40-per-cent vision in my upper left eye. I hear on Tuesday what has to happen. They could put something up into my heart."

"You've done all the active things you've done," I said, "gone on Concorde faster than the speed of sound and surfboarded without knowing you've had this hole, and you've suffered no ill effects. So if you act sensibly you can carry on with no ill effects."

"Yes," he said. "I'm actually better off than Emma." He mentioned our niece. "She's had TB, and I heard last week she's still got it, they can't eliminate it. She's on nine antibiotics, and she's got it latently. There's criticism of the hospital for not picking up that you can't get rid of it."

"In the 1940s and 1950s there were rows of beds in the open air to get the oxygen," I said.

He nodded.

"I had to drive past a small hospital in Midhurst where they did that," he said. "You could see the patients in beds on the flat roof."

For our next course we had halibut, and we sipped glasses of red wine. The subject moved to Europe. He told me the UK would be better off leaving Europe and joining the European Free Trade Area with Norway, Iceland, Switzerland and Liechtenstein.

He showed me a picture of an organ he had installed in his house. "It cost me as much as a small car," he said. "I play it every day. It's got all the organs of all the best churches in the UK on it, so you can have the experience of playing on different organs each day."

"Will you give any more recitals?" I asked.

"No," he said.

We finished our halibut and ordered Black Truffle ice cream.

We had agreed to split the bill. He had difficulty in arriving at the total. He elected to pay in cash rather than by card, and when I put my share of bank notes into the communal kitty on the table he had difficulty in counting the exact amount. I wondered if his 'event' had affected his mental processes.

I rang him on the Tuesday evening to enquire about the results of his tests. He said, "My heart's in good condition. I don't need an operation. My consultant said, 'You've been doing all you've been doing for sixty-five years, I'm just going to let you go on doing it.' He said that my 'event' was 40-per-cent statistically likely due to the hole in my heart – which is called PFO – and 60-per-cent likely due to other things. So it might not be my heart. Siblings are supposed to have a test to see if they have it too. The condition doesn't show up on an echocardiogram, only on a Doppler ultrasound bubble test."

I wondered if I had a hole in my heart which I had inherited from my parents.

"You've had an 'event'," I said. "You may never have another one. But as it's your artery and blood pressure, I'd find out what foods to avoid and quietly avoid them."

"Yes," he said. "I will."

"Did he say if your vision may improve?" I asked.

"It's likely it will never improve," he said.

I said, "The brain repairs itself when people have had dreadful motorcycle accidents and have steel inside their skull, and perhaps you'll find your eye will heal itself."

"Perhaps. Thanks for ringing and being concerned."

He was going to turn a blind eye on the hole in his heart. He was too realistic to be in denial, and he had faced what had happened to him and relegated the 'event', regarded it as unimportant.

Jack had suddenly aged in his own mind. He had lost 40 per cent of the vision in his upper quadrants in his left eye and had a hole in his heart. He had decided not to give any more recitals. He had moved into a time of his life where he would be nursing his health. The hole in his heart had made a hole in his life, and while understandably living carefully around it he had decided to turn a blind eye and disregard it and live as if it had never happened. I admired him for this.

A Bandage and Narghiles

I discovered I had varicose veins behind my knees, in the place where it is impossible to see unless one stands between two mirrors. Eczema crept from the backs of my legs to the sides, and I found the veins while investigating its cause. I went back to the Belgian lady who stripped my veins in two operations seventeen and nineteen years previously. Her clinic was in a large house round the corner from Harley Street. She had an apartment upstairs and patients were seen on the ground floor.

I encountered the double-barrelled receptionist, who was large and had a loud voice. Above where she sat was a notice in large letters: 'I'm not bossy, I just have better ideas.' I sat in the waiting-area round the corner.

There was one other patient waiting, an Irishman. He announced, "I'm investing on Thursday in Cheltenham."

"Clients' money?" I asked.

"Investing in the horses," he said, and he laughed.

"I hope the clients get to choose the horses you're betting on," I said.

He laughed again. Then he asked what I was having done.

"Foam sclerotherapy," I said. "Pumping foam into the backs of my legs to kill veins, guided by ultrasound. Then a compression bandage for fourteen days."

"You'll be all right on that," he said. "You've got the right build. You'll be fine. But you know she uses staples now. So many do, staples not sutures. She staples the bandage to the skin at the back of your leg."

I pretended to make a move for the door. "You're winding me up," I said.

"No. It doesn't hurt too much. The first couple of days are a bit difficult. Here's my card. If you want to make a reservation I'll find you a table even if it's fully booked."

I read his Irish name and his position: 'Head Concierge, Scott's.' I knew Scott's was a restaurant that specialised in sea food.

"I was at the Ivy for ten years and then moved to Mayfair. I do a lot of standing in my job, so I've had my veins done."

Eventually he left.

I was called in for my consultation. The Belgian lady, Margot, had my notes from nineteen years previously, and told me what I had had done and what had been tied up. She stood me on a stool, daubed gel on the backs of my legs and studied her ultrasound screen. She confirmed that I would need foam sclerotherapy: the left leg the next day, the right leg at a later date as the body can only absorb foam for one leg.

"I think you need to be covered for thrombosis," she said. "There is nothing in writing on this, but it would be wise."

She gave me a prescription for anti-thrombotic Clexane.

I bought twenty syringes from the pharmacy in Marylebone High Street nearby. I gave myself my first injection the next morning.

That late afternoon I returned to her clinic. As soon as she led me into her room, I asked, "Do you staple the bandage to the skin?"

"No, we've never done that. I've been doing this procedure for ten years and never once have I done that. Why do you ask?"

I said, "The Irishman who was in yesterday said you did."

"Oh, he's a character. He says all sorts of things. But he *will* find you a table if the restaurant's full, he actually does that."

I lay on my front.

"Catheter going in," Margot said, and I felt a sting above my ankle. "Foam going in." Again I felt a sting. "One more catheter above the back of your knee." I winced as it went in. "And one last one the other side of your leg. And one more last one just higher. And one final final last one. Now turn over for your bandage."

She stretched out my left leg so my sole pressed into her bosom. Then she bandaged my left leg from toe to groin, covering the knee, and stuck the bandage together with sticking plaster.

"At night, put a stocking over it, nylon or a loose elastic stocking, just to stop the bandage catching on sheets." She gave me instructions as to how to remove the bandage after fourteen days, and I left.

I sauntered back down Marylebone High Street on my way to Bond Street station. Although it was early March there were people dining in the open air at every restaurant, sitting at tables on the pavement. Every window was interesting. In the Lebanese restaurant, customers were smoking narghiles (or hookahs), while they waited to be served, puffing on a pipe attached to a long tube through water that cooled the smoke.

My leg had stiffened up but the discomfort eased as I sauntered. I thought of people who bandaged in their pain and of people who puffed at narghiles. The pain-limiters and the pleasure-seekers rubbed shoulders in the Marylebone High Street. Once I would have been a pleasure-seeker but now I was glad to be in a bandage as it would liberate me from the itching behind my legs. Narghiles were interesting but in my mind I had a bandage stapled to my skin and I was grateful for my toe-to-groin bandage and sticking plaster that would restore my enjoyment of the moment.

Strokes and a Dying Order

I was set to attend a memorial service for Walter Grayling at the school. At 6.30pm the previous evening the chaplain rang and said, "I'd like you here by 2.15 tomorrow, please."

I said, "The memorial service. I *am* coming. But why the precise time?"

"Because you're on the service sheet as giving a tribute," he said.

I said, "Oh." It was news to me.

That evening I cobbled together some handwritten notes. The next day I duly turned up at the school chapel shortly before 2.15 in a suit, white shirt and old school tie. I was greeted by the chaplain and shown to a seat in the second row next to the bald President of the Old Boys' Association, who was giving the tribute before mine. On my other side sat another Old Boy who had been deputed to read the contribution of a former master, who was unwell.

"He's had two mini-strokes," the Old Boy explained.

"TIAs?" I asked. "Transient ischaemic attacks?"

"Exactly. It was considered he would be unwise to travel so I'm reading his speech."

At that moment Arthur Sargent, a former master, shuffled in holding a stick. Each shuffle only covered inches, and it took him a couple of minutes to turn and sit down. I was shocked, I had not realised he had had a stroke.

There was a welcome from the chaplain and then from the Head, who read the reference given Walter Grayling by J.L. Austin, his tutor. There was a prayer and a hymn, and my bald neighbour read a long tribute. Then it was my turn.

The lectern was a folding stool with sagging canvas straps positioned at the front of the sanctuary before the altar. It came up to my knee. I lay my notes on it and stood, hands behind my back, in the sanctuary with the chaplain at one elbow and the Head at the other and the school choir sitting on both sides behind me. I addressed the packed congregation.

I said that Walter Grayling had come to the school in May to get to know the staff and school, and that I was in his first 'O' level set the following September. I said that he had made us learn and chant the first four lines of Euripides' *Alcestis*. I recited them and offered a translation. The lines were from Apollo's opening speech and described how he had been forced to dwell in the halls of Admetus as a slave, though being a god. I said there was a debate about whether children should learn chunks of literature by rote and that Walter had known the answer more than sixty years ago.

At the end of the service we talked outside the chapel and wandered up to the dining-hall for tea and cakes. I spoke to several Old Boys who I had known at school, and to Arthur Sargent who told me about his stroke.

"It happened when I was working in a library near our village," he said. "I felt unwell."

"Did you know you were having a stroke?"

"Oh, yes."

"Did you dial for an ambulance?"

"No, I went home," he said. "I'm paralysed all down my right side."

I said, "Well done for getting here."

He said, "My wife drove me," and shrugged.

Then I saw Joe Nail standing like a Victorian with bouffant grey hair puffed out and swept back like an 18th-century wig. He turned to me and greeted me, looking up, for he was quite small: "We belong to a dying order. I've got lines of Sophocles, Aeschylus and Tacitus, but no Euripides. That faculty is just not around today. We belong to a dying order."

I nodded. "The younger generation is missing out on a lot," I said.

"It is. How's Paul?" he asked of one of my sons. When I had updated him, typically quirkily and Victorian: "Give him my compliments but not my respects." It was a sardonic farewell he had sometimes used in his pre-retirement days and was supposed to be humorous.

I thought about the old masters. Two had had strokes and one felt he and I belonged to a dying order as no one quoted in Latin and Greek any more. The truth was, we all belonged to a dying order. We grew old like Walter Grayling and died, sometimes having strokes along the way, and we recalled things lodged in our youthful minds. I saw a generation dwindling towards the grave.

The One Like a Hidden Sun

I was to be interviewed about my experiences of the One on a minor TV channel. The interviewer invited me to dinner to discuss the route the hour-long interview would take. I found the Saatchi Gallery Mess restaurant in what used to be the Duke of York's barracks at the top of the King's Road not far from Sloane Square. I was early and was shown to a table, and soon afterwards the interviewer, Andy McTaggart, arrived, balding with a pleasant smile, and his Viennese wife joined us. We ordered pea-and-mint soup and I followed up with salmon cakes and fruit salad. He asked me a lot of questions and we agreed a direction for the interview.

Two days later I arrived in Sloane Square at 9.15 to wait for a lift to the studios on the other side of the river in Andy's car. There was about to be a solar eclipse, but few people were looking heavenwards as they bustled about. In fact, there was cloud cover, and although at 9.30 the street lights came on and the temperature dropped slightly so I could see my own breath – it was still March – there was little sign of an event, the moon passing between the sun and the earth, that would normally arrest and inspire.

Andy and his wife glided up in their blue Chrysler and ten minutes later I was in the Battersea Studios, which were a bit ramshackled. I was fitted with a microphone and a battery, and seated near a vase of mauve tulips and glasses of water. The producer gave us a signal from his window and, looking at a clock over my shoulder, Andy introduced me. We talked about the One for 45 minutes.

Then the door burst open and the producer was striding towards me. "The battery's run out," he said.

"And the clock's stopped," Andy said.

The producer fell on my microphone and replaced the battery. "Start again where you were five minutes ago."

"I can't remember the question I asked," Andy said.

"I'll just start where I think," I said.

The producer returned to his room and gave me a thumbs-up from his window. I started again. But I was no longer in mid-flow, I was trying to remember what I had said and was reconstructing, and the ponderous end was of poorer quality than the earlier inspired flow.

Outside I met the next interviewee, the fifty-ish sister of a famous rock-and-roll wife.

"What are you speaking on?" I asked.

"I'm going to talk about my spirituality," she told me.

I sat in reception and waited for a taxi to take me to a tube station. I had talked about the One, and she was now talking about her spirituality, but did our words actually matter? The One was hidden like the sun behind an obscuring moon, and in our country there was cloud cover and no one was aware of the hidden One among the street lights and drop in temperature of our secular Western world.

Blood Clots and Nylons

I took a tube to Bond Street and walked to the house in Upper Wimpole Street where I was to have sodium tetradecyl sulphate foam pumped into the varicose veins of my right leg, my second sclerotherapy in a month. I was recovering from my first operation. I was out of my bandage and into a compression stocking on my left leg.

I reported to the New Zealand receptionist and took a seat. There was no one else in the waiting-room. Then Margot came out and said in her Belgian accent, "You can come in now." As I entered, her husband Jim came through the front door in a pink shirt and pink trousers. He had white hair and was in his early eighties.

"May I shake your hand from nearly twenty years ago?" I asked.

He recognised me and pumped my hand.

I said, "You told the New Zealand trainee nurse, 'Bring the stabber.' She said, 'This one?' You said, 'No, that one's too small, a bigger one.' She brought a stabber like a six-inch nail. You cupped it in your hand and said to me, 'People with blue eyes don't feel pain – '"

"They don't," he interjected, interest all over his face. "It's true."

"I thought you were hypnotising me by suggestion," I said. "Then you asked me, 'Where did you say you visited in Rome? Did you visit the Pantheon?' And as I replied you stabbed me."

He laughed and said to Margot, "Did you hear that? I asked for a bigger stabber and said people with blue eyes don't feel pain."

"You can take your trousers off and then stand on the blue box," Margot said.

I took my trousers off. Jim was reading my notes.

"Who do you resemble more, your father or your mother?" he asked.

I thought. "Both, I would think," I said.

"I was looking at their early deaths. I might be able to tell you when you're going to die."

But I didn't want to know that.

"I hope it's not in five minutes' time," I said, "from your wife's use of the stabber...."

He laughed.

"I have to use the stabber," she said, "on your left leg. Can I have my patient back, please. Lie face down on the couch."

I gripped the couch with both hands and eased myself on to it face down.

Margot worked very quickly. She squirted me with a spray. "Local anaesthetic," she said. "One here." She stabbed me with the stabber. I winced and bit the side of my hand. "Just squeezing the blood clot out." I could feel it like a marble under her fingers. "That's out." She put a plaster on my wound. "One here." I felt the stabber open a vein. "Squeezing it out."

So it went on for another three blood clots. Soon she had removed five, slitting my vein and squeezing the clot out like a pip from a juicy orange. She put a plaster on each.

"One last one," she said. I felt the pain of her pressure and squeezing.

"I can't get it out," she said. "I've done five out of six. That will just disperse under your Clexane, your heparin. I'll just mop up this blood."

"Is there a lot?" I replied, lying on my front.

"Yes." She sprayed the couch between my legs and dabbed with a cloth and then wiped.

"Yes, a lot of blood. Now I'm doing the right leg. Spray, local anaesthetic. This may hurt a bit."

I felt a sharp stinging pain as she injected the foam into the back of my right leg.

"One more here. And here."

I had six stinging injections in the back of my leg. She seemed to put a plaster on each.

"Now it's time to turn over," she said.

I turned awkwardly onto my back.

"One here."

She injected a vein and I felt the foam sting as it went in.

Then soon I was finished. "Now bandages," she said. "Left leg first."

She put my left foot on her breast and bandaged it from my toes to above my knee.

"Now I'm putting a nylon on to hold the bandage in place," she said.

She rolled a nylon stocking over my foot and pulled it up to my knee.

"Now the other leg," she said. And soon I had another bandage and was wearing another nylon stocking. I dressed.

Outside Margot was talking to the New Zealand receptionist. "We're going to Cornwall," she said to me.

"On the night train," said the New Zealand receptionist.

"Jim knows the owner of the harbour at Porthleven."

I expressed surprise and said that Pippa had relatives there.

"We're going to stay with a view of the sea. We're looking forward to it."

"What a pity we're going at separate times," I said. "Or you could come to see my harbour."

"I'd love to see it."

As I left I thought how accomplished she was. She had removed five out of six blood clots in one leg and filled the other one with foam, and now I had bandages and nylons on both there was no difference between my two legs. Neither really hurt, I was over my pain.

I said goodbye and set off for the Marylebone High Street and knew I would look out for young ladies smoking hookahs, like the caterpillar in *Alice in Wonderland*.

A Tray in her Lap

We approached Stockholm between wooden creeks and islands. I went up to the sun deck for a panoramic view of the narrow channel our ship was following. It felt cold despite the sunshine, so I went down a deck to breakfast in the veranda. It was crowded. One of the Filipino waiters sprayed my hands with sanitiser and said, "It's full. At the back, or on deck." I threaded my way to the back of the restaurant, past the self-service trays, and spotted two empty seats.

"Are these free?" I asked an elderly, stout Jewish gentleman sitting the other side. He was in his eighties and had fuzzy, white hair.

"Yes," he said. "You're more than welcome."

I smiled, deposited the orange juice I had picked up as a sign of ownership, and went off to the line of people queuing. I took a Weetabix and sprinkled on oat flakes, All-Bran, sultanas, nuts and two kinds of seeds.

When I returned his elderly wife had joined him. She was large of girth with an open face. After a few cautious sparrings about the view and the weather, the Jewish gentleman said, "We've chosen the waterways tour of Stockholm because it was the one with the least walking but now I hear there are steps down to the boat. Neither of us are as young as we used to be – "

"We've done a lot of walking in the past but we're not able to do it now," his wife interjected.

"We just want to be looked after," he continued. "My mother flew to New Zealand for the first time when she was eighty-one. She was completely blind and had no one with her. No one on board looked after her, no one helped her into her seat, and she sat on her case and cried. She died when she was ninety-nine."

I pulled a sympathetic and commiserating face.

"We went to Canada and the lady in front of my wife pushed her seat back into recline and it went back into my wife's lap. She couldn't push her seat back to compensate as it didn't work, and she couldn't use her meal tray. The lady refused to move her seat, so we asked the steward. He said the lady had every right to recline, and wouldn't do anything. He didn't want to know. So we asked the tour leader. She didn't want to know either, and wouldn't do anything. So we asked the steward again. He threatened to throw us off the plane. No one was interested. So she had to have lunch as it was handed to her – "

"I had to have it loose because the tray on the seat in front was in my lap," said the wife of ample girth.

"So now," her husband continued, "we fly business class."

"It's better," his wife said. "It's quicker at check-in and through customs, you have your own room to wait in, and there's more space between you and the seat in front on the plane."

"We went to New Zealand to see my brother," her husband continued. "We flew business class. We took a train for twelve hours and my brother met us at Wellington and drove us to his house. When we left I said goodbye to him for I reckon that's the last time I'll get out to New Zealand to see him."

His eyes misted over. It had been like saying goodbye on his deathbed.

"Then after that we took a ferry and hired a car and drove right round the island," he continued. "We stayed in guest-houses. It's good there. They've different levels. Some have a Jacuzzi. They looked after us very well. We don't want to be with people who don't want to know," he said.

They were two vulnerable elderly people who just wanted to be treated reasonably. The family had had bad experiences going to New Zealand and Canada, and they were prepared to pay for business class so they could have good experiences in their remaining years. I was sad when three days later the Jewish gentleman lost a hearing-aid while on a coach excursion from port. It could have happened anywhere in St Petersburg, and the ship's administration went through the motions but did not really want to know.

A Russian Invasion and a Defiant Estonian

Our guide in Tallinn was a roly-poly old lady who greeted us at the port, and said over the microphone as the coach pulled away, "My name is Kristi. You will be shocked to see such an old woman as your guide, but you will be seeing other ruins on this tour." There was laughter. "A younger guide will give you political correctness and say the right things but even though our driver is Russian I will not say anything politically correctly but will tell the truth." There were murmurs of approval. "Estonia is a very small country in terms of population, we are only 1.3 million. 400,000 – one third – are here in Tallinn. We are 1 million Estonians and the rest are ethnic minorities: Russians, Ukrainians and Belorussians, Russian-speakers. The Russian-speakers have to learn Estonian. I am Estonian and I have had a lifetime and although the Russians think their language is better than ours I think it is good that they are made to learn Estonian at schools. They have their own schools and they have complained to Moscow that they are being made to learn Estonian, but I think that is good. As you will have realised, I am outspoken." There was more laughter. "Parts of Tallinn are nothing to write home about, they're neither here nor there."

There were smiles from the mainly elderly passengers at her use of English idioms. Soon afterwards we stopped near the brow of a hill to look at a medieval wall. We got out and walked up to Maiden's Tower to look down from the Upper Town at the Lower Town from the 1475

Kiek in de Kök (Low German for "Look into the kitchen"). I engaged the old lady in further conversation about the Russians.

"Do you feel the Russians might try to take back Estonia?" I asked.

"Oh yes. It could happen at any time. By land, sea and air. They overfly us with their planes, invade our airspace. We are members of NATO and they advise us. They were here yesterday. We are ready. NATO will help us."

"Could the Russian-speakers ask Moscow to come in and protect their language from the Estonians?"

"You have the hit the nail on the head," she said, relishing another idiom. "That is exactly what they are doing, and how the invasion will happen."

"Could Russian militias arrive and pretend to be Russian-speaking Estonians, just as they have pretended to be Ukrainians in Eastern Ukraine?" I asked.

"They could. We don't believe them when they say they're not in East Ukraine. We know they'd do the same here. At present the Russian-speaking Estonians have no militia or army. We've prevented that. Oh look, there's a member of our Defence League." She pointed to a man walking on the other side of the road dressed in khaki and wearing a khaki flat cap.

We continued the journey on the coach and stopped at the Song Festival Grounds, where in 1988 300,000 Estonians sang national and patriotic songs forbidden under Soviet rule calling for Estonian independence. Our guide said, "I was here at one function in the Soviet time when there were visits by Soviet astronauts – cosmonauts. Our national anthem played and they did not stand up. Several old ladies poked them with their umbrellas and then they stood up and showed respect for the Estonian national anthem."

I tackled her again. "If the Russians come, will you fight?"

"We will fight. My parents' generation did not fight and regretted it. We were occupied by the Germans for three years and then the Soviets for fifty. My father was a Soviet prisoner. My mother taught history but was not trusted as her husband was a prisoner, and when asked 'Which do you prefer, Germans or Soviets?' she used to say, 'Which would you prefer to have, bubonic plague or smallpox?'"

We drove to a manor house in the countryside just outside Tallinn. When we stopped our guide said, "Two Estonian girls will play a very old Estonian instrument like a zither. I will not say more as they will give you an explanation and I do not want to steal their fire." She meant 'steal their thunder'.

We sat at dining-tables and drank coffee and ate slices of cake while the two Estonian girls in national dress played kannels. A kannel is a two-thousand-year-old instrument related to the zither. As one of the girls explained, originally it had five strings and was developed to have sixty strings. Theirs had fifty strings.

On the way back to the ship our guide talked about her defiance of Parliament. "It is corrupt," she said. "I cannot say that the white in our blue, black and white flag stands for sincerity and honesty. I was talking to a group outside our Parliament, saying this, and an MP came out. He was one of my students from twenty years ago when I was a teacher. He listened but did not say anything. Perhaps he knew I am right."

I got off the coach and as I tipped her said, "Thank you for talking about invasions and I hope they don't happen."

I walked away. She had lived her life in defiance of the Soviet Union which had imprisoned one of her parents and dismissed the other, and she had been a teacher herself. And now she revelled in the freedom of speech that came with living under the European Union. Her idioms weren't always quite right but she was proud of her independence. She expected Estonia to be invaded by Russia any day – an expert on the cruise had told me that our ship might be one of the last cruise ships to visit Tallinn before the Russians sealed off the country – and I knew that if they came she would be just as defiant to the invaders as she had been in the stories she had told us.

A Colonel in Tears

I attended the Old Boys' lunch hoping to have five minutes with the guest speaker, a Colonel who had had a distinguished army career in Northern Ireland and Bosnia and who now spoke on defence from the back benches as an MP in Parliament. It was drizzling, and the drinks that should have been set out in the chapel quad were at the far end of the dining-hall, where about twenty Old Boys had gathered. I shook the Colonel's hand and asked if he was going to take a drink. He said, "Oh, yes." We helped ourselves to champagne and he stood with me, stout and plump in a suit, white shirt and tie, although the dress was on the invitation as smart casual and I was wearing a blazer.

I told him I had just returned from Russia and Estonia, and that the Estonians had made the 300,000 Russian-speakers learn Estonian. I said they had complained to Moscow, and that the Kremlin were considering what to do and were overflying Estonia with their aircraft – hence the last NATO exercise involving 5,500 troops that had just taken place in the Baltic. He said, "I won't be a Minister because I don't believe in cutting defence, I'm better off speaking from the back benches."

I said, "Perhaps you *should* be a Minister, and argue with the Prime Minister from the inside."

Then he told me, "I'm sick of the criticism of MPs' salaries. The Press have distorted things. The duck-house 'invoice' was for an estimate, it was never bought. It was wrongly included and crossed through, and under the Freedom of Information Act the press got hold of it and made out that it was bought. The MP lost his seat as a result. MPs are not overpaid. I've run out of money. I've had to take my children out of private education, I can't afford it any more. I'd like my twelve-year-old to come here, but I can't pay the fees."

I said, "Why don't you ask the Head if something can be done?"

"No, I'm not going to beg."

"Would you like me to mention it to him?"

"Oh, yes please."

The Head was lurking beside us and after a few pleasantries I retreated to my table with my sipped-at champagne. There were nine tables of six with name cards, and I sat with contemporaries I knew distantly and a quiet man with stuck-out ears I did not know, Tim. We ate smoked salmon and duck-egg salad, roasted cod and a mousse with two creamed scones. I finished my champagne and sipped at half a glass of red wine. Coffee was served, and then the Head spoke and a senior girl introduced the Colonel by running through his career.

"I didn't know I'd done so much," said the Colonel, and everyone laughed. He moved away from his table and stood in the open floor and described how he was first shot at when he was five in Aden, where terrorists fired on a lorry he was travelling in. He had come to the school as a boarder speaking fluent Arabic, but imperfect English, and he said the school had given him everything. He wanted to go into the RAF like his father, but he went to the opticians Bird & Fairley in Loughton for an eye-test, and they found he was colour-blind. He asked his father if he could go into the Navy. No, he would not be able to see a red and green ensign. The Army? "Oh," his father had said, "the Army will take anybody." Everyone laughed.

He broke off to pick up his glass of red wine from the table, and then continued. He went to Sandhurst and was commissioned as a Second Lieutenant and then promoted to Lieutenant, and did an in-service degree in International Politics and then a tour in Northern Ireland. He said, "I was shocked to be using my military skills within the UK. I had thought when I was trained that I would be using them in places like Aden." He was promoted to Captain and then guarded Rudolf Hess in Spandau Prison in Berlin. He returned to Northern Ireland as Intelligence Officer and became Company Commander. "I was Incident Commander in Ulster at the Droppin Well disco bombing in Ballykelly. I heard the Ballykelly explosion in 1982 and arrived three minutes later. Seventeen were killed, including six of my men, among them my clerk and storeman. I was on hand and saw the victims."

He served in the Ministry of Defence and was promoted to Lieutenant-Colonel. He was military attaché to NATO in Brussels, did two more tours in Northern Ireland and then commanded the UN force in Bosnia.

"I was told there was a fifty-fifty chance I would be killed and that I would lose forty per cent of my men. It was terrible. We were billeted in a school and I slept in a bed behind the Head's desk in his study. But I was better off than my men. They were in tents in minus 20. Our progress was slow. The Prime Minister, Major, came. I said, 'You look bollocksed.' He said, 'I am, but you shouldn't be saying that to me. I should be saying that to you. They're saying you're not guarding our convoys enough, you're not on top of things.' I said, 'If there's any criticism, it's of me, not of my men. I'm responsible, not my men.' The next day I fired 150 rounds of the highest-explosive bullets at those who were attacking our convoy, and caused mayhem, and our convoys had no trouble after that. When the television reporters interviewed me, trying to find out what was going on, I said, '*I'm* responsible, not my men. If you have any criticisms, direct them at me, not my men.' There were frequent skirmishes and in one of them one of my men lost a foot. I was shot but didn't realise it for a day. I took my trousers down in the loo and saw my upper leg, which was a complete mess, and thought, 'What's that?' I pulled the bullet out of my flesh. I've got a metal plate in my upper leg and a metal hip. And I was shot in one arm. In Bosnia I discovered the Ahmici massacre in which a hundred and three people were killed. I never expected to come out of Bosnia alive. I'm so grateful to be here." He was promoted to Colonel and after working in the Supreme HQ Allied Powers, Europe he retired.

He became a commentator and spoke up for compensating injured soldiers. He criticised the government for not supplying more troops and helicopters in Afghanistan. "I went into politics because my men asked me. I said, 'If I did go into Parliament I'd be a Tory.' They said, 'We don't care what party you're in so long as you're in and can say things for injured soldiers.' I'm in politics for my men."

Cameron said at the Conservative Party conference that all the Conservative MPs should be on Twitter and Facebook. The Colonel had said, "Prime Minister, can you imagine me on Twitter? On Facebook?" Cameron had said, "Unless you are angry, embittered or drunk I think you shouldn't bother." There was laughter.

The Colonel returned to his seat to deafening applause for a very powerful speech and was presented with a bottle in a gift bag. I was passed a message that I was the senior Old Boy but it was now too late to thank him on behalf of all listening. It was announced that there would be a tour of the pre-school, and some of the Old Boys set off.

I congratulated the Colonel on the power of his points. I had a word with the Head and led the Colonel over. They were engrossed for five minutes and I saw the Colonel looking at his phone. Then he broke away and came over to where I stood in the window. "There may be a deal in a few years' time, for the sixth form," he said. "Shall we catch them up and join the tour?"

I walked with the Colonel across one field and over another field where Sports Day had just been held. We talked about Russia and Tory politics, and his role as an intelligence officer. He told me McGuinness and Kelly had both been in the IRA. We found the tour in the pre-prep and we stood in a classroom and talked about the deficit. Then we all walked back to the school. It began to rain and the Colonel and I broke off and sheltered in the lobby. We sat in comfortable chairs talking about this and that and then Tim, the quiet fellow from my table, appeared.

The Colonel had explained that Tim had lost his son a few years back. His son had gone out for the evening and did not return. "I feel guilty as his father was with me at the Army and Navy Club that evening, and his wife contacted him while he was with me to say their son was missing. His body was found the next day. He'd been hit by a train at a station where he should not have been, and one of his arms was ripped off. He wasn't found until the afternoon of that day because his body looked like a pile of rags. I think what happened was that he fell asleep on the train coming home and passed his station. He woke at the end of the line, got out, needed to pee and went down the end of the platform onto the track, and didn't hear a quiet train coming the other way. I'm staying on to attend an event at 7 with him, to remember his son."

The Head appeared with his wife and asked, "Would you like a cup of tea up at the house?"

There was a thunderstorm in progress. The rain was pelting down and jumping in the lakes of puddles and splashing our legs as five of us walked under three umbrellas while lightning flashed. We entered through a porch and sat in sofas while the Head's two children played Monopoly with his wife's mother on the carpeted floor.

I sat beside the Colonel. The Head sat in a nearby sofa with Tim alongside him and further away from us, looking at the children. We talked across an expanse of carpet. The Head's wife came with cups of tea on a tray.

The Colonel was unstoppable. "When I was in Berlin," he said, "I had this torrid affair with a woman who worked as a clerk in a large office, and after eighteen months she said, 'Oughtn't we to get married now?' So I reported this to the Army and went back to her and said, 'I've got a form for you to fill in. You have to be vetted by the Army.' She said, 'Haven't you worked out what I've been doing?' I said, 'You work in an office as a clerk.' 'Yes, but what languages do I speak?' 'German and Russian.' 'Haven't you worked out from my languages what I've been doing? *I've* been vetting *you*.' She was in MI6. My mother was in the SOE, trained in parachuting and to kill Germans in the Loire, and my first wife was in MI6. I was unhappy, and I had to write a book about Bosnia. It earned me a quarter of a million, it all went in the divorce settlement. I remarried a Countess, and three weeks ago the Deputy Director of MI6 visited me and said he'd like my daughter by my first marriage to join MI6. I said 'All right,' and put it to her. She thought about it and turned them down. She said, 'I don't want to live a lie, I don't want to pretend to be doing something I'm not.'" He laughed. "I lecture on leadership at the MI6 'school' – training headquarters – down on the south coast, I won't say where. They do courses – shooting, James Bond stuff. But she said No."

His daughter had chosen his path of being open and truthful in Parliament, not her mother's path of being duplicitous and deceitful.

Then the Colonel got on to Northern Ireland "I knew Captain Nairac. He was killed on a mission in 1977. And I knew Paul. He was surrounded by four IRA men, they were all round his car, and from inside his car he fired through his windscreen, killing two, wounding one and one ran off. I had to go and clean up. It was remarkable, he was unhurt."

He showed me a picture on his phone of the marriage of one of his men who had been badly wounded. He said, "The worst thing I witnessed was the explosion at Ballykelly."

Tim said, "We should be going soon."

I stood up. The Colonel stood, and the Head and his wife also stood. The Colonel said very hauntedly and very quietly, "I knew something terrible had happened. I arrived within three minutes and saw the carnage. There were two girls of about eighteen lying on the ground. One of them had no legs, and her arms.... She murmured to me, 'I can't move, what happened?' I said, 'There's been a bomb.' 'Have I been badly hurt?' 'Yes.' 'Will I die?' 'You may.' 'Soon?' 'It may be soon.' 'Will you hold me?' So I held her and she died within two minutes, she just slipped away. Then I was at a memorial service for those killed at Ballykelly and I was approached by an old lady. She said, 'I think you held my daughter after the bomb.' I said, 'There were two girls. I held one of them. I'm sorry to have to ask, but do you know if your daughter lost her legs?' 'Yes, she lost her legs, I've been told.' 'Then I held your daughter. She died very quickly.' 'Thank God that she died quickly,' her mother said."

The Colonel's eyes were red and had filled with tears. A tear trickled down one of his cheeks. The Head and his wife were silent before his rush of emotion, appalled at the scene he had described. I said quietly, "You'd make a good Secretary of State for Northern Ireland."

The Colonel was still in tears. He just looked at me and said nothing.

We took our leave of the Head and his wife and left. The thunderstorm had passed. Outside I shook hands with the Colonel and Tim and said I was going in the opposite direction. As I walked back to my car I thought of this past pupil who had learned his values from the school and lived for his men. He was sixty-six and had been retired from the Army nine years, but the men he had led were still uppermost in his mind. He had witnessed dreadful things in Northern Ireland and Bosnia, and they were still vividly in his mind and welled up as strong emotion he could not control. He drank too much, probably to dull the rawness of the sufferings of the dying he had witnessed and not been able to come to terms with.

Tim had suffered in the loss of his son. I did not know if he had seen his son in the morgue. I knew there had been an inquest, and possibly he had had to identify him. The Colonel's dead were not relatives, just the men he had been responsible for, who he felt it was his duty to protect. He was a good man, and his country had paid him to be a Colonel and cope with the torn-off limbs that come with keeping order in our troubled time. We paid our Army men to do a job and they had to live with the dreadful things they had seen for the rest of their lives, and the memorial services they attended brought it all back each year. He was sixty-six and in the first chill of winter, and though still a working MP he had entered early old age with memories that were tearing him apart.

A Chapel and a Bath
(Or: Irritations and Escape)

Opposite the ruined chapel as I walked to the post I encountered Joan, stooping, hobbling and frail, and making her way towards her house the other side of the road.

"Hello, Joan," I called.

She looked at me myopically.

"It's Philip," I said.

"Oh, I haven't seen you for ages. How are you?"

"Well," I said. "How are you?"

"Not good," she said. "I can't see properly. I'm losing my sight. I've had three operations in three years. First, my hip, then I had a hernia. Then I had adhesions and I had to have another operation. And my knee's dreadful. I need a knee operation. But I'm eighty-nine. I'm too told to have a fourth operation. So I'm just going to keep going until I collapse.

"What do you think of the chapel over there?" she asked. "The owner had good plans at the beginning, but they were rejected. Two lots of plans were rejected. The Council wanted to preserve two original stained-glass windows. And look at it now. It's a ruin, occupied by birds, and the two windows – the reason for the rejections – have been smashed. It's such a pity that a man who had plans to take care of it should have been told No. I'm sure the owner thought, 'Right, I'm not doing any more. If you want it as it is, have it as it is.' And it's opposite me. I could see it from my window if I could see that far. Yet there are plans to build another restaurant in the only boat-building yard. If they go through there'll be nowhere to build boats any more. And you know the public toilets facing the sea were bought by a model? She submitted plans and was rejected because the new building was to be all glass, and downstairs had a room with just a bath. Imagine, it's on the coastal footpath, and the model wants to sit in the bath and admire the view, and it hasn't occurred to her that there will be spectators looking through the glass windows. But she'll get permission for something next time round, and it'll be out of keeping with the conservation area. This old chapel can't be maintained, but it's all right to shut down boat-building for a restaurant, and public toilets for a model's bathroom. I don't know what the world's coming to. Anyway, I shall just keep going until I collapse. I'm definitely not having any more operations, I'm just too old."

I watched her hobble to her gate. She had had enough of the world, and I thought she did not want to remain in it any longer than she need. I thought that by choosing not to have a fourth operation she was speeding up her release from the irritations that surrounded her, both within her body and within the village.

An Ache and a Beach
(Or: A Run-down Battery)

I parked and crossed the road to collect Pippa. I lifted the long brown gate and swung it enough to get in. Bill was sitting in a low chair in shorts and an open-necked shirt, the ex-sailor now balding and grey with a ballooned-out stomach. He was sitting at the bottom of the slope with his two grandchildren, playing remote-controlled cars.

I stood with my feet astride, making an arch or a tunnel, and Jack, aged seven, steered a blue car between my feet to his delight and rushed round to steer it back.

"The battery I've got's lasted since Christmas," he told me. "It's now July. I've got two reserve batteries."

He had spoken matter-of-factly rather than boastfully, but life has a habit of deflating any remark approaching a boast. His three-year-old sister watched as the blue car crawled at snail's pace.

"It needs a new battery," Bill said. "I'll change it in a minute."

"How are you, Bill?" I asked, sitting on one of the flight of steps to the back door.

"So-so. You know I had temporal arterial inflammation. I had part of my temporal artery removed as a biopsy. I've been on steroids five years, and that's causing me other problems, so I'm getting myself off them, gradually."

I knew he had had a brain operation and that his medication had brought new problems.

"But as I come off them," he said, "I ache all over. Everywhere. Shoulders, neck, back. Each time I reduce the steroids and replace them with my new drug, I ache more. But I've got to get off the steroids and get this down." He patted his protruding stomach. "Anyway, I'm still here. And I can still do things. We're taking the grandchildren to the beach this afternoon. To Par. There's a cross on the beach and people leave rubbish in front of it to symbolise the rubbish they're getting out of their system within. We took the new Methodist Minister to Dartmoor last week. She's an anthropologist and she was very interested in some of the Bronze-Age sites we showed her. But there was a lot of walking and I thought I wasn't going to make it back to the car."

Then Jack came up to me. "For my eighth birthday," he said very politely, "I'm having a car this long and this wide." With his hands he measured three feet by getting on for two feet. "It will take real diesel. I'll have to fill it and run it. That's in December. I'm looking forward to December and my birthday when I'll have a really good car."

"You're lucky," I said. "You won't need a battery, you'll be using diesel." And nice boy that he was, he nodded.

I turned back to Bill.

"Yes, I'm still here," he said as if he too had been lucky. "I can run their cars for them and we'll have a good time this afternoon on the beach. I used to go down there when I was younger and run about, but now I'm just content to be there."

He was younger than me, and his battery had run down. His whole body ached every waking minute, but he would be returning to the beach of his childhood and would have a good time with his – it has to be said – exhausting but polite grandchildren.

A Message from God

"We have to be so careful with what we say to people," Pippa said. "Carol was in tears today. She hasn't been able to get something out of her head for twenty years, words spoken to her by a vicar. Twenty years ago her father and brother died close together, and she was upset. She went to a church near her, St Elizabeth's, and the relief vicar spoke to her and comforted her and said 'There, there' and asked, 'Do you want to come and speak to me?'

"She told me, 'I knew I should have said "No", but I said "Yes". I went along and he told me that my father and brother were all right. He said he had been praying and he had had a message from God in his prayers. The vicar said, "The message is, 'Watch your daughter'." There was nothing about my son, just my daughter. "Watch your daughter." I didn't know what it meant – watch out for a disaster happening to my daughter? Watch out for what? My daughter was about ten then, and ever since those words have rung in my head. Now she's having IVF treatment and I'm worried for her. I keep hearing that vicar's words, the message from God.'"

Pippa said, "I told her, 'You've done a good job in bringing her up. She's had a rubbishy boyfriend but she hasn't turned to crime or to drugs, she hasn't left her husband, she's got on and worked and done well.' Carol said, 'I know, but I still hear those words and their tone. They ring in my ears.'"

Pippa said to me, "That relief vicar wants shooting. We have to be so careful in what we say for our words can echo for twenty years. She won't be consoled. Carol said, 'That vicar ruined my life. What he said has ruined my life.' I could shoot that vicar. A balanced person would put the words out of her mind, but she's obsessed by them. She said, 'I'm often in tears when I think of those words.' Her daughter's got an IVF meeting on Wednesday and Carol is fearing the worst. IVF is being linked to ovarian cancer. She's convinced that her daughter's going to die."

Pippa shook her head. "It's terrible," she said. "What was he thinking of, delivering a message from God like that? Her father was a vicar and so deep down she's thought her father was behind the message, that's what I wonder, that he's looking after his granddaughter. She's got it in her mind that God knows of a disaster that's about to befall her daughter, and she just collapses into tears when she recalls those words."

The relief vicar had received this message in prayer. I had no doubt he was sincere and had felt a compulsion to convey a contact he had had with her dead father and brother. But he had not considered her fragility and how she would react to news from the beyond. It would not have occurred to him that his message would blight her life for the next twenty years. Sometimes a message from God is best not delivered.

A Providential Sale

At the beginning of that summer term Simon was approached by an elderly man, a Henry Brown, who looked after a local school that had been one of our competitors. He asked if we would buy his school with effect from the coming September. He had been a stockbroker and, having been involved with the school in different capacities for some years, had become a director in the school's company to help the Head out. Soon he found he was calculating and paying the monthly salaries, and as the years passed and staff retired he found he was in sole control of the financial running of the school. No one else – not the Head or any secretary in the office or any of the other management personnel – knew what needed to be done. All decisions to redecorate and all general school maintenance were left to him. He had no experience of how other schools coped with maintenance, and he paid what he was quoted. So, £26,000 was spent on installing cupboards in one classroom, many times more than the going rate, and much more was spent on decorating the senior school's assembly hall. Yet the two sites still looked tired and were under-resourced. Once the money available for improvements was spent, he had to wait a term for new funds to flow in.

Simon met Henry Brown all through that term. He was seventy-four and felt it was time to involve a younger management. There were many things to discuss and it was soon clear that we should do as he requested, if only to save the staff from a disastrous situation if anything should happen to him. It was agreed he would come in during the autumn term and transfer all the knowledge he had acquired during the previous fifteen years.

He had felt increasingly tired as the negotiations proceeded, and two weeks before contracts were due to be exchanged he went for a check-up at his doctor's. What he was told shocked him.

His doctor said, "I'm sorry to have to tell you this, but you have cancer of your liver, your pancreas and your stomach. In fact you have cancer in five places. I'm sorry to say it's inoperable. You need to be admitted to hospital now."

Reeling, Henry Brown asked, "How long have I got?"

"Two weeks."

He went home and told his wife and daughter, and then rang and asked to see Simon urgently. He told Simon. He said, "I want contracts to be signed while I'm still alive. I've rung my solicitors and there's to be a Power of Attorney."

For legal reasons, contracts would *have* to be signed while he was alive. Otherwise the Power of Attorney could not be implemented and the transfer could not take place.

Simon got on to our solicitor, and the contract was prepared immediately. There was not time to have a detailed survey, and we had to take a view on some aspects of the buildings. The partner preparing the contract came to London for a weekend conference, and in his hotel room at night, instead of sleeping, he prepared a document with dozens of articles and clauses and sent it through to Simon, who received it at 3am and returned it, read, by 7am. The contract was ready for signing within two weeks, still in August.

By now Henry Brown was lying on his back in a hospital bed, slipping in and out of consciousness. He was alive, and so the Power of Attorney operated. Through the Power of Attorney the contract was deemed to have been signed.

Henry Brown died three weeks after being diagnosed, a week after the signing of the contract, by which time the school was in our hands and the staff had been rescued and part of the purchase price had gone to his widow.

Looking back, I cannot help feeling that the whole transaction was Providential. Some nudge from Providence had inspired Henry Brown to approach us. Intuitively he knew he could not continue and that he had to make haste to place the school in safe hands. And so when he was given two weeks to live, he had already taken steps to head off what would surely have been a catastrophe if he had done nothing. For without financial steering and ability to pay salaries, the school would have foundered, whereas it has now gone from strength to strength. Henry Brown had made a Providential sale.

Truth Like a Clattering Crash

I arrived at the Stable block at 7.30 on a warm October evening, took a glass of champagne from the tray held by a waitress, saw people in a room and entered.

"Hello," I said to elderly Jack Meadow. He shook my hand warmly. There were about twenty in the room. I could see the Secretary of State for Health, tall and in a dark suit, posing for a photo with Edith Small, blonde and white-faced, and a man in a suit.

"I didn't know you were in the patrons' club," said Hilda Strawson.

"Nor did I," I said. "I've been directed to the wrong room." And I turned and made my way out and along a corridor to a very large sitting-room with a pale fawn carpet where there were already getting on for a hundred guests, the men in suits.

Pippa had followed me and we stood near the door and talked to a couple who had entered at the same time. Looking round, I decided I knew nobody. Pippa was still recovering from her latest operation, and she sat down at a table alongside a ninety-four-year-old man who had reached out to shake my hand.

Then Jack Meadow came in with a man I recognised but could not name. We stood together and chatted while Jack Meadow's wife, who had a stick, sat down at the table near Pippa.

"You have an empire now with your latest school," Jack Meadow said.

"It's not really an empire," I said.

"Yes it is," said the man I could not recognise. "If you want a pedestrian crossing, let me know. I'm Chairman of Highways, we have an annual expenditure of £700,000 and we've still got £300,000 to spend."

"Oh," I said, "can you write down your phone number?"

I gave him pen and paper, still holding my champagne glass. He wrote a number.

"Can you put your name by it?" I said, "in case I take another number and it gets muddled up."

I watched as he wrote 'David Kipling'.

Of course, it was David Kipling who lived part of the year in Turkey.

But it was worrying that I had not recognised him. I had spoken to him in the street at some length only a few months previously. I had to face the fact that in my early evening sunshine I might be experiencing the first symptoms of forgetfulness.

The Secretary of State for Health had entered and been escorted to the middle of the room, so I excused myself and set off towards him. Nearby stood Edith Small.

"I'm delighted you've got your latest school," Edith said.

I said, "I watch the Parliamentary channel when I can and I've caught you being Deputy Speaker several times. You seem to be coping very well."

"I've had a very busy week," she said.

"I saw you sitting behind the Prime Minister and the Leader of the Opposition when President Xi addressed both Houses in Westminster Hall," I said. "Lip-readers said the Leader of the Opposition told the Prime Minister, 'His ex-wife was a prostitute.' Did you hear who he was referring to?"

"No, I couldn't hear what they were saying," she smiled.

"Hopeless," I said. "We expect our MP to bend forward and eavesdrop on what the Leader of the Opposition is telling the Prime Minister."

She laughed. Then I was being introduced to the Secretary of State for Health. I told him my wife was sitting the other side of the room as she had had a recent operation.

"Your wife's over there?" he asked. "Let's go and meet her." He bounded across the room with me in pursuit and crouched by an invalid who was sitting in front of Pippa and listened intently to her story about her operation until his escort tapped him on the back and indicated Pippa. Pippa briefly told him of her experience of the NHS.

Then the Secretary of State for Health was asking me about my schools. I said, "In 1966 I discovered the Cultural Revolution in China. I mention this because I know you have a Chinese wife and you will have discussed the Cultural Revolution with her."

He looked at me in astonishment, and said, "She's told me that several members of her family suffered greatly during the Cultural Revolution."

I nodded.

Then order was being called and we were told that the Secretary of State for Health was about to address us.

The Secretary of State made his way to an extended part of the room where there was a microphone, and Edith Small introduced him. She said, "The Secretary of State for Health has the most difficult job in the Cabinet. We are fortunate to have such a good Secretary of State for Health."

The Secretary of State for Health spoke. He had a pleasant, polite tone and delivery and appeared very relaxed. He said, "No, the Prime Minister's job is the easiest in Cabinet because no one wants it." There was laughter. He said, "I introduced Ofsted-style inspections into hospitals because in schools they bring standards up and tell schools what they need to do to improve and I want the same for hospitals." He said twenty-four hospitals had been put into special measures, including a local hospital whose staff had told him, "We welcome what you have done as we know what we have to do."

He said, "Four-hundred-and-fifty people die unnecessarily each year, mostly at the weekend. It's broadly the same figure in all countries but we need to be better than them. Dying on a Sunday is more likely than on a Wednesday, and we need to put a stop to that. We need a full supporting staff every day of the week. A junior doctor in a weekend A & E without support from senior staff will have a miserable time."

I noted that only consultants were senior to junior doctors. As A & E and paediatric consultants always worked weekends, was he blaming consultants for deaths on a Sunday?

He said disarmingly that the BMA, a trade union, had misled doctors. David Kipling was standing next to me. He whispered, "The junior doctors are in uproar." "It is disappointing," the Secretary of State continued, "that the BMA walked out of the negotiations two months ago and haven't heard the government's final offer. They have misled doctors, telling them they'll be thirty- or forty-per-cent worse off. But I don't want any junior doctor to have a pay cut and it's not going to happen."

I was watching his face. Was he being sincere? It seemed so. Was he lying? It did not seem so.

Then there was a clattering crash. Everyone turned and looked. Pippa who had seen it happen later told me that a young man had stepped bumptiously back into a tray of wineglasses being held by a young waitress. Several glasses of red and white wine fell over Jack Meadow's wife and onto the pale fawn carpet all round her. I saw the waitress picking up empty glasses and escorting Jack Meadow's wife out of the room, her dress stained with red and white wine. Pools of wine were soaking into the pale fawn carpet. The owner of the Stable block moved to the stain, and politely shrugged.

It was unfortunate that the crash of glasses should coincide with the Secretary of State's assurance that doctors would not receive a pay cut. The crash sounded like a statement of a conflicting view, a protest. The stains on the carpet were seeping outwards like blots on his assurance. The junior doctors believed their lives had been stained by the policy of BMA-leaked pay cuts. Perhaps sensing this, the Secretary of State wisely brought his remarks to a swift conclusion. He had come across as a pleasant minister and there was prolonged applause. Those holding champagne glasses pretended to clap on the backs of their hands that held their glasses. Had he been telling the truth? The crash suggested something unsaid, the counter-view.

There was then an auction. Edith Small announced that the Secretary of State started work at 6am every day of the week and would be leaving in five minutes' time at 9pm as he would not be home until 11pm. He would be starting work at 6am the next day. The Secretary of State was asked if he would stay for the first five minutes of the auction. He hesitated and reluctantly stayed to witness the auction of a couple of prints, which raised £400 for party funds, but left before the auction of two paintings of Thatcher and Churchill, which each fetched £1,500.

After the auction I found myself near Edith Small. We discussed my visit to Athens and I told her the philosophers had backed my vision of what the UN should become as the UN at present was unable to solve the world's problems such as the war in Syria and the refugees from the

Middle East and North Africa.

"I'm very interested in that," she said. "Write to me and I'll introduce you to my friend who's an Under-Secretary in the UN, and also to the Foreign Secretary."

She wanted to talk further but a party activist came up and said, "I need to take Edith away and it's time for the raffle."

Edith continued talking to me about how I should write to her and she would advance my initiative in the UN. "It's worth a try," she said. "There may be opposition, but it's worth a try."

Then she *was* dragged away and the winners of the raffle were announced. Names had been written on cards the organisers held, those in the room who had bought tickets had been given no numbered tickets. Four of the eight names read out were of the organisers, including the name of the man who had dragged Edith away.

On the way out I reflected on the evening. As we walked slowly down the short drive to the gates in the warm October night, I thought of the Secretary of State for Health who had spoken after a protest march by junior doctors, which had taken place the previous weekend, and before a strike by junior doctors which was looming in a week's time.

He had made a statement with apparent sincerity and it had been answered by a crash. The falling tray and stained dress and stained fawn carpet suggested the truth was otherwise. There was no evidence that the truth was otherwise, the crash had somehow created the impression of opposition.

He had appeared to be telling the truth and most of his receptive audience held champagne glasses or wineglasses as they stood, but the real truth seemed to have intervened like a clattering crash on a fawn carpet whose immaculate cleanness seemed indelibly stained.

A Foot in the Door

I returned to my old college for a gaudy. I parked near the orchard, collected my pack from the porter's lodge and walked to the Linfield block. The key in the pack would not open the outer door at first but after struggling I got it open and climbed stairs to room 6 and dumped my bag and suit carrier on the bed.

I went down to the entrance to the Linfield Room and found a few of my contemporaries. I chatted over a cup of tea. Our Provost, Jeremy Boxham, thin, bespectacled and spiky-haired in an open-necked shirt, came in and said "Hello" to me. Several of the Old Boys wanted to speak to him while he found tea, but we were able to chat briefly about his biography of Ted Hughes, which was about to come out.

Jeremy Boxham led us into the Linfield Room and addressed us about the college's finances for an hour. He asked Old Boys to make donations.

Afterwards we had a further chat. Hughes' widow had withdrawn her support and consent, and after spending four years reading 100,000 pages of Hughes' journals in his archive he had been told he could not quote from Hughes' literary works and letters, leaving him only able to write a biography and paraphrase what he would have liked to quote. He told me that generally speaking some letters can be quoted despite withdrawal of consent if there is a public interest, but that private letters by a poet cannot be deemed to have that public interest.

I sauntered back down to the lake and encountered the Ambassador to Iraq when Saddam invaded Kuwait. We had a chat about Baghdad. Then I sauntered back to the Linfield building's staircase 21 to change into my dinner jacket. I struggled with the door, and just as I succeeded in opening it I was called from behind:

"You've managed to get into your door. I can't get into mine, the next one along."

Keeping my foot in the door I turned and saw a little old man.

"I ought to be able to open doors," he said, "I was an engineer. I was up here during the war, 1943. I had an eighty-year-old tutor who lived in Headington. He wouldn't come into the college so we had to go to Headington. He wouldn't answer our questions. I was eager to learn and I'd ask a question and he'd just look at me and ignore me. Sometimes the tutorial was cancelled for no particular reason. We'd travel to Headington and have to turn round and come back. We had a lousy tutor and what I learned was in spite of him, and so I only got a pass degree.

"I've crossed into physics and written dozens of papers. They're all online, all a hundred and forty-three of them. But I can't get anything published as there has to be peer review and I'm against the way they think. I worked in Avro – the British aircraft manufacturer and aviation engineering company that became Hawker Siddeley Aircraft – for nineteen years. I worked on Vulcan. It was secret work, so I had no reference at the end and that made it hard to get another job when I left. I researched the air displaced by jets like Vulcan. I researched Maxwell's ether. You know, in the 1860s it was thought that the air consisted of ether. That's how I see it. The universe is infinite, it has no beginning or end, there was no Big Bang and it's composed of electrical charges that are substanceless, a network of ether. I'm with Maxwell and Lord Kelvin. Einstein disregarded ether in 1905 and later, but I think he's wrong. So you see, as I came to physics through engineering research and had been into aerodynamics and am an original thinker I've a different view from what peer reviewers think and so I can never get published. I'm ninety but I'm still writing papers which I put online."

"I thought you must be ninety," I said. "If you came up in 1943, that was seventy-two years ago. You were eighteen in 1943."

"I was," he said, "and I had great curiosity, but I never had my questions answered and so I struck out on my own and conducted original research and I've come up with original answers that reject the conventional way of thinking."

I still had my foot in the door.

"I'll see if I can get my door open now," he said. "I'll have to bring some original thinking to it as it's not responding to what they put in my pack. Look, here's my card. You can find me online. You can read about my view of ether online. You can always give me a ring and come and see me. I'm in Surrey. I've enjoyed talking to you."

"Good luck with your door," I said, pocketing his card.

As I changed into evening dress to go to chapel, then the champagne reception with my contemporaries and the older Old Boys and then dinner in the hall, I reflected that he had been unlucky in the timing of his time at college. He had been a wartime undergraduate at a time when tutors were a law unto themselves, and he had not been taught as well as would happen today. But the good thing was, he had in consequence learned to be original, to go off and research the air and find a network of electrical charges that contradicted post-1860 science.

During his work on Vulcan he had discovered that the universe is full of ether, contrary to what the post-Einsteinian textbooks say. And because he was so different he had not managed to get his foot in the door. Perhaps one day he would be regarded as a genius like Newton, another original who discovered the properties of light, gravity, calculus and mechanics when he was only twenty-four. I was full of admiration for this old man's solitary research and a hundred and forty-three papers that had disregarded the views of scientists and his peer reviewers, and was sad that he would die without getting his foot in the door.

An Evangelical Tone and a Trick

The first half of Derren Brown's one-man show *Miracle* was tame: a game of consequences in which an answer from a member of the audience had been predicted and was within a blown-up balloon. He had a patter, he talked non-stop, and in encouraging a member of the audience to choose 'at random' page 177 from a book and then find the page torn out and in his pocket suggested that the member of the audience had been fed the numbers in the patter. Certainly 'seven' was mentioned several times.

Somehow Brown was encouraging the audience to make 'free' choices in response to a ceaseless patter which had lodged in their subconscious and influenced what they said. To put it another way, Brown encouraged the subconscious to make choices of which the conscious was not aware.

After the interval things hotted up. He made the packed audience stand and he adopted the role of an evangelical preacher and faith-healer. (Brown had been an evangelical Christian before he decided he did not believe.)

"Hold hands with your neighbours," Brown called, "both sides. Close your eyes and see your ideal healthy self-image and your own face on a seashore with the sea behind it. Look at your ideal self-image, healthy, no pain. Let the face come towards you so you can see it's brimming with health. Now become that face."

Suddenly there was a terrific sound that filled the theatre and many lights flashed. Raising his voice like an evangelical preacher and faith-healer, he called out, "Become your ideal self-image, feel no more pain, you're cured. If you have sciatica, you're cured. If you have poor eyesight, you're cured."

Then there was another blast of sound and more flashing lights. His voice rose and without attributing the healing to God he assumed the tone of a faith-healer but using secular language. There was another blast of sound and more lights.

"You've been cured," he announced, "now make your way to the side to come up on stage and tell me how you've been cured."

A dozen people filed and formed a queue on the left of the theatre. The first went up on stage, a lady in her fifties. She broke down in tears and told how her sciatica had gone. A man followed. He described how he could now walk. All of those who spoke had received a healing experience during the blasts of sound and the flashing lights. Brown put out a hand and pushed each on the head and one after another they fell back hypnotised into the arms of a helper behind them, who laid each on the floor.

A lady came up who had been dependent on her spectacles and was nearly blind.

"Read this without your spectacles," Brown said.

A newspaper was shown on screen with a headline. She took off her spectacles and read. She was able to read the words. Then he turned to the audience.

"Who's sceptical?"

A man in his late forties raised his arm.

"Come up."

The man went up and was given a child's book which was shown on screen. There were simple one-syllable words on a page.

"Read them," Brown said, pushing his head.

The man tried but was completely unable to read the words. He had been hypnotised not to read words that were very easy.

Like Christ Brown had healed the sick, but by manipulating their suggestibility from a secular point of view, using the tone of an evangelical preacher and demonstrating that healing had nothing to do with faith or evangelicalism. The implication was that the healing was a response to a suggestion.

"If I were you," he said at the end, "I would still get your sciatica treated and I would still use your spectacles for reading."

Brown was admitting that no one had been healed fundamentally, they were suggestible and had responded to suggestion in the moment and had not had any long-term cure.

Later Brown hypnotised six men sitting on the stage to bow their heads and look down while a man was levitated among them, hanging in the air in the floodlit dark apparently without wires. But I was still thinking about how he had convinced a dozen people that their long-term ailments and disabilities had been cured when they had not been cured.

Brown had manipulative skills that enabled him to be one step ahead of his victims, who did not realise what he had done to them. He was a trickster. He had used an evangelical tone and had produced results of faith-healing, but his whole approach had been a trick.

Fortune's Wheel
(Or: A Membership Secretary and a Foreclosure)

Pippa said, "I had dinner with Stella Wrighter. She was hilarious about Edith Small. Stella runs an annual bridge group for a cancer charity and Edith greeted her like a long lost friend, 'Oh, it's so nice to see you, I've been thinking of you.' So Stella said, 'I'm selling raffle tickets.' 'Oh, come to our table, we'll have some.' So Stella went to the table with a strip of tickets for £5 and Edith got out a £20 note. Stella said, 'Oh, thank you, Edith,' and put the note in the tin and gave her four strips of tickets. 'Oh, oh, oh, yes that's all right,' Edith said, realising she would not be getting any change. 'Have you met my brother?' 'Oh,' said Stella, 'are you having £20 worth too?' and the poor bloke had to put his hand in his pocket and hand out £20 as well."

Pippa laughed. Then her face looked serious. "Stella is on the committee for NADFAS. The membership secretary for NADFAS for years has been Pamela Mountjoy. You've met her, she was at the dinner given by Rosie many years ago. I've seen her regularly at meetings. You're supposed to go every time, but I've had operations and I've said to her, 'Won't be able to come next time,' and she's said, 'I'll put you down as being here.' She kept a long and wide sheet of paper that covered the table and you could see at a glance who attended when and who didn't. She was very efficient. Her son was at Charterhouse and her daughter at Cheltenham Ladies' College. She lived for NADFAS and her immediate surroundings. She lived in a large house and everyone thought how fortunate she was.

"I saw her in September and said I couldn't go in October because I would be in Greece. Stella said Pamela wasn't there for the October meeting, and the sheet wasn't there. She'd sent in a letter: 'Because of my personal circumstances I won't be able to attend.' The committee didn't know what it meant. She lived in one of the large houses opposite the golf course, and one of the committee members went and.... Stella said, 'It was awful. Her husband was supposed to be the cleverest man many had met. He'd forged her signature on documents and taken out a loan without her knowing, and the business the loan was for failed, and the bank foreclosed on them. Pamela heard on a Tuesday and was out of the house the following Friday. She's not seeing her husband any more, she's living with a friend, stunned by it. Her husband seems to be living with his daughter, who married a man who is into horses.'

"We don't know what happened. Perhaps the bank had been writing to him for months and he ignored them and they got fed up and foreclosed. Her mother had a cottage in the grounds and that went too.

"Anyway, a member of the committee found the foreclosers throwing everything into a skip, including the NADFAS membership books. The books were rescued from the skip. Pamela said that she'd come to terms with it all. She may come back, but she was too shocked to come back immediately."

I pondered the efficient membership secretary and her pride in her sheet of paper, her large house and the sudden change in her fortunes which had plunged her down from a great height and humiliated her in front of those whose attendance she had monitored. No matter how well off we seem to be, Fortune's wheel can turn at any time and plunge us into ruin and homelessness.

A Wheel and an Allotment

I found the car park for the woodland cemetery and parked between trees. I walked through drizzle to the Gathering Hall, which was in a wooden complex. The Hall was packed and I greeted Angela Mason, who said, "Thank you for coming."

I kissed her and said, "I was very sad to hear about your husband."

She said, "He had cancer and it spread everywhere and he tried to carry on. He went to his allotment and carried on doing his volunteer work in wildlife and the cubs, but it just overwhelmed him."

"And you sustained him during that last illness," I said.

She said, "I was doing things every day, yes, but it got too overwhelming and he went."

"It's a release for you," I said understandingly, and she nodded without saying anything.

I spotted three ladies I knew and I crossed to have a chat.

"We were just saying you haven't changed in twenty years," one of them – Stella Wrighter – said.

"Peter Pan," I said, "forever young, though under the present circumstances I should be careful not to boast of such matters."

The ladies laughed. We chatted and then allowed ourselves to be swept along by a slow flow of people taking all present to one of the woodland halls across a courtyard. There were chairs near the back and we took our seats. Many behind us had to stand.

We were asked to rise for the arrival of the coffin. Kevin Mason was borne in on the shoulders of four undertakers and placed on wooden trestles near a lectern with a microphone. In place of an altar there was a view of bracken, trees and woodland. A spoked cycle wheel, decorated with evergreen to make a wreath, was propped on the top of his coffin.

The service sheet, a booklet, had a picture of Kevin Mason cycling by the sea on a bicycle with drop-handlebars. I looked through the booklet and was startled to see from an outline of his life with dates that he had been a professional cyclist in Holland, Belgium and France for two years in the 1950s. There was a record of his road races from 1949 to 1955, and of the position he came in each. I had known him as a quiet man, very much Angela's husband when she was Chairman of the Council.

A funeral director stepped to the microphone and greeted us. He gave us a very slow account of Kevin Mason's life: how his parents were teachers and how he was evacuated to Devon during the war, how he stayed on down there with his parents and went into a bank and then became a professional cyclist; how there was no money in cycling in those days – a prize was a puncture repair kit or a saddle-bag – and so he had become a teacher of deaf children. He was known as a good listener and a kind man, and tirelessly worked in his allotment to fill his fridge with 'home-grown' food.

One of his three sons spoke next, reminiscing about things he and "Dad" had done when he was a boy. Towards the end his voice broke with emotion and he blinked back tears.

Angela Mason read a poem ('The Glory of the Garden' by Rudyard Kipling) and one of his grandsons, who was over from New Zealand and aged thirteen, read another poem. There was no singing. There were closing sentences, then the floor-to-ceiling windows in front of us miraculously opened and the four undertakers returned and hoisted the coffin onto their shoulders and slow-marched out into the woodland, turned at right angles and disappeared into trees.

We sauntered back to the Gathering Room for coffee. There were sandwiches and sausage rolls by a wall, and photos of scenes of his life, including his cycling. I spoke to the three ladies and to Angela Mason's grandson.

"He's played cricket with men and was man of the match," Angela Mason said.

I saw the lean, mature look of a future star within his thirteen-year-old face.

"You can play for New Zealand," I said.

He nodded.

"If you want it enough and if you practise enough."

Then I saw Jack Meadow. He waved at me and we stood together, taller than the others in the room, and we agreed that bearing in mind Angela Mason had been a local political figure there seemed to be no one from the political scene present. It began to drizzle again, and I said goodbye to Angela Mason.

"Thank you for coming," she said, "and for speaking to my grandson about cricket. I'm really pleased you could come."

As I walked through the woods back to my car I pondered the humanist funeral. A secular society had collectively dumped Christianity, and there was no resurrection or after-life in the service, just a focus on what Kevin Mason had done: worked in a bank, cycled professionally, taken part in road races in Britain and Holland and worked in a school for the deaf. He had become a good listener because he had taught the deaf to speak and to lip-read and he had had to pause while he assessed their efforts.

His had been an ordinary, modest, local life but he had done voluntary work as a scout leader, youth leader, trainer for the local football club too and volunteer for the local wildlife trust in the meadows by the local river. With his cycling and his allotment and now his retirement work he had lived much of his life in the open air.

Later the coffin would be taken to Parndon for cremation. He would not be buried in this woodland cemetery, but he had lived close to Nature and we had paid our respects to a life that expected no immortality and took heart from the closeness of his family, some of whom lived in New Zealand.

The Wheel of Fortune had turned, and fate had handed him a cruel allotment. But he had borne it bravely and had been regaled by the simple enjoyments of an ordinary life.

A Pancreas and a Quiz
(Or: We're all going to Die)

At the Forest supper I spotted elderly Henry standing near a table offering Christmas cards, tea towels and Forest calendars.

"How are you keeping?" I asked, peering into his eyes and noting his hollow cheeks.

"Not so good," he said. "I've had cancer, in my back. In my pancreas. I had some blood in my urine but I'd had prostate trouble and I thought some had leaked. Anyway, I had an operation two weeks ago. And I'm feeling all right. But I've got to have dialysis. Three days a week. I go to Whipps. Two till about five. I'll have to do that until I die. We're all going to die, you know. We're all going to die."

"We certainly are," I said, "but not yet. Don't die yet. Be here next year with another quiz."

He looked at me strangely.

"You're right," he said. "Not yet."

"See you here next year," I said.

On the tables were photocopies of his latest quiz. But actually, I later learned, it was a quiz everyone had done in 1996. "No one'll remember," he had said. "It's nearly twenty years ago."

Yes, I thought, we're all going to die. We all carry within us the seeds of our own destruction, as did his pancreas. But before we face our end, which we will all have to do some day, there were things to learn about the fascinating universe, and life was exciting, like rising to the challenge of an exercising quiz. Life was interesting, and we had all postponed facing our deaths for the immediate enjoyment our lives gave us in the present moment. Life was good, and we did not have to think about leaving it yet.

Roots and a Shock

I went to the dentist, Dr Clerihew, to have a crown fitted. I was reclined back to a lying position and opened my mouth.

"Relax for me," the dentist said.

Drilling and then fitting took a quarter of an hour.

"You're going to do my roots now?" I asked.

I had had a bit of broken tooth at the back of the right side of my jaw, and she had put a skim over it which had broken owing to sharp food and had had to be done again. It had fragmented again, and the roots beneath the skim seemed to be near the visible surface.

"Yes," the dentist said behind her mask, "open wide. Injection going in now."

I felt a stab on the outside of my lower gum.

"Sorry." She changed the position and stabbed again. "That's gone in," she said.

Then I felt a stab on the inside of my gum. "I wasn't expecting that," I said.

"Oh, we're full of surprises. Now rinse." I rinsed and sat while the dentist and the nurse pored over a screen behind me and talked in whispers.

"Your bottom lip should be numb now," the dentist called.

But it wasn't at all numb.

"It hasn't happened," I said.

"Oh."

"If you like, we'll just proceed without it."

"No, we need to do it."

She came and probed my lip and asked if I could feel her prod. I could.

"I'll have to do the injection again," she said.

I felt another stab on the outside of my bottom gum, but less this time as my gum had gone a bit numb. Then I felt another stab on the inside of my bottom gum.

"Now I'd like you to return to the waiting-room downstairs. I'll just take an X-ray of my next patient's teeth, it'll only take a couple of minutes. Go and sit in the waiting-room while your lip gets numb."

I made my way unsteadily down the stairs and sat and read a book on Shakespeare's sonnets I had brought. I was oblivious to the rest of the surgery waiting-room, another patient and my teeth, lost in the Elizabethan time.

Ten minutes later Dr Clerihew returned, still wearing her mask. She beckoned me to follow her upstairs.

"Is it numb now?"

"Yes, it's worked."

"Good," she said.

I sat back in the chair, avoiding the tray set out with instruments, and she reclined me to a lying-down position.

"Open wide," she said. "Nice and relaxed for me. Just having a look. I'm going to poke around. Can you feel that?"

With my mouth open I shook my head.

I felt the suction machine the nurse operated suck out my saliva.

"All done," she said.

She had only looked in my mouth for about ten seconds.

"Bite on the muslin pad between your teeth."

I bit.

"Keep it until you get home," she said. "Read this."

She handed me half a sheet of A4 headed 'Extraction'. Shocked, I read that I should keep my socket dry for twenty-four hours and then wash my mouth out in hot salt water every three or four hours to stop the socket from becoming infected.

Now, and only now, did it dawn on me that I had had an extraction. 'Removing roots' had been a euphemism for 'extraction'. No wonder she had wanted to get the injections right.

I thanked Dr Clerihew and the nurse, still biting on my muslin pad, and descended the stairs holding the rail and settled up with the receptionist. Not long before I had been sitting in the waiting-room waiting for my lip to go numb without the faintest notion that I was about to have a tooth removed. Had I been over-trusting? Or just very (literally) laid back in her reclining chair? Had I been too involved in Shakespeare's sonnets? Or was I getting old and no longer had the instinct for danger and survival that I had had as a younger man?

I did not know the answer, but it was astonishing I could accept removal of roots without thinking that the broken tooth above them would have to come out too, leaving a gaping socket that would have to be treated with hot salt water for a few days. But then I thought it was a good thing I had not known as the mental ordeal, the fear, of having an extraction had been completely removed and I had offered a relaxed mouth as she had wanted.

An Afghan and Refugees

I knocked on the window of the first taxi at the rank in Berlin's

Alexanderplatz, and told the swarthy driver, "Kaiser Wilhelm Memorial Church, the Christmas market next to it." He nodded and Pippa and I got in. He spoke English, so we had a chat about the international situation.

I said, "We were told before we came there would be armed police in the Christmas markets following the Paris massacre, but there aren't any."

He agreed and said, "Berlin is safe."

I asked, "We've heard there were eight hundred thousand refugees. But I haven't seen any. Where are they?"

"In the beginning, outside Berlin in villages. But now in the Tempelhof airport barracks. Ex-military. They've been put where the military used to be. It's difficult, they keep coming."

"And Angela Merkel has been criticised for letting them in?"

"Oh, yes, there are so many."

We approached Potzdamer Platz.

"The wall used to be here," he said. "Here we cross from East Berlin to West Berlin."

"Which are you from?"

"Oh, I'm from Afghanistan. But not recently. I've been here twenty-five years. I was a refugee from the Russians."

"In the late 1980s," I said. "When bin Laden was a hero for fighting the Russians."

"That's right," he laughed.

"Do you go back to Afghanistan?"

"No, I've never been back. My children were born here. All my family are out. Some are in Canada, some in the United States. None of my family's in Afghanistan."

"You've done well," I said.

"Yes," he said. "I have a small company. I employ drivers. Not enough come forward. I will have to employ refugees, maybe, I'm not filling the positions now. But I have work."

"And Afghanistan?"

"It's in a terrible state. It may fall to the Taliban. But IS are there too. It's in a bad way. I'm glad I am not there. I'm glad I became a refugee. The Russians were terrible in those days but Putin has shown pictures of hundreds of lorries taking oil from IS to Turkey. The pictures were taken by one of his planes. One was shot down because it was taking pictures. Turkey has been given three billion euros to stop the refugees from leaving Turkey, and they're buying cheap IS oil, double-dealing.

"The Russians were terrible in those days but Putin's right about the Turks. You know," he said, "the Afghans have never really liked the Turks. I became a refugee because of the Russians but I'm on the Russians' side against the double-dealing Turks. They should be stopping the refugees from leaving, not encouraging them to leave and adding to the problem. There have been so many refugees here, the villages of Germany can't cope and nor can Berlin now. We just want the flow of refugees to stop."

A Minute and Eternity

"Look," Pippa said, "Jennifer's in the paper." I saw a picture of an elderly woman. "We used to go down to the harbour in Porthleven, Breage-side. I was often with her. She later had a husband who was virtually bedridden and she called upstairs, 'Just taking the dog out, I'll be up in a minute.' She went outside the front door and fell down and died. So he was stranded upstairs. Then the dog died. I don't know how much later. Look, the paper says the dog and Jennifer have been buried in the same coffin."

It was a slight story but I found it haunting. That's what happened. You called up the stairs to your disabled husband that you won't be a minute, and fell dead, and the minute became all eternity. When she did not come up he must have called down from upstairs and when there was no answer he must have got himself out of bed and dragged himself down the stairs and opened the door and found her outside in the cold with the dog beside her. If she had known that when she opened the front door she would be taking leave of her life, what could she have done? There is so much organising of our affairs we have to do before we move on.

I thought of my aunt, who had an operation in her nineties. She asked me to visit her and opened her bureau.

"If anything happens to me," she said, "there's my chequebook and my pension book. And there's my will. And the order sheet for my funeral service, the hymns I've chosen."

I said, "I'm sure it won't come to any of that, I'm sure you'll come safely back," as she indeed did.

But given the choice wouldn't we all plan our departure, or would we think it best to go suddenly and leave the planning to those who are left behind, even if they are disabled?

A Fall and a Physio

Pippa returned slightly late from one of her groups. "I've just driven Mandy to St Margaret's," she said. "She's had a terrible time. Her husband's in his mid-seventies and he fell and broke a hip and he had to go into Whipps to have it pinned. He bruised his wrist at the same time. A physio was sent to his hospital bed to exercise his hand. He said, 'No, please, it's not ready, it's very painful.' But she was very domineering and brushed his objections aside and said, 'Push against the table, really hard. Push. Come on, push.' He did as he was told – and broke his wrist. Now he's bedridden. He can't get out of bed because of his wrist. He's been in bed for five weeks because of his hip and his wrist and now he's got bedsores. He's been in all three hospitals round here, and she's got nothing good to say about any of them, not the doctors, not the physios, not the nurses.

"He's in St Margaret's at present. She visits him every day. She's got no car, I don't think she drives. She was going to walk from the group to the station, well over a mile, and get a tube two stops and then walk to St Margaret's, another two miles. I couldn't bear to see her set off and do that when she's so surrounded by suffering.

"I took her to St Margaret's. The road to the M25 is cordoned off. There was a shooting in the Marriot car park this morning and a young man died of gunshot wounds in the Volunteer car park. Gang warfare, the murdered man was being paid back for attacking a man a couple of months ago. There was a feud involving drugs and he had a man's hand cut off outside Nu Bar. The man who did the cutting took a local taxi wearing a tracksuit inside out, and the driver noticed blood on it and after dropping him at his home heard about the incident, put two and two together, told the police and the attacker was arrested. The organiser fled to Spain and returned to the Marriot. He booked a room there and came out to get in his car and was shot. He staggered into the road and flagged down a passing car driven by an elderly couple, commandeered it and was driven to the Volunteer. Those paying him back pursued him and shot him dead in the car park. The elderly couple must have been completely traumatised. Anyway, the traffic was horrendous but I'm glad I took her. She's got enough to be getting on with without having to walk three miles to make her daily visit to her husband."

I shook my head. I had been hearing about a fall that had broken a hip and then I had been hearing about man's fallen state, a ruthlessness that had succeeded his gentleness in paradise and was beyond the help of any physio. I put the Fall out of my mind and pondered on what Pippa had begun to tell me.

Mandy's husband's health had been reasonable until his fall and his broken hip. Physiotherapists are supposed to ease constricted limbs, not damage them further. His broken wrist had set him back and made him bedridden. He and his wife had been all right before the fall, and now, following the appearance of the physio, they were in daily crisis.

Of Mice and Muscles

I rang Derek and told him, "Mice are gnawing the wires of our outside clock. Have you got any poison they eat and then go outside to die?"

"Before you go any further," he said, "I'm not doing it any more for a bit. I've got a muscle problem in my legs. I can't stand up and so I can't work at present. But no, I haven't got any poison where they go outside and die. You need to set more traps. And you can buy poison yourself and put it down in trays. You can buy sandwich bags and tip some poison in and lob them in the corners where you can't reach. Tie the bags at the top. The mice gnaw through to the poison."

"Thanks," I said. "So what happened to your leg muscles?"

"I was in the kitchen six weeks ago and my muscle above my knee gave way and I would have fallen over backwards and hit my head if I hadn't clutched onto the sink. Then it happened again three weeks ago and tore another muscle at the back of my knee. I can't walk. I'm getting old. I'm seventy-one next birthday, you know. My body's not functioning as it used to. If it weren't for Myra I wouldn't be able to get around. I've got mice in my muscles."

"You're five years my junior," I told him. "You're like a footballer who's got a muscle tear and can't play for six weeks. You need to strengthen your muscles with glucosamine – joint protection. You need to go to a gym once a week and try to reform your diet."

"Yes, you're right. I'll get some of that stuff. I should have gone to a gym already. My legs might be more supple then. My cholesterol's all right, it's five. We eat good food, chicken and stuff. Yes, thank you, I'll discuss what you said with Myra and put some of it into practice."

"Doctor Rawley has spoken," I said. "Next patient, please."

After I rang off I realised that I had rung him to help me eradicate mice but had ended up providing him with help for his muscles. We all have our problems and turn to each other for help, sometimes for a fee and sometimes out of human sympathy. I was glad my advice had not involved a fee.

A Disguise like a Stove-Pipe Hat

We drove in front of Audley End in early January, parked in the muddy car park and tiptoed back to the shop, turned the corner and Emma greeted us with her three children and husband. Her mother came out and joined us, and her husband. Then we wandered slowly to what had once been the housekeeper's room, where a long table in the bay window had been reserved. We drifted through to the old servants' hall, now a restaurant, and ordered coffees.

Theo said to me, peering through his spectacles, "I was your way recently. I was a candidate for the Headship at a school near you, one of your competitors." He named a local school. "I came second."

"Oh," I said, "in the early days they took pupils from us."

"They're a hundred pupils short now," he said.

"I'm glad you didn't get it as you'd have poached a hundred of our pupils."

He smiled. "I've met the Heads of two of your schools at ISA conferences," he said. "I had a long talk with one of them about your latest school. She's looking forward to working with them."

We took our coffees through to the bay window. There was a view across the green sward to the river, which had recently flooded: there were pools of water on the grass. About a hundred geese stood by the distant river.

Our lunch order had been taken, and I went through to the servants' hall to contribute to the payment. We then set off with the children to watch a riding display, leaving Pippa and Theo to guard the table. By the stable block a girl was riding a horse round a poled enclosure and describing how she was steering to some twenty lookers-on. She explained how she controlled the horse's direction by pulling on the reins and kicking with her heels. An older lady nearer the spectators summarised what was being said in a clear voice. Then Theo rang to say, "The food is on the table."

Back in the bay window I tucked into carrot and parsnip soup, bread and butter, and then a sausage roll.

I said to Emma, "I was hearing from Theo how you nearly moved. How's the partnership going?" She was a GP and she had bought into a partnership.

She said, "I'm part-time. But the virtual paperwork is time-consuming, anything from updating records to dealing with prescriptions. It's an extra eight hours a week. I'd like to be bought out and then be a salaried GP elsewhere."

"So you'll blame Theo," I jested. "You'll say, 'I'd like to stay but my husband's just got a job elsewhere and I have to go, so please buy me out.'"

"Something like that," she agreed, smiling.

"You like the practice?"

"Oh yes. It's interesting. We have quite a few Syrians."

"Do they come with blisters, having walked as refugees?"

"No. They seem well off. They have smartphones. They don't speak much English, they bring an English-Arabic dictionary with them and I have to communicate with them through that. Some bring another Syrian who speaks a bit of English and acts as an interpreter."

I nodded. Then I listened to her elder daughter who told me about her pets. "We have five fish and we've had three kittens. The first one, Oscar – no," she said, interrupting herself, to her mother, "I want to tell the story – was sadly run over by a car a month ago. Now we've got two more."

Emma said, "She was deeply upset at the death of her kitten a month ago but now she's telling the story her account is matter-of-fact."

"She's empowered herself by telling the story," I said. Emma nodded.

After lunch we walked through the kitchen and scullery, and the wet and dry laundry, to the dairy. Videos of past servants talking about what they did were projected onto walls from hidden projectors. We walked down over the stable bridge to the playground and watched as the children climbed up inside a small house and looked out of the windows, and then clambered onto a wooden horse and cart. We sauntered on to the stable block and looked at a couple of horses.

I found some dressing-up clothes and helped the children into jackets and skirts of the 1880s. They found a scrubber and scrubbed a wooden horse and rubbed it down and then sat on saddles and 'rode' it. I found them hats and put a stove-pipe hat on my head and bowed and touched the brim to the ladies, who laughed.

It began to drizzle and we walked back to the car park and said our goodbyes and drove off.

"I had a long chat with Theo while you were looking at the riding demonstration," Pippa said. "He told me why he had the interview. The roll at his school had fallen to a hundred and fifty before he took over and the governors deemed it dangerously low. No one else would take it on. It's now a hundred and seventy, but though the nursery's full there aren't enough in the junior school. They're leaving at five and going into the State system and the fees haven't been coming in. Three of the hundred and seventy are free – his children – and other staff have children there and don't pay fees. There hasn't been enough to pay the staff, and Theo's had to impose a pay cut. There isn't the money to decorate and attract more parents and new teachers, and he and Emma have been doing things to save money. Emma has been going in and Hoovering and cleaning to save money. They fixed up to amalgamate with another school, but the other school owns its buildings, whereas Theo's school doesn't, and the other school pulled out. The other school is anyway in a bad way and is expected to close in the next few months. There isn't enough to keep Theo's school going and it's expected to close in the coming months. That's why he's been applying for other jobs. They're very worried. Emma is very worried too. They're planning to move and sell their house and start again elsewhere."

I was quite shocked. "Were we invited today so they could tell us that?" I asked.

"No, I don't think that. I think they wanted to see us. But they're very worried."

I nodded. I pulled a warm padded coat over my body-warmer and switched on the seat-warmer and settled back into the flow of hot air Pippa had turned on. I thought of how we had gone back in time by frequenting the servants' hall and how we had dressed up in the clothes of grooms to bring their heavy workload and the servants' lives to life in the children's minds.

But in fact besides taking children back to past times the clothes were a disguise. I had dressed the children and had put a stove-pipe hat on my head but the real stove-pipe hat had been worn by Theo, who had disguised the seriousness of the situation that had led to his interview. He had worn a disguise like a stove-pipe hat.

Prosecco in Artillery Lane

We were in to the restaurant in Artillery Lane and sat at the reserved table and were served mint tea and sparkling water. The others came in during the next few minutes. Florence said, "I've just been asked, am I one of the brothers? I mean to say...."

I said, "You should have said you were transgender," and everyone laughed.

The restaurant was a third full and we stood and chatted until Jack, who had found the restaurant and made the reservation, came in.

"You should have ordered Prosecco," he said, and when the nine of us were sitting down glasses of Prosecco arrived. We sipped the sparkling wine, and while a selection of tapas arrived our conversation sparkled.

Jack was up the far end of the table, opposite Pippa who had laryngitis and sinusitis and was trying to nurse her voice. I sat opposite Rupert and asked him if he was fully retired.

He said, "No, I'm still working full time as a solicitor. The fifty thousand I was owed for forty years has theoretically been paid," he continued, the Prosecco loosening his tongue, "but it hasn't fully happened yet, and nor has my retirement. I'm fed up. I haven't had a retirement. A man I have known for many years died recently aged ninety-two. He left me twenty-five thousand to spend on myself. He said, 'I don't want you to save it for something or give it to your children. It's for you to spend.' I've always had a chip about not going to university. Others had university holidays and travelled, I was working and couldn't go. I want to travel."

"A cruise?" Florence asked.

"No, I wouldn't want to go on a cruise. There's a problem with going abroad. Being a diabetic I have to take needles, and they might be confiscated at an airport. I've got to think about it."

"A cruise company will take care of that side," Rex said. "You need to book."

"I need to think about it," Rupert said. "Anyway, I'm working full time and I can't go for the time being." And I doubted whether he would go.

The tapas and succulent arancini Jack had ordered was replaced by our main dishes. I had hake. I asked Rupert about his nephew who had been confirmed as a diabetic.

He said, "Families are difficult. You are kindly and domineering, but I have let my children be and do what they want to do. And Henry has strong views. When I was found to be a diabetic, mother controlled my diet and set me up for life. I've stuck to that regime and have always weighed my food and never had to vary the twice-a-day injections. But today, 'times have changed'. You can have what you like and then inject yourself with insulin. I have taken the traditional way, Henry wants to go the modern way. I see more of Kathleen. I like her partner and we watched the Conservatives' election victory together." Then he said, "My memory is getting bad. I can't remember names, and I can't remember how to spell some words. I don't use a computer. I write a letter and read it and have difficulty in identifying my thread."

There were memories of our childhood days. Tales were told about me to great mirth, and I recounted how Rex, lunching above the family shop with Rupert and me when he was about seven, did not like the fat on his ham and threw it out of the window, and how it landed on a lady's hat as she walked underneath. There was hilarity. We ordered puddings. I had ice creams, saying to mirth, "We didn't have ice cream during the war so I have to make up for it now."

The Prosecco and red wine had fired us up and there was a swapping of places and Jack came and sat next to me. He told me how the Bank of England had done unreported quantitative easing and had created £375bn of new money more than a year back and had lent it to the Bank of England Asset Purchase Fund at 0.5%. The Fund had purchased gilt-edged debt at 2.85% and had made a profit of 2.35%, which on £375bn was £8.81bn.

"That's where they found the money to pay for the tax cuts," I said. "I reckon the £375bn is a safety fund to prop up the British economy if there is a Brexit, a British exit from Europe."

We talked about Europe and the wine emboldened Jack.

"The European Union doesn't work," he said. "Nor does the United Nations."

"Because it's nation-states negotiating with nation-states," I said. "There needs to be a supranational, federal level to sort out Syria and the immigrants. A democratic World State is ahead."

He shook his head. "The EU and the UN don't work," he repeated.

He was stuck in the nation-state and nationalism, and a believer in national self-assertion.

After cappuccino a thin Italian waitress with watchful eyes and her hair in a pony-tail brought the bill and Jack, by career an accountant, did a calculation. He divided the total bill, £532.47, by 9 and announced, "Can I have £60 each."

We all counted out our £60s – I passed him £120 to cover Pippa's contribution – and, having gathered in ten £20 notes he looked at the pile and said, "There's £400 here."

"Ten twenties?" I asked.

"We only did tables up to twelve," he joked.

"Ten twenties," his wife said, "is two hundred."

"It's just gone down," Jack said.

There was laughter. Mark paid £120 by card for himself and Florence and more notes were passed down the table. There was now £420 in notes before Jack.

The Italian waitress came and Jack showed her the bill. He wrote on it £532.47 minus £120. He explained the £120 was covered by the card and said to her: "I want some change. £5 will do. The bill is £532.47 including service, and you've got £420 and the payment by card. I just want a fiver."

The waitress looked doubtful. She took the bill away. The fiver was not forthcoming. So Jack attracted her attention.

"You owe me a fiver," he said.

She looked even more dubious and left. She returned with the manager.

"Is everything all right?" he asked.

"No," Jack said, "it isn't. I'm owed a fiver."

"Come to the till to discuss it?"

So Jack stood up and I saw him talking to the manager near the doorway.

Pippa and I said goodbye to the others. We had a car waiting outside in Artillery Lane. We advanced on Jack who seemed to be firing heavy artillery.

"It's *not* all right," Jack was saying, holding a £5 note. "She should have given me the fiver."

To diffuse a tense situation I said, "I witnessed the situation, I think it was a language problem, a misunderstanding. The waitress did not fully understand."

"I believe that," the manager said, relieved. "But the problem is, there is only £400 in the till."

"Well," I said, "I saw it being collected. Seven put in £60 each, seven sixes are forty-two, £420 was put in and I saw it counted."

"I must investigate why there is only £400 in the till," the manager said.

It occurred to me that the waitress – or someone – had pocketed £20 but I thought it was time to bow out. I said goodbye to Jack and we headed for the door and walked to our waiting car where our chauffeur was waving. I did not then know that the manager would ring Jack to say that a £10 note – not £20 – had been found under the cash machine.

Reflecting on the situation on the back seat of the car I thought Jack had overreacted. He had been too strong and had made a scene. The waitress could have misunderstood his instruction about the £5 and where the missing £20 had gone could have been handled gently at the level of patient explanation. The sparkling Prosecco had brought out the artillery in both Rupert and Jack, and Jack's fierceness and the manager's insistence had briefly threatened to mar the pleasant occasion. Jack saw things from how they affected himself and the nation, and censoriously demanded good service, which did not include disobeying instructions about change; whereas I, from the chill of my early old age, saw the waitress's and management's difficulty and tried to smooth the situation down, bring about a reconciliation and restore harmony, wheel the artillery out into the lane.

An X-ray and Chaos

"You're looking well," Dr Jalal said as he showed me into his room, smart, besuited and bespectacled. "And your X-ray's looking good too. You're still working hard?" He pointed to his screen. "Look, there's your X-ray two years ago, and alongside there's your current X-ray. There's no deterioration in your lungs at all, in any way. You're doing really well. I think you'll be working until you're in your nineties. There's a famous medical Professor whose lecture I attended not long ago. He was ninety-two and he spoke completely fluently. Then he went on holiday to Australia and came back and gave up medicine. He said, 'I realised when I was in Australia that I should stop now.' And he didn't do medicine any more, just retired."

"Where did you get your professorial knowledge about lungs?" I asked.

"I studied in Glasgow, and then in London. I specialised after I came to this country. I'm an Iraqi," he said.

Surprised, I said, "Oh, I worked in Baghdad, in Kaseem's day."

"We Iraqis respect him now," he said. "When he died he had a dinar and a quarter in his pocket and had no land or possessions. He acquired nothing for himself and just tried to benefit the poor. He was honest.

"I trained at the University of Baghdad," he said. "And I practised in a hospital half a mile from Waziriyah. I left Iraq in 1988. It's terrible what's been happening. It's chaos. In my time Sunnis, Shiites and Kurds all lived and worked together, but the politics have split them up. We Iraqis think IS is an American-Israeli creation with troops trained in Turkey. It's to create Greater Israel."

"There's a story on the internet that al-Baghdadi is really a Jewish actor, Simon Elliot," I said. "He's only appeared in public once, in a mosque. He could be an actor playing a caliph. It's possible."

"We Iraqis believe that, definitely," Dr Jalal said. "It's the Americans who've messed Iraq up. They're ruthless and cruel. They want to split up Iraq, create Kurdish, Shiite and Sunni zones. That's what IS have done. We know what's going on. We don't believe IS is Iraqi. It's the Americans who are manipulating them. I'm a Shiite," he said. "We must talk. I have your email and your phone number. We will meet outside and talk about Iraq. I'll write you out a form for next year's X-ray."

He scribbled onto a form on a pad, tore it off and gave it to me. He was moving me on, he had his next patient to see and could not talk the afternoon away reminiscing on Baghdad. As I left I thought he had analysed an X-ray of my lungs and I had X-rayed his brain's attitude to the chaos in the country of his birth.

Pilgrims and Lorries

My printer was printing paper with smeary smudges on it, so I made an arrangement with a company in Waltham Abbey for an engineer to visit. He came punctually at 8.30am, a broad-shouldered man in a suit with smart black hair, and followed me up the stairs to my room, carrying his service bag. I showed him a sheet with a grey smear I had printed off the previous day.

"It's the roller," he said, and he slickly opened up the side and extracted the roller and dabbed from a bottle and began to wipe it dry.

"Have you come from far?" I asked.

"Sittingbourne," he said, and when I looked blank, "near Faversham and Canterbury in Kent."

"Quite a long way," I said. "You're near the Roman Watling Street and you were a hostelry for medieval pilgrims to Canterbury," I recalled. "Kent's a nice county."

"But it's got the lorries," he said, as he dried the roller with a cloth. "They park overnight in Sittingbourne Road, and there are problems of human waste and litter. They come to Tribune Drive as it's on a website as having no parking restrictions, and cause access problems. They make driving very difficult. Sometimes it's hard to get out of the town. It used to be a country life but now it's cluttered with Continental lorries. Sometimes they come through the main street. When there's a problem with the ferries Operation Stack impacts on us. Getting into London along the A2 is a lorry jam.

"Yesterday it was windy and the Dartford Bridge was closed. I was in Leicester and the M25 was jammed. Ten hours it took some to complete their journey. I spotted the difficulty and ended up going the long way round the M25. Five hundred and fifty miles I did yesterday. You see, normally there's an engineer who covers the Aylesbury side of London and another who covers the Wanstead side. But the Aylesbury one's on a course this week and the Wanstead one's left. And so they asked me to cover for him. I don't know where I'm going to be today. You're near Wabbey – we call Waltham Abbey 'Wabbey' – so I've come to you on the way in. I'll go into Wabbey next and they'll tell me where to go. It may be somewhere as far away as Leicester again. I'm all over the place. I get up at the same time every day and leave at the same time every day and find a route that's not plagued with lorries and when I come back I search and find a route that bypasses the lorries.

"Well," he said, "it's working now." He had replaced the roller and he touch-typed buttons and printed out a Menu Map. "This is a health check," he said. "You've printed sixty thousand copies, and you won't need a service and parts replaced until you've done two hundred thousand copies. You should be fine now."

I thanked him and walked him down to the door. I watched him drive off to 'Wabbey'. He lived in a deeply historical part of the country with Roman associations and medieval inns that put up pilgrims to Canterbury, but now he hurtled round Southern England dodging Continental lorries and I was sad that a traditional way of life revolving around pilgrims had been overtaken by a modern way of life revolving round cars and lorries.

Horror amid the Camaraderie

The Shrove Tuesday Old Boys' reunion was a sell-out. It was held on a mild night. I walked past the chapel, where I knew the corpulent Reverend Martin Barnet was giving a sermon. I entered my old sixth-form classroom and greeted the Head's wife and was bought a glass of red wine by an Old Boy I did not know, who (the Head's wife explained) had organised a visit of Old Boys to the Tower of London the previous evening. He had spivvy hair and wore a short overcoat and told me he had taken about fifty groups to the Tower, but a Beefeater always gave the guided tour.

Then there was an influx from the chapel and soon my old classroom was packed. I was greeted by Mervyn Innes, who was six foot five and taller than anyone else. He used to be my fast bowler in the Under-15 cricket team and I asked him if he had bowled "reverse swing".

He said, "I used to bowl out-swingers by gripping the seam in a certain way, and occasional inswingers with my right arm coming down on the right side of my body instead of across it, but I don't know what reverse swing is."

I stood with His Honour Judge Henry Cardew, who had been a brilliant mimic at school. I asked him, "Were you ever tempted to mimic your fellow judges in the course of a judgment?" He smiled. I said, "If I elect to go and live in the Ecuadorian Embassy, will you give a judgment saying I should be given compensation for arbitrary detention?"

"Don't get me started," Henry said mock-heatedly, as Mervyn laughed. "I feel strongly about that."

Then I pushed through a *mêlée* and shook the hand of Derek Minstrel just as we were called through to dinner.

I sat between Derek Minstrel and His Honour. I shook hands with Lance Rivers, who was sitting beyond Derek. Grace was said by the portly Reverend Martin Barnet, owlish in build and round spectacles: "*Benedictus benedicat per Jesum Christum, Dominum Nostrum,* Amen." And we sat to smoked salmon, salmon fillet and mousse. Opposite me was the oldest Old Boy present, who had arrived at the school during the Second World War and could not hear properly. I talked to Derek.

"How's your wife?" I asked.

"Not well," he said. "She was dragged into a hedge by one of our horses and she had to have a skin graft, and it's left her with a terrible weeping rash round her hip. She has to have regular dressings and take tablets and she doesn't feel up to much. And look, I've got a brown mark on my nose. Do you think I should get it seen to? It might be skin cancer.

"She wants to move. She wants to be in a village, within walking distance of the shops. She's found a house in Coopersale that's on the market. It's on at £2.5 million. I don't know whether I'd get that for our property, it's 13th-century and needs things doing to it. And I like the view. I must have a view. And as if that isn't enough to be coping with, we're going on a cruise, in October. Round Spain and up the other side. Denis Saccharine and his wife asked if we'd go and we all booked and paid, and then Denis died. It's in the Old Boys' magazine. He died in Portloe, Cornwall, of a heart attack. There was nothing wrong. He had things planned, he was forward-looking. His heart just stopped. So his widow is going on the cruise but she's looking for someone to share her cabin and pay her for the cost of Denis's ticket. I'm not sure my wife is up to going, but we'll do our best."

The next course was a round fillet of beef shin with shallot beignets and a potato croquette. I poured glasses of French red wine from one of the bottles on the table, and spoke with His Honour.

"You live in Majorca," I said.

"Yes, I'm a tax exile. I have ninety days here, and I go back there the day after tomorrow. I was paying 83 pence in the pound. I was working for 17p with a business in Spain. I've been involved with Majorca for over forty years, since 1972. It was so easy to get to. I was a London solicitor before I became a circuit judge – it's rare for a solicitor to become a circuit judge – and I could fly out on a Friday night and fly back on a Sunday evening. When you get out into the countryside Majorca hasn't changed much since Robert Graves's day in the 1920s and 1930s, except that there are no mules or donkeys now. Graves's son is around. I've met him. He has nothing to do with poetry. I can still use the NHS, doubly, as a European citizen as well as a British tax exile. I'm pro-European but anti-EU, don't get me started on that. I retired when I was sixty-one. I didn't expect to live this long. So many of our contemporaries have died."

We were served a pudding of pancake and burnt cherry ice cream, and then coffee and *petits fours*, and then the Head addressed us, a smallish man in a suit with thinning hair. He read out the names of seven Old Boys who had passed away including Denis Saccharine, and he said the school's ethos, which we had all known, was still strong.

"There's a story attributed to Tony Markham, who was Head and left and went to another school," he said disparagingly to laughter – Markham had gone on to Eton – "about a drinks party. Markham was asked, 'How do our pupils turn out socially?' Markham said, 'They lead. Imagine a drinks party. It's buzzing and senior boys from local schools are present. An elderly lady is taken ill and one of our boys calls for a chair. A Forest boy brings it and a Brancroft's boy sits on it.'"

There was laughter as the school's two rivals had been presented as producing pupils who lacked initiative and were selfish.

The President of the Old Boys' Association spoke and then the Head Boy. Then corpulent Reverend Martin Barnet, in his cassock, struck up on the piano and we all sang the school song lustily. It was about following in the footsteps of the founder, treading "the way the founder's gone".

That was the end of the evening. Still standing, we shook hands and said our goodbyes. I left the table and encountered the Reverend Barnet.

"Welcome back," I said, for he had recently left after thirty-seven years at the school. "I'm still catching up on your departure."

"Thank you," he boomed, treble-chinned in his cassock. "The Bishop rang up and offered me a parish, and I said, 'Yes.'"

"You'll be a Chaucerian priest," I said. "You'll visit them all, even the most distant in the parish – "

"Yes, I will."

"Trudging through snow if needs be. You'll keep the highest standards."

"I've got my books," he said. "The sixty-three crates of books."

"That's a lot," I said.

Then I saw Robin Roach, who had emailed me in an automated letter asking me to be LinkedIn.

"I'm sorry," I said. "I don't do LinkedIn. But it's nice to see you. Are you still a notary?"

"I've retired," he said, "but I still do some advisory work."

Then Lance Rivers was alongside near his twin, squeezing my hand.

"He's just advised me," he said, holding out his visiting-card. "This is his colleague. He knows I've just been given a power of attorney by the Royal Family. His firm did the document."

"Make sure you're not liable for repairs to Windsor Castle and Buckingham Palace," I joked, deliberately misunderstanding him as Robin Roach laughed.

"No, it's for the ruler of Qatar."

"So you can write out a cheque for each of your friends, starting here," I said, and Robin Roach and Lance Rivers laughed.

Lance turned to me.

"The ruler of Qatar likes you," he said to me. "You know that, you kindly sent him – "

"So if the World Cup is going to go ahead in Qatar in a temperature of 50° Centigrade in an air-conditioned bubble, perhaps he can invite us to be in the royal box," I said. "Are you still building in Morocco?"

"I was," he said, "but then what happened to Adrian stopped the work."

I looked blank.

"Adrian, your son?" I asked.

"Yes."

"What happened to Adrian?"

"He died," Lance said simply, expressionlessly.

"*Died*? I didn't know that, I'm so sorry. Where?"

"In London. It's all right, but he died, and that slowed the building project down."

"I can imagine," I said. "I'm so sorry, you've been through a dreadful time."

"Come and meet Jonnie, my other son," he said.

And I found myself shaking hands with a good-looking besuited young man.

Later I reflected on Lance Rivers. He had always supported the school and he had done well as advisor to the Royal Family of Qatar. But what had been a reunion, old friends chatting and reporting on their lives, had suddenly lurched into horror, and a completely different register. Horror had surfaced amid the bland banter of the Old Boys, and I had been wholly unprepared for it and had been caught off guard.

I turned away to talk to the Head wary of what the banter concealed and still reeling at the horror amid the camaraderie.

Limp Mode and Full Power

We drove off the M5 to the A30 and basked in the ruggedness of Bodmin moor, full of inner energy at the green sweeping landscape. We were about ten miles from our destination in Cornwall in her Mitsubishi Shogun when Pippa said, "There's a light on. It says 'ASC off'. There's an image of a car with two skids underneath."

I stiffened. My openness to the scenery outside was immediately closed. I reached for the manual and leafed through pages about warning lights.

"It's the Active Stability Control function," I said. "It says, 'Stop, turn off the engine and the light might go out. If not, the car needs to be inspected.'"

We agreed to continue. But we were losing power. It was an effort for the car to get up hills. We focused on the road and our speed, ignoring the scenery outside.

"Now an orange light's come on," Pippa said.

Again I hunted in the manual and found a diagram with perhaps forty lights, all labelled.

"It's the engine warning light," I said.

We agreed that's why we were losing power.

With difficulty we reached the house. The tide was out and the sea was still quite rough after the storms. I unlocked our front door, picked up the key and unlocked the padlock that held a chain between two granite stones. Pippa reversed onto the parking area on the small green. She turned the engine off. I unloaded. She turned the engine on again. The warning light was still on. Our consciousness was still dominated by the light.

"I'm going to drive it to the roundabout and see if I can lose it," she said.

When she returned she said, "The power has come back, the light's still on. I don't know what to do."

We conferred and she agreed to ring the garage that serviced the car. I read out the number from the back of the vehicle licence and she called the garage on her mobile, sitting in the car. Luckily Richard was on hand, the man who knew most about the car.

"There's a fault," he said on the loudspeaker. "It's sensed a fault and sent out a warning and gone into limp mode. When it's stopped it resets itself but your light's still on. There's a fault stored. It's 4.30 on a Saturday afternoon, your best bet is to call the AA. They can read the fault on a laptop and may be able to repair it."

So I went indoors, took out my AA card from my wallet and rang the AA. They knew where I was ringing from and after some questions the fellow said, "The response time is by 5.20."

The AA man came at 5, a thinnish engineer in his thirties with a sharp aquiline nose. He put the bonnet up and bent over the engine. Eventually he said, "There's boost pressure control deviation." He worked on and then said, "There's a pipe to the manifold pressure sensor. It's blocked with carbon. I've cleaned the pipe. The fault code was PO299 and I've cleared the code. I'm just going to road-test the vehicle."

He drove off. He returned and said, "It's all right now. The light's out. It's on full power."

"Thank you very much," I said.

He filled in his form. "How have you found my service?"

"Ten out of ten," I said.

He ticked a box with a smiling face above it.

"Your response time was very quick. Ten minutes."

"Yes. I was sat in St Austell. I was having a cup of tea. The truth is, we're glad when a call comes in, we don't want to be sitting too long. When nothing's happening on a Saturday we read everything several times to pass the time. Better to be busy. I'm off at seven, so we'll see if there's another call."

He held out a hand and we shook hands, and he drove off at 5.35, our problem solved.

The car had gone into limp mode, and we had gone into limp mode too, searching through the manual to little avail and wondering if we should stop. But this "sat man" had responded within ten minutes and we were on full power now. I unloaded the freezer bags inside on full power. Things were working, I was full of energy and warmed to the booming sea.

Cramp and a Dazzling Christmas Tree

On Boxing morning I was woken by cramp in my left leg. It was excruciating. I threw back my covers and raised my leg. I gripped the back of my left thigh. The pain was relentless. I put my right foot down and somehow got to my feet in the dark and tried to walk. My hamstring muscle was in agony. I had a searing pain. I switched the light on and hobbled backwards and forwards. I could hardly put my foot to the floor. I raised my toes to squeeze the muscles of my leg. I stood on my right leg and swung my left leg gently backwards and forwards. To no avail. Was it in fact cramp? I wondered if I was having a thrombotic attack. Was there a blood clot above my knee at the back of my leg?

The pain really hurt. I gritted my teeth and walked down the passage to the bathroom and back, several times. I had it in my mind that I could walk the cramp off, but also in my mind was the possibility that walking would dislodge a blood clot and send it to my heart. After twenty minutes of persistent walking to and fro the pain began to ease and soon I was able to get back into bed, having coped with the cramp. I fell asleep almost immediately.

Simon had us to lunch that day. We were to arrive early, about 11.30, as we would be eating early. He was extending rooms in his house and had already moved the main staircase, and there were signs of building work round most corners. I sat in the main room with the grand-children. Unopened presents covered the carpeted floor and gathered round a tall Christmas tree with jumping lights. My younger grandson brought a book for me to hear him read, and then I chatted to my older grandson. Simon's in-laws had arrived, and every seat in the room was taken.

About 12.20, as lunch was being prepared, I felt the cramp coming on again. My younger grandson was reading to me again, and I could not continue listening to his story. Without a word I stood up and, not wanting to spoil Boxing Day for the family, walked to the door, hobbled down the passage to the front door and let myself out. I bent in agony and rubbed my hamstring muscle at the back and wiggled my toes and swung my leg. I hobbled to the road and walked up the pavement and turned into the school entrance next door, my face screwn-up with pain. I walked about, stamping and trying to ease the pain. Again I wondered if I was having a thrombotic attack.

The pain got worse, and I thought how silly it was of me to be away from the house. If I passed out and collapsed no one would know where I was. I ought to get back at least to within view of Simon's front door. Should I call an ambulance? That would disrupt Boxing-Day lunch, it was better for me to cope with my own pain if I could and not allow it to impact on the others.

I hobbled back to Simon's front garden and the pain abated. I felt the attack receding. Quietly I opened the front door, which was on the latch, and let myself back in, hobbled down the passage and then walked back to the seat I had vacated a few minutes earlier. No one commented. Perhaps they thought I had been to the loo.

I sat down in the present-filled room. Inviting boxes were wrapped in Christmas paper. My five-year-old grandson, Al, put his book in my hand and I heard him read about the three billy-goats. I paid attention to his story. It was as though the cramp – or thrombotic attack – had never happened.

"Right," Simon announced, "it's time to open one present each before lunch."

The family were harmoniously together and I had outlawed my cramp without going to hospital. I had coped with it on my own without impacting on the others and spoiling Boxing Day and their present-opening. The Christmas-tree lights were jumping, and the room was filled with warmth and a loving atmosphere as the children reached for their presents. I was glad I had overcome my pain.

I had no doubt that there would be more unexplained cramps in the coming days and years as I experienced the first chill of winter in my ageing arteries and veins, but I had not spoilt the occasion. I reflected that as we grow old we appreciate the enjoyment of others more and diminish our own discomfort and live more selflessly. I had ignored my symptoms of growing old and revelled in the wonder in the children's faces as they opened their presents under the jumping lights of the dazzling Christmas tree.

A Slip and Empty Days

Mr Riley was a dentist. I went to him for several years when I was a teenager and then an undergraduate. He was balding and had sallow, yellowy skin. He always wore a white mask over his nose and mouth, and when he examined my teeth I would see his two brown eyes peering over the rim of his mask, concentrating intensely. He said very little, even when it came to drilling for a filling. He only spoke when necessary and in a very quiet voice. He lived for his work, and he concentrated really hard to give his patients the best treatment.

I went away and lost contact with him over the years, but I occasionally heard reports of him from some of his other patients. One of them was Lucy Lerner, a classroom assistant. She told me she had changed dentists.

"It was terrible," she said. "His surgery was in his front room, he lived in the house where he practised, by the pond off the High Road, opposite St John's church. He lived alone. He was in his kitchen when he had no patients and he slipped. As he fell he caught hold of the side of a kitchen unit with one hand. He twisted round and fell heavily on his back and couldn't get up. He was in acute pain and knew something was wrong.

"He called for the gardener in his quiet voice. It took a long time for the gardener to hear but he came to the back door which was locked.

"'Break the door down,' Mr Riley called.

"The gardener got a wrench from his shed and broke in and called an ambulance. The ambulanceman said, 'It looks as if you've broken vertebrae in your back.' They put him in a neck brace and took him to hospital. He was X-rayed and they found two vertebrae broken.

"He had an operation. It was successful and he recovered and was able to walk. But he had lost the feeling in his fingers and this never came back. So he couldn't practise. His career as a dentist had come to an end. It was terrible, he was such a caring man, so quietly spoken and sensitive to the pain of his patients. He was such a considerate dentist. So he's been sitting at home and his patients have all gone elsewhere.

"He's lost the profession that filled his days, and when I last saw him and asked how he was getting on he said, 'The days are so empty.' Just that. 'The days are so empty.' I reckon we would all feel our days are empty if we didn't go out to work to fill them. It all came from a slip, and now he's sitting round with nothing to do, lamenting his empty days."

A Travel Plan and a Helicopter

That early December evening was mild. We had the restaurant to ourselves, and hosted our company's dinner for the top dozen. Gale and James were the last two to arrive. James, ruddy-faced and in a suit, said he had come straight from work. It was the first time he had attended our dinners and I asked him what he did. He said, "I'm in security in London." He meant that he looked after the security of buildings there.

The Italian waiters were very attentive and there was a relaxed atmosphere and a lot of laughter. We all sat round one long table, and I was nearly opposite Gale, and was able to talk to her, but was out of range of James. After our three-course dinner with bottles of wine we stood, left the table and talked individually.

James looked even more ruddy-faced. He told me, "I've had some promotion. My new job means I'll have to travel. This coming year we're going to some exciting places."

Gale, composed, elegant and self-assured, said, "I've always wanted to travel. We're trying to work out how I can join him, for example in the holidays."

I sensed that she would be giving in her notice soon.

She gave in her notice a few days later at the end of term. She said she wanted to be free to travel with James, and they would do his foreign tours together. It was what she had always wanted to do.

She had given the contractual two terms' notice, and she was still working for us in mid-February. On a Saturday morning, about 10am, they were preparing to drive into the village together. He said, "I'm just going to take an aspirin before we leave," and a few moments later she found him keeled over.

Gale realised he had had a heart attack and raised the alarm. A helicopter landed in playing-fields near his home and air-lifted him to hospital. He died in the helicopter, and sadly their plan to travel would not now happen.

Box-Leaf Caterpillars and Nature's Plan

That morning I showed my fifteen-year-old grandson Bernard the knee-high crenellated box hedge near the front door. The front of the box hedge had shrivelled grey leaves. I put my hands on the top of a crenellated battlement and parted the tiny woody branches. A box-leaf caterpillar showed, green on a leaf, and there were tiny black eggs on the underneath of nearby leaves.

"The caterpillars came from China," I said. "They came over here about four years ago, in Chinese box-leaf plants for Kew Gardens, and they've spread. Last year they were unknown in Essex. This year they're in every garden round here. They feed off box leaves, nothing else. The moths lay eggs on box leaves, the eggs hatch into caterpillars, they eat the box leaves, turn into silk cocoons and new moths hatch from them. And if we're not careful they'll lay more eggs. We won't have any box hedges left, not here at the front or round the back."

I found a couple of metal folding chairs and two pairs of gardening gloves and a plastic tub, and carried them to the hedge. I opened the chairs and sat at the left end of the crenellated box hedge, put on the gloves and parted the leaves. Each time I did this we found a caterpillar. I picked it out and nipped it between my fingers and dropped it in the tub. We worked painstakingly, clearing each section of the crenellation, the higher and lower levels, section by section. We had not even reached a third of the way through and we had over a hundred caterpillars.

I said, "If they do this every year, there won't be any more box hedges anywhere."

Bernard said, "You'll have to pull it up and plant another hedge, but not a box hedge."

I said, "I'll have to do this for ten minutes a day and then go to the knot-garden and do the same there."

It was a blight. But I marvelled that each tiny caterpillar could only survive if it ate box leaves. It had no other food. As I found caterpillars in the depth of the hedge, parting tiny woody branches and peering down from my sitting position, I reflected on how wonderful it was that Nature provided enough food for each species. I said to Bernard, "No other caterpillars eat box leaves so there is enough to go round for this species. Other species eat other leaves of other plants, and the box-leaf caterpillars, by concentrating on box hedges, leave the leaves of other plants to other caterpillars. So there's enough for everybody. It's wonderful, isn't it?"

"Yes," Bernard said thoughtfully. "It's almost as if it's been planned."

"God's plan," I said. "Or rather, Nature's plan. There's an intricate system in Nature. Everything is cared for. Every creature has its place and its habitat and food. And the box-leaf caterpillar's place is box hedges. But not in our garden."

"No," Bernard said, "not in your garden. But it is wonderful."

He was looking at Nature in wonder as he sat over the hedge. I, his grandfather, had shown him Nature's plan, and though only fifteen he had grasped the place of box-leaf caterpillars in the system and had glimpsed the order of the universe and its unity.

Histrionics and Mould
(Or: A Thingy and a Fire-Engine)

I had an email informing me that the Rt Hon. Denis Everley was to be guest of honour at a dinner for Leyton and Wanstead Conservatives, and as I had had many talks with him some years previously I sent off a cheque for two tickets. I heard nothing, so on the morning of the dinner I rang the contact number. A woman answered.

"Donald McSwain?" I asked.

"I'm afraid he's not here. Can I help? I'm his thingy."

Not sure what a 'thingy' was, I gave her my name and asked if Donald McSwain had received my cheque.

"Oh yes," she said, "we're expecting you tonight."

We arrived at the Wanstead Golf Club at 7 and were greeted by a couple of elderly men in an entrance hall between a bar and the brightly-lit function room that was lined with photos of past golfing presidents round the tops of the walls and had two rows of three circular tables laid for forty or fifty guests. Each table was laid for six guests, and there seemed to be a seventh table at the farthest side of the room. Donald McSwain came forward, a smiling balding small man with a demotic accent.

"How are you?" he asked. "Where are you from? I didn't rec your names on the guest."

I realised as he chattered that he omitted the second half of long words. 'Rec' should have been 'recognise', and 'guest' should have been 'guest list'. He had some sort of a speech impediment. Then a little very old lady who was bent forward approached.

"We spoke on the phone," she said.

She was his 'thingy'. She had a clipboard, and in view of her advanced years I decided that a 'thingy' was a volunteer rather than a PA.

We went into the function room and helped ourselves at the drinks tables. I took a glass of Prosecco, Pippa an orange juice. We sipped near the radiator.

Pippa said, "Everyone here is very old, I'm the youngest. The Conservatives here are ancient, there's no young blood."

I saw Denis Everley arrive, early sixties and slightly overweight, jowly with a creased face in a suit, hair smart with a parting. After initial exaggerated greetings, his hands thrown out and up, he made his way towards us and I advanced to meet him.

"Hello Philip, how are you?" he asked, pumping my hand. "Good to see you again. Hello Pippa." He kissed her cheeks twice. Then he turned to me.

"There's a lectern at the far end," I said, "and we're looking forward to hearing all about Europe. I found a list of MPs online who are in or out, and you're among the 'unknowns' – "

"I'm a Whip," he said, "I have to appear neutral."

"A Whip," I said. "Do you have a black book? Do you blackmail Tory MPs into voting how the government want them to vote?"

"No," he laughed, "but I could tell you some stories that are very scary."

"We're waiting to be enlightened by you on what's really going on regarding the referendum on the EU," I said. "We want to know whose lawyers are right, Gove's – who say that Cameron's deal can be overturned – or Tusk's and their advisors on the European Council. And if Cameron is going to sack Gove as Justice Minister, whether he's asked you as Whip to sack him."

He laughed. "All the MPs are allowed to express their real view," he said.

"And we want to know if Johnson was wrong to say an out decision could trigger an immediate second referendum. We want you to tell us if invoking article 50 *will* trigger a two-year leaving period during which there can be no new referendum – or negotiating of new trade deals."

"The PM gave me a duty to perform," he chuckled. "He said, 'I want you to look after Boris Johnson.' That's quite a thing to have to do. Anyway, I'll see you later." And with a theatrical flourish he turned and shook hands all round a nearby group.

I talked to a long-white-haired man with a ruddy face and a floral tie. He was peering at my place card.

"Is that you?" he asked. "I'm sitting next to you."

He told me he had come from a village near Colchester, "between Wivenhoe and Brightlingsea". He said, "I'm a councillor. We've got a dormitory town coming on our borders. There's only a hundred and fifty in our village and there are going to be many more than that in the new town. We'll have to expand our hospital and school space. I'm a specialist surveyor. I specialise in damp and mould," he said. "Damp and mould."

We sat at our table and he introduced his partner, who was sitting next to him. "She's been Mayoress of Redbridge and that's Colin. He's been Mayor of Redbridge, at a different time."

At that moment Donald McSwain, Chairman of the Association, gave a welcome speech in his demotic accent. "Wel to Ley and Wan," he said. Then he called for grace.

We stood up and Colin pulled a sheet of paper from his inside breast pocket and, full-faced with spectacles and balding, he read a grace.

"I found it on the internet," he said as we sat down.

"We thought you were a Reverend," I said, and the others laughed.

We had pre-ordered and were served smoked salmon and prawn with spread bread and butter. Pippa's neighbour told me she had been to Conservative conferences. "I sat next to that man who had an affair with Sara Keays," she said. "What was he called?"

Pippa turned to me.

"Cecil Parkinson," I said.

"Oh, yes," she said, "and Ann Widdecombe. I didn't like Iain Duncan Smith. He's not very warm. They're all wandering around and you can sit with them and talk."

The specialist in damp and mould said, "My partner and Colin are Rotarians. As part of Cameron's Big-Society help for the Third World, we clubbed together and bought a battered fire-engine. We had it serviced and done up, and we sent it by ship to Ethiopia. Sending it cost more than the fire-engine. We all went out to a village outside Addis Ababa. We were greeted like celebrities. We stood and observed. The fire-engine came out of the distance and raced along a road, an African fireman ringing its bell. It was in action almost immediately, as there was a car crash and a driver had to be cut out. It holds a ton of water, that's how many cubic feet there were in that fire-engine. It has to be serviced once a year."

"So the three of you went out together?" I asked.

"Yes," he said. "We're also helping an Albanian orphanage."

I said, "I know someone who was listening to the Albanian Prime Minister yesterday. He said Europe's given Albania 1.5 billion euros even though it's not in the EU: 917 million euros from the European Central Bank, and 650 million euros from the EU. The EU's grooming Albania to be a future member of the EU."

The main course arrived. We were served chicken asparagus in white-wine cream sauce. The ex-Mayor of Redbridge stood up, left the room and returned with a bottle of white wine and a jug of water, and everyone was able to have a drink. The damp-and-mould expert passed him £10. I did the same expecting it to be declined, but to my surprise the ex-Mayor took both notes. Was the wine really £30?

I held forth on the referendum. "It's a very complicated decision, the vote," I said, talking neutrally but trying to stir up the Mayor and Mayoress. "Vote out and you're voting for Scotland to leave the UK, secure independence and join the EU. There's Putin's expansion to consider, now's not the time to fragment Europe."

"There are too many immigrants," the ex-Mayoress said flatly.

"Yes," said the ex-Mayor.

"And there's keeping the peace," I said. "Europe was in ruins in 1945, there'd been a war every thirty years since the nineteenth century. Thanks to NATO and the EU there's been peace for seventy years. It's Churchill's vision. He called for a United States of Europe in 1946. The Outs are turning their back on Europe, and on Churchill. They're looking backwards, not forwards. Back to little England, not regional and global union."

The ex-Mayor and the ex-Mayoress said nothing.

Then Denis Everley appeared behind us. He grasped Pippa and me on our shoulders and leant forwards and said, "Smile, your picture's being taken." The unsuccessful Parliamentary candidate for Leyton and Wanstead at the last election was trying to take our picture on a mobile phone. It was not working, so he left the room and returned with another mobile phone. "You can't get the staff," Denis Everley joked. We all stared with frozen smiles while he took the photo, and then there was some more banter.

"You mustn't heckle me when I speak," Denis Everley said.

I said, "I listen religiously to *Prime Minister's Questions* every week, and I've modelled my behaviour on how the MPs behave so I couldn't possibly heckle."

He smirked. I stood and said, "You're a Treasury Minister. I've discovered the Treasury created £375 billion by quantitative easing and sold it on and made a profit of over £8 billion, which paid for the Tax Credits. I think it's a fund for Brexit, for if our trade suddenly stops. It's a sensible thing to do. I'll send you the papers if you like. It's secret."

Denis Everley said, "You'd better not send them. I'd better not see them. You'll be able to tell which way I hope the vote goes from what I say shortly."

We were served lemon torte with raspberry coulis. The damp-and-mould man told me, "I'm writing my autobiography. I've reached 1974. My parents told me I was conceived on the first day of the war. My parents wanted a child before the war got too dreadful. I was in Mill Hill during the war, and we came to Leyton in 1952. Then later to Ilford. I shall write about my specialist work in damp and mould, and about my volunteer work."

Coffee was served with mint chocolates. Then there were toasts, first to the Queen, then to the Conservative Party. And then a youngish councillor with an East-End accent was introducing Denis Everley, and Denis Everley was standing in the aisle between tables, waving his arms, speaking, turning to the left with a bow and then to the right with a bow, and extending his arms.

Denis Everley talked about his political career. There was nothing about Europe, just about himself. He told how he was eager to debate at his school, how he was elected in 1983 and Margaret Thatcher used to say, "De – nis" (the 'nis' rising). He had admired Thatcher very much and so did the audience. There were murmurs of approval. He talked about Heath and Blair, histrionically waving his arms. "I didn't like Blair," he said. "He was a superb actor, he should have won an Oscar. He wore make-up. In the chamber our skin can sometimes look pale because of the lighting there. He solved it with a bit of eye-liner and a bit of something to give colour to his cheeks." He waved his arms and looked even more of an actor than Blair. He turned to Cameron. He said, "I've been able to observe the Prime Minister at close quarters, and I think he'll go down as one of the great Prime Ministers one day."

Now a television in the bar outside the function room was turned up and an excitable football commentary drowned his words. I watched Denis Everley as he turned from side to side, bowing for emphasis, holding out his hands. I watched his histrionics while the roar of the crowd and the excitement of the commentator obliterated Denis Everley's sound.

Eventually he finished to applause. There was a vote of thanks, and everyone talked. Donald McSwain was trying to start the raffle draw. "Raff," he called, but no one listened. Eventually the 'raffle caller' called, "White two hundred and sixty," and slowly, after many repeated calls, the forty present fell silent.

I looked at my neighbour, who was an expert in mould, and at the mouldering faces in the room and contrasted them with the vigorous-looking past presidents' photos on the walls. Most of the guests were really old, like Donald McSwain's 'thingy', who was supervising the raffle table. It looked like an old people's home. And I thought of Denis Everley's energetic and dramatic arm-waving and exaggerated gestures, an actorish act designed to impress. The number of one of Pippa's raffle tickets was called, and she rose, drew the next number from the ticket box and walked to the 'thingy' and returned with Roses' chocolates.

Another of her tickets was called – she had only bought £2 worth as we had nothing to do with the Leyton and Wanstead Conservatives – and I wondered if she had drawn her own number from the box by coincidence. This time I went up, drew the next number and the 'thingy' pointed to the last five prizes, all uninteresting except for a medium-sized diary with a British coastal scene on the front. So I returned with that.

We were in a Labour constituency with a candidate, who had been unsuccessful, rather than an incumbent MP, and the standard of organising was poor. The raffle caller droned on, waiting for unclaimed tickets to be claimed, and I wished that Denis Everley would return to the front and wave his arms in another virtuoso theatrical display so that some of the mould-encrusted faces would sit up and come alive and form a view on the mouldering response to the actor's Oscar-level performance and histrionics.

A Chauffeur and the Death Seat

I chauffeured Pippa to Haywards for our anniversary dinner. We sat near the fireplace at a table for two. Pippa sat on a long seat that extended the length of the wall. It was a Saturday evening and pretty full.

We started with a glass of champagne each and talked about this and that while delicate courses were placed in front of us: a pre-starter, a pumpkin (or butternut squash) velouté with a thin goat's-cheese-like cracker containing squid ink, and arancini; then our starters, crab and crab bread for me, beetroot salad for Pippa; then our main course, John Dory with underdone broccoli and carrots, and baked creamed potato tasting of garlic; then a pre-pudding, a lemon posset; and then our pudding, in my case chocolate bavarois with hazelnut ice cream and honeycomb. I was now drinking water as I was driving.

Then a glass plate inscribed in chocolate 'Happy Anniversary' round its rim was brought with two madeleines (small sponge cakes) and two square jellies. I thought of Proust tasting madeleine and of the involuntary memory it brought of Combray and his aunt Léonie in *Swann's Way* in *In Search of Lost Time,* which appeared in 1913 before the First World War.

As I looked at the glass plate and the madeleines a white-haired man in a sweater and an unzipped blue body warmer passed by my elbow, turned and sat down on the long seat between Pippa and the lady on the next table. I instantly recognised him: Daniel Rivers, a bully at school and now self-effacing and shy.

"Hello," I said loudly, extending my hand. "Are you chauffeuring?"

It took him some seconds to grasp the situation. He was now holding a large glass with a tiny amount of red wine at the bottom.

"Yes," he said. "Hello."

"Perhaps you can chauffeur me when I've finished my water?"

He grinned. "This is my son, have you met him? And my daughter-in-law."

I said to the couple at the next table, "He had a word with me beforehand when he dropped you off and said, 'Keep an eye on them for me when I'm not here.'"

They all laughed.

"Oh, it's your anniversary," Daniel Rivers said, reading the chocolate on our glass plate. "It's their anniversary too."

His son and daughter-in-law had a chocolate-inscribed glass plate containing madeleines and jellies as well.

"Is it your first anniversary?" Daniel Rivers' son asked, smiling.

"Yes," I said. "Your dad will back that up. We Old Boys stick together and support one another."

Daniel Rivers' son smiled.

"Isn't it strange?" Daniel Rivers said. "I was here before Christmas and Denis Saccharine was sitting where you are, on your chair."

Denis Saccharine had died of a heart attack while on holiday in Portloe, Cornwall just before Christmas. I affected to move rapidly. "This is the death seat," I said.

Daniel Rivers laughed. "Yes," he said. "You're sitting in the death seat. And my brother Lance was here at lunchtime. Sitting down the far end."

"Now you say he's your son, I can see the likeness," I said. "It's in the profile."

Pippa asked, "Did you go to the same school as your dad?"

"No," Daniel Rivers said, taking charge of the question. "He went to Stortford College."

I ate my madeleine cake, thinking of Proust, and Pippa sipped an amaretto coffee while I tippled my water, preparing to drive. We talked between ourselves, and then Daniel Rivers, his son and daughter-in-law stood up to leave. I stood and shook hands with all three.

"I'm going to the Old Boys' lunch on Wednesday," Daniel Rivers said. "You don't go, do you?"

"No," I said. "No, I don't. Too busy working."

Daniel Rivers went to the till and paid the bill. I followed. The co-owner of the restaurant, a lady with hair done up the back, took my payment card and said, "It's strange how everyone knows everyone, isn't it?"

"I used to know him at school," I said.

"Yes, he told me. And his brother Lance was in at lunchtime."

"Just put this on the Qatar account," I said, thinking of Lance Rivers' links with Qatar, and everyone laughed.

Outside I reflected on the death seat. Of all the chairs I could sit in, why Denis Saccharine's? The chances of that happening if life was an accident were very slim. Was it Providential? Had I chauffeured so I could sit in the death seat – would I be next? But no, all feelings about seating were superstitious – like batsmen when a cricket side is batting, who do not leave their seats in case doing so brings bad luck – and not Providential. Coincidences may happen but I was free from them – the deepest me beyond the world of time, that is – and I could expect to live many more years yet. The death seat was no different from the chauffeur's seat I sat in to drive Pippa home.

Earth Floors by the Loire

"I've inherited a house," said the osteopath as he massaged my back. "It's in France, in Oudon. It's a thirteenth-century French house. My mother's given it to me. She and my sister weren't speaking so my sister's been given a small house in Oudon and a flat in Nice, and I've been given the larger house in Oudon. It's got one large room up and down with compacted earth floors. Much of the furniture has disintegrated to dust. The walnut's disintegrated, and the pine. The mahogany is OK. I want to restore the house. I'm going to spend ten days there in

September. My sister wants to carry the mahogany furniture from my house to her house but my mother's said 'No'. My sister's excitable, she's French.

"It's a wonderful setting. There's a floodlit tower behind my house, and there's a slope two hundred yards down to the Loire. It's a place I can go to and be quiet. I'll carry on working here. But I'm really looking forward to savouring the thirteenth-century atmosphere and thinking of all the people who have been through the downstairs room during the last eight hundred years. I shall live in my soul and be aware of the history the house's past occupants have known."

A Queue and a Lord

The bank queue was short. Pleased, I took my place in it. The man in front of me turned round. "Hello," Nutty Bray said, "fancy seeing you here. How are you?" He shook my hand and I smelt his foul breath and noticed his unshaven throat, and frowned. Then he was called by a cashier and I followed to another cashier.

He waited for me until I had finished my transactions. He followed me out of the bank.

"I live in Buckhurst Hill now," he said, "in a maisonette."

I held on to my plastic bag very tightly, aware that I was vulnerable as I was standing outside the bank holding a large amount of cash.

"I don't cycle any more," he continued. "I went to Jim Dawson's funeral and also to Brian Tremlett's funeral. I had a birthday card from Lance Rivers for my birthday. I was so pleased, we were boarders together. My family owned a newsagent's and tobacconist's, and it's still operating under different owners. I go in in disguise, otherwise they'll call me 'Lord Bray'." He grinned.

Eventually I was able to shake him off and proceed on my way. I reflected that he had never really done anything with his life and, feeling inferior to some of his contemporaries, tried to impress them with accounts of improvements in his own life. His parents had owned a shop and in his own mind he could be a Lord. Now he did not cycle (as he had done since leaving school). He travelled by bus for he had never had a car. I felt sad as I watched him walk to the bus-stop.

A Crossword and Alaska

Charles Nones shared a room in my college with Rupert. It was a large room overlooking the grassed quadrangle, and as Rupert often invited me for after-lunch coffee I got to know Charles. He had powerful brown spectacles that magnified his eyes and he spoke in a loud and very forthright way. His subject was history, but he told me he was learning Italian so he could read Dante in the original.

He once told me, "My father travels to London each day by train. He was an adviser to Anthony Eden when he was Prime Minister. So at that time he wore pinstripes and a bowler hat. He always did the *Times* crossword on the train. He didn't look at it before starting it on the train. There were several commuters who had always travelled in the same compartment. They all got on at the same station and they all did the *Times* crossword. My father always finished first, inside ten minutes.

"Then one of the others started finishing before him, in just over nine minutes. This happened consistently and my father couldn't understand his sudden improvement in speed. Then my mother met the other man's wife at a social event, and the wife said, 'George starts breakfast really early and does the crossword with a dictionary.' So he was doing it at home first, then just writing it out on the train and pretending he hadn't seen any of the clues until then." He laughed.

I said, "You have a very high-powered father."

"Yes," he said. "With it comes expectations."

"About you?"

"Yes, he has expectations of what I'm going to do."

We were out of college during our third year and I lost regular contact with Charles. I saw him sometimes in Hall during supper, and Rupert occasionally mentioned him. I was not sure what happened to him when we left. Then I heard from one of the alumni that he was teaching in Alaska. Over the years when his name came up I would hear, "Oh, he went to Alaska, he must still be in Alaska."

Then one year when I was invited back to a gaudy I sat with Peter

Halford, a contemporary of mine. He said, "There's a list in the Buttery of who's died during the last year. 'The dead list.' Coming to have a look at it afterwards?"

I said, "Yes. Who've you heard has died?"

He mentioned a couple of names one of whom, he said, was "friendly with Charles Nones".

"Oh, what happened to him? Is he still in Alaska?" I asked.

"He never was in Alaska," Peter Halford said. "He committed suicide at the end of our final year. It was hushed up, and those who wanted to save his reputation said he had gone to Alaska. His father had high expectations of him and of what he would do, and somehow he felt he had not lived up to his father's high expectations, and killed himself. His address is now Heaven. Or Hell."

I was amazed. Fifty years had passed since his death, half a century, and most of his contemporaries thought he was still alive. Hushing up his suicide was in keeping with fulfilling his father's expectations, I reflected. I shook my head. He had undoubtedly had a brilliant father who could do an unseen *Times* crossword every day within ten minutes, but he had been saddled with expectations that had proved destructive and had annihilated him.

I said, "If only he could have broken free from the harness of those expectations."

"I agree," Peter Halford said, "I agree."

Window-Dressing and Make-Believe

That winter there were storms in Cornwall, and the waves pounded the wall below my window, fountained higher than our roof and crashed down and flung shingle at our side wall, pitting our pale pink paint. I would need to redecorate the outside of the house. While I was arranging this I was contacted by a film company. A new television series, *Poldark*, was to be filmed in Charlestown and they would like to use our house. They wanted to paint the front a muddy colour to suggest the 18th or early 19th century, and they would pay for the outside to be redecorated and made good after filming. They would need to do things to the windows. Could I be at the property to open up for them and let them make these changes? They would pay my return fare.

I signed a contract and Pippa and I drove to Cornwall two days before filming was due to start. The outside had already been dressed. A carpenter added wood to the sash-windows to turn them from four panes to sixteen and a team came in and dressed the windows from the inside with muslin and a night-light. I arranged for a drainpipe to be removed. The road outside was covered with cement-like dust that suggested an unmade muddy track. A small tent was erected by our front door as a rallying-point for the crew.

The filming took two days. Charlestown was Truro in the film, and there were shots outside our house and by the harbour reflecting all times of day and all weathers, so that in two days they had snippets that covered several months. The star, Aidan Turner, walked around under our front window between scenes in period costume. Small crowds gathered to watch in policed areas. I spent the days writing on the first floor and keeping my head out of camera shots. The deal was that only the outside of our house would be used. The actors could be on the front steps and look as if they were coming out of our front door, which belonged to Captain Blamey in the film, but they could not come into our house.

In the early evening of the last day of filming I was downstairs having my evening meal in the front sitting-room. I said to Pippa, "I can hear somebody in the hall."

I opened the sitting-room door and encountered Captain Blamey in wig and period finery standing beside a lady in a wig and finely dressed, with two dressers in front of them.

"Hello," I said, surprised that they were in our house.

"Hello," said Captain Blamey, matter-of-factly as if he had every right to be there.

We stared at each other. Then the front door opened and the two dressers pressed back to the walls and Captain Blamey and his lady left the house down our porch steps. The dressers followed as soon as they were out of camera view.

I returned to my meal. Then there was a loud knocking on the door.

"I'm the producer," a fellow said. "Did they come into your hall just now?"

"Yes," I said.

"I'm terribly sorry, they had no right to do that. They misunderstood. I'm sorry about that. I'll make sure you get an extra £250 for the inconvenience."

"Thank you," I said. "No problem."

And I returned to my meal.

The next day was strike day, when the film-company staff packed, made good, Hoovered up the cement-like dust on the road, restored the harbour to how it had been and left us a muddy-looking house to put right. I reinstated the drainpipe and gave the painter the go-ahead, knowing the film company would pay his bill. Pippa and I then drove back to Essex.

I was struck that I had taken part in a gigantic illusion which had involved considerable deception, muddying-up our house to turn it into something that it was not, suggesting a time that was not our time. All this had been done to entertain the public on Sunday evenings. There had been a collective lie to tell a story that would entertain and amuse. We had profited – we would receive over £3,000 to redecorate, plus our fares and the £250 for the actors and dressers wrongly entering out house – but the whole village had been inconvenienced. I wondered at a culture that delighted in presenting escapist make-believe while the real problems in the world, which were addressed by true poets or story-writers, were put out of mind.

Stabbings and Mushrooms

In Douglas on the Isle of Man I hailed a taxi. To be pleasant I asked the driver how long he had lived on the island.

"Six years," he said in an East-End accent. "I was born a Cockney, I lived in London's East End. I'm from a gangland family. I was a cabby in the East End. I did a lot of driving but it suddenly became unsafe. I was stabbed twice by fares, once in my stomach and twice in my neck. I wasn't sure why, it seemed to be immigrants and the National Front but I thought it might be gangland-related. I had to carry a pick-axe handle in my boot to defend myself. I was driven out by the increasing violence and decay in London. I said to my wife, 'I can't go on doing this. I'll get killed.' So I've hidden myself away from London.

"My wife's Thai. She doesn't speak English. I don't speak to her much. She speaks to mushrooms. Her job's growing mushrooms. At home I'm on my computer and she's thinking about her mushrooms. We've got an apartment up the road, not overlooking the sea. Our rent's over £200 a week, but we get an income from England, from the council, for letting my Dagenham flat to Africans. I had to invest £2,000 to get here but I've had the money back in rent. I might want to retire in Thailand. If those who want to do me violence find me here, they wouldn't find me in Thailand.

"I can't trust anybody. I had an Indian fare. He quizzed me about my Thai wife. He said, 'Have you got a lot of money?' I said, 'Yes.' He said, 'How much?' I said, 'A hundred and eighty thousand pounds.' He said, 'That's not a lot of money.' I said, 'It is to me, it may not be to you. So f— off and leave us alone.'"

I could see that his paranoia about being found had led him to address the public in a way unbecoming to a professional cab driver.

He was on the side of the Isle of Man. He said, "The UK is accusing us of massaging the figures, of hoarding £1.4 billion. We need a strong Chief Minister who will stand up to the UK."

Then he asked me, "Would you like to retire here? You don't want to settle in a large property. You could find an apartment like mine and live very comfortably here. No one will find you here."

I thought of how he had fled gangland stabbings and reprisals to live anonymously while his wife grew mushrooms, and how the mushrooms were a kind of front for him, that hid him from his (either real or imaginary) pursuers. And so keen was he to convince himself of his own safety that he was now projecting his ideas onto his fares, trying to persuade his fares to settle in the Isle of Man just as he had.

A Walk and a Shut-Down

I saw Lady Myrtle at the Friends of Epping Forest sitting at a table near the stage and I went over to her and bent and told her about my forthcoming book on the Forest. She was white-haired in her late eighties.

"Oh," she said, "Lee would be so interested." She was referring to Lord Myrtle.

"I was sorry to hear the news about him," I said, bending over her. "We often met in the village as he walked a lot, and he always stopped and had a chat. Once I was getting my oldest son into a car that was taking him to school. He was holding a violin case and he came by, walking up to the Forest, and took the violin case from his hand and helped him into the back seat of the car with it. I had a lot of time for him."

"He walked to Epping Forest the day before he died, you know," she said, looking up at me and looking frail. "He went about 3 and came back saying, 'I feel a little shivery. I'm going to have an early night.' He got up the next morning and got worse. One organ after another shut down. He was dead by three. Emphysema and pneumonia. Legionnaires' disease was what I was told. If it wasn't that, I don't know what caused his death. It's a mystery. But he went from normal at 3pm one day to dead by 3pm the next day, every organ shut down."

She shook her head.

I looked down into her watery widow's eyes. She had been a firebrand left-winger in her time and Lord Myrtle had been a union boss before being awarded his peerage but death was no respecter of rank. Whether you are a peer in the House of Lords or a homeless man sleeping in doorways, death calls when it will.

Double Vision and Strokes

"Doreen's in hospital," Jack said. "She's been uptight. She didn't want to leave Loughton for the flat in the complex where she is now, and she feels she's on top of Arthur. The flat's so small they can't have time away from each other. Anyway, she had double vision and in hospital she's been diagnosed as having had a TIA, a transient ischaemic attack, a microembolism that has affected her sight. She's all right, she's healing, but she couldn't meet her friends from Probus who were at a function just fifteen minutes away.

"Arthur's doing his best. He's permanently in a wheelchair but is able to transfer to his 'three-wheeler' and ride along the path to the complex shop. It at least enables him to get outside into the fresh air. He's had two strokes. The last one was when he was having an operation on his prostate. He needs another operation, he's got prostate cancer. But on the day of the operation he won't be able to take his tablets and not-taking his tablets caused his last stroke. So he's dreading the time ahead." I recalled how light and limp he was when I last lifted him into his car after a visit.

After I rang off I thought of the elderly couple in their late eighties who hated being on top of each other yet were dependent on each other in different ways, after decades of marriage. There was only room for one television in their tiny flat and they wanted to watch different programmes. I thought of the give-and-take that went into a marriage, and of the double vision and strokes (not to mention prostate problems) they had to encounter, and I was sad at the chill of winter encountered in old age.

A Fox and Bites

When I opened the front door to go to my car I had a shock. A small fox was standing on the doormat inches from my legs. It was trying to come in, so I pulled the door to and watched. It sloped off and sat down under a nearby car, and then walked to the blue box for discarded newspapers near the front door. It returned to the doormat and then stepped down and waited three feet from the door. I thought it was a cub, a large cub rather than a fully-grown fox.

There was a broom propped by the newspapers for sweeping leaves. I cautiously opened the front door, took the broom and gently extended it to guide the fox on its way. It tried to bite the broom's brush. It took a few paces into the flower-bed by the porch, beyond the palm tree, then staggered and collapsed. It was trembling and seemed to be having a fit. Then it was docile, but it would not move. It bared its teeth like a wolf.

I did not mind the fox being in our garden so long as it did not bite me. Then I thought of my grandchildren. What would happen if they came round and were bitten? Could the fox be rabid? Can a fox have rabies? I recalled reading that foxes can be reservoirs for rabies.

Its behaviour was strange and could threaten visitors, so I rang the Royal Society for the Prevention of Cruelty to Animals. They came very quickly in a large van that had an in-built cage at the back. The RSPCA man got out and approached the fox slowly to examine its condition. It tried to bite itself.

"It's sick," the man said to me. "Something neurological."

He went back to his van and returned with a kind of bag on a pole with a hand-operated trigger. He somehow scooped the fox up and carried it to the cage in his van, released it into the cage and closed the cage door.

Now the fox chased round and round. It fought with the cage and at one point bit itself.

"It's neurological," the RSPCA man repeated to me, "and self-harming. It will have to be destroyed to put it out of its misery."

I felt sad. Its problem was that it wanted to enter my house and would not retreat to the wild. And it had bitten itself twice. It had not bitten anyone – yet. I was not sure that what it had done warranted putting-down. The RSPCA man was adamant that his diagnosis was right.

"I'll drive it away," he said. "You won't be seeing it any more."

I watched the van disappear through our gates. I felt sad. A noble creature that had been living in our main field had strayed into our domestic routine and had exhibited a willingness to bite. It could not be trusted. It had to go but not to its death. I was sad that there was no halfway house in the RSPCA's rules regarding animals that had exhibited a desire to bite.

Incas and Doodlebugs

"I was a boarder during the war," said the elderly man opposite me at the Old Boys' reunion Shrove-Tuesday dinner. "I was in Harsnett's. Our housemaster was the legendary J.S. I can see him now, his shock of white hair.... He read to us boarders every night. I remember him reading about the Incas. We loved his bedtime stories. I've always been interested in the Incas, and I went to Peru not long ago to find out more about the people in those bedtime stories. We used to hear the doodlebugs go over, and he was always reassuring, it wouldn't drop near us. I remember the night a doodlebug fell on the nearby golf course. We heard the engine and ran to our bedroom window and we heard it cut out, and we heard the bang. J.S. appeared and said everything was all right, it was a long way away. But he'd told us doodlebugs wouldn't drop near us, and after that I no longer felt safe. I felt insecure and I could not trust what J.S. said."

I noticed he was dribbling. He was old now and drooled, but he could relive his memories of the war with an immediacy that suggested they had taken place only yesterday.

A Wrench and Dignity

The plumber arrived at our Cornish front door. "Hello, Mr Rawleys," he said, "Gordon, I've been before. All right?" He was a thin man in his late fifties with thinning hair.

I showed him the leak in the loo and the taps that needed washers.

"I'll need my wrench," he said.

He went out to his van and returned with an old cloth bag containing his tools and found a wrench. He opened the cupboard doors under the sink and bent and turned the stopcock to turn the water off and used his wrench. Then he returned to the bathroom and worked on the loo and taps. I joined him.

"This may be the last time I come to you," Gordon said. "I've had a pain in my chest. I thought it might be my heart so I was sent to Treliske Hospital. They said I hadn't had a heart attack. They gave me a CT scan and found I have asbestos in my lungs. Asbestos dust. Asbestosis. Got it from the work I had to do when I was young. It may have been dormant since them days and come out now. My lungs aren't taking in oxygen. It's not good, I've been feeling ill. I've had tests, a biopsy. It's strange, others in the firm worked in the 1970s and they don't have it. It must be a particular job I did and they didn't. It's one of them things. No one knew asbestos wasn't safe in them days. We tore it out with our bare hands if it was in the way. Maybe things today seem safe but aren't, for example mobile phones and computer parts. I'm told it can be dormant for sixty years. What makes it active after all that time? Is there a suppressor in the body? I can't get my head clear, but I'll face it with dignity, I'm determined to do that. But if I have to stop working very soon, as seems likely, it'll be a wrench. There," he said, "you've got new washers and your loo's fixed. I'll go and turn the water on now. That's all you can do, isn't it, face it with dignity when it comes, and it'll come to everybody."

I was full of admiration for his simplicity, his plain-speaking honesty, his dignity and his uprightness. He had instinctive qualities that have eluded many more sophisticated men. Men like Gordon were the salt of the earth. I never saw him again and in due course I heard that he had died. I never heard the circumstances.

Scarlet Blood and Lost Letters
(Or: Scarlet Letters)

Thirty-seven years ago I heard a screaming and looked out of the front door into the dark and saw our 'neighbour' opposite, a builder, propelling an old lady into his gate. I crossed the road and saw the old lady sit on a chair inside the lit-up front door, scarlet blood pouring in five streams down her head and on to her coat.

"Mugged," the builder said to me. "She lives just up the road. Tall fair youths hit her on her head and snatched her handbag."

"It's not the money," the old lady gasped between dry sobs, "though there was £14 in it. It's the letters. I've got letters I've carried all my life. They're irreplaceable. This blood'll dry and I can get more money from the post office, but those letters mean more to me than my life."

I wondered if she had hung on to her bag because of the letters, and provoked the bludgeoning.

I reassured her and tried to give her hope. What good would letters be to a young thief? Young thieves were like the footpads and the highwaymen of a former time. They took the money and threw away everything else. The tall fair youth would throw the bag away, letters and all, and she'd get it back. Was her address in the bag?

"Oh, yes, I've got other letters in it with my address on. But *those* letters...."

It occurred to me that the thief might visit her address and mug her again, but as she sat on the chair, indifferent to the blood that made great scarlet streams and rivers round the side of her face and on her coat, her fingers helplessly intertwined, I could not say that. Instead I stared at her, struck by her subordination of her physical pain to a romantic attachment from long ago, whose memory the scarlet letters kept alive.

The Sun and Icarus

As the ship approached Goa I sunbathed on the top deck. I knew I shouldn't but the sun was warm and I lay on my front on a towel on the wooden sun-lounger and gave myself to the sun's nourishing rays. Like Icarus I flew too near the sun.

When I returned to England I had an annual check-up and a nurse fitted electrodes to my back and sides for a routine ECG test. She said, "You've got some lesions on your back in three places. You should have them looked at."

I could not see the lesions without standing between two mirrors and had not been aware of them until then.

I saw my doctor, who said, "You have three patches I'd like looked at. Two are where your wings would be if you had wings."

She referred me to a consultant, Dr Bewers. He was a youngish man and he asked me to strip to the waist. He fingered my three patches, two by each shoulder-blade and one below. He said, "I think you have three basal cell carcinomas. It's a form of skin cancer caused by sunlight. You've got skin cancer on your back, near your shoulder-blades and lower down. You're not going to die of this. I'll take a biopsy now to confirm my diagnosis and when you come back I'll scrape them off for you."

He scratched and peeled off bits of my skin from where my wings would join my shoulder-blades if I had wings. The sun had melted my wax wings as they did Icarus's.

A letter came through confirming his diagnosis and making an appointment to have the lesions removed. I returned to his room and climbed on to an examination-table and lay down on my front. He gave me local anaesthetics and I could feel him picking and tugging at my skin, curling and scraping it off. I had plasters. I had always loved the sun and had often sunbathed in my Cornish garden for three-quarters of an hour after lunch. I would go into a kind of daze and have what amounted to a siesta, the warm rays of the sun permeating my skin (as I saw it) and imbuing me with the sun's invigorating power. But I was also exposing myself to the sun's destructive radiation. At one and the same time the sun was life-giving and filled me with energy while radiating me with destructive skin cancer.

As the sun set, I saw that the sun was an ambivalent force for both good and bad, for health and ill health. Once again I had encountered the basic law of the universe, +A + –A = 0: +A (invigorating energy) + –A (destructive cancer) = 0 (the sun reconciling the two opposites within its rays). I had lived my life between opposites within the universe's dialectic, and I now had to extend these opposites to the sun.

In the early dusk I knew I would never again be able to sunbathe and missing the sun's warming power on my cheeks made me feel sad. I was now a grounded Icarus, I had vivid memories of my flights but could never fly again.

A Vicar and a Nephew

"Ernest did so much for his church," Penny said, "but no one visited him during his final illness. He had lived alone at home. He gave me a key and I often shopped for him. I knew his wife very well before she died, she was at the church. He was like a grandfather to my children, he often came to Sunday lunch when they were younger. He collapsed and was taken to hospital by ambulance, to A & E. A registrar and consultant both examined him and he was under constant observation, attached to monitors. His blood test showed he had renal failure. He was moved from A & E to the Acute Assessment Unit as there were no beds on the ward.

"I was with him. My daughter looked in when she could. A curtain was drawn round his bed. All his organs started to shut down, nothing could be done. I held him until 11.30. The vicar came and said loudly the other side of the curtain so he could hear, 'He was a cantankerous so-and-so.' He died soon afterwards.

"He had put off making a will, and his house went to his nephew who lived in Milton Keynes and who never visited him. I went to his house to tidy up as no one had been in since the ambulancemen were there. His nephew and his wife and dog turned up at the front door by arrangement. They were looking for the will. They asked for my keys and I handed them over.

"I found out who Ernest's solicitor was and she opened up for me so I could take back the photos of me and my family. They had gone. I'm sure they were thrown away. I managed to retrieve a wedding photograph of Ernest and his wife.

"The nephew made contact through the solicitor. All he wanted was to ban me from going in any more and to sell the house. The cleaner still looked in to do round for him, and was owed some money.

"It's horrid. He knew so much about Loughton and had access to all the church records and its local history, but no one visited him and through the vicar the church insulted him while he was dying. And his greedy nephew wasn't interested in him. They hadn't spoken for years. He was a widower, and those he helped turned their backs on him, except for me, and now they've used the law to turn their backs on me. Why is life so unfair?"

A Vicar and Autism

"I went to a wedding in Crete last week," said Stan. "The groom was my cousin Penny's son. Penny, the groom's mother, was staying on a package in a really good hotel by the sea. The bride's father had booked a complex inland in the hills without consulting the family, and he expected the groom's parents to take rooms there. He's a vicar, and he has an autistic son, Benjie, who lives in a home near Portsmouth. He's in his twenties and can't be still and he can't speak. He grunts and jigs about, he's always moving. Looking after him is a full-time job. So Benjie stayed in the complex and was looked after by his family. The vicar's wife shows signs of being autistic, I think that's where the son gets it from.

"Anyway, the vicar held a barbecue before the wedding up in the hills. He made no arrangements. My cousin's ex-husband, the groom's father, arrived with all the meat and fish which he'd bought fresh in the local market that day, and did most of the cooking. Without him the barbecue would not have happened. The vicar was very unwelcoming, he completely ignored my cousin. Imagine the groom's mother not being greeted at such an event. My cousin doesn't drink alcohol and there was a toast. She raised a glass of sparkling water. The vicar made a remark which she overheard: 'People who toast without alcohol are party-spoilers.' He then complained to her about her ex-husband's drinking: 'It's terrible that some people don't know when to stop.' He made her feel uncomfortable. She left at 9, and he said as she was leaving, 'It's bad manners to leave so early.' He's a Christian, but he didn't consider her feelings.

"Autistic people are unaware of others' feelings, and perhaps having an autistic wife and son has eroded his vicarly sensitivity towards others' feelings and their point of view. According to his daughter the vicar doesn't believe in God. I don't understand it. How can you be a vicar and not believe in God and not be considerate towards people?

"His daughter could have got married in his church in England, near Oxford. But *she* doesn't believe in God. She's a humanist, like the groom, so they were married in a Venetian Fort. The groom loves Greece, it was a beautiful setting. They all stood on uneven ground and threw rose petals. The wedding breakfast was in a hotel near the Fort, the Veneto Hotel, one of the most elegant boutique hotels in Rethymno and one of the oldest buildings of the Venetian era. It was part of the 14th-century Dominican monastery, Santa Maria Magdalena. The vicar spent every minute looking after his autistic son. Benjie's a grown man but can't speak and he was jigging to music the whole time.

"My cousin's hotel by the sea had a lovely garden and I shall always remember a row of large coloured urns on a wall. They were self-contained, they weren't aware of each other. I think Benjie's like a coloured urn."

A Stark Reality and Three Hundred Dreams

Prize-giving was on a hot afternoon. I left my jacket in the boot of my car and walked to the marquee. I was seated next to the Deputy Mayor of the Town Council and relished the breezes through the marquee sides. There was an introduction and the school hymn was sung, and then there was a welcome and a Headmistress's address. There were Speech and Drama recitals, school captains' reports and piano recitals. Then the guest speaker spoke, Annie Marlborough. I knew one of her sons had been found to have leukaemia at the age of three and had died at the age of nine, I knew her tragedy had inspired her to open a hospice for children, for which she had been fund-raiser and events manager.

Annie Marlborough had blonde shoulder-length hair and a very brown suntan. She told how she had left the hospice and was working full time bringing dreams to children with life-threatening illnesses or severe disabilities. So far she had brought dreams to two hundred children. The school had supported her charity and she was presented with a cheque for funds that had been raised at various events during the year.

After the prize-giving there was a gathering for the staff in the Studio behind the assembly hall, which she attended. I spoke to her. She said, "I'm in Hainault now, with an office, a car and two helpers. A man offered it and I've done it and it's worked. I'm trying to bring happiness to ill or disabled children, fulfil their dreams. It's in memory of my son who died when he was nine. My other son is eighteen now, and is shadowing me. He may take over from me eventually. I'm so pleased this school has supported my charity."

A teacher was retiring after forty-one years in schools. She had a problem with her hip she did not want to have seen to, and was bent double. She had just entered, negotiating the step down with great difficulty, and had lowered herself into a chair at the back. I had to go and speak to her.

When I turned back Annie Marlborough was leaving. I went over and thanked her for coming and watched as she walked to her car. She had been a normal mother, an attractive blonde, and disaster had struck and removed her first child and she had been propelled into running a charity for other children who were ill, something she had not dreamt would be her lot when she got married. I thought, 'Our paths in life are very strange and often end up far from where they began.' I wondered at how the stark reality of her son's death had morphed into fulfilling the dreams of children she did not know.

A Sandblaster and Beautifying Tracery

The bowl of our round fountain was covered with a circular iron wheel with elaborate tracery that had once been painted black. It was in four segments and some of the iron tracery had pulled away from the frame. I needed the ironwork sandblasted, re-soldered and then repainted, and I found a man in a firm in Tottenham who would come out and take the ironwork away.

Gary turned up with his van, quoted and carried and stacked the four segments in the back. He told me, "My father and I had our own company in Bath. We had venture capital to fund us. When my father was eighty-two he was found to have bladder cancer, and he died. The venture capitalist wanted his money out and we had five days to put new funds in. It didn't happen and we lost everything. I worked for a firm in Birmingham for two years, and then came back down south to Tottenham. I now employ four people."

He drove off.

He brought the four segments back sandblasted, re-soldered and covered in new black paint. He fitted the segments back round our fountain, which had the Three Graces round its side along with Aphrodite.

Gary said, "We had these out in our workshop and sandblasted them one after another. It's very dusty in our workshop. It's a lovely wheel and I love the tracery. We care for what we do. I'm sorry to be giving it you back as I enjoyed looking at it. The four segments look fantastic back in place. I'd like to come and see it when the reeds have grown through. You should enjoy the work you do, it's about more than making money, isn't it? It's creating art-like objects like that fine tracery that beautify Nature."

Lake Garda and Chaos

"Amy has been in Italy and had an eventful last day," Pippa said. "She was with a group of twenty-eight, staying at Lake Garda. Their flight was at 5pm from Venice. They all wanted to go to Venice early and spend the day looking round. Transport was laid on if the whole group was going, but one grumpy man wouldn't go and so they had to go under their own steam. So Amy and two other women and two men took a taxi to the station. There were self-service tickets and not many trains according to the timetable Amy found. A train came and they all piled in and sat down. There was a screen with Italian on it. The Italian suddenly changed to German. They realised they were heading to Germany. The train came to a stop at a station and they piled out. There was no one to speak to so they ran to the driver's cab and spoke to the driver. The driver made radio contact with a train coming the other way and persuaded it to stop. They had a ride in the cab, and climbed down and crossed the line and climbed aboard the other train when it came. That train took them back to Lake Garda and on to Venice.

"It was very wet. At Venice they walked through heavy rain to a museum. One man wanted to go on to an art gallery, so they all went. The other man attached himself to Amy and wouldn't leave her. At the art gallery Amy went to the loo and dried her clothes under the hand-dryer, and he was just outside the door of the Ladies, waiting for her. He went to the Men's loo and locked himself in a cubicle and couldn't unlock the door. He was thundering on the door with the palm of his hands. Amy went in and got him out by shouting instructions.

"It was so wet they went back to the museum. Amy was unable to see what she wanted to see so they decided to take a water-taxi to the airport. Now the rain turned to snow. One of the two women slipped on the quay and fell into the water-taxi. The water-taxi couldn't cross the bay to the airport because of the snow. They got off at the next stop. They took taxis to the airport. The man who wanted to go to the art gallery went with Amy, and the two of them had a laugh about the other three, who seemed 'mental'. When they got to the airport they found their flight was delayed by the snow. They couldn't take off until 10pm. They arrived at Gatwick after the last train had gone. They had to stay in the Travelodge there.

"Amy's car was at Reading station. Amy was told, 'The next train to Reading is ten past five on platform 8. No, I've told you wrong: ten past eight on platform 5.' In the end she caught her train and picked up her car. What a palaver. It's enough to put you off going anywhere ever again. When *we* go abroad it's all straightforward. We've had to catch trains and battle with rain and snow but it's never turned out as chaotic as that."

I wondered if some people attract chaos by not being careful and wary, by not having sufficient mental self-control. What was it Eliot had said? Something along the lines of: when the hand is expert with sail and oar, the sea is calm. When the mind is in control, life runs smoothly.

There was not much anyone could do about the weather, but the art of travelling was to control events by detailed and meticulous planning and research, not to be at the mercy of accident. I reckoned some people have meticulous temperaments and others act on impulse and are buffeted as they muddle a way through.

A Blank and a Back

There had been a lunch on a Saturday for the Old Boys to recognise Jim

Dawson's sixty years as a teacher in the school. He was now in his mid-eighties. I attended in the dining-hall and saw Meg sitting on a table with her back to the stairs that led up to the corridor. Towards the end of the lunch there were speeches. The Head spoke, and then Jim Dawson was called up, the ex-football star who had played in the Amateur Cup Final at Wembley in 1951.

He stood by the kitchen hatch at the rail and began to speak and I listened, recalling how he used to address us in Geography at school, expecting him to thank everyone for attending.

He said, "I didn't know I'd be asked to make a speech." Then nothing was coming out. He had faltered, it was as though he had forgotten who he was and who he was with. He later told me he temporarily forgot where he was and could not remember why he was there. He had gone blank, and there was a silence.

A quick-thinking man who was younger than me put his hand up and asked a question as if he were a boy in class. I could not hear what it was, but Jim Dawson mock-told him to "pipe down". There was laughter. The 'boy' stood up, walked over to the rail and bent down to be punished. Jim Dawson pretended to smack his bottom, and again there was laughter. The 'boy' had broken the awkwardness, but, seeing something was wrong, the Head stepped in and thanked Jim Dawson for his sixty years of service and called for applause. Jim Dawson was encouraged to return to his seat next to Meg, and two minutes later they slipped out and left.

Meg later told me, "Doug Insole was there, his friend from the old days, the cricketer. And that was the moment I realised Jim had Alzheimer's. He already had muscular dystrophy, as if he hasn't got enough problems."

I later heard that his muscular dystrophy was incurable prostate cancer, and that he had not been told this as, having Alzheimer's, he would not understand it properly. "Come round and see him," Meg said, "but don't let on about his prostate cancer."

So I went round to his house and climbed the steep garden path and sat with him in his front room in December. He seemed pleased to see me but complained he had a pain his back.

"You know an osteopath," he said. "Could you get me an

appointment so I can sort out the pain in my back?"

Knowing it was prostate cancer I was vague and said, "I'll do what I can but I know he's pretty booked up."

I gave him a book about the Forest I had written and dedicated it to him. I read out the dedication, which referred to him as a 'maestro' for his footballing prowess. (It was said in the 1950s that he and Johnny Haynes were the two most accurate passers in British football.) When I read out the word 'maestro' he stood up and gripped my shoulder and burst into tears.

"I am so grateful to you," he said, "I think of you every day. You're so kind to me." And he groped for my hand and gripped it with tears rolling down his cheeks.

I found his tears embarrassing and felt uncomfortable as, at Meg's request, I had withheld information from him. I did not visit him again. I was not surprised to hear he had been put in Forest Place. Many Old Boys visited him once but none returned as he either did not recognise them or was tearful and they felt uncomfortable. Sometimes he did not recognise Meg. It was very difficult for her.

Because he was so fit – he had gone to the gym every day until the onset of Alzheimer's – his heart was strong and he lived longer than expected. The thought crossed my mind, in Arthur Hugh Clough's words:

Thou shalt not kill; but needst not strive
Officiously to keep alive.

Then his prostate cancer took hold and he tearfully told the nursing staff he did not know why he was there. It was very difficult.

While I was away in August I received an email from the school saying that he had died. The funeral had taken place by the time I got back. I was relieved for him. It had to happen, and his passing was a merciful release. But I can still see him standing before the rail at the lunch celebrating his sixty years of service at the school, when he was the strong, confident man I used to know before his illnesses overtook him.

See also 'A Trolley and Stress'.

A Transplant and a Claw

Rosemary had had multiple health problems after a complicated birth at a cottage hospital. She had had gangrene and had had toes amputated, and her liver functioned at 30 to 40 per cent. She had been on dialysis soon after the birth, and it was wearing her down. She had to spend four hours in a hospital three times a week, and with the travelling to and from the hospital she had not had much time left of the three dialysis days to herself.

She found a donor of a new liver, a woman she had worked with twenty years previously. There was a match. The donor's mother lived and worked in Switzerland and fostered children. She had the liver transplant. Two weeks later I rang Jack for news.

"There's been rejection," he said. "Her new liver's functioning at 10 to 20 per cent. She's turned blue and one of her hands has turned into a claw. She had to have a fistula, a pipe, screwed into her arm. She's now off dialysis but on Thursday she has another operation to remove the fistula and undo the operation, otherwise her arm must be severed. The two children will be in an after-school club that day."

"She's suffered so much," I said before I rang off. "Henry has done very well to cope with her and the children."

Neither of us knew that her son would shortly be diagnosed as a diabetic, like his grandfather Rupert, and that she would be suffering even more on his account.

Rosemary had trained as a nurse to help others, as had her husband Henry. Between them they needed all their nursing skills to cope with the health issues that clawed within their family. Rupert had had his problems in securing his 'pension', and now they would need his support for his grandson, a need which had clawed into his attention.

A Fall in a Home

"We visited Geoffrey in his home," Susan told me. "Ronnie's mother's partner. You remember, you sat next to him at the wedding. He was in the home because he'd got Alzheimer's. He was diagnosed as having an ulcer and after three or four months he was told that it was in fact stomach cancer. He went into a home on the South Coast. He was over ninety. He was in a wheelchair. He couldn't drink. He seemed confused, not sure why he was there. He was being watched by the nursing staff, he was supposed to be escorted to the bathroom.

"After we left that evening he tried to go to the bathroom on his own. He fell over. He died that night. It's hard to understand, how someone who's being watched and escorted can fall like that and die. You're not safe at home and you're not safe in a home, so where are you safe? One fall and you're gone."

It was the stomach cancer that killed him, I reckoned. It weakened him and made him unsteady on his legs, which is why he had to be escorted. It must have been very advanced to make him so frail that a fall could kill him. And when one is that frail there is no safety anywhere, and a fall may be Nature's way of ending the misery of being sapped by cancer. The fall may have been Nature's way of ending his pain and torment, and may have been a blessing in disguise.

Shopping Bags and Tragedy

"We're going to a funeral in Sutton," Susan said. "Something terrible's happened. Ronnie's mother lost Geoffrey, as you know. Now she's lost her sister-in-law. Her brother got into his car in Tesco's after loading the shopping bags into the back. It was parked near a wall. His wife had stayed in Tesco's. She came out of a side entrance and he didn't see her. What happened's not clear, but we think she wanted to go to a shopping bag and she bent into the car with the door open. He was in reverse with his foot on the brake and she was bending into the car with the door open. He reversed out of the space so he would be ready to set off when she joined him and she was dragged under the wheels. He ran her over and killed her. He's distraught. Over the phone he said he doesn't want to talk about it. It's a freak accident."

I shook my head. What could be more ordinary than loading shopping bags into the back and going to the back to remove something from a bag? And what could be more tragic than for a husband to kill his wife? Somehow the registers of the ordinary and of tragedy had got mixed up and the effect on the driver's life was devastating. He sobbed throughout the funeral. His wife was in a wicker coffin, which remained where it was at the end of the service, and he was still sobbing when he went back to blow her a final kiss.

A Wedding and a Fall

"Carol's daughter was married last week," Pippa said. "I saw the photos. She planned the reception very well. After the church service the bride and groom were served champagne in the car that took them to the hotel reception. There was a 'pearl' on the menu. The hundred and fifteen guests sat at tables for their wedding breakfast. Carol was on 'top table', up one end of the room. There were speeches. Carol said she could see the bridegroom's nerves. Eventually Carol wanted to go to the loo. She stood up and didn't see that an usher had hung his morning-dress jacket on his chair, and that the tail trailed on the floor. She, the mother of the bride who has to be perfect, tripped over the tail and fell. She crashed headlong to the floor. She was embarrassed. She was raised to her feet and managed to get out of the room. But she had a swollen knee and had to have a cold compress and Arnica, which the hotel provided.

"When she limped back into the room no one seemed to have noticed. Because Carol was up one end of the room and they were all down the other end of the room, most were unaware that it had happened. They had been immersed in their table's conversation and had not paid attention to what was going on elsewhere, and there was a hubbub that had drowned the noise of the crash. So the fall happened and Carol was treated for a swollen knee, and the great majority of the guests were none the wiser."

"People are unobservant," I said. "A poet, a writer, is always looking and notices everything. But most people live in a dream connected to their own situation and thoughts and notice nothing. As Eliot said, humankind is unable to bear much reality."

Stunted Toes and a Joined-Up Head

"Did you have a good weekend?" I asked Carol, our domestic help, after she had stopped Hoovering.

"I saw, and held, the new baby," she said, of her granddaughter. "I won't drive on motorways, I haven't got the confidence, so I took buses. It took me three-and-a-half hours to get to Rayleigh. Poor little thing, she's got so much wrong with her. You know she was born with a tongue-tie, and they sorted that out by cutting it. And she's got a problem with her toes in one foot. They got entangled in the string-like amniotic bands in the womb. When limbs get entangled, their growth is stunted. They've got to go to Southend Hospital about that and also see a consultant. The baby's got Amniotic Band Syndrome.

"And now she's got a problem with her skull. Normally children are born with their skull open at the top and the fontanelles, the soft spots, close over a period of time: the posterior between eight and twelve weeks after birth, the sphenoidal after six months, the mastoid six to eighteen months and the anterior twelve to eighteen months. Hers all seem to have closed within three months, if I've understood it correctly." I frowned. *Had* she understood it correctly? "And that may mean the head can't grow as it should so there are appointments to cope with that. They have so many doctors' appointments and consultations about parts of her, poor little thing.

"And Ronald's having to do it all, as his wife's depressed. She's been sitting at home crying about the baby. Her mother left Derbyshire to go down and look after her, and she had a mild heart attack soon after she arrived and was in hospital down here for four days, so they've had to visit her every day in among the medical appointments.

"I got to hold the little thing but she's not keeping her food down, she's sick after feeding, and that's another problem. I can't get my head to be on top of it. And then, as if all the rest weren't enough, my daughter's having IVF and that's not worked. It's all very upsetting. I don't know, you get married and your husband turns out to have dementia; you have children and they have their problems; and they have grandchildren, and there are problems there too. Sometimes life seems just one endless problem."

"I'm sure everything will sort itself out," I said. "It generally does. Your husband's coping well and it's only gradual – "

"That's true."

"And your granddaughter will be able to operate with reduced toes. She may not be a ballet-dancer but would she want to be? She'll be able to function reasonably normally, she's got her balance and she can walk and run. She may not be able to be an athlete but that needn't matter. And the head – children grow and her head can still grow even though the top has closed. And the tongue's already resolved. And I'm sure they'll sort your daughter out eventually. All the problems will be Hoovered up. You will come through all this and you'll have a clean carpet."

"I hope you're right, Mr Rawley," she said. "I hope you're right."

A Chef and a Backhand Cut

I went to the Queen Elizabeth Carvery for Sunday lunch. There was no queue and I greeted the chef, who was in white with a chef's hat behind large mounds of beef, turkey and gammon. He was sharpening his long knife criss-cross to get ready for serving, a thickset fellow in his fifties who had served me before.

"Hello again," I said. "I'm pleased to be served by the master of the backhand cut."

He grinned.

"Turkey and gammon, please," I said. "How are you keeping?"

He expertly began cutting backhand, a technique I always associated with him.

"Not so well," he said. "This restaurant's changing hands. There's still going to be a roast but it's going to be done in the kitchen. They're closing this Carvery, so this'll be the last time you see me. They're closing it next week and doing changes for four months and it'll reopen in August without me.

"I've been laid off before, in the army. I was in Ireland, Bosnia, you name it. I was given an MD, medical discharge. I had cancer, and the army didn't want to know, laid me off. It's not right that they do that when you're ill. It's backhanded. So now I'm redundant again."

"I'm really sorry," I said. "We shall all miss you. I do hope you'll find something quickly and keep your backhand serve in training."

He smiled.

"Stuffing, sir?" he asked, holding my plate.

A Toenail and Torture

I had an ingrowing toenail on my right foot, and in the 1980s I went into the Royal Masonic Hospital and had one side sliced down and removed. The trauma of the operation left it encrusted underneath. With hindsight there was fungal growth under the nail from the day of the operation – perhaps an instrument was contaminated – and I lived with an encrusted fungal nail for thirty years. The Indian lady in my foot clinic drew my attention to it. She said, "You've got fungus under the nail. You need our new laser treatment. It will kill off the fungus and return your nail to normal. It costs £250 for at least two sessions, and it always works."

So I booked myself in with her partner, Jake, a Sri Lankan who treated cricketers' feet. He was always attending Test Matches and treating the feet of fast bowlers in several Test sides. He was in his thirties and had a smiling face. I lay on his couch and took my sock off my right foot and he switched on his machine and held a probe that gave out an orange glow. "You have to have four hundred shots," he said. These would be signalled by four hundred pips, which the machine would give out.

I sat, relaxed, and had the first fifteen. Then a burning intensified on my toe. I groaned before we reached twenty and he stopped.

"It's boiling me," I said. "It's like dipping my toe in scalding water."

Jake laughed.

"We'll try again," he said.

I counted another fifteen pips and again I was in agony and gasped: "Aaah."

And so he went on, stop-starting our way every fifteen pips until, biting my hand to control the pain, I reached four hundred. My toenail had glowed orange on several occasions.

"That'll kill the fungal infection under your nail," he said. "You need to come again in no more than six weeks."

Jake led me downstairs.

"How did you get on?" the bespectacled receptionist asked guardedly.

"It was torture," I said. "I was ready to confess to anything."

Jake laughed.

"If I'd been an England cricketer, I'd have given him all the secrets of the English dressing-room."

He laughed again.

"This should be used on terrorists. Give them twenty shots and they'll be screaming to talk."

He laughed again.

I went back six weeks later and sat in the waiting-room. Jake, the Sri Lankan, came down the stairs and put his head round the wall.

"Time for your torture," he said. "Another four hundred shots."

He was a humorous torturer. He giggled and laughed as I gasped and writhed after fifteen shots. He always stopped the torture to allow me to recover. While he gave me shots he told me what went on in the cricket dressing-rooms. One English fast bowler had to have his foot strapped before playing, and another had such a bruised toenail that he cut a hole in his right plimsoll and played with his big toe visible.

"Four hundred, all done," he said at the end.

I limped downstairs.

"One more session to finish it off," he said.

"I thought I was going to escape with two."

"One more. No more after three."

I went a third time and again my big toe glowed orange.

I am pleased to say it worked. I now have no infection under my big toenail on my right foot. The third session was free, included in the original price. And I would recommend his laser and the orange glow of the probe to anyone. It is strange that we do not remember pain. I know I was in agony but I would still recommend it for nothing else gets below the nail so effectively. Sometimes torture has our best interests at heart.

Four Bereavements and a Tortured Life

"Jane's granddaughter died," Maud said. "She's had a terrible life. She's ninety and four have died. First her husband. Then her first daughter. Her first daughter married and she and her husband opened some sort of a children's home near Coddenham in Suffolk. There was talk of sexual abuse involving one of the children there, and the mother of the child involved went to the home with a gun and shot them both, Jane's first daughter and her husband. It was a terrible scandal. Then the other daughter died, I'm not sure how. And now her granddaughter. She had cancer. She was given eighteen months to live and she died recently. The funeral's in Devon, or Somerset. Her husband, her two daughters and her granddaughter have all predeceased her. That's terrible.

"The worst thing that can happen to anybody old is for their loved ones to die before them. She had that four times. Four bereavements. She's had a tortured life. Why do some people go through life without any bereavements and others have four, when they've done nothing to deserve it? Why do some people suffer more than others? I don't understand it. But that's life. Some plants thrive and do well and others get killed off by the frost. It all has to be accepted. But even if she accepts what's happened to her, *four* when many others have none. It's hard to make sense of it, isn't it?"

Collapsed Veins and a Deer

Pippa left to have her third hip replacement, an operation to replace her unsatisfactory second hip replacement which had dislocated twice, once in front of our Cornish house and once in Germany while she was talking to the owner of a shop in Aachen. I waved her off early in the morning as she left by car, and she rang me later to say she was going down around 10am. I wished her good luck.

Around 10.15 I went to the kitchen to make myself a cup of coffee and saw a beautiful, slender deer standing under the apple trees by the bird feeders. It was timid and was looking at me as I stood the other side of the window: a doe with round white spots. It had come into our garden from the forest and was just standing. I put my head outside the door and it continued to look at me. Irrationally I thought, 'Pippa's soul has taken the form of a deer and has come to give me a message, to assure me that everything will turn out well.' I had a strong feeling that this was the case, but put it out of my mind as being ridiculous. Then it bounded off into the undergrowth and I saw it heading across our field and disappear into trees.

Around 11 the phone rang. A lady asked for me and said: "It's the King Edward VII Hospital. Your wife hasn't had her operation and she's not having it this time. I've got the anaesthetist on the line and I'm putting you through. He wants to speak to you."

It was highly irregular for the anaesthetist to ring. What had happened? In some trepidation I said, "Thank you. Hello."

The anaesthetist told me that he administered the anaesthetic and that everything was proceeding normally. "Your wife was unconscious on a ventilator. Then I noticed her pulse had dropped to thirty-five and suddenly your wife's veins collapsed. We immediately fought to revive her. The surgeon and an assistant frantically pressed on her heart. The registrar gave her heart massage. We were all doing things. I had to give her an injection to counteract the collapsed veins. I was looking for a vein that would take a needle but we couldn't find one, they'd all collapsed. In the end I injected her jugular artery in her neck. We nearly lost her. We all agreed that we could not proceed with the operation and she was wheeled to Critical Care and she will be there for forty-eight hours, being thoroughly monitored under day-and-night observation. We will aim to try again in a month's time when we have all the data from Critical Care." 'Critical Care' was the hospital's terminology for 'Intensive Care'.

The anaesthetist spent an hour on the phone to me, talking through every aspect and inviting me to suggest what had caused the collapse of her veins. Had she contributed in some way? What tablets had she been taking and when was the last one she had taken?

I rang Critical Care. A nurse told me: "She's the only one in Critical Care, she's got our full attention. There are four of us monitoring her. She's full of tubes, she can't move her arms so you can't speak to her, I'm afraid." I gave her a message to repeat to Pippa.

I visited Pippa at the hospital. I was told I could speak to her for a short while and was led into a forest of plastic tubes. There were many dials round her.

"You nearly lost me," she said, lying down. "I'd had the anaesthetic, I was out, I'd no idea what was going on. The registrar's a pupil of mine when I was Head. He was in the Garden Room when we took over. He was an angelic little boy when he was about four and used to come to me for daily cuddles. He told me, 'You really gave me a fright.' He massaged my heart. The whole operating team fell on me and resuscitated me. Sheila, my surgeon, looked in on me when I came round and said, 'You escaped.'" Pippa laughed. "She said, 'Ninety-nine per cent of our job is boring standing around and doing things, and one per cent is interesting panic, and you provided us with some one-per-cent interest.'"

I said, "I'm glad I didn't lose you, and you've got a lot of individual attention here. You're in good hands. Have they said why they think your veins collapsed?"

"No. They don't know. They hope these tests will find out."

A nurse had appeared. "I'm afraid that must be all," she said. "We have to continue the monitoring."

So I said 'good-bye' and left.

When I got home I went to the kitchen to make a cup of tea. I instinctively looked out of the window at the bird feeders by the apple trees. There was no trace of the slender deer.

Pippa had her operation a month later, courageously going through the procedure again, and her veins were fine, and no deer approached my window while she was unconscious.

Disarmament and a KGB Man

Fyodor was a Russian. He emailed my website with an attached constitution for a World State he had drafted and invited me to a conference of international philosophers in Athens the following October if I shared his views. I printed off his document and took it with me on a cruise of the Baltic and skimmed through it. It was in uncorrected English, some of it turgidly written, and too materialistic for my view and culpably unlinked to the UN. There was no hint of a vision. But I was intrigued at the idea of international philosophers meeting near Plato's Academy to approve the creation of a new 'Republic', a World State, and despite my reservations I agreed to attend the conference.

I had to register before 4.30 on the first floor of the Cultural Centre of Athens on a Sunday. I flew to Athens on the Sunday morning and with Greek time being two hours on I just made it. I met Fyodor, who was bespectacled in his sixties, and his blonde plump Russian wife, Sonia. He introduced me to a Chinese lawyer he had allocated as my assistant. He was a warm, dominating figure who clearly held the international philosophers together. He invited me to a reception at the Georgian Centre, where some of the international philosophers stood around drinking.

For the next three days I met him within the context of the conference. I began sitting in the audience away from the lectern but he swiftly asked me to be Chairman and on the second day – in a nearby lecture-room with fixed semi-circular tiered seats that had been made available free of charge by the City of Athens – I sat next to him on the platform. Soon afterwards I chaired fifty international philosophers into adopting his constitution and bringing in a new World State which now required a mass movement to draw in a billion people. It declared war illegal and called for universal disarmament. I read out a declaration of the creation of the World State and everyone present queued at the front to sign it on my desk.

We stayed in the lecture-room from early in the morning until late in the evening. At that time Athens was beginning to be crowded with refugees from Syria and elsewhere, and at dusk the garden outside the Cultural Centre contained groups of sitting young men who were injecting themselves with what looked like heroin.

The first opportunity I had to speak to Fyodor alone came on the fourth day of the conference (not counting the registration day) when there was a coach tour of places in the Peloponnese. He insisted on sitting beside me and I was able to ask him about his life. From what he said it was apparent that he was a dialectical materialist. He said, "I have written three books. My first book picked up a sentence in Engels. All living things are in a chain of being and obey the same laws of Nature, including humans." His view of a World State was humanist and materialist, and ignored the 5.8 billion who believe in one of the established religions.

I asked, "When did you get your first computer?"

He said, "A KGB man showed me his new PC. I said, 'Can you get me one?' He got me one and I didn't know what to do with it. I typed up my first book on it. I fell foul of the Soviet Committees but got it accepted in the early 1980s."

I wondered how he came to be with the KGB man in the first place but did not ask as asking might have spoiled the atmosphere.

We visited Mycenae. I climbed to look at what my research indicated was the bathroom where Agamemnon was stabbed and killed by his wife Clytemnestra on the night of his return from Troy. Later we stopped at Agamemnon's tomb.

At Nauplia (the modern Nafplio) we stopped at the fortress of Palmidi, and wandered past cyclamens, and we then went down to the main square, which had Venetian features. Fyodor, Sonia and I found an outside sitting area in shade that was served by a nearby restaurant, and we ordered cheese, smoked salmon, ham and egg club sandwiches, chips and diet cokes, and he told me how he had been a diplomat "working on commercial trade, including cars", in Egypt for eight years, and also in Greece.

Later that evening we returned to the Georgian Centre, and he took me to the Centre's computer and showed me a timeline he had put together. It was on the need to disarm before there is a nuclear explosion and a nuclear winter.

I saw Fyodor as an ex-Communist dialectical materialist like Lenin and Engels, and as a diplomat who had branched out on his own and founded the forum of international philosophers. No one seemed to have funded the six annual conferences of international philosophers he had put on, and the City of Athens had given him the lecture-room with fixed seats free for part of the time. So why was he doing it? To act out his ideas? Or was he doing Putin's business by masterminding political initiatives under the guise of discussions on philosophy? I did not know.

Fyodor was an enigma, promoting a political agenda that included Western disarmament (within a context of universal disarmament) under the guise of philosophy. I knew I would be wary of promoting an ex-Communist programme under the guise of political Universalism.

Menelaos and Ancient Stones

Menelaos was a Greek actor who was well-known for his appearances on Greek radio and television. On the first day of the conference in the Athens Cultural Centre he showed a video of himself shot at the previous year's conference. He was in Plato's Academy, a ruin of ancient stones on a low hill, and he brought down the Light by intoning to the gods in Greek. He had grey hair shaped in the manner of statues of ancient Greek philosophers and Roman emperors, and he startled us by chanting live the words he was chanting in the film. He chanted with tremendous power and invoked Mnemosyne, the goddess of memory. He said, "I am chanting to the spiritual Light, and have based my chant on ancient Greek practices."

On the second evening Menelaos put on an entertainment for us, a one-man show: Katsivelos's Greek version of *Avgerinos* by Romania's national poet Mihai Eminescu. He looked very smart in a white suit and shoes and white bow-tie, and he postured and cried out to a musical accompaniment. He recited the verse very theatrically – it could be said, excessively theatrically – and appealed directly to the audience in the manner of the performance of a classical Greek verse play by Aeschylus, Sophocles or Euripides.

On the last day a coach took us past Corinth to the Peloponnese and we stopped at Epidaurus (the modern Epidavros) and walked up a long path to the theatre. On the way Menelaos joined me and said in faltering English, "If you are no.2 next year, can you please think of me. I have received nothing for what I have done for the conferences. My services are given free. But I need money, I have to eat."

I said I would bear this in mind and would do what I could next year.

In the Epidaurus theatre (where I spent a night in a sleeping-bag when I was nineteen) I sat on the President's seat and surveyed the semi-circular stage and tried to imagine what it would have been like during performances of the classical Greek plays of Aeschylus, Sophocles and Euripides. Suddenly Menelaos was before me in the stance of a Greek actor. He declaimed classical Greek, flowing words that could be heard in the topmost tier of the ancient stone seating because of the acoustics, and I listened to the rhythms of the Greek words. At the end he said, "There were Doric words in what I have just recited." The Doric words were very old, pre-7th-century, a kind of 'Old Greek'.

I watched Menelaos after his impromptu performance. He clearly loved the place and derived energy from the ancient stones. He lived to convey the beauty of the Greek language, especially classical Greek, and though short of money freely gave from his talent. He reflected the tradition of ancient Greek verse plays and amid his posturing was a sincere and almost naive desire to strike attitudes and arm positions. I was not surprised to receive a Christmas card from him for he regarded anyone he had met two or three times as a lifelong friend. And he was counting on me to arrange some reimbursement next year.

A Church and a Pension

Jack rang me. He told me: "Rupert wants to be alone this Christmas, he doesn't want people to ring him. He needs to think. He's acting as a solicitor for a very complicated transaction. It's been happening for forty years. Forty years ago he agreed not to receive a penny in fees until completion, and the fees would be £40,000. He's regarded it as a retirement package, a form of saving, a pension. It's really complicated.

It involves buying five adjoining properties from separate owners near Sevenoaks, demolishing them and building a huge tower block after obtaining planning permission. There was a lot of local resistance but they now have planning permission. Exchange took place in 2008, and planning permission was in January 2014.

"Under the local deal there has to be a new access road to the car park of the local church, and the church was to contribute £80,000 towards the cost of the road. The church have had a meeting and the committee members have been greedy. They want the buyer to pay more towards the road. The buyer has said there should be a new contract, that the old one should lapse.

"The new building will give eighty care-home beds. The builder has scheduled building to start in the first week of January, but the church has put a spanner in the works. Building can't start until the church have agreed the access road. Rupert was in tears when I last saw him. He said, 'I'm in a bad way, I'm not in control. I can't enjoy any leisure or any sort of retirement while this is going on.' He's in tears four times a day. If the whole thing collapses it will be a catastrophe for him. He will have worked forty years on it without being paid a penny. It's given him mental problems, he just wants to get away from it and from people over Christmas and sit alone – and try not to worry. So don't ring him."

After Jack had rung off I looked out of the window. A blue tit was on the bird feeder. A jackdaw flew and perched on a nearby railing and the blue tit fled. The church was like the jackdaw, and Rupert was like the blue tit seeking nuts. The jackdaw flew off.

Two weeks later the church was appeased, the care homes were built and Rupert received his 'pension'.

A Scheme and a Petard

The first time I met Patrick Foot was at the accountants. Pippa, Simon and I were led by an office girl into a room where three people seemed to be having a meeting, two from the firm of accountants and a man in white shirtsleeves and a tie with grey hair, about sixty-five, who I took to be the client before us. He extended a hand, and thinking he was vacating the room I shook it. He did the same to Simon and Pippa, who also shook his hand. The office girl asked if we wanted coffee or tea and invited us to sit down. As soon as she left Patrick Foot barked, "I've got some information about you all. Let me make sure I've got it right. Philip Rawley," he said accusingly to me. "Address? Date of birth?"

Thinking it strange that a previous client should be interrogating us but in a social situation with two from the accountants' firm, I confirmed the information he had, as did Pippa and Simon when he turned to them. Then he wanted to know about other members of the family.

Seeing our perplexed expressions, Jenny, the lady accountant, interrupted and said: "Patrick Foot is a consultant. He worked for HMRC for seventeen years and I've asked him to come and give advice on your wills, trust and tax affairs and look at your position."

"I wish you'd said that earlier," Simon said humorously.

"I thought you were the last client," I said, and Patrick Foot and everybody laughed.

"I'm terribly sorry," Patrick Foot said, "I thought you knew I was coming."

"No one told us," Simon said, and all eyes turned to Jenny, the lady accountant.

Patrick Foot then conducted a review of our wills, trust and tax planning, during which there was much talk of what would happen on "first death" and "second death". It was assumed that as I was older than Pippa, the first death would be mine.

After the meeting Patrick Foot set out his thoughts in a paper, which he emailed through, and he came to a meeting at our house a fortnight later. Jenny arrived first and I sat her at the table. I greeted Patrick as he parked his car. He told me he had come across Tower Bridge. He had been in Arundel and the previous night he had seen a play in the Haymarket. He was doing a lot of travelling. I offered him coffee but he asked for water and immediately took a large round tablet.

Pippa and Simon joined us and Patrick Foot led the meeting. He began by apologising formally for interrogating us at the previous meeting. Again there was talk of first and second deaths. He said, "I've done what I'm suggesting regarding my own wife. I've put in place what I'm suggesting to you." He added, "I've got two daughters. One of them has a mortgage she has difficulty in meeting payments for, so I've taken it over and pay it. I'm deducting what I pay from her share of the proceeds on the second death, so there will be overall fairness of my treatment of my two daughters."

Three weeks later Patrick Foot came again. He arrived early and he and I had a chat at the table. He had sent an agenda and he ran through his proposals again. At one point, while explaining his ideas, he said, "That's the novel I'm writing, the transaction I've just described." I gathered he was writing a novel about a lawyer who (like him) offers his client a particular scheme. Just before 4pm he looked at his watch and said, "I ought to be going now. I've got to get through the Blackwall Tunnel before the rush hour. I've got another meeting to go to after that." I escorted him to the front door and watched as he turned his car, and waved him off as he headed for our open gates.

Another fortnight passed and then Simon rang and said, "I've just heard from Jenny that Patrick Foot was taken ill before the weekend. He has a brain tumour and is being operated on today. He's finished the trust document and his partner can complete the work. Jenny says realistically we won't be seeing him again. His working life has come to an end."

I was shocked. His brain tumour must have been advanced for him to have an immediate operation. I felt sad. His novel based on his scheme wouldn't be happening. If he did not survive the operation then ironically all talk of a "first death" – based on what he had expected to happen to me – would apply to *him*. The scheme he had proposed for us, which he had implemented in his own life, would now be tested within his own circumstances. The adviser was going first, setting an example. It could be said that he had been 'hoist with his own petard', and his client would be carrying on as before, unaffected by the schemes that had been triggered in the life of the adviser by news of his brain tumour.

'Hoist with one's own petard', 'affected oneself by one's schemes against others'. (*Concise Oxford Dictionary*.)

A Red Universe like the One

That evening there was a phenomenal sunset. I looked across the fields from my study and the sun, still well above the horizon, had turned red and had reddened the few clouds in the darkening blue sky. The red sky was breathtaking. Then I noticed that our lawn had turned red. Startled, I hurried downstairs and stood on the terrace near the bird feeders to get a better view. The fruit trees had turned red. In wonder I looked individually at different apple trees, all red as was the grass beneath them, as if I had never seen them before. I looked at the conifer hedge behind the herbaceous border. That too was now red. And behind me, the house was red. Everything I looked at was now red. Even the blue tits and long-tailed tits on our bird feeders had turned red. I had somehow entered a universe in which everything is red. I stood for a long time in wonder and watched the red sun slowly sink below the western horizon, and only turned back into the house as dusk fell.

Later I pondered what I had seen. I had seen the same universe but coloured red as I had never seen it before. What if one day I looked out and saw the same universe not red but showing the One like a red glow, so it was apparent there was one energy pulsing through it? Then I realised that instinctively seeing the universe as an emanation of the One was no more implausible than seeing the universe transformed by the colour red. The red universe was like the One I instinctively knew: there all the time but only apparent now and again.

Angels in Gloom

I arrived at the office near the Angel station in a biting wind and climbed the stairs to the first floor just after 7.30pm, wearing a blazer and an open-necked shirt. I found myself in a long room with desks in gloom up one end and a lit bar at the other end, where a half-circle of publishing staff were waiting for guests to arrive. A small boyish young man with an angelic face and long hair that curved round his cheeks on either side stepped forward. He looked like an angel. I said my name.

In an American accent he said, "I'm Eustace."

I knew he was the new owner of the firm. He introduced me to nearly a dozen young ladies who interrupted their talk between themselves to shake my hand. I accepted a disposable glass of red wine and asked if he had settled in.

"Oh, yes," he said. "I've been here more than a year now. My desk's back there. Look, I've got a poster of one of your books on that wall."

I followed his finger and saw three posters on the wall. My name was across the top of the right-hand one.

Eustace introduced me to the publicist, a Canadian girl with long hair who said she wanted to Skype me or talk over the phone on publicity plans for my forthcoming books. Linked to publicity was whether or not there was an Appendix of maps and charts, which the copy editor had said should be included but which a Dinah had said should not. Dinah had not answered my emails for three months and had written that day to say she had been ill with a lung-related condition but was now back and central.

"Is Dinah here?" I asked.

"No, she's not tonight."

The publicist introduced me to the Development Editor who was standing further into the gloom. She told me she approached people who had not written a book but had something to say, and helped them with what was often their first book.

The room had filled up. Earnest women and detached bald, thin men were talking to some of the twenty-seven staff who were present. There were over fifty in the room, some in the gloom and some at the lit end, and in the confined space the hubbub was so loud it was hard to hear what was being said.

There was another room, the library, and I went through to see who was there. It was dingily lit except for one spotlight, under which Eustace was standing, surrounded by authors near shelves lined with books. I spotted the new Publisher standing in the gloom and introduced myself.

"You're above everyone," I said, "except Eustace? You're above Dinah?"

"Yes," she said, "insofar as it's possible for anyone to be 'above'

Dinah."

I said, "You worked with HarperCollins."

"That was more than ten years ago. I was ten years with HarperCollins and then ten years with Hay House."

I talked with a couple of authors in the gloom and turned and found myself alongside Eustace, who was still standing under the spotlight. I said, "Your head is by my last two books." They were on a shelf just beside him.

He took down one of them and looked through it.

"Very good," he said. "I want to publish the sort of book we're well-known for. You're in that tradition."

He introduced me to his wife who was standing nearby, a youngish lady with shortish dark hair who shook my hand. She had been one of his authors and she also had an angelic face.

"I am from Ukraine," she said.

We discussed how the struggle was going in Ukraine.

"I think Ukraine will split in two," she said, "one part West-looking, one part East-looking."

Both Eustace and his wife said at different times, "We will be doing something in October when your books come out."

I found myself talking to Eustace again. Standing under the spotlight he asked me, "How do you think of Universalism?"

"As the One, unification," I said. "It's seeing history – all civilizations – as one, and philosophy as one, seeing the universe as a unity, and literature as presenting images of the One behind social situations like this."

He nodded.

"Here's my card," he said. "You can email me at that address if you have any problems. I want the books to be in the tradition we've always stood for."

I sensed he was on my side. He turned away and soon he was surrounded by other authors.

I stood between the two darkened rooms, in harmony with the One. It did not matter about Dinah. I was laid back, events would take their course, I would leave the Appendix for the universe and the angels to sort out. I was in touch with the unity behind the universe, and conflicting social situations did not matter. (I would learn three weeks later that Dinah had left the firm.) I finished my red wine, thanked Eustace and his wife and headed off down the stairs into the gloomy street.

A Room and a Deed

I had to set up a Trust to deal with the University that would be storing my papers. I had visited a local solicitor and explained what was required, and I now had to go in and sign the Trust Deed. I arrived at the solicitor's office five minutes before the appointment and announced myself to the receptionist, a quiet young girl who picked up the phone and told the solicitor I was in the waiting area.

The solicitor appeared, thin, bespectacled and in a suit. We shook hands. He said, "I've booked the room over there, let's go through."

The door had a narrow strip of glass in it, through which heads could be seen.

"Oh," he said, "there's someone in there." He looked at his watch. "They're overrunning."

He returned and sat on a chair opposite me. There was an awkward silence.

"Perhaps we should knock and say, 'Your time's up,'" I suggested to lighten the atmosphere.

He laughed nervously. The receptionist looked down, embarrassed and determined not to giggle.

"Perhaps you should instruct the receptionist to knock and put her head round the door and say, 'Sorry, your booking time has run out,'" I suggested.

Again the solicitor laughed nervously and again the receptionist looked down, determined not to be drawn into the situation.

"There's no phone in there," the solicitor said. "So we can't ring them. They've booked the room and they're overrunning."

But he did not have a solution as to how to deal with the problem.

Then his face lit up.

"If he's in there," he said to the receptionist, "he won't be in his room. So we can take over his room for a short while. That's what we'll do. Come this way, please."

I followed him into a room with a large, low, black desk, before which I sat.

The solicitor produced the Deed and explained the paragraph he had added, and I duly signed. We had a brief discussion about the way forward. Then he stood up and we went to the door.

Outside the meeting-room door was wide open. A man in a suit was sitting where I had sat. He had been locked out of his room by our deed. The solicitor and he greeted each other and the man smiled briefly at me as he returned to the room we had just vacated, from which he had been banned.

The solicitor and I shook hands.

"Goodbye," I said to the receptionist.

She nodded to me and, knowing her place amid the smash-and-grab of rooms, looked down. As I left the waiting area through the door to the stairs she was still looking down.

Pasties by the Lighthouse

For Maud's ninetieth birthday Pippa, Paul and I drove to Porthleven. Maud was waiting for us in the open front door. She waved and ushered us in for coffee, delighted to see us. Paul left his dog in the car. She opened our cards and added them to her mantelpiece, where some twenty cards proclaimed '90'. She opened our presents. She said, "I'm going to enjoy every minute of today. I've been really looking forward to it."

We all returned to Pippa's Shogun. I sat in the back with Paul, the dog was behind his seat in a nylon 'kennel' in the boot.

We drove to Marazion and found a pasty shop. Paul and I bought four pasties red-hot from the oven and four bottles of water. Then we drove past St Michael's Mount in bright sunshine to Pendeen lighthouse, where Maud's father had been lighthouse keeper before she was born. We parked the car by a bench and Maud, Pippa and I draped a rug over it and sat while Paul distributed pasties, napkins and water and opened a jar of pickle and put in a fork.

"I knew these cliffs when I was a little girl," Maud said. "I often came here. And my father used to take a pasty to work and eat it on these cliffs all those years ago." I reckoned it was before the First World War.

It was a beautiful March day: a cloudless sky, warm sunshine and cliffs before us that fell away to a sparkling blue sea. A wind blew clean air round our faces, and we screwed up our eyes in the dazzling sunlight and bit into our still-hot pasties, peeling back the paper bag which held each and spreading pickle with the fork. The pasties remained hot to the last mouthful. Paul had wolfed his, and we watched as he ran towards the sea end of the lighthouse wall with his dog.

When I had finished my pasty I stood and walked down across the turf of the cliff slope and joined him. The wind blew in off the sea and we gulped pure Atlantic air and looked at the squat, domed lighthouse Maud's father had maintained as a coastguard before he left to become a miner in Geevor mine, which lay on the horizon. We saw the hazardous clusters of rocks offshore, to which the lighthouse drew attention with its beams.

Later we returned to the Shogun and Pippa drove past Geevor village school, where Maud had been educated, and Geevor mine. We drove on to Cape Cornwall and Paul and I crossed a field and climbed a steep promontory to see the view from the chimney that dated back to the 1850s. I sat on a stone seat below the summit and watched the sea dash against the rocks of Whitesand Bay three-quarters of a mile from Land's End.

We ended up in St Just, which Maud had known as a child. We parked and had tea in The Cook Book. There were books on sale and I bought a first edition of T.S. Eliot's *Poetry and Drama.*

Maud was enjoying revisiting her childhood haunts, but I was still thinking of the lighthouse, in the old days a workplace for coastguards, and of the pasties Maud's father ate there, perhaps on the very spot we had eaten our pasties. We had been celebrating Maud's ninetieth birthday with a trip back into her childhood, but we had also been continuing a tradition older than the First World War. Timeless in her old lady's memories were her recollections of pasties by the lighthouse.

Ninety like a Buddha

The next day Pippa, Paul and I drove to Trevaskis in Hale, Maud's favourite restaurant. She went there each week with Age Concern. The group always sat at the long wide table at the back – three others in the group were over ninety and the nonagenarians always sat together – and Maud was waiting for us in the centre of that table. On the wall behind where she sat a poster said, 'Happy 90th Birthday'. I sat opposite her.

At one end of the table sat Maud's son Richard and daughter-in-law Sue and her two grandchildren. At the other end Pippa and Paul sat with Bill and Daphne, Pippa's cousins.

"How are you?" I asked Bill, standing as he arrived at the table. I had noticed he had put on weight.

"Not good," he said. "I'm breathless. I'm having an operation on April the nineteenth to have a new aortic valve put in my heart. I can't wait for it to happen. Then I can start getting my weight down. I'm fourteen stone. I'm usually under twelve stone. I'm not looking forward to the operation but I am looking forward to afterwards."

We sat down and Maud ordered her favourite: lamb and beef, half-and-half, with vegetable. Now all Maud's family were talking animatedly to each other. Sue was telling me her company was involved in the building of the Hinkley Point C nuclear power station. Maud's grandson had been for an interview with the same company that morning and his sister had made him remove his student's ring from his nose. Daphne was telling me about the engagement of her granddaughter to a teacher who happened to have been at school with Maud's grandson. She told me that another of her daughters had Ehlers–Danlos syndrome, which she had inherited from Bill's side of the family, and one of her thumbs was consequently loose.

The conversation continued through pudding: a choice of many kinds of cheesecake, pavlovas and meringue pies. Maud sat removed from the animated to-and-fro discussion, enjoying being with her family and contented at being in her favourite place but tired and isolated and too old at ninety to take part. She sat as still as a meditating Buddha amid the scraping of plates and laughter around her, detached and serene and perfectly still.

Boxes into Store

The day came when fifty boxes of my works, tranche 1 of my archive, were to be moved to the University on permanent deposit for at least the next hundred and twenty-five years. The 64-litre plastic boxes were all catalogued and stacked in my cramped archive room. Two removal men turned up at 9.30 with a woefully small van. I could see immediately it would not take all the boxes. But they had been delayed in bad traffic and rather than send them back through traffic for a larger removal van I agreed to proceed with loading and see how many we could cram in. The space in the back of the van would only allow stacks of four boxes, so I told them to take out their golf clubs and other bits and pieces and we agreed to start loading.

They were two willing fellows, both rough diamonds but good at what they did. They decided that each box should be double-handled, one of them at each end, and understood they should carry each box down two flights of stairs without tilting it so papers did not shift from one end to the other and make nonsense of the catalogue listing.

I stayed upstairs to make sure the right boxes went. There were frames with wheels – dollies – on which the boxes fitted, and I wheeled a dolly with four boxes on it to the door for the two fellows to lift off in the course of four journeys, and I then slid more boxes onto dollies so the men always had a box to lift off when they returned.

Halfway through I heard a raised voice.

"It's f — g stupid," the smaller fellow was saying heatedly on his mobile at the foot of the top, narrow flight of stairs. "You're telling us to go back to the yard with a half-load and reload onto the bigger van. That's double-handling and the boxes are delicate, they mustn't tilt, and it'll take us until after 3 by the time we've got through traffic back here. We're not doing it. You need to get someone to drive the bigger van here. You haven't got anyone? You should have told us to take the bigger van in the first place."

The other fellow, who was tall with a careworn face, said, "We're not doing it. We'll keep going and do as many as we can."

"It's f — g stupid," the smaller man said and concluded his call. "Pardon my French," he said to me, "but the management don't know what they're doing. I was talking to the owner's wife."

"Jamie, the owner," the careworn man said, "inherited the firm. Someone should have sent him out to do what we do, then he'd know the problems. But he wears a shirt and tie and he's no idea of measuring boxes or the insides of vans, or of lifting. He's never had to lift any furniture in his life. He's just in his office, and he's not there that often. If it weren't for what he inherited he'd be in a dead-end job like us."

The men agreed to continue but were warning me, "Our maximum's going to be forty-three. How many boxes can you take in your car?"

"Four," I said. "Two in the boot and two on the back seat. We'll be three short."

"Hmm."

"The Lord will provide," I said light-heartedly, jollying them along, keeping them positive. "It's like the loaves and fishes. Miraculously they went round. Trust in the Lord and you'll find you can take forty-six."

The men laughed.

There were many more journeys up and down the stairs, and eventually the careworn man said, "Come down and have a look. We're shutting the van doors."

I followed him down and stood outside the porch.

"How many did you get in?"

"Forty-six."

"The Lord be praised," I said, and they laughed again.

I parked my BMW alongside their van and opened the boot and a side door to the back seat, and soon my four boxes were in. The two on the back seat were stacked, one on top of the other. The two in the boot were side by side.

We drove in convoy to the University. We took a back-street route as the van was overloaded and the two men were afraid of being stopped by the police. I followed them. At the campus we had to request over an intercom that an unattended security gate should be opened, and we drove into a tunnel dark enough to require headlights under University buildings to the loading bay for the new block where the Deputy Librarian was waiting to greet us, a well-built man in spectacles who wore a sports jacket and tie. I shook hands with him through my car window and told him there were four boxes in my car.

"Let's get those out first," he said to a thin balding warehouseman.

My two men watched as he bent over my boot and lifted out one of the boxes single-handedly without any difficulty and walked with it to the waist-high concrete loading platform. The warehouse man then bent and lifted out the other box single-handedly without any difficulty and walked with it to the waist-high platform.

My two men looked at each other and then at me. They were thinking, 'How come we professionals were double-handling, one at each end of each box, and these puny-looking fellows can lift them out and walk without staggering as though the boxes are really light?'

I watched as the boxes on the concrete platform were loaded on to dollies and on to trailers and wheeled a few yards into the storage area: a long room with a low ceiling lined with black boiler pipes and green metal shelf-units containing spaces large enough to take a box. The boxes were labelled with numbers, and they selected the small numbers first and lifted the fifty boxes onto the shelves so they were in numerical order. I grasped the boxes were in a temperature-controlled environment afforded by the central-heating pipes for the new building which ran along the ceiling.

I tipped my two men well and waved them off. Then the Deputy Librarian led me to a lift and took me up to a spacious floor with large windows that overlooked greenery and a lake. He took me into the Library and then showed me the room where special collections like mine could be read. You asked for a box, it was loaded onto wheels in the storage area and sent up in the lift. You sat at a long wide table with power points and opened the box and did your research.

The Deputy Librarian explained the system and showed me current displays in glass cases: letters by Freud to his family, signed 'Papa', in one case and woodcuts by Blake in another. We visited other parts of the Library, talking in undertones so as not to disturb students who were working at screens. There was a timeless peace in the Library and I was relieved that my archive had been handed over into safe keeping and content that it should rest here and be looked at if there was interest in this serene yet vigorous atmosphere.

The next day Pippa, who was in Cornwall, rang and spoke to Penny, my PA, while I was at the bank. They discussed the move. When I returned Penny told me: "Pippa asked, 'Is Philip now in a box?'"

I laughed. I thought of how we had seen the mummy of Ramesses II in Cairo, lying on his back with a brown face and hooked nose in a glass case. I had more tranches to deliver, and perhaps the last one should be my dead body, which could be stored in a large box in the storage area to supplement my works and my life.

Pippa's question was typical of her mordant sense of humour but when all the tranches were in, my life and works would be in boxes and in a sense I would be in a box. In a real sense I had put myself in the boxes that had gone into store.

Quality like Blueberry Cheesecake

"I went to the Café Belgique yesterday," said Penny. "I wanted a slice of blueberry cheesecake and I called the girl over to serve me. She was in the shop's uniform and she said, 'Hello from Zumba.' And she did a little shimmy, acted out a dance. I was so surprised to see her. She's very thin and slender and a natural mover and everyone at Zumba hated her. I didn't, but everyone else did. She's foreign, no one knows where from. Someone said she's Hungarian. And we knew she worked in a shop but not where. Now she's there. At Zumba she's no idea of seniority. She went up to one of the more senior in our group and said, 'Can I stand in front of you because you're tall.' I mean, fancy saying that. No, she can't stand in front of her. She's just the sort of person women hate, a naturally good mover and in your face and showing you up at the same time. She stopped coming to Zumba. And then one day she came back. She said, 'I'm back,' and everyone thought, 'Oh, no.' She was still disliked. She stopped coming again and we were all relieved.

"Yesterday she said, 'I'm coming back again, I'm going to be there tonight.' But she doesn't realise you have to give notice, so she didn't turn up last night. I saw her earlier, putting the chairs and tables out single-handed, and she looked very competent. She wore plastic gloves to handle the slices of cheesecake and she put my slice in a box, and sealed it very professionally. She was all on her own. And she asked me if I'd like to take part in a raffle. I said 'No' to the raffle and got out as quickly as I could. She's very young but she has a manner above her years. She's had a struggle as have many at Zumba and she's a loner. But she's vibrant, she's got energy, she's got something. She's quality, like blueberry cheesecake. If you knew women, you would know exactly why women don't like her."

A Funeral like a Dress Rehearsal

We arrived in Lewes, found St Anne's church and parked in a side street. Paul and I walked up the hill, wearing suits, white shirts and black ties and along with other elderly people filed through the churchyard to the porch and entered the church. The oldest parts – the tower, nave and south chapel – were early 12th-century, and it had been a centre of pilgrimage on account of its healing well.

We took service sheets and found one of the few empty pews. A couple asked if they could squeeze past us, and while we waited, listening to piped Mozart, Beethoven and Bach, the man asked Paul if he was a friend of Lord Clipper's and revealed that he was the architect of the Royal Opera House. The lady next to him, his partner, had been a student of Lord Clipper's. She had been a well-known BBC and ITV newsreader a decade back. I scanned the congregation for Alan's surviving Bletchley-Park colleagues and fellow Oxford academics and historians, but did not recognise any although there were many familiar faces I could not place.

At 3pm the music stopped. Sentences of hope were shouted from the church door. A white satin-clad coffin was borne in on the shoulders of four pallbearers and placed on a wooden bier before the altar and we listened to Purcell's stirring 'Music for the Funeral of Queen Mary', written for the funeral of Queen Mary II in 1695.

There was a welcome and the well-known actor Erwin Deer, now bearded and very wrinkled, advanced to the front and read theatrically from *Ecclesiastes* chapter 3 in the King James version: "To every thing there is a season, and a time to every purpose under the heaven: a time to be born, and a time to die; a time to plant, and a time to pluck up that which is planted; a time to kill, and a time to heal; a time to break down, and a time to build up; a time to weep, and a time to laugh; a time to mourn, and a time to dance; a time to cast away stones, and a time to gather stones together; a time to embrace, and a time to refrain from embracing; a time to get, and a time to lose; a time to keep, and a time to cast away; a time to rend, and a time to sew; a time to keep silence, and a time to speak; a time to love, and a time to hate; a time of war, and a time of peace." (A recent interview with him in a Sunday newspaper quoted him as saying that his wife, with whom he was still living, had had lovers during their marriage.)

There was a hymn and then a tribute from Alan's eldest son. He spoke of his shock at Alan's death at ninety-four, and of his family life. His earliest memories were of the clicking of his father's typewriter. He said, "We played table tennis because he had learned to play at Bletchley Park. I especially remember playing on the top floor of the Provost's Lodgings at Oxford." He described the parties his father and mother gave, which he loved, and said: "Although he was said to have the highest IQ of his generation he was absolutely hopeless in practical matters. He never learned to drive but that did not stop him criticising the driving of others. He was a lifelong back-seat driver." There was amused laughter among the congregation. "His tennis serve was contorted and elaborate. It included raising his front leg, but it was extraordinarily effective." Again there was amusement from the pews.

One of Alan's grandchildren read a 1681 poem by Richard Baxter ("He wants not friends"), which Alan had always liked, and after a hymn there was a tribute by his second son, who described how Alan had involved him in his library when he was a child: "'Could you put that book up there. Could you take that one down from up there and put it here.'" He said, "He wrote four books after he was ninety, and in the last few years he was unable to move and when I visited him it was: 'Could you take that book down from the top shelf? Could you put this one in its place?'" He mumbled and I could not hear everything, but his affection came through and he seemed to be affected by the loss of his father and several times wiped his nose with a tissue while speaking.

There was a reading from *A Pilgrim's Progress* and a fetching young lady sang Purcell's 'Dido's Lament' from the opera *Dido and Aeneas*, an aria 'When I am laid in earth', suggesting that Alan was an Aeneas and that his widow was like Dido, abandoned by the death of her husband.

There were prayers, then a friend of the family read a poem Alan had written for his wife. It began, "The pathway may bend/but my love will not end." There was a hymn, a closing prayer and blessing. Then to Bach's 'Prelude and Fugue St Anne' the coffin was hoisted by the four pallbearers and borne down the aisle on their shoulders, their hands folded in front of them. I was standing by the end of our pew and as I bowed my head it passed within inches of my hair. His two sons supported their mother, who was in her early eighties.

We had written our names and addresses on cards put out by the funeral directors and left them in our pew. We queued in the aisle to sign a large leather-bound book of remembrance. Then we filed down the path and sheltered from light drizzle under a tree and watched the family gather round a grave for the interment. Someone near us said, "It's the first time in forty years there's been a burial in this churchyard. It's full but they've found a space." In the distance I could see the South Downs.

Soon the family returned and Paul and I advanced. Alan's widow stopped in front of me, supported by her eldest son, abandoned Dido. I stepped forward and introduced myself.

"I visited him last year when you weren't there," I said. "I dedicated a work to him. He told me I should write it in 1978 and last year I said, 'You were urging me to write it then and you were urging yourself to write your book about your secret work in Bletchley Park.' And he said, 'Yes, I was.'"

"Yes," she said. "He wanted to write that book in 1978."

Alan was on record as saying that his wife did not know about his secret work at Bletchley Park until it came out when he was ninety, but now she was admitting to knowing about it in 1978.

"Thank you for coming," she said. And her son led her across the turf, over other people's graves, back to the path. (I did not realise until later that she was nearly blind and would have seen me as a dim outline.)

Paul and I walked across the turf to the grave, which was surrounded by wreaths. The drizzle had almost stopped. I looked at a prominent wreath of white lilies and read the card his widow had written, "To my precious Alan."

I looked down into the grave. The satin-clad coffin lay at the bottom, about eight feet down. A few daffodils were strewn across the top. As I looked it came on to rain.

We turned away, passed other members of the congregation and walked back to the path. There was no tea laid on for the congregation. There was tea back at the house for the family: the children and grand-children. There was now a chill in the air. It was 4.30 and so we crossed the road to a pub, sat in the window in the warm and were served tea. We had a view of the entrance to the churchyard and watched the steady rain.

Alan had given his life to founding and serving institutions but his successor at my college had not attended and I seemed to be the only representative of my college. He had written many reviews and had written many books. We watched his family leave in a long car, and I thought of him lying alone at the bottom of the open grave in the steady rain, out in the chilly air with a distant view of the South Downs having shed a lifetime's striving. He had been writing a review half an hour before his wedding and was well-known for making use of every moment with ten-minute appointment slots, and now he had slipped into the past. He was in a timeless mode and had all eternity ahead of him in which to review his life's achievements without any paralysing ill health.

I had paid my respects to what he had done for me, but apart from his widow no one was any the wiser. As I looked out at the chilly rain from the warmth of the pub window it suddenly dawned on me: had I not just attended a dress rehearsal for my own funeral? Would it not be long before I would be lying in the bottom of an open grave with all eternity to reflect on all I had thought and done, all my words and deeds, all my ambitions and achievements, and all my questing and legacy?

Slumped Passengers and a Dark Tunnel

For my journey back to Cornwall on Good Friday I had booked well in advance in the first-class quiet carriage. I arrived early at Paddington and found the first-class waiting-room, showed my ticket and poured myself a mug of espresso coffee. I sat and sipped with my bags by my feet and watched the screen until my platform was flagged. Then I walked to the train and found my window seat, L24. I was surprised at the number of passengers milling about in the aisle, some talking quite loudly and others speaking on mobiles in the quiet carriage.

I had a table and I buried myself in my work. As the train pulled out I was aware of a lady standing at my elbow looking down at what I was writing. Then I realised there were a dozen passengers ahead of me without seats. They were standing, sitting or lying in the aisle, mainly young girls. One with long hair was sitting reading beside my knee, one with her knees showing through her torn jeans was lying on her back with her head on the crossed legs of another girl. Several of the seatless passengers held mobiles or tablets, which they studied while the seated passengers read newspapers or dozed.

A lady's voice came over the intercom: "We apologise for the overcrowding, that some of you are having to stand or sit in the aisles. Good Friday is a busy day, and the booking arrangements mean that not everyone can have a seat."

I was travelling backwards. I watched fields with sheep slide before me; ponds with Canadian geese; and a hawk, probably a kestrel, gliding with outspread wings, seeking prey. I watched wheatfields slide past me and then clusters of newly-built houses, crowded together. Above the hedges that rushed past was a blue sky with occasional small puffy clouds.

I looked back at the aisle and was struck by the good nature of the seatless travellers. Several were smiling, one girl stretched out was very relaxed. They all seemed to have accepted their predicament and were making the best of a bad situation.

I turned round and looked at the crowded aisle behind me. I was shocked. There must have been twenty contorted bodies in the aisle. No ticket collector could get through, it was quite hopeless to go to the restaurant car next to our carriage and bring back coffee, or go to the loo. Each step anyone took would involve treading on supine or sitting flesh. I was glad that I had made a smoked-salmon sandwich the previous evening and that I had brought a banana and had added a packet of shortbread biscuits from the first-class waiting-room.

As I munched my lunch I looked out of the window. A farm slid by, and then a country lane with a cyclist wearing a helmet. Then there were fields of stubble with oak-trees scattered about, and a line of poplars: a hedged countryside and arable system going back to the 18th century, perhaps the Middle Ages.

I looked across to the table for four across the aisle. A couple were playing Scrabble. (They made ephemeral words, to be broken up at the end of their game, while I made permanent words in my writing.) Another couple were munching sandwiches. The girl by my knee was reading *Red Sky at Sunrise* by Laurie Lee. Further up the aisle a buxom elderly lady was sitting on the table of a seated gentleman, a complete stranger, her legs on the aisle floor. The gentleman had paid a first-class fare to have a table, and her rear now covered it so he could do no work.

I looked out of my window again. A plane had left a trail across the blue sky. There was a crack in the sky. I suddenly realised: my life was passing and slipping into the past. Each field and lane and farm was like an experience, and I was watching my experiences loom and recede. Each sheep and hedge, each weir and group of grazing cattle – my life was slipping by. Then suddenly we entered a long tunnel, and outside all was black. The bodies slumped on the floor did not seem to realise that we were all hurtling past wonderful sights towards a dark tunnel from which we would never emerge.

A Twitch like a Wink

At Plymouth the voice announced over the intercom: "This train is overcrowded and is going nowhere until some passengers get off. There are only five allowed on the vestibule. There are between ten and fifteen on some vestibules. There is an empty train standing at the next platform. It leaves at 1.42. Will some passengers please get off this train and get on the other train."

No one moved, and the train remained stationary for twenty minutes. Then suddenly there was a jolt and it began edging forward, and there was applause from the seatless passengers on the aisle floor. (The next day Television South West announced that there would be an inquiry into an incident at Plymouth station when the police had to turn a hundred and fifty people off our train.)

A couple across the aisle had got out at Plymouth, and two men had taken their seats. They had a dog which strained at its lead to cross the aisle and get between passengers' legs. The two men tried to restrain the dog.

One of the men, who had a crew-cut and wore a sweater with a design of patterned squares, had a twitch below his left eye, which looked like a wink. He removed a small bottle of rosé from a bag and the other man poured it into two glasses, which they chinked. He produced sandwiches which the other, who had sun-glasses perched on top of his middle-aged head and wore a thick grey sweater with sleeves rolled above his elbows, bit into. Chunks of bread fell from his mouth and the dog between his legs caught the bits in its mouth and chewed them.

"Where are you from?" the man with the twitch asked the girl opposite him, with a wink.

She said, "From Cornwall. I do this journey regularly, to London and back. It's getting worse."

"As crowded as this normally?"

"It can be," said the girl.

"We booked on the internet a week ago," the man said, winking connivingly. "You couldn't get a seat, but you had a ticket to travel. It's bad they let you book without a seat."

The girl said, "If you can book six weeks in advance you can get a seat, if you can plan ahead and be forward-planning."

The man winked and produced his phone. He turned to his partner and winked again. Then he started texting a message.

"I'm so afraid of treading on his tail," the girl said, looking down at the dog. "He's being very good."

"He's amazing, isn't he?" the man with the sun-glasses on his hair said. "His first-ever train journey."

"Really?"

"Someone trod on his tail earlier and he gave a whelp."

The man with sun-glasses on his hair turned and smiled into the other man's eyes and offered him a crisp from a bag he had produced. The man with the twitch smiled back, took a crisp and winked. Their two empty glasses stood together on their table. The dog lay contentedly at their feet.

A Widow and Ashes

Len came for his money. He had tacked back a cable that was hanging down our sea-side wall and had done some work on the rear roof.

"WD40 on the stairs," he said, thin with cropped hair in his thirties, as I gave him his envelope. I showed him the front-door lock I had oiled. It was still catching as I turned the key. He turned the key backwards and forwards.

"The mortice isn't working properly," he said. "Look, it's not coming out even though I'm turning it. I may have to replace the mortice and realign it with the plate on the doorpost."

"Claire looked in to see Pippa while I was away," I said in the hall.

"Yes," Pippa called from her chair in the sitting-room through the open door. "She was thinking. She came down to think. She parked her car up the hill and walked down and came and tapped on the door. She wanted to think and so we had coffee. I helped her to think."

"I look in to see her every week," Len said as he and I entered the sitting-room. "And the last two times I've been in she's been a bit weird. I hope she isn't giving up. She's been talking about her funeral."

"Yes," said Pippa, "she's planning her own funeral. She's still got Harry's ashes and she's talking of where both their ashes can be scattered together."

"Perhaps she's being practical," I said. "Perhaps she's thinking of paying for her funeral so others don't have to do it when the time comes."

"No," said Len, standing in the sitting-room doorway. "She told me, 'I don't really care if I go now.' She was saying she wants to be with Harry."

"Yes," said Pippa. "That's what she was saying to me. She's ready to go and join Harry. She misses her children. Certainly Kay. She complains that the boy never comes to see her. And she's very involved with the grandchildren. I was trying to get her to be positive."

"That's what I try and do," Len said. "She's been fund-raising for Mount Edgcumbe Hospice, which looked after Harry. She's raised funds for them for the last two years at the football ground. But there was a problem last time."

"Yes," said Pippa. "Something to do with a knife."

"That's right," said Len. "A man slashed out and ripped someone's T-shirt. He could have slashed someone's chest."

"The man's been arrested and there's to be a court case," Pippa said.

"Oh, I didn't know that," Len said. "I think it was to do with drink. I don't think she'll do that kind of fund-raising any more. That incident has set her back, unsettled her. She seems to be giving up. All this talk of *her* ashes being mixed with Harry's and scattered somewhere together, I don't like to hear that, it makes me feel uncomfortable. I hope she doesn't give up. I'll continue to keep an eye on her.

"We've just moved into an old lady's house up the hill. I sold our house within five days and the old lady's house was empty. It's larger and has garage spacing for three cars, which I need. I've got a classic cream Volkswagen Beetle with a curved screen, early 1970s, and there's room for that there. It's an old-fashioned house, it's got dado rails. You know, picture rails, only halfway up the wall, with two kinds of wallpaper, one below and the other above the dado rail. There's a lot to do. But I'll keep going in once a week. Claire's alone a lot of the time, she's got no one to talk to and things go round and round in her head. She wants to become ashes, she wants to be with Harry and for her ashes to be mixed with his and to be scattered somewhere because it wouldn't make any difference to her if she wasn't around any more. But she's forgetting about Kay and her grandchildren, and I'll keep mentioning them. Yes, she's a widow who wants to be ashes."

Shadow on the Cliff

That night I went for a late-night walk by the Cornish sea. A storm was on its way and the wind gusted by the roundhouse. I gulped fresh Atlantic air and walked across the bridge, the only human visible in the seaside village, and sauntered round to the harbour wall, relieved that my life's work had been delivered for safe keeping for at least a hundred and twenty-five years. The outer harbour was floodlit from a floodlight near the roundhouse, and the waves and 1790s stone walls were all illuminated.

I climbed the stone steps and stood on the harbour wall and looked out to sea. The Longshore lighthouse light was flashing – six pulses and a seventh long one – and there were distant lights on the ships along the dark horizon. There was no moon, and clouds had covered the stars.

I turned to look at the headland and started. For on the lit cliff face above the sea three hundred yards away was a gigantic shadowy figure. It reached nearly halfway up the cliff, a dark, well-defined silhouette, and was completely still, a clear black figure from its head down to just above its ankles.

I shifted my position as I looked, and it too shifted its position. I moved again, and it too moved. It was copying me. I now realised the enormous shadow belonged to me. The floodlight behind me had thrown my shadow three hundred yards across the waves and beach and projected it onto the cliff.

I walked towards the end of the pier. The shadow walked with me. I turned and walked back. It walked back. It was a giant. Somehow I had been projected onto a cliff as a giant. On the pre-historic cliff I had the stature of a giant. I had an *alter ego* that reflected my life as my writing did but in a way that magnified me. I thought, 'Perhaps that is what happens to every writer. He writes down his experiences in normal everyday size, but on the wall of history he appears larger than life and is accorded the stature of a giant.' Perhaps it was always thus and will always be so.

Then I recalled ascending Mount Brocken in Germany, on whose summit soon after dawn the rising sun can cast one's gigantic shadow onto the clouds. The weather the day I stood on the summit did not permit me to witness this phenomenon, which is known as 'the Brocken spectre'. Here in Charlestown the floodlight had acted as the sun, and I had seen my spectre on the cliff.

My shadow and I were inseparable. When I walked in the sun it walked beside me or (if the sun was behind me) ahead of me, as if leading me, pointing my way. I had thought of it as a future self, a wise self to whose knowledge I had to ascend. Now my shadow and I had separated. I was on the harbour wall, in life, and a gigantic image of myself was across water on the cliff face as if after my death.

Then I suddenly felt I was in the Underworld, and was looking back into life at my posthumous image. I stood and surveyed my Shadow across water. From the Underworld I looked across the Styx at the image of my self that would survive me.

A Swept Desk and Green Grass

The funeral of our sometime neighbour Sarah, who had died at the age of eighty-nine, took place in Glynn Valley Crematorium, Bodmin on a Wednesday at 9.30am.

We arrived early and sat in the car park until her son Patrick drew up, and immediately afterwards her daughter Abigail, a neatly dressed blonde lady who had come from Washington DC. Her husband Steve had a job connected with the Ministry of Defence there that we should not talk about. We had a word with Abigail, who thanked us for coming, then filed into the small chapel and sat in a pew halfway back. Sarah was in a wicker-basket coffin on the left, and through the wall-to-ceiling windows before us was a panoramic view of hills, fields and distant woods. In the centre turned the top of a wind turbine, nearly spoiling the view.

We had been handed a sheet containing a photo of Sarah as a young lady. It had probably been taken just after the war. The sheet was headed 'A Celebration of the Life of Sarah'. There were about forty of us in the pews.

The celebrant stood at the lectern at the front, a smiling middle-aged lady, and welcomed us. She said several rainbows had already been observed through the windows, and she hoped there would be more. She announced that it would be a non-religious service to celebrate the life of Sarah in poems and music; a kind of mixture of a funeral and memorial service. She read a poem, and said she had been given an account of Sarah's life by her daughter Abigail, which she read.

She described how Sarah had spent her childhood in Polkerris with her three brothers, who rolled her pram full of dollies down the hill to make her cry. They succeeded. Only the eldest brother had survived. He was sitting in the aisle near the front in a wheelchair, aged ninety-six. There were three pews of relatives, in the last of which sat an enormously fat man whose trousers could not keep his shirt in under his jacket.

She told how Sarah had become a nurse and had helped with operations. Her consultant was subject to mood swings and in a fit of anger sometimes swept all the operating instruments onto the floor. He only did it once in Sarah's presence. Later she marched into his office and swept all the items on his desk on to the floor and announced that if he did that again to the instruments she would walk out of her job. It never happened again. She became a midwife in the 1950s and then worked for the RAF, and opened a hospital in Germany. In 1958 she met and in a lightning romance married Les, a merchant-navy captain. He was away on ships for much of their early married life, and she brought up her two children single-handed and engineered several house moves, finally the move to Charlestown, where we were neighbours, and to Par, where I visited Les just before he died in 2005.

In 2008 the first signs of her vascular dementia surfaced. She was found wandering outside her house and was convinced she was about to be attacked from outside. She was admitted to the Royal Cornwall Hospital, Truro and tried to escape several times. On one occasion she flooded the building from her top floor, deliberately leaving the taps running. On another occasion she threw china out of the window together with a note appealing for help, so she could be rescued. Eventually she was well enough to be discharged back to her house, but her mental condition deteriorated and she was admitted to Coombe House, where she was well looked after: one of the staff watched over her while she slept.

Abigail had written to Pippa from Washington to say she was deteriorating rapidly. She could no longer tolerate food – she vomited up everything she ate – and grimaced from pain in her stomach. She went downhill rapidly. The celebrant tactfully said that while her death would have saddened all, there must be relief that she had escaped the trials and confusion of her old age.

There was a song, 'The Green, Green Grass of Home', and after a final committal of Sarah "to Nature" the curtains slowly drew and hid the wicker coffin. Les, a humanist who could not stand the Church, had been buried in a field on Fowey Point under green grass – a field the family secured permission to bury him in, with a view over the sea – and now Sarah was following him in being committed to Nature. Pippa dabbed under her eyes with a tissue. There was more music, 'Barcelona', and then the celebrant announced that all present were invited for refreshments at the Carlyon Bay Golf Club.

The front row stood and filed towards the celebrant, followed by the next two rows, and above the conversation an announcement was made, which we did not hear. One of the standing ladies said, "The Golf Club's off, there are no refreshments at the Golf Club." I wondered how the announcement came to be made. We had all been invited, and a minute later we were all disinvited.

We now stood and queued. The enormously fat man's trousers had given way at the back and he was showing his underwear to those behind him as he stood, unaware, in the aisle. A note at the front said that donations could be made and would be shared between Coombe House and the Alzheimer's Society.

Slowly the queue moved outside. There was a small garden with some wreaths under signs stating weekdays. There were no flowers for 'Wednesday'.

We talked again with Abigail, and I said I had often met her dad during my late-night walks by the sea and that he had explained how he steered by the stars: "The old seaman's lore of ancient times handed on by word of mouth and now probably made extinct by computers." I shook hands with Steve and invited him to look in. He said they had to get a train later that day and fly back to Washington the next day, and they wouldn't be able to look in during this visit. I also spoke to Patrick.

Pippa and I drove off. Lanhydrock House was round the corner, where 'Chirpy' was a stable-boy during the First World War, and we stopped for cappuccino and desultorily discussed Sarah's life. I said she had had great strength to sweep things off her boss's desk, bring up her children single-handedly and organise her house moves to get her family down by the sea. Pippa nodded.

"So which would you rather have," I asked, "a Christian funeral and then a memorial service; or a 'non-religious' service that committed you to Nature?"

Pippa was silent.

"And would you rather have a wooden coffin or a wicker basket?"

"I don't suppose I'll care," Pippa said.

Had Sarah's soul witnessed her funeral and was it on its way to a new life? And did a 'non-religious' funeral service fail to take account of the journey of the soul to a new phase of existence? In the West we were in an age of secular disbelief while out in the greater world 5.8 billion of the 7 billion world's citizens were religious.

Sarah now knew the answer, and only she of those in the Crematorium could now say whether the 'non-religious' service was right or wrong.

Sheep and Screens
(Or: The Way we Live Now)

The field near the Charlestown church was full of sheep. I stopped and took in forty or fifty, some sitting, many frisky lambs, many black-headed sheep and three black sheep, and I thought of the nursery rhyme I used to chant: "Baa baa black sheep, have you any wool? Yes sir, yes sir, three bags full." (No doubt at shearing time a black sheep provided three bags of black wool.)

I returned to the harbour and outside my house, on the green in front of it, were forty or fifty white daisies. They were scattered about like the sheep, and in a strange irrational way I saw a correlation between the grazing sheep and these daisies on the grass.

I was transported back to my Essex garden and the daisies on its lawn. In my mind's eye I would see the stitchwort and vetch, the clover and golden dandelions that put up their heads along with the daisies between mowings. And I could see the meadow of wild flowers beyond the main field. In my mind's eye I was feeding my carp and roach, I could see my five big fish surfacing for the pellets I had lobbed in, no longer hibernating from the winter chill at the bottom of their pool. And I could see the cupped white water-lilies rooted in mud and shining in the sun. And I could see myself scuffling through yellowed and reddened Forest leaves.

So much of Nature is in the mind, images before the inner eye when the eyelids are closed. We are often unaware of our surroundings when we are within them. Many drive past without noticing the sheep or the daisies, many come and go without seeing the plants at their feet or the fish. I thought of the way we live now and the sitting and lying bodies in the aisles of the crowded train, each clutching and fixated on a mobile phone, a tablet, an iPad, a laptop, reading messages or texting or searching for information and taking occasional pictures to be stored. Not one of the thirty in the aisle beside me was without a piece of technology to consult. The more we look at a screen, no matter how small, the less we notice the huge variety of life going on outside our immediate consciousness. And starved of Nature's forms around us by our phones we fail to see the universal One that is behind the physical world and controls its routines. Our consciousness can gaze at sheep and at screens, and the way we live now habitually prioritises technology above the wonderful images of Nature.

Myriad Splashes and Stars

That Cornish March morning was perfect: a clear blue sky, a still sea, warm sun and an untold number of jumping, dazzling lights on the surface that formed several lakes of splashing light stretching like a causeway from the horizon to the shore. As I screwed up my eyes, dazzled by the exploding lights, it seemed as if rain was pelting on the sea. I could see the diagonal lines of rain as they splashed into the lakes.

I looked for the black cormorant that had sat between the curling waves the previous day and dived for fish into each approaching crest of a wave, but it was not to be seen.

Late the previous night I had stepped outside my front door and wandered down towards the roundhouse and looked up, the sole human on the harbour, and all round my head and shoulders were falling stars like leaves of a weeping willow under which I stood. The planets were bright and glistened, and the question mark of the Plough was immediately above my head. There had been almost as many twinkling, winking stars as the jumping lights before me now.

Near me each flash was like a blinding reflection from a mirror. Each splash flashed and was gone. The whole sea seemed to be rejoicing in the warm morning, proclaiming, 'I'm here, I have shoals of fish below just waiting for you. I've survived the winter chill and am looking forward to warmer weather.' As I watched, the lakes shifted their position. One lake's splashes died back and new splashes formed a new lake nearby. And now the lakes blended into each other so there were no lakes, just one dazzling causeway leading to the distant continent of Europe. And I had a strong irrational feeling that the 'Remains' would win the coming referendum on the EU.

The sun, the dazzling sea and the blue sky seemed indivisible, and my soul leapt to the leaping lights of the sea's myriad splashes, utterly convinced that what I beheld was a pulsing and rejoicing One.

'Myriad', adj., 'Of an indefinitely great number'. (*Concise Oxford Dictionary*.)

An Uneven Path and a Clock Tower

When I was a teenager I cycled to school and back. I would cycle to Avondale Drive and cross the meadow full of wild flowers to the brown river Roding. I would dismount and wheel my bike across the humped-back bridge. I always looked down into the river for fish and for signs of wildlife in the reeds by the banks.

Then I would cycle up the narrow path between two sets of wire netting that took me alongside the field of a boys' school whose land extended to the hedge by the Roding. The path was very uneven, stones protruded from the dried mud and I had to steer round them. I passed the large main building with its clock tower and many windows, and the old wartime barrage-balloon station where an old wartime gun pointed at the skies. (This space is now occupied by the David Lloyd Club.)

I came out on the bend of Roding Lane and cycled up the steep hill past the Pratts' house (where Lord Sugar later lived) to the school. I parked my bike in the bike shed behind the Gym, took my books from the saddle-bag and proceeded into school.

On the way home I cycled down Roding Lane at great speed. The sun was between the trees and flecked my eyes as I sped down – and I would then cycle back down the narrow path past the boys' school with playing-fields. Very often there would be a game of cricket in progress – I once played for my school there – and I would keep one eye on the cricket as I cycled over the uneven stony path. It never occurred to me in those days that I would own a school, let alone several, and I never saw this building as waiting for me one day. But Providence is very forward-looking. It has a habit of showing you what it has in mind for you to run. I was shown my first school several times as if being nudged towards it. Now I wonder if one day I'll find that I was being shown the clock tower and many windows for a reason and an approach that have yet to unfold.

A Coffee and a Cosmic Plan

I went to have my annual hearing consultation near the Wigmore Hall in early April. 'Nessima', the Canadian-Algerian, came out smiling and ushered me into her room. She looked at my ears through her otoscope and changed the heads of my hearing-aids. She turned my swivel-chair to face the wall, put earphones over my head and gave me a button on a lead to hold. I had to press it each time I heard a sound.

"The lower sounds have got worse," she said, looking at her screen. She explained at some length how I heard sounds, and she changed the settings on my digital hearing-aids to cope with these new findings.

As she worked, I said, "Have you travelled recently?"

"I went to Turkey," she smiled. "No sign of any refugees where we were. But the main problem was my father. He went to Indonesia in January to open a hearing care unit and he went into Starbucks to have a coffee and there was a terrorist incident that was in the international news. He was killed with three others. IS claimed responsibility. An Indonesian extremist living in Raqqa, Bahrun Naim, masterminded the attack. They were targeting a police post near Starbucks. Two attackers were killed and two back-up men were killed in a shoot-out. Four attackers and four victims. It was a great shock to my mother, who was in Montreal."

She was nearly in tears. Appalled, I said, "I'm so sorry. How dreadful for him and for you and the family. Having coffee in Starbucks, it could have been anybody. He just happened to be there, in the wrong place and at the wrong time, a random victim of an attack on a police post. The whole thing is senseless. IS must be stopped, but it may take a generation to stop them. Meanwhile, I'm really sorry you've had this shock."

"He was killed by crazy men," she said. "People think all Muslims are like that, but they aren't. And I'm pregnant," she said, "five months pregnant."

I said, "I hadn't noticed, but I wasn't looking." She was not obviously pregnant.

"I'm glad you didn't notice. But in another four months he'd have been a grandfather. I'm going to be off on maternity leave for a year in June. Can you come again in June before I go, and then I'll see you in June next year as soon as I get back."

As I walked back to Oxford Circus station I was struck by the way one member of her family had been taken and a new member would be coming, almost as a replacement. Life appeared to be maintaining a balance – one out, one in – and before her screen and earphones I detected an echo of the workings of the universe, of Nature's system and of a cosmic plan.

Haunting Images and an Exorcism

I am tormented by images which haunt my mind like ghosts.

There is little Johnnie Horner, who was in my class at school where he was king of marbles and came and had tea with me in my garden wigwam. Near the end of his life he did a daily egg-round from a farm in Stapleford Abbotts, where he lived. He fell ill and told me, "I won't live to see the daffodils next spring." He did live to see them, but he died soon afterwards. I am haunted by his simplicity in reducing his aim in life to seeing daffodils in the spring.

I am haunted by Hookie, who was at my college and was our Ambassador in Iraq when Saddam invaded Kuwait, telling me in the college grounds by the lake, "I have dementia." I am haunted by his simple acceptance of a condition that apparently undermined memories of his diplomatic career.

I am haunted by Joe Makers, who lived within the grounds of the school I founded, telling me outside his house, "I've got cancer in my liver. I've been told it's incurable. I'm still going to have chemotherapy just in case it works." I am haunted by his hope – his clinging to life – within the finality of his condition.

I am haunted by Archie taking his doctor wife and two small sons into a Muslim country, Kosovo, to found a church there, going in like Daniel going into the lions' den with a young family that would have to learn Albanian in school in order to be taught in Albanian; while he learned Albanian so he could attempt to convert his everyday contacts – his barber, a shop assistant – to Christianity, at the risk of being beheaded by IS. I am haunted by the way he risked his family and by the questionable trust he placed in the Lord while taking this risk.

I am haunted by simple things. My grandson Al when aged five said to his mother while he was making slow progress with his vegetables at lunch, "I shouldn't have broccoli, it might make me a little bit naughty." I am haunted by his use of his potential naughtiness to bargain for getting out of eating broccoli, when only five.

I am haunted by the chatelaine of Cliveden during the Profumo Affair telling me in a Starbucks about Stephen Ward's links with Soviet Communism – and at that exact moment a robin with a red breast flew in through the open door and perched on a stair opposite her. I am haunted as the robin's red breast seemed to symbolise Red Communism and in some irrational way embodied Ward.

I am haunted by things that have gone wrong. One day the two underground pumps that pumped our sewage where I lived were both burnt out and had to be replaced, and I had to hire a tanker in heavy rain to pump the manhole clear before new pumps could be fitted. I am haunted because the cost and effort left me where I was before, with two working pumps, and the sequence of events did not make sense.

I am haunted by the Royal Mail. When I sent a package guaranteed delivery to arrive by 1pm the next day, a Wednesday, it was caught up in the system and went backwards and forwards from one sorting office to another and back again before being delivered on the Friday. I am haunted because the hindrance slowed my work and there was no satisfactory explanation as to why it happened.

Such images nag and haunt me until writing them down (like this) purges my mind of them, loosens their hold and their power to haunt. I have loved life. I have had a great curiosity and fascination with things that have happened, and a desire to understand them and fix the ephemeral into an enduring pattern, and I have always had disparate images from my embracing of life crowd into the corners of my mind, vying for attention, pleading to be used. Many I censor and shut out. But when I sit with a blank page and begin writing a story without knowing what is coming next or how my story will end, I am vulnerable. They clamour like persistent children wanting to be photographed, and though they are too slight to warrant a story of their own, I am aware of their merit.

And so this story is a bit unorthodox. It is a ridding myself of clamouring images that demand to be included, that are striking in themselves but do not warrant full works. By admitting them I consign them to oblivion in this act of writing them down: this sharing, this purging, this exorcism.

A Stag and Wire-Cutters

I came downstairs just after 7 and set about preparing my high-fibre, cholesterol-lowering breakfast: Oatibix, Clusters, All-Bran, granola, flax-seed, wheat germ, ground almonds, walnut halves and semi-skimmed milk; Benecol drink and Actimel; a slice of bread, Benecol 'Buttery' and honey; and orange juice. Something was moving at the bottom of the lawn. I looked and saw a commotion in the wire fence. I picked up the binoculars and had a close look.

A stag was bucking and kicking. Its antlers were tied up in the wire fence that stopped deer and rabbits from entering our garden and eating our plants. Clearly the fence had failed to keep the stag out as it was on the inside and trying to get back out into the field to return to the Forest.

I did not know if it had been eating our heathers and roses, and munching our low-hanging apples. These had been munched during past nights. Part of me thought, 'It deserves to be trapped. Perhaps this will teach it a lesson and it will not come in and eat all our plants.' As I looked through the binoculars it sank down in exhaustion and lay still. I wondered if it had just died.

I thought of going down myself to release it but then remembered my age. What if it broke free and attacked me with its antlers? I might need wire-cutters and did not have any. Wisdom persuaded me to ring for help.

A couple of fellows from the schools in dark blue uniforms turned up half an hour later with long-handled wire-cutters. I briefed them. They marched down with a broom, and the heavier of the two fellows plonked himself down on the supine stag's back and held the two antlers near where they joined its head. The other fellow warily cut the wire in several places with his wire-cutters. Looking through the binoculars I could now see that some chicken-wire was so entangled in one of the stag's antlers that it was wearing it like a kind of sleeve.

Now the stag rose and bounded free through the hole in the wire fence they had cut. It was away into the field, and ran sedately towards the woods. It disappeared and had returned to the Forest.

The fellows walked back.

"It had a gashed leg," the heavier one said. "And we couldn't get the chicken-wire out of one of its antlers."

"But you did brilliantly," I said. "You're a really good sitter. I was very impressed by your technique, to sit on it and hold its antlers to prevent it from moving them with its head."

They both laughed. I thanked them and waved them off, and they returned to the schools.

Now there was a gap in the wire fence.

Later I reflected that I could have turned the stag into venison and exacted a drastic revenge for its invasion. Instead, imbued with a sense of my oneness with all living things, I had released it at the expense of our wire fence. Those in harmony with the universe put their own situation and themselves last and instinctively act to preserve the oneness of Nature.

A Wildlife Garden and the One

Garfield Myers had ginger hair at school and a freckled face and he excelled in playing the piano at break. He strummed out 'When the moon's upset' and sang how the moon gets dolled up in a sky-blue shirt and a rainbow tie.

He became a surgeon after he left school and in the 1980s I heard that he had bought a large four-hundred-year-old house in Devon which came with a wild garden.

I went back to school for the annual Shrove-Tuesday reunion and was standing in my old Classical-Sixth classroom, the former library, when he walked in, wearing a dark suit, white shirt and tie, and shook my hand. He still had his head of hair, although it had greyed. I had not seen him since he left school, for nearly sixty years, and I reminded him of his piano-playing. We sat near each other in the dining-hall and he told me about his garden.

"I'm semi-retired now," he said. "I still do some operating. I spend most of my time in my garden near Tiverton. It slopes steeply down to the river Exe. It was free from pesticides but it needed a lot of work, weeding and new planting. I love butterflies, and we've got more than a hundred species of wild flowers, including purple orchids, corn-cockles, campions, pignuts, foxgloves, pasque-flowers and sanicles. Many of them attract butterflies. We've attracted thirty species not seen there before, including white letter hairstreaks and marsh fritillaries. I've been chairman of the Devon branch of British Butterfly Conservation. There are all sorts of reptiles: glow-worms, snake-like slow-worms, lizards and grass snakes. We have otters. I love Nature, and we've got nestboxes. We've got kingfishers, dippers, herons, treecreepers, titmice, flycatchers and siskins. We've got fifty nestboxes for birds. We've got Daubenton and pipistrelle bats. We've got log piles to encourage insects and they're feeding sites for woodpeckers, nuthatches and treecreepers. We've got a natural pond and a flood pond. We've got amphibia, copses, a river, a meadow, cornflowers and dead wood. It's a fantastic habitat. I'm really interested in plants that provide herbal remedies: St John's wort for mild depression, feverfew for migraine and goat's rue which helps diabetes. My love of plants and wildlife go back to my childhood here in Essex. We used to have picnics in a meadow at the back of where we were living."

"I remember," I said. "You had me to tea and we had a picnic in the meadow. The sun was shining."

"The sun was always shining in those days. Those picnics set me off on what I'm doing. We have two or three thousand members of the public round each year. You must come if you're down. I love Baroque music now. Albinoni. I play Albinoni in the garden and also in the operating theatre. I operate to Albinoni."

I had created a garden the public came round and I knew how much time it took and the thought and care that had to be put into it. We had both loved wildlife in our childhood. I too had loved butterflies and learned about each species. He told me he had also created a wildlife garden in the grounds of Tiverton Hospital and been its President. I saw him as a pillar of the local community, a still-practising surgeon who was a member of the Exe Valley Rotary Club and a public figure, but (he told me) he was at his happiest in an open-necked shirt and shorts, sitting in his rowing-boat on the Exe. He had nurtured local *flora* and *fauna* and was as much a naturalist as a surgeon, and whether or not he knew it he was very close to the One.

Silence and a Green Curtain

We were in North Norway and drove to an igloo hotel near Alta. We had reindeer burgers for lunch and went out on a dog sleigh. Pippa rode in the sleigh and I steered at the back, bending over the seat and standing on the footbrake as we skimmed over 10km of snow between trees along a frozen river. It was nearly minus 20C and we had warming hot currant juice and ate chocolate-chip biscuits in an Altaic tepee made of skins. It was of the design in rock carvings c.7000BC. It was large enough to seat a local community. Twenty-two poles met at the top and had a smoke-hole for the smoke from the birchwood fire to escape.

We returned to our igloo hotel and at twilight we went out on a horse-drawn sleigh. The sleigh driver was very old. He nodded gravely and did not speak. He was well wrapped-up in skins. Pippa and I lay back in the sleigh, and sitting on high before us the driver shook the reins and the horse began to trot. We were drawn along a wide snow track between wooded pine trees. As dusk turned to early dark we arrived at a snow-covered clearing. There was a cloudless dark sky and the stars were very bright. They twinkled and dazzled in the frosty air, which was now minus 20C. We sat in awe, our hands under a rug, peering at the stars without speaking, completely still. Then for the first time the driver spoke, in English: "Listen to the silence."

We listened. There was no sound at all. The air was still and I was aware of the silence beneath time. This silence extended beyond the stars and throughout eternity.

The sleigh driver said, "It is beautiful."

We returned to the igloo hotel. We would be sleeping on an igloo bed of ice on reindeer skins in sleeping-bags, and in preparation we had something to eat in the hotel restaurant. Then we went out for a final look at the night sky above the wooded pine trees through which we had been drawn.

As I looked up at the night sky it stirred into life. Out of the silence behind the stars emerged a green haze and it gathered into a green curtain which veiled the silence: the Aurora Borealis, the Northern Lights. I watched spellbound as the curtain faintly moved and was full of wonder at the heavens which veiled stars and stillness and silence in dark space beyond our atmosphere's green curtain.

Indexes

Dates of Stories

Dates of stories in *The First Dazzling Chill of Winter*, in contents order

Part One The First Dazzling Chill of Winter	Date
The First Dazzling Chill of Winter	22 December 2012; 2 November 2015
A Dapper Man	24 January 2009
A Corpulent Barber and an Angry Son	3 June 2009
A Roundabout and a Crashed Life	November 2009
A Rickety Stepladder and a Dreamer's *Chaise Longue*	9 August 2010
A Leaving Party at the Osteopath's	24 August 2010
Wild Boar	30–31 August 2010
A Plane on the House	31 August 2010
A Nurse and a Bleeding Consultant	1 September 2010
The Moors' Paradise and a Sigh	2 September 2010
A 1399 Home and Dolphins	2 September 2010
An Angry Old Man in a Passing Order	4 September 2010
As Unyielding as a Slab of Granite	6 September 2010
A Black-Out and Table Tennis	9 September 2010
Nemesis in Naples	9 September 2010
A College and Cowboys	4 October 2010
Noah's Pageant	5 October 2010
A Chapel on the Bend	29 October 2010
Two Silver Jugs on a Tray	31 October 2010
A Backward Boy and Mining	2 November 2010
Grouted Boulders and Encroaching Waves	4 November 2010
A Turkish Palace and a Smirk	5 November 2010
The Landlord and the Pie	5 November 2010
A Brother at the Window	8 November 2010
Maestros and Managers	13 November 2010

Fromages pour les enfants	19 November 2010
A Parakeet in our Garden	21 November 2010
Cranes and a Natterjack Toad	27 November 2010
A Hospice Donor and a 'Pompous Twit'	27 November 2010
A Candle and a Squashed Mince Pie	30 November 2010
Gold and a Grumbling Undertaker	19 December 2010
A Tray and an Offhand Vicar	19 December 2010
Lycoris Buries her Friends	30 December 2010
A Family Skeleton	3 January 2011
Treasure in Heaven	3 January 2011
A Coffin like a Packed-Away Christmas Tree	6 January 2011
A Mute Question	19 January 2011
Teeth and an Outside Water-Supply	24 January 2011
Two Backpackers and a Film	13 February 1011
An Owl Handler out in the Cold	20 February 2011
Thirty Dogs and Forty Tortoises Downstairs	29 May 2011
A Buzz and an Iron Axe Head	20 June 2011
A Last Glimpse of Childhood	20 June 2011
Cobwebs in a Storeroom	22 June 2011
Tea in the Museum	22 June 2011
A Suntan and Blue Jokes	23 June 2011
A Gutted House and Far-Away Eyes	24 June 2011
Spilt Wine and Mersea Island	29 June 2011
A Hip and a Rebuff	3–4 July 2011
Critical and Early	5 August 2011
Christmas Day and a Grandchild	11 July 2011?
A Headache and a Locum	11 July 2011
A Broken Hand and a Thunderous Look	28 July 2011
A Brown Envelope and a Bach Fugue	29 July 2011
Two Vines and a Nonagenarian	29 July 2011
A Herkimer Diamond like a Milestone	29 July 2011
Flat Battery	5 August 2011
Chocolate Curls and Chunks	5 August 2011
A Hornets' Nest and Folded Clothes	27 September 2011
A Bulgarian Kick and a Line Dance	29 April 2012
A Warm Log Burner and a Latch-Pinned Door	7 May 2012

Black Sheep Like Pets	7 May 2012
A Wheelchair and *Bible*-Reading	After 18 October 2012
A Singing and Murder	10 March 2013
The *Maître D'* and a Submarine	11 March 2013
Encomiums and Imperial Purple	13 March 2013
A Mask and Five Plasters	23 March 2013
An Electioneering Widow and a Splashed Carpet	10 May 2013
Wisteria and Hot Stones	25 May 2013
A Chimney and Christmas	28 May 2013
Leaves and Nectar	3 June 2013
A Clockman and Cuba	4 June 2013
Strangers and Friends	28 June 2013
An Athlete and a Monk	2 July 2013
Hazelnuts on a Keyboard	3 July 2013
A Captain and a Baha'i	4 July 2013
Gentle Mr Grayling and a Blurt	5 July 2013
Missionaries like Wind Turbines	14 July 2013
A Wheelchair and Stony Hill	9 August 2013
A Working Harbour and a Dream	9 August 2013
Veiling Cheeks and a Wimple	3 November 2013
An Elagabalus Coin and a Yacht	21 November 2013
A Funeral and an Isolated Mourner	22 November 2013
Fines and Spills	17 December 2013
Glittering Gold off the Black Head	17 December 2013
A Sore Point	28 December 2013
Missionaries like Zealous Carol Singers	29 December 2013
Caviare and a Rat	11 February 2014
Like Four Spikes after a Storm	21 February 2014
A Berber in Civilization	25 February 2014
A Turk and *Shariah*	8 March 2014
A Trolley and Stress	30 March 2014
A Grab-Rail and Birdsong	18 April 2014
A Silence and a Bulging Stomach	5 May 2014
Fits and a Bath	6 May 2014
A Swimmer and a Medal	1 July 2014
A Stiff Upper Lip	2 July 2014

Wounds like Carrots	26 July 2014
A Peregrine like a Chained Soul	26 July 2014
Paper Boats and Kettles	26 July 2014

Part Two

In the Early Evening Sunshine

In the Early Evening Sunshine	26 October 2013
"Huh, huh" and a Waved Sole	19 August 2014
Bluster and Bluff	7 September 2014
Leather Gloves and Bat Bags	23 September 2014
A Ninety-Year-Old Cricketer and Rows	4 October 2014
Twinning and a Rodeo	9–11 October 2014
A Ruin and a *Boudoir*	11 October 2014
A Hedge, Green and Brown	27 October 2014
Partridge and a Tomb	1 November 2014
Bruises and Pickle	28 November 2014
A Lost Ruby and a God	29 November 2014
Galaxies and God	10 December 2014
Champagne and Order	13 December 2014
A Tooth and Cholesterol	7 January 2015
A Heart and a Blind Eye	27 January 2015
A Bandage and Narghiles	7 March 2015
Strokes and a Dying Order	24 March 2015
The One Like a Hidden Sun	24 March 2015
Blood Clots and Nylons	1, 9 April 2015
A Tray in her Lap	29 May 2015
A Russian Invasion and a Defiant Estonian	3 June 2015
A Colonel in Tears	21 June 2015
A Chapel and a Bath	11 August 2015
An Ache and a Beach	11 August 2015
A Message from God	20 October 2015
A Providential Sale	28 October 2015
Truth Like a Clattering Crash	25 October 2015
A Foot in the Door	28 October 2015
An Evangelical Tone and a Trick	Idea: 12 November

	2015. 16 December 2015
Fortune's Wheel	18 November, 12 December 2015
A Wheel and an Allotment	24 November, 12 December 2015
A Pancreas and a Quiz	26 November, 12 December 2015
Roots and a Shock	29 November, 12 December 2015
An Afghan and Refugees	5–12 December 2105
A Minute and Eternity	12 December 2015
A Fall and a Physio	12 December 2015
Of Mice and Muscles	14 December 2015
A Disguise like a Stove-Pipe Hat	2 January 2016
Prosecco in Artillery Lane	23–24, 26 January 2016
An X-ray and Chaos	25–26 January, 6 February 2016
Pilgrims and Lorries	9 February 2016
Horror amid the Cameraderie	11 February 2016
Limp Mode and Full Power	13 February 2016
Cramp and a Dazzling Christmas Tree	17 February 2016
A Slip and Empty Days	17 February 2016
A Travel Plan and a Helicopter	21, 28 February 2016
Box-Leaf Caterpillars and Nature's Plan	24, 28 February 2016
Histrionics and Mould	26–28 February 2016
A Chauffeur and the Death Seat	27–28 February 2016
Earth Floors by the Loire	30 March 2016
A Queue and a Lord	30 March 2016
A Crossword and Alaska	30 March 2016
Window-Dressing and Make-Believe	31 March 2016
Stabbings and Mushrooms	30 March 2016
A Walk and a Shut-Down	29 March 2016
Double Vision and Strokes	30 March 2016
A Fox and Bites	29 March 2016
Incas and Doodlebugs	29 March 2016

A Wrench and Dignity	29 March 2016
Scarlet Blood and Lost Letters	c.1979/28 March 2016
The Sun and Icarus	31 March 2016
A Vicar and a Nephew	27 March 2016
A Vicar and Autism	27 March 2016
A Stark Reality and Three Hundred Dreams	29 March 2016
A Sandblaster and Beautifying Tracery	30 March 2016
Lake Garda and Chaos	27 March 2016
A Blank and a Back	29 March 2016
A Transplant and a Claw	28 March 2016
A Fall in a Home	27 March 2016
Shopping Bags and Tragedy	29 March 2016
A Wedding and a Fall	29 March 2016
Stunted Toes and a Joined-Up Head	29 March 2016
A Chef and a Backhand Cut	29 March 2016
A Toenail and Torture	27 March 2016
Four Bereavements and a Tortured Life	27 March 2016
Collapsed Veins and a Deer	17 February, 28 March 2016
Disarmament and a KGB Man	28 March 2016
Menelaos and Ancient Stones	28 March 2016
A Church and a Pension	28 March 2016
A Scheme and a Petard	26 March 2016
A Red Universe like the One	31 March 2016
Angels in Gloom	26 March 2016
A Room and a Deed	26 March 2016
Pasties by the Lighthouse	25 March 2016
Ninety like a Buddha	25 March 2016
Boxes into Store	26 March 2016
Quality like Blueberry Cheesecake	26 March 2016
A Funeral like a Dress Rehearsal	25 March 2016
Slumped Passengers and a Dark Tunnel	25 March 2016
A Twitch like a Wink	25 March 2016
A Widow and Ashes	25 March 2016
Shadow on the Cliff	26 March 2016
A Swept Desk and Green Grass	30 March 2016

Sheep and Screens	31 March 2016
Myriad Splashes and Stars	31 March 2016
An Uneven Path and a Clock Tower	31 March 2016
A Coffee and a Cosmic Plan	7 April 2016
Haunting Images and an Exorcism	31 March 2016
A Stag and Wire-Cutters	30 March 2016
A Wildlife Garden and the One	1 April 2016
Silence and a Green Curtain	28 March 2016

Index of Titles

(Stories in alphabetical order, part titles in italics.)

BOOKS

O-BOOKS

SPIRITUALITY

O is a symbol of the world, of oneness and unity; this eye represents knowledge and insight. We publish titles on general spirituality and living a spiritual life. We aim to inform and help you on your own journey in this life.

If you have enjoyed this book, why not tell other readers by posting a review on your preferred book site?